REMAINS

A FICTIONAL ACCOUNT OF A TRUE CRIME

JIM CHENEY

Copyright © 2025 Jim Cheney.

All rights reserved. No part of this publication may be reproduced, distributed, or transmitted in any form or by any means, including photocopying, recording, or other electronic or mechanical methods, without the prior written permission of the publisher, except in the case of brief quotations embodied in critical reviews and certain other noncommercial uses permitted by copyright law.

ISBN: 978-1-7366855-4-9 (Paperback)

ISBN: 978-1-7366855-5-6 (eBook)

Library of Congress Control Number: 2025905663

Any references to historical events, real people, or real places are used fictitiously. All characters, incidents, and dialogue are drawn from the author's imagination and are not to be construed as real.

Prufrock Communications, LLC.

Franklin, TN

For my mother and father

AUTHOR'S NOTE

THIS IS A WORK OF FICTION. THE CHARACTERS ARE based on real people, as are the locations in and around Noble, Georgia, where this story takes place. The characters' names have been changed as I have never met or conversed with any of them. My work here is based on research that exists predominantly in the public domain. Any resemblance to anyone associated with the investigation of the Tri-State Crematory is the result of my imagined personification of their sensibilities, motives, and crimes. The discovery of hundreds of discarded bodies on the 16-acre wooded property where Tri-State operated, while inconceivable, is true.

In addition, I would like to offer my deepest thanks for the help in completing this book. Specifically: Leah Handelsman for her assistance in editing the manuscript, David Higdon for the cover design, Jon David Hedrick for a first read, and Irish novelist Alan Glynn for his generous and insightful critique of my overall writing and delivery.

Finally, a wink and a nod to my good friends HL and TB for the use of their names—you know where all of my bodies are buried.

J. CHENEY

CHATTANOOGA, TENN. SEPTEMBER 2024

Death does not concern us, because as long
as we exist, death is not here.
And when it does come, we no longer exist.

-EPICURUS

1.

SHAWNA'S COFFEE WAS ALREADY COLD.

"You want to what?" she said, picking up a chipped mug. She started to stand and then sat back down, scratching the chair across the floor and dropping the mug back onto the table with a ceramic thump, oily black coffee sloshing.

"You want to do what?"

Rollie was sitting on the other side of the table. His legs were out beneath it like khaki girders, his frame swallowing up the chair back, his head a massive granite thing on his shoulders. He sighed, shifted his legs beneath the table, accidentally kicking her bare ankle with his boot in the process. He put his hands over his face and leaned back in the chair and looked up at the ceiling, exhaled. She waited, had seen this act before. *Woe is me. Here it comes.*

"Look," he said, letting the chair down and lowering his frame over the tabletop, intimate, needing to explain himself. It was his sales posture, trying to look less imposing despite his bulk. "It's not something that I want to do either, but the machine is broken, Shawna, which means that we can't do the job that we get paid to do by people in three states who need our services." She stopped him, got up for a refill from the cheap pot gurgling on the countertop next to the microwave with the blinking green time read out.

"Oh," she said over her shoulder, hair not done yet, robe still on. He did not look at her. Knew she was going to hit him with both barrels.

"So now, this, this . . . . this plan you're talking to me about is because of our professional and no doubt moral obligation to people all over the South who—how did you put it—*need our services?*

Goddamn, Rollie, I tell you what. The way your mind works is just fantastic. And I don't mean like . . . "

"I know what you mean," he said. They were talking around each other now. Circling it until somebody gave. He had to win this one. They were closer than they had ever been to the bank coming to the house. Standing on the front porch: *Hi Mr. Davis. Are you aware that you are six months behind on your mortgage?* Twenty-something Sheriff's deputy standing behind him in case things got unpleasant. Hoping it might. "We got to do it," he said. "Just temporary, Shawna. But I don't take the money up front like nothing has changed, I can't get us out of the hole we're in and then it won't matter what's out there in the woods, cause the woods won't belong to us anymore. You understand what I'm saying to you?"

She turned around with the fresh coffee, stared at his back, muscled in the sleeveless undershirt. Ropey arms dangling.

"Sit up," she said, and he straightened his shoulders and turned to look at her. "How bad is it?"

"Bad."

"How much time?"

"For what?" he said. "The bank, or the machine getting fixed?"

"Both," she said.

"Couple months, maybe," guessing, but sounded realistic. She knew anyway—was feeling him out to see if he was being honest with her. Catch him lying now and he might lose more than the house. Things had been testy. She took a sip of the coffee and watched him over the rim.

"What you're talking about is not just illegal, but it's wrong in the eyes of God."

"Yeah, I know, Shawna. But Jesus ain't gonna come down off the mountain and pay the bank what we owe. Far as I can tell around here, God and his son don't see fit to do much for black folks. That goes back a long way. They probably see foreclosure as cleaning up his house."

"He is not petty like that."

"Who, Jesus? Shit."

She went back to her seat at the table, folded her robe tighter. Looked again at him. Handsome man with a good heart. Meant to do right by all of them—her, the kids, the land that they had scratched enough together to acquire so he could start the business. Good reputation in the community, even if most of them were polite to their face and whispered cracker bullshit behind their backs. They were established and they could protect that or risk it all disappearing like so much dust. And how they would talk when the sheriff and his deputies pulled up in the yard for the last time, Rollie toting shit out in boxes with open lids, furniture that had belonged to her mother and father. Shame as thick as the humidity in the air. No. He was right. Had to bend.

"Okay," she said.

"Okay what?"

"Just okay.

"Shawna."

"Give me a second Rolland May," more serious than before. Dialed in tight. Not taking her eyes away from his. A hint of fear, maybe. "It's not like this is an easy thing to get your head around."

He tipped the chair again, locked his hands behind his head. She'd said what he needed to hear. Conceded, but there would be terms. There were always terms with her, but he had cleared the first hurdle, and he knew that he needed to let her work things out. He could wait for that. His plan, or lack thereof, would take on a life of its own and she would decide how and when she would be involved. Maybe turn a blind eye when she needed to. Fine by him. If he was being honest, the audacity of it made him want to hang the whole business up. Let the bank have the house. *Fuck it.* But there were real obligations. His son in school, playing football. Matt just now making his way. His daughter wanting more out of life than Noble, Georgia had to offer. He could make it work. Keep

Shawna and the kids clear of it in the interim. Get things back on track. Fake it and get paid. Clear the books up. Shove it forward.

"Tell me again how it works," she said, pushing the mug of coffee away, the bitterness making her stomach churn.

"From the outside," he said, still leaning back in the chair, trying not to grin, "Nobody's gonna know anything different. We just got to be cool how we go about it, Baby. Know what I'm saying? Got to keep our story straight until we can get it back to normal. Nobody but us got to know what's going on. You understand, Shawna? This is us working our way out of a problem. Working together. You see?"

She said, "Normal?"

2.

WALKER COUNTY SHERIFF HI LEWIS PUT HIS CRUISER
in park and looked through the windshield while he fished through
the glovebox for a roll of Tums. He found a torn sleeve of the antac-
ids and pushed two of them free with his thumb and popped them
in his mouth, the scene in front of him its own type of indigestion.
His deputy, a kid barely out of high school named Ellis Carver, was
leaning against an outdoor ice machine at a Quick Stop on State
Route 193, talking to a man who looked to be in his late sixties. The
old guy was dressed in jean shorts, a cut-off t-shirt and a baseball
cap that was tilted back on his forehead. Canvas tennis shoes. Lewis
could count three cans of tallboy Icehouse lined up on the sidewalk
next to the ice machine, and a rumpled knapsack leaning against the
building. To their left were the restrooms, one of the doors partly
open. The old man had not bothered to put out his cigarette while
talking to the deputy and he was gesturing wildly with it, stabbing
it back into a wire nest of beard to pull on it and blast a cloud of
rancid breath and smoke that lingered between the two men like a
wad of grayish couch stuffing. The deputy looked at Lewis through
the windshield and then back at the vagrant, obviously exasperated.
Lewis chewed the last of the chalky tablets and got out of the car,
shifting the gun belt and pulling the underwear out of his ass in
one practiced motion. He closed the door and the old man noticed
him for the first time. Lewis looked over at his deputy and raised
his hand slightly, then walked to the curb of the sidewalk, standing
a couple feet from the old man.

"Delbert," he said.

"Sheriff," the man said, dropping the cigarette.

"What's going on here?" Carver started to speak and Lewis hushed him with a sideways glance. He'd left his sunglasses in the passenger seat and had to squint for the light coming off the metal doors of the ice machine.

"Minding my own," Delbert said, scratching at his beard. "Been in the woods is all. Got thirsty."

Lewis motioned at the bathroom doors. "You go in there to wash up?"

"Yes sir." Lewis nodded. "I got eat up with bugs and was trying to cool off some." Lewis nodded again.

"And the store owner called us."

"I reckon."

"Mr. Patel ain't that mad about the washing up, but he's been out here drinking and asking people for money," Carver said.

"I never," Delbert said.

"How you explain those beer cans," Lewis said, taking off his hat and waving the heat away from his face. "Looks like you had at least three cylinders of that stuff. Damn if that brand don't give me the worst kind of headache."

"Don't bother me none," Delbert said. "They got it in there on special in that tub of ice up next to the magazines and such. I never bothered no one. Just, you know, trying to cool off is all. Eaten up with all these bugs." Lewis looked at Carver and the kid deputy shrugged.

"That about everything there is to the story then?" Lewis said, seeming to ask them both at the same time. Neither answered and Lewis suddenly felt very tired. He put his hat back on and tapped his chest, feeling the acid coming up like coals in a kettle grill.

"Delbert. This makes the third time that we've been called out here cause you're upsetting Mr. Patel's customers, drinking on the property, and using his restrooms to wash off the filth. I'm tired of it. Deputy Carver has not been in the department long enough to be tired of it, but he'll get there, and the owner of this store is within his rights to press charges. Now, I can ask him not to do that because all it means for Deputy Carver here is a lot of tedious paperwork and a trip to the Scenic Suds to get the smell out of his car. For you, it means at least a couple days in the tank and probably a fine that you can't pay which means you'll go back in the cell and serve out your penalty that way. You following me here?"

Delbert nodded, looking at his shoes.

"When is the last time that you ate something?" The old man shook his head. "You got some place that you can go that's not here?"

"Can go back to my camp along the creek. Got some things there."

Lewis searched in his pocket and pulled out a money clip and peeled off a ten, reached out and handed it to Carver.

"Go in there and get him something to eat. Couple of those red hot dogs or something and tell Patel that we're gonna run him off and that he won't be back," and here he looked at Delbert, "and if he does come back and causes any more trouble, we'll arrest him on the spot. That clear Delbert?"

"Yes Sheriff."

Carver took the bill and turned to go inside.

"You want me to spend all of this on him?"

Lewis grimaced and nodded.

"I think he has some canned goods in there. Just get something that soaks up beer." He returned to Delbert.

"Clean this mess up here, including those butts and when Carver gets out with your things, you get gone and don't come back unless you can act respectably." The old man bent to pick up the beer cans and Lewis went to the patrol car. He flinched at the hot metal door handle and slid inside and turned the engine over and flipped the fan switch on high, letting the semi-cold air wash over his face. He picked up the radio and clicked the talk button.

"Tanya?"

"Yes Sheriff."

"Anything pressing for me back at the office?" A pause and then a harsh crackle.

"Not unless looking at these budget numbers again is pressing."

Lewis thought of the budget approval at the county commission and reached around for the Tums.

"No," he said into the handset. "That can wait till tomorrow. Unless we're invaded by the Soviets, don't bother me till the morning. I'm going to the house."

"Rodger that, Sheriff. Contact only in the event of invasion. I'll leave a note for the night dispatch."

"You do that," he said and put the handset back in the cradle. Delbert was carrying the beer cans to an overflowing trash can between the pumps. He was almost there when he dropped one and trying to catch it, sent the other two scuttling across the parking lot in opposite directions.

"Jesus," Lewis said under his breath before backing out and turning onto the highway toward home.

3.

Special Agent Traian Thomas Sat In An Almost empty office in the Georgia Bureau of Investigation's Atlanta headquarters. He had taken his suit coat off and hung it on a coat rack in a corner behind the door and taken a seat in a torn leather chair that had been abandoned by the previous tenant. He swiveled in a circle and loosened his tie. He had been through a full day of orientation and was waiting on the operations guys to bring in a computer that would sit idle more often than not. He was looking out the window at the shimmering parking lot when a soft knock came from behind him. He spun around to see the Director standing in the doorway. Thomas stood up, but the man motioned him to sit, stepping into the room, observing the emptiness with indifference.

"Settling in I see."

"Yes sir."

The Director seemed to be looking for a chair. "Got a minute for me?"

"Of course, Sir."

The Director turned and went out into the hall and came back rolling another office chair. This one a simple black number that probably belonged to one of the cubicles that were spread throughout the Investigative Division's space in the building. He pushed the chair into the middle of the room and sat down in it with a groan.

"Traian," the Director said, looking at him. "I'm not familiar with that name. What is it?"

"Romanian, Sir. On my father's side."

The Director nodded. "Mean something?"

"Warrior, Sir. At least that's what I have been told. Not many people get it right."

"Lose that third vowel I'm guessing. Bet you had a lot of nicknames in school."

"Quite a few, Sir."

"Any stick?"

"Not the ones in school. People in the Florida office called me Loco, for . . ."

"I get it. Not bad. I'll file that away. Use it once we see which track you head down." Thomas smirked.

"Anyway," the Director said, loosening his tie as well. "I hear good things about you. I've read up some but got most of it in a briefing from the assistant director. Cindy's a good agent. I trust her. Told me about an insurance fraud scam that seemed like it might have been dreamt up for the movies. Where was that?"

"The big player was in Tampa running things out of a brokerage headquartered in Ybor City, but it was all over the place in South Florida."

"And you ran lead on it?"

"Yes Sir. Well, until D.C. took it over."

"After you did all the work, no doubt." Not a question, but something that he seemed familiar with.

"Well, you'll have to tell me about that sometime."

"Certainly, Sir." The Director paused, looked at a spot on his shirt, then licked his thumb and rubbed at it.

"You take a drink, Traian?"

"Yes sir."

"How 'bout we get some of the people who you'll be working with together and we'll get cocktails after work on Friday. Good spot just down the street. Loosen things up a bit. I'm sure that you're glad to have today behind you."

"It was fine, Sir. Everyone very accommodating." The Director stood and walked around the back of the chair.

"That's good to hear. I've been in this office for going on fifteen years. Can't say that I like how much the city has grown. Pain in the ass to get anywhere and we got more drug and violence bullshit than we can shake a stick at. But the office is a good one, and the agents are, for the most part, sharp people. You'll find the ones who hide in the periphery soon enough." He tapped the back of the chair.

"Good night."

"Good night Sir."

•

Traian Benjamin Thomas was born in Ohio in 1958 to parents who both taught at the College of Wooster. His father a world history professor and his mother head of the English lit department, specializing in classics and Medieval studies. As an only child, Traian grew up with the smell of books and an on-going family dialogue that fostered an insatiable hunger for knowledge, debate, and intellectual superiority. He was a normal enough kid, with a paper route, a decent fastball, and a healthy fear of the Catholic Church—a convention that his father guarded fiercely and that his mother merely tolerated and occasionally prodded with her sarcasm and love of tormenting her husband for the mere pleasure of it. They were good, somewhat distracted parents, consumed with the daily rituals of education and the theories that came along with it, applying their fields of study to a child who patiently listened, and dreamt of a world far beyond the sleepy streets of Wooster, the nuances of Medieval England, long-fallen empires or dead Russians at the siege of Leningrad.

Traian often wandered out of the house after an impromptu lecture on the French Revolution or Sir Gawain and the Green Knight and circled the yard aimlessly, considering whether or not his parents' students got as bored with their interests as he did. Then forgetting it entirely as he mounted his bike and rode down the tree-lined avenues looking for a pick-up game or maybe a glimpse at Shelly Cantrell who was older than he was, but always smiled at him when he caught her eye, her reading on the front porch of her family's house on Stevens Avenue, just up from the park. Shelly with her pale skin, sometimes on the porch, sometimes leaning against the massive tree that sat in the front yard, book propped in her lap, black curls on her shoulder and him going by like he had happened that way by mistake. Looking cool and aloof on the bike. Had not been seeking her, but the gang of ball players he ran around with. Pretending not to see her until she called to him going by and he would almost turn the bike over trying to stop. Startled and painfully adolescent. Speaking to her in awkward boy language without eye contact and juices moving through him like hot sap, inexplicable and exciting.

But what caught Traian's attention more than Shelly Cantrell's snow-white skin were the stories coming out of Youngstown and the Mahoning Valley region—a quick jump up to Akron and then 76 straight east through farm fields and then into burnt out towns that had shown promise but were beginning to rust at their centers, people sulking around the streets like their hearing had been blitzed, meandering through downtowns in a daze, filthy awnings over dismal bar entrances, whores holding up street lamps, expressions blank with worry over what happened to their non-existent marriages and livelihoods and prospects for any kind of future at all. Gray clouds from smokestacks parting to glimpses of ironic blue sky. Mob families from Pittsburgh and Cleveland had both laid claim to the area in the mid-twentieth-century, before the rust paralysis, Youngstown not being large enough to support its own crime family and being almost equidistant from the two larger cities that fought for and ran the rural Ohio territory like it was a getaway for well-dressed thugs. And with the two factions both looking to control the valley, the violence was a siege that Traian found more real than anything that had happened on the eastern front of Hitler's failed war or the impending conflict in Korea. He would sit in the family room of his parents' home with the Daily Record and read wire reports from around the country, soaking up the stories and realizing at a young age that they were bolder and stranger than any fiction, and his affinity for crime and crime fighting rose in him until it was all-consuming. *Baffled my parents,* he would tell an FBI instructor in the training academy's cafeteria on a cold November afternoon when the rain splattered the windows, the trees skeletal and menacing through the smeared glass, the room sparse and thick with smells from the kitchen that was loud with people cleaning up after the lunch crowd. Tables not yet wiped, pot roast mixing with disinfectant and cackling laughter bouncing off stainless steel surfaces.

He studied Criminal Justice at Ohio State in Columbus, missing the war in Vietnam by the skin of his teeth, skipping over dropouts who'd lost their cause and were tripping on memories of pseudo revolution, Traian leaving the weed and blotter alone. Just the occasional can of beer. Sticking to the books. Then he ditched the idea of law school to land in the FBI's new facility in Quantico where he excelled to the extent that they wanted him to stick around, teach some classes, help move the thinking along at the federal level. He considered the offer and decided that he had no capacity for teaching people things that he had not undertaken himself. Asked to be assigned somewhere and they sent him to Miami to help catch white collar criminals who had a penchant for killing people who did not agree with them. A hotter version of degradation. He'd requested Cleveland or Pittsburgh and the same instructor he'd told about his parents not understanding his ambition asked him if he had something against sunshine, rum, and Cuban pussy. He had not answered. Just took the assignment and figured he'd get back that way once he showed them what he was capable of. Bring the whole thing full circle. Invite the folks down for the weekend and brown-up their midwestern faces.

Now he was in Atlanta in an empty office, thinking about having drinks with the new team, mostly smart. *Some on the periphery*, the Director had said, or something along those lines. Nothing new there. Having to talk about the insurance scam he'd busted wide open in Tampa. Thinking about the short version instead of the long one that he found boring to the point that it made his teeth hurt, but others always found exciting enough to stop him mid-sentence to ask the waitress to bring more drinks. *A double for my Romanian friend here. Can't believe this shit? Go on Loco. What happened next?* Now thinking about his wife at home, setting up the small apartment on one of the Peachtree streets—so many variations of the same name that he could not keep them straight. His wife, Kim. Beautiful woman who may as well have been picked off the dangling limb of an orange tree outside Orlando, full of brilliant color, health and optimism. She had graduated from the state school in Tallahassee with a double major in Psychology and Education. Could outwit just about anyone and then reprogram their thinking. She had come along with a forced promise that he would not sign on to anything that would require him to pull his gun or have her answering the door to uniformed cops informing her that he was not coming home for dinner or anything else for that matter. Been real clear on that. Wanted kids and not to be a widow before she turned forty. He had promised her, and he tried to keep his promises.

4.

SHERIFF LEWIS PULLED INTO THE WORN DRIVE OF HIS house and had to stop short for the bike that lay overturned, blocking the wrought iron carport where his wife Sherry's wagon sat, ticking in the late afternoon sun, the rear hatch open and several bags of groceries visible. The dog was circling the wagon's rear end and Lewis tapped the horn, making Jester jump and then scamp out of sight into the back yard, tail tucked between his legs and glancing back over his shoulder. He put the cruiser in park and got out and walked around the front and picked up the bike and moved it into the grass.

"I told him not to leave it there." Lewis looked up to see Sherry come from behind the house in shorts and a faded t-shirt. He put the kickstand down on the bike and went back to shut the cruiser off. Then he walked down the drive. Hand on his gun belt, putting on the law enforcement stance, peering over the gold sunglasses.

"Need some help, Miss?"

"Sure, Sheriff," she said. "You taking a break from catching bad guys to come and help me? I'm so flattered."

Lewis took off his hat and started toward her.

"You're something alright. Where does it hurt?"

She posed, tossed her hair, smiled. Her body was like watching a gymnast tumble, all legs and fluid movement and concentration. Grey-green eyes and yellow hair, worn long.

"C'mon, Matt Dillon, the ice cream is melting in the back of the wagon." She turned and went down the drive, Lewis watching her saunter, wondering if the kid was home.

"Robbie home?"

She looked over her shoulder. Knew what he was thinking.

"Just asking," he said, putting up his hands.

"He's here," she said, picking up one of the brown sacks and hefting it on her hip. "But he's been invited over to Matt May's house to spend the night." He picked up the last two bags and she shut the back hatch.

"How's Shawna?" he said, the two of them walking up the rutted brick path to the back door.

"She's good. Told me how well Levi is doing playing football at UTC. Says that Rollie thinks that he might even have a chance at playing pro ball. Wouldn't that be something."

"No shit," he said, stepping around her and opening the screen door. Watching her walk up the short run of steps toward him. Followed her into the kitchen.

He said, "So then tonight we'll have this fine castle to ourselves," gesturing with the sacks of groceries at the low slung ceiling in the kitchen, tight hallways like a dog run to the two back bedrooms and shared bath. The whole house about eleven-hundred square feet of brick ranch. A tornado's bullseye, his dad had called it when he'd supervised their move three years before after Hi had accepted the job with Walker County. A little piece of heaven in the valley below Lookout Mountain's shadow.

"Maybe play knight and damsel, that kind of thing. Get the steed out."

"Jesus, Hi. Help me put these away." She paused, looked around the kitchen. "Better yet, why don't you go take a shower. You stink like you've been in the sun all day" then a pause and she says, "and I can smell the cigarettes in case you were getting too proud of your undercover skills. You can keep your steed and your Winstons in the barn together. Puff away."

"Lights. I switched to the lights. Did you buy some beer," but he did not wait for her to answer. Went out of the kitchen and found Robbie in his room, sitting on the shag carpet and playing with a handful of plastic green army men. He watched from the doorway and listened to the boy make war sounds. Sweet kid. Too timid, but his father had thought the same of him and had tried to pull the softness out of his personality like a loose tooth. It had all worked out okay—the softness being gone. Helped him to not second guess himself or overthink. Had been an asset when he was young and thought he was impressive. Now it was an absence he was working to fill back in with measured amounts. Hi felt like he had reached a point where he was assertive lawman and a reliable husband and father. Not bad. At least he believed Sherry thought so. With Robbie it was harder to say. He thought kids were just a shade easier to read than criminals.

"Who's winning?"

The boy turned around, one of the soldiers in his hand. "I don't know. Just messing around. Anybody give you shit today?"

"We've talked about that Robbie."

"Yes sir."

"No," Lewis said. "Nobody gave me any shit. Well, one old man, but it was nothing. He's a harmless old drunk living in the woods."

"You said there was nothing harmless about a drunk."

"Jesus Robbie. I just came in here to ask you how your day was and tell you that if you leave that goddamn bicycle in the driveway again I'm going to bury you with it."

The boy laughed, dropped the army man into the jungle of carpet and came to where his dad was standing in the doorway. Then looked up at him and hugged his middle. *Progress,* Hi Lewis thought.

•

"There was this boy who we used to play ball with who got a scholarship up to Alabama in Tuscaloosa. Never seen anyone play third base and hit like he did. Came from good stock is what he said, but he hit doubles and triples like he let the devil have his way with his sister any way she could bend."

Rollie May was standing at the check-out counter at Turner's Feed and Seed, watching out the big front window as two men hefted sixty-pound bags of lime off the forklift, lifting them into the bed of his Ford that he had parked out front. Rocker panels rusting out. Bad brakes. His work truck. The clerk, a redneck boy named Lester Peacock, was talking while he punched in the order onto his standing account. Rollie watched the Ford sink under the weight and hoped that the bald tires would not explode in the morning heat. The dust on the store window looked like smeared ash and Rollie wondered if anyone ever thought to clean it.

Lester said, "We called him Scatter Gun on account of how he shot balls all over the field like he was knocking down birds. Anyway, he blew out his shoulder throwing side-arm on a slow-roller bunt. They was playing," paused, stopped punching in the order. "Tennessee maybe? Anyway, he's done in Tuscaloosa almost as soon as he gets there and then he's got nothing but time on his hands. So . . ." He stoped, peered at the read out on the register. "Gonna be seventy-five even, Rollie." Lester adjusted his hat.

"Didn't you play ball, Rollie?"

"Nah. Not baseball. Played football some in high school."

"Yeah, I remember now. Tight end right?"

"And linebacker. Uh-huh. Blew out my knee. Went to work for my daddy after that. My son plays up in . . ."

"Anyway, Scatter starts on pain pills for his shoulder and gets hooked. Starts buying and selling little white tablets, and next thing you know, he goes from big show prospect to small time criminal."

"That right?" Standing patiently at the counter. Watching Peacock.

"Yep. Went into some country club in Mountain Brooke in Birmingham—that's this hot shit neighborhood around there—and tries to rob all the people eating in the dining room. He and some colored fella . . ." Lester looked at Rollie, offered a shy grin. "Sorry about that, I mean black fella. They is standing in there with their guns and telling all those people to put their jewelry and wallets in this pillow case the black fella is passing around, and one of the guys eating is a federal marshal or some shit and he stands up and pulls his gun and they have this stand-off in the dining room of the country club. Scatter ends up shot and the colored fella run out through the kitchen. They never did catch him."

Rollie said, "That's some kind of story, Lester."

"Ain't it though?"

"Sure is."

"How come you need all this lime anyway?"

"Beg pardon," Rollie said. Lester looking over the top of the register at him. Dead expression like he'd forgotten the question. A black mole that probably needs to be checked on his lower neck. North Georgia cracker talking about country club robberies and baseball. Asking questions. Seeing Shawna at the kitchen table. Head in her hands while he talked her through it. Rollie talking fast and her nodding slow like she could see him going crazy right there in front of her.

"Whatever happened to that boy Scatter you talking about. He dead?"

"Naw. Took one in the leg, if memory serves. Sent him to the hospital and then to Reidsville. Not sure what kinda stretch he got. At least he gets to do his time in Georgia. Even with a limp." Lester handed Rollie his receipt, looking to the door when the chime went off. Mechanic from up the street named Ricky Tate. Oily jeans and a stained undershirt. Hat tipped back on his head. Eyeing Rollie as he went up an aisle.

"Thank you Lester," Rollie said

"Looks like they got you loaded up out there. All that lime and such."

Rollie checked out the window at the sagging truck.

"Looks like it."

"You go on now, Rollie. Ricky's one of these racist assholes that settled the county back in the day. No need to wait on him to come back up here and start some bullshit." Lester said. Rollie moving to the door, Ricky calling from the back of the store.

"I heard that bullshit you're talking up there, Peacock."

"Well, it's true ain't it." Rollie went out.

5.

SHAWNA MAY PULLED HER BLUE TOYOTA INTO THE parking lot of the Baptist church and parked in the spot closest to the door that was not reserved for handicapped people. It was a simple building, squat red brick tucked back in spindly groves of pine trees that were bare of limbs until they got closer to the light above the needled canopy. The parking lot was loose gray gravel, full of potholes that held water that turned a milky slate color as it pooled, splashing up onto the bumpers and rims of the clean cars that piled in for the Sunday services. Made young men take the arms of grandmothers making their way to the front door in uncomfortable shoes, old men trailing behind. She put the Toyota in park and sat listening to the engine idle, rolled down the window hearing the loud birdsong. No one there but her. What she had anticipated and prayed for after her conversation with Rollie that morning in the house. He'd left for Turner's and she had taken her time to get ready. Wanted to stop by the church before heading over to the school to work in the administrative office. Been there for years. Could run the place in her sleep, those men step out of her way. White kids and black kids alike. Was nothing more than a numbers game to her. How many seats, how many teachers, how much budget, how much shortfall. Noble, as it had always been, and how it always would be.

She opened the car door and went up the steps of the church and then went back down and looked around the side of the building to see if the Reverend's white Cadillac was parked along the side or if Wilson's truck was sitting down by the dumpster where he liked to park so he could hit a joint after taking out the trash.

Unnoticed, but also all-noticing of the congregation's coming and going. Wilson. In and out of county lock-up like it was his auntie's boarding house. Coming back to the church and putting something on for the reverend. *Bad breaks, man. Can't seem to get right.* Never mind the weed and the bottle of whatever was handy underneath the seat when the sheriff's cruiser pulled him over for weaving all over the state highway. Grew the pot back behind his place on Sunset Road. Little slanted shack that had been around since the Yankees came through on their way to Atlanta. Could have been around when the Cherokee were minding their own business before they packed them off to the badlands or wherever those white men with guns made them walk.

Shawna did not see truck or the Caddie and went back around to the front of the church, up the steps and then into the vestibule— small little room that got dark when the door closed behind her. Faux wood walls and pictures of Jesus cradling lambs or reaching down to take a little black girl's hand, light behind him like he'd stepped out of an exploding star. Little black girl looking up at him like she was not so sure about this bearded dude in white robes taking hold of her. Whole place smelled of outside and what she guessed was probably mildew. Wilson was not much on upkeep, and the Reverend not much on discipline. Not like he had been when he first got to Noble. Fresh off the road, marching around with Dr. King and full of everlasting hope and the rest of those sermons that amounted to a Jim Crow pile of horseshit.

"Don't matter," she said out loud and went into the chapel to sit and think. Stained wooden pews on both sides with a red carpet aisle running between them, slight decline in the floor as you made your way to the altar. Podium front and center and then the waist high railing that made a semi-circle in front of the altar itself. Worn burgundy-colored cushions for kneeling and looking up at the suspended Jesus-on-the-cross that hung above all of it. Mostly they stayed in their seats and hollered back and forth at the Reverend who somehow managed to look pale some Sundays despite being cave black. Outside, pallets were stacked against the side of the building next to torn bundles of shingles, a wheelbarrow with a flat tire, a rusted out fifty-five-gallon drum that was half full of trash and rainwater. Pieces of a dismantled swing set. *Brothers and sisters, I stand before you as a man of God,* the Reverend Righteous would call. People nodding their heads, hot in their suits and ties. Little kids fidgeting, maybe sucking on a piece of candy. It was her community, and while it was not perfect, it was hers and the place gave her peace.

Shawna walked half-way down the aisle and then dropped into one of the pews, took her purse out of her lap and set it beside her. Quiet above all else. She took a deep breath and let it out.

"Lord," she said.

"What you doing in here?" She started, looked around thinking, *That was quick,* then turned and looked back to the double doors. Wilson stood there, a torn t-shirt and what might have once been a khaki pair of pants. Boots untied and a durag over his shaven head. Could not tell how his eyes looked. Probably yellowed with fissures of red like old atlas maps, liquor stench dampened by the sweat.

"Aww, it's you, Shawna May," he said and shifted his slouching frame. "You leaving?"

"Wilson. Don't you know better than to sneak up on someone like that?"

"Weren't sneaking up on nobody. I got to clean the restrooms and the kitchen in the back. Can't help that you come in here on my way to do something else. You leaving?"

"No," she said. Bit too panicky. Sounding guilty. "I just came in for a minute."

"I come in an empty building, and someone likely calls the Sheriff. Ask me what I'm doing," he said. She stood up, turned to face him. "Anyway, I got to clean these bathrooms where these goddamn kids put things down the toilet and make them back up.

Think it's funny. And you know what else? These women come in here and flush they sanitary napkins down the commode and it likes to cause a flood. They put up a sign that tells them not to flush them nasty things, but they ignores it and guess who gets to come along behind and clean-up the slop?"

"I didn't see your truck when I came in," Shawna said, picking up her purse and putting the strap over her shoulder.

"I wrecked it. Went in the ditch coming back from . . . Well, never mind where I was coming back from. Deer run out in front of me on Sunset and I turned the truck right into that valley the street department boys call a ditch. Had to get it hauled out. Axle's bent all to hell. It's up at Tate's garage getting straightened out. I can't catch a break no-how. Gonna cost me like everything else. That redneck motherfucker Ricky gonna say, 'Well, Wilson, you want the bad news or the bad news first?' What you doing in here anyway?"

"Reverend R. been in today?"

"I ain't seen him."

"Tell him I was by if you would."

"Alright." He came around the left side of the pews and they passed each other, her going up and Wilson headed down to the door that lead to the kitchen in the back. She was almost out, when he called to her.

"Y'all got any work up your way?"

She turned, pulled the purse against her side.

"How you mean, Wilson? Ain't you working here?"

He grinned. "Yea, but it don't pay that much. I got this truck to get fixed and I know Tate's gonna stick it to me. Tell me there's about five more things that need to be repaired that I can't afford. You know how it is."

"I'll ask Rollie when I get home." She went out and got into the sunshine and her heart felt jumpy. Could feel cold sweat on her forehead and went slow to the Toyota. Knew what was wrong without having to name it. She put her hand on the top of the car to steady herself and looked back at the church like it had been watching this all along.

•

Clarence Warren unspooled his six-foot-four frame out of the driver's seat of the hearse and stood his full height beneath the porte cochere of the Holy Family Funeral Home. His boss, Tyler Arnold, told him that morning that there were no services scheduled that day, so Clarence had taken his time getting the hearse washed and then gone down to the diner to eat the roast beef special with fried okra, white beans, and a side of corn bread that had bits of bacon in it. He reached back in the hearse and got the Styrofoam cup of iced tea he had ordered to go. He put the cup on the hood and reached in his suit pocket for his cigarettes and plastic lighter. Tyler forbid him to smoke in the hearse, and when Clarence had insisted that dead people didn't care one way or another if he smoked in there, Tyler told him it was about the appearance and that nobody wanted to see their loved one carted off by a six-foot-four black man smoking cigarettes with his arm hanging out the window. Not to mention that the nicotine stained the white curtain lace separating the driver from the coffins in the back. They'd had a similar discussion about the music that Clarence liked to play loud when he was running a body, but Clarence had won that argument saying he'd keep the windows rolled up when people were around. Said, "You got me wearing this suit that don't fit and I got to wear this fucking cap that looks like I'm a tugboat captain. I can't listen to Buddy Guy moving a body up the road?"

Clarence surveyed the parking lot. All of the islands had these little trees planted in them. Supposed to be evergreens. Tyler said that they made people feel more welcome, but half of the trees had died three months after they had been planted—some kind of beetle secretion or something, and now they were just dead sticks poking out of the mulch. Looked like a Christmas tree people left up in their living room till July. Clarence knew it would be a matter of time before Tyler handed him a shovel and told him to dig the dead ones up. He was too cheap to hire anyone else and Clarence thought his job description grew like ass cancer.

"I hope that cigarette didn't ignite in my hearse." Clarence turned and looked over the unblemished top of the black vehicle, shiny white spots winking off the wax where the sun snuck under the overhang. *Jesus Christ*, he thought, *ignite*? Like he was talking about dynamite.

Tyler stood looking at him from the open doors of the funeral home. He was a short little man, tucked snug into his own suit that pinched him in the crotch and road up his ass after he sat. Coat sleeves too long and the back more like a cape. Was holding a ledger book in his hand, glasses perched on his nose. Big broad tie with a knot the size of a fist, and his hair combed over his scalp in little thin wisps that went every-which-way if he walked by one of the big fans they set up in the visitation rooms when it was hot. Would only turn on the air conditioning if *he* started to sweat. Never mind the guests. They could handle it for a couple hours, was his thinking. Even when the old women's makeup would start running with tears and stale humidity, told Clarence to leave the thermostat alone, like it was the dial on his safe or some big deal shit.

"I ain't smoked in the hearse, Mr. Arnold."

"I 'have not' or 'I haven't' smoked in the hearse, Clarence. We've been over this a dozen times. We don't use 'ain't.'"

Clarence pulled on the cigarette, let the smoke move around in his body, savoring it, picturing himself putting the red coal out on the bald man's head. Pound him deeper into the suit and then wrapping up his body with the clean lace. Leave him in the broom closet for his sister to find next time she came to visit from St. Louis, sleeping down the street at the motel cause she's afraid of the bodies in the cooler.

"I have not smoked inside of the hearse, Mr. Arnold." He'd like that, repeating it back like a pupil or some fucking thing. White man teaching this big nigger how to talk straight. Be ready to receive the dead in style. Make him the Angel of Death with manners, listening to blues on the Alpine speakers.

"See that you don't."

"Most certainly, Sir," Clarence said and dropped the butt on the ground then ground it out with his glistening black shoe, leaned over and picked it up and walked around the back of the hearse and dropped it in the trash can. Little cylinder next to the door with a circle of sand for the mourner butts, but he used the big can since he had to clean out the sand when it got even one lipstick-stained filter in it. He saw Tyler looking at him. Man knew sarcasm when he heard it.

"Got the automobile all shined up, Mr. Arnold. She's running good. I mean *well*. Want me to put it down in the garage?"

Arnold looked the hearse over, walked around the sides like he's the man going to buy it off of Clarence. Making sure he's not paying too much. He stopped around the front. Opened the ledger and ran his finger down a list he's made earlier that morning.

"No, Clarence. Might as well leave it out. We've got a body later this afternoon. Mildred Parsons. Eighty-six. Died this morning crossing the street downtown. A young man ran a red light and hit her in the cross walk with his Mustang. She'll be a mess, I'm guessing. But she wanted cremation, so I'll need you to pick her up at the medical examiner's office and then take her to Tri-State."

"Today?" Clarence said looking at a long shadow on the parking lot, thinking about the bottle he had put aside in the freezer back in his apartment. Girl down the street who wanted to get to know him better.

Arnold looked up from the ledger. "I don't know, Clarence," he said, closing the book. "Either today or tomorrow morning. She has no family, poor old thing, so it should go quick, but the police are involved so you never know. Either way, is this going to be a problem?"

Clarence did not answer. Watched Arnold take his short little man steps back to the open doors of the funeral home, letting in flies. *Cheap motherfucker,* Clarence thought.

•

How he got there was on account of his grandmother. She kept house for an old couple in Gadsden, Alabama where she had raised Clarence after his father left and his mother moved into his grandmother's house when she could not come up with the rent, then left with a man that she met at a K-mart one night when she was supposed to be picking up groceries. Clarence was sixteen, already pushing more than six feet, squatting more than three hundred and fifty pounds. Trying to make his grades in school. His grandmother left in the morning for the big three-story Classic Revival on Turrentine Avenue where she cooked and cleaned and was sent home after the dinner meal. She got fired one night when the husband came back from the golf course, half-way through a bottle of Early Times, and broke her arm after biting into a piece of chicken that was not cooked all the way through. His grandmother came in their house holding her arm like a bird with shot in its wing and slept the night on the couch. Clarence woke the next morning to find her whimpering and drove her to the hospital to get the arm set, and on the way home, he raised his voice to her for the first time in his life demanding to know what happened, not buying her story of falling over a root in the sidewalk. Woman was sturdy as bank vault.

He went to the house on Turrentine, but the man was not home. Back on the golf course, house maid told him, keeping the door ajar, talking through the opening like she was ashamed of being in the apron. The wife came up behind the little maid and pulled the door open, said "I've already called the police." Clarence left a few minutes before the deputy got there, the wife saying that a large Negro had tried to assault her on her front porch. He drove over to the country club and found the husband putting on his golf cleats in the parking lot. Clarence broke his leg in three places with a four wood from the man's golf bag, still resting on its side in the trunk. He was on his way to working on the other leg when a caddie from the club hit him in the back of the head with a piece of rebar he'd found on a wood shelf in the cart stand. He woke up in the Etowah County jail on Forrest Avenue with seven stitches in the back of his head and blurry vision in his left eye. The judge gave him ten years, acting like he was letting Clarence up his skirt on the first date. Went into lock-up figuring he'd do the whole stretch. Did two of his years in juvenile detention before they moved him over to St. Claire Correctional when he turned eighteen. He was keeping things in order, working out and staying close to the black men who were empathetic enough to take him in. Took on some jobs inside and got a reputation as an inmate who'd listen and do what he was told. When the medical examiner's office back in Etowah asked for a trustee to help clean up around the place, they gave him Clarence, and he was shipped back to Forrest Avenue where he worked under the county coroner who turned out to be the only decent white man he'd ever known. Two years there and the coroner, a man named Dr. Horn, went to the court and got his sentence reduced saying he'd keep Clarence in line. He stayed on, sleeping easy on a green leather couch in Dr. Horn's cramped little office. Medical books all over the shelves, stacks of papers and old journals piled on the desk, posters of the human body in old frames, crooked on their nails poking their bent heads out of the plaster. *Spooky.* Up in the morning to wait on his bodies, talking to Dr. Horn smoking Camels with no filter out by the ambulance drop off. Then inside on a delivery, watching Horn cut them open, explaining what he was doing the whole time like Clarence was doing his residency. *Jesus, look at that. Doctor holding a heart in his hand talking about egg salad for lunch. God damn.*

Horn let him attend his grandmother's funeral and visit with family when they came in to pay their respects. Cold October day. Men and women in shabby suits and coats, him in the jumpsuit, a deputy smoking back on the road, talking to the guys that dug the grave. No parents. The deputy let him stay a while longer, Clarence standing over the grave, one of the men waiting with a Bob Cat to fill in the hole, Clarence crying and telling his grandmother that he was sorry for all the trouble that he'd caused her. Swore he would make it up to her. Then Tyler Arnold came into the office in November and asked if he'd like a job. Dr. Horn kept him for six more weeks until he could secure another trustee, gave him five hundred dollars in an envelope, and let him walk out into the winter sunlight, unattended, six years after swinging a four wood like Calvin Peete having a come-apart at August National.

6.

SATURDAY MORNING. TRAIAN COULD NOT RECALL exactly how many of them had been at the table. His head cottony and his mouth just as dry. Thinking it over, coffee in his queen-sized bed, bedroom still unpacked. Boxes on the floor. A dresser in the corner with a picture of his parents in front of the arch overlooking an autumn quadrangle at Wooster. Kim's hanging clothes on the floor as well, and a plastic tub of mismatched shoes. There had been Director Haskins and his wife. Jene he thought her name was, or Jenny, maybe. She had left early to pay the babysitter. The assistant director by herself. Not married and no boyfriend. Couple other agents who just happened to be there. Kent and Gillis. One of their wife's name was Susie, he thought, laughing too loud. Traian trying on his humor for the Director, Susie looking bored in a nice blouse and hair that looked like it had been done earlier that morning, still smelling of the hairspray that they had used in the salon. Told Kim where it was and who to ask for if she didn't want her hair fucked up. And of course Kim, cool and refreshing as the white rum and lemon in in her squat glass. Nursing the drink, watching them watching Traian. Top button of the white shirt undone. Showing little and a lot at the same time. That had been it, he thought. Sipped the coffee and dripped some on his bare chest.

He'd ordered another bourbon over crushed ice when Kent jumped into a pause, knocking over a saltshaker reaching for his drink. Tossing the flakes over his shoulder. Something bright red in the glass, faded out like fruit punch. Said, "Tell us about this famous bust in Florida, Thomas." *Thomas*, like they were teammates. "I hear, well, that . . . " Kent said, wiping the salt with the side of his palm.

"Let him tell it," Susie said, sipping her drink, cutting an eye at Traian, moving the straw around in the glass in a slow circle. Kim taking notice. Calm through the glance.

"Well, I'm sure that all of you . . . "

"Yes, tell it," Kim said. Liking him on the spot. Having fun with it, storing up the attention. Would uncap it when they got home, brushing their teeth in the bathroom. *Yes, Agent Thomas, please tell it.* Big smile in the mirror, looking at him in a reflection in his underwear and t-shirt, following his eyes moving over her bare legs. The waitress dropped off the bourbon and went away without asking if anyone needed anything. He sipped it, felt the warmth and saliva gather. Took a breath.

•

The way that Traian landed the biggest bust of his fledgling career was on account of a man names Allen James who ran a small insurance agency in Bonita Springs, Florida. The agency was named after his father—James Financial Services, or JFS. Allen had grown the small shop into a big regional player along the I-75 corridor, diversifying the product portfolio and being creative with tax planning and reporting. Helped retirees make the most of their savings and then figured out how to flip the coin over by selling financial products to the banks and credit unions themselves instead of making shit-money off mutual funds, life insurance policies, and inflated annuity fees. Over cocktails one night at a seminar in Tampa, he met a mid-level executive with a big firm out of Washington state called Puget that specialized in cobbling together agencies like Allen's all over the country and leveraging their collective client base and buying power to make investment and insurance products that would be exclusive to Puget. No one really understood what went into the products, but they worked and sold like free hand jobs. Allen got rich.

"You guys . . . " Traian conscious of not using 'y'all' with the Southern accents surrounding him at the table, the place quiet now. Just a few diners left, the rest drinking steady. Moody Van Morrison overhead. Low lights and mirrors along one wall. Waiters with aprons putting down place settings. He could feel the Ohio nasal in his voice. Sipped the bourbon, trying to get into the part. "You remember when that private plane went down in Tampa Bay? 'Bout five, six years ago?"

"I was in Kansas, then," Kent said. "Nice gig there, eh Suz?" Kent's wife looking at her empty glass, seeing open plains and smelling rib meat and wood smoke. Skylines thick with tornado wind. Hiding a Valium habit from the kids and her husband.

"I remember," Haskins said. "It was full of executives. Heading to Chicago, I think."

"That's it, but it was Detroit." Traian said, nodding, looking over at Kim, her watching him back. He thought she looked pleased. Maybe the two of them showing off a little bit. "They helped run a big UAW credit union office in Tampa. There were four of them. On their way to play golf down in Naples and then up to Detroit for an earnings report to the Board. Plane went down in the Bay. No one came out of the water, including the pilot. All C-Suite guys." Traian sipped his drink, thinking about the most concise way to tell it.

"So this board up in Detroit was full of made guys working the credit unions to hide money. All but three of the members were part of the same crime outfit run by . . . "

"Frank Bonanno," Director Haskins said.

"No shit?" Kent said. "Related to the other guy? What's his name?"

"You're thinking of Joey Bananas," Traian said. "Could have been, but a big gap between the two careers. I never got in the room with Frank after this all went down. Got kicked up to the DC and NYC offices." Had their attention now, big name mobsters sitting in the middle of the table like an exhibit. All of them leaning in. Even the wives.

"So, it turns out that one of the products that Puget cooked up was a life insurance investment plan that a company—in this case a credit union—could take out policies on their employees and when the employee died, the benefit came back to credit union. All perfectly legal, albeit a little unethical considering the exec who dies probably leaves behind a wife and kids. So it also turns out that Allen James was up in Detroit for a meeting with a client and one of these credit union board members sat in on the discussion. Allen has no idea who the guy is. Finishes the meeting, gets a cab to the airport and flies home to Florida to do the enrollment paperwork.

"But a couple days after, his receptionist buzzes him and says there are two guys in his lobby that would like to see him. Allen says that they can make an appointment for tomorrow, and a few minutes pass and the receptionist—a cute twenty-something blond girl working an internship—comes into his office and says that they insist that Allen see them right then. She looks worked-up about it, so Allen gets up, walks out to the reception desk and these two guys in matching suits get off the couch and come over and introduce themselves as board members for the credit union in Detroit. Allen says, 'That's nice. I was just in Detroit, blah blah, blah,' and they say 'Yea, we know, that's why we're here,' and so they go back into Allen's office and shut the door." Traian took a break, waited for questions, but the table just looked at him, wondering why he's dragging things out. *Get to it. Jesus.*

"So, what happened was that the Detroit guys want to buy life insurance policies on two senior executives in their New York office. Say that they heard through a mutual friend—Allen's client—that he can underwrite these insurance policies and that they, meaning the credit union, gets paid when the executives die. When I interviewed Allen, he kept making that point. Says, 'They kept asking me what happens when the insured dies. We get the money, right, right, right?' and Allen tells them yes, they get the money, but the policy has to mature at least six months. Almost like he's guiding them on the protocol, but he has no idea that they are connected and that the credit union is one big front for laundered money."

"Wait, I thought we were talking about the guys that went down in Tampa Bay?" Kent said.

"We are," Traian said, holding his empty glass.

"You want another one?" Kim said

"Get him another one," the assistant director Cindy said. Traian had almost forgotten she was there. Quiet, but listening to his story. Kim got up and began to walk to the bar. Then turned back to the table.

"Anyone else?" They all said yes, please, they all wanted another and Kim laughed and went to the bar and told the bartender to send over their waiter who had disappeared somewhere in the back of the restaurant.

"Go on," Cindy said. "I'm starting to remember some of this happening."

"Right," Traian said. "So Allen writes the policies on the two guys in New York and when he gets the signed paperwork back, he files it away and thinks nothing of it. Only eight months later, he gets a call from the provider that both men died in a car accident coming back from a meeting in Philly and that the payout is three million apiece, back to the credit union.

"So Allen says 'Holy Shit' but still doesn't know anything and he just chalks the whole thing up to coincidence, cause, I mean, what are the odds, right? And of course he's a darling for the client. This is Allen thinking his way through it. So, he goes back to work and a few weeks later, guess who shows back up?"

"Joey Bananas," Kent's wife Suzie said, giggling. A little drunk, slurring the words just a bit. Elongating *Jooooooeeeee*. Cindy looked at her, pursed her lips. The waitress came back, following Kim who had gone to the bathroom. She set the tray of drinks on the adjacent table and served. Traian looked at the fresh bourbon in front of him.

"No, not Joey."

"The two thugs from Detroit."

Traian looked past Director Haskins's shoulder and saw that a man was sitting half in shadow holding a beer glass.

"Sorry," he said. "Just been listening in. I'm agent Randy Gillis. Could not help but overhear the story. Hope you don't mind."

"I'm sorry," Director Haskins said, turning around and looking at the agent, seeming confused to see him there, hanging on the story like the rest of them. "I should have introduced him. Would have said something, but he snuck up on us." Now looking more irritated than confused. Gillis did not seem to notice. Calm.

"No," Traian said. "The more the merrier. Nice to meet you Agent Gillis." He picked up the cocktail glass and tipped it. Young guy. Good looking with a full head of wavy brown hair, styled with product. Neat suit with white shirt and no tie. Traian guessed he might be thirty-five.

"So, yeah, Allen gets another visit from the boys in Detroit, only this time they call ahead and make the appointment. Wanted to take Allen out to dinner down in Ybor City. Allen says 'Okay, fine, but what are we meeting about and the Detroit boys tell him not to worry about it. They can talk over dinner. They book a room in the downtown Hilton and have Allen meet them at the bar. They have drinks and then head over to Columbia to eat. I get all this from Allen in the interview. He thinks things are going great. They seem happy about the policies, and about the time the fried Calamari shows up, they drop it on him like a wet bag of cement—tell him that they want to take policies out on the four of the executives in the Tampa Bay office, three million on each. Allen says that maybe this won't look so good right on the heels of the other guys in New York and they say, again, not to worry about it. That was an accident and taking out the policies is not illegal, and can he just write them up, like they asked. So, Allen does it, only now he's thinking maybe he's into something he can't get out of. At least not clean, and so he goes back to the office in the morning and because he's scared, he tells this intern named Regina about what's going on, thinking she's not even gonna really understand all of it and will just be someone he can unload on until he gets his head around it. All of this in twenty-four-hours and Allen is fighting headaches and heartburn the whole time, knowing that his gut is right on this and that he's in a world of shit."

"Was he screwing the intern?"

Traian stopped talking and looked over at Kim who had asked the question. Cynical, amused, using her eyes. Toying with his limelight. "I don't know," he said.

"You didn't ask? Seems strange that he would confide in her, don't you think?"

Traian nodded.

"I did. I mean I *did* ask."

"And?"

"And it wasn't really relevant to the case."

"I see," Kim said and sipped from her glass, still looking at him like they were alone and talking about something that they had talked about before, but never really resolved.

"So, Allen calls Puget and gets it in the works and after a couple of tense back-and-forths and Allen being adamant that there's nothing screwy going, they agree. And of course they do that cause they are going to be collecting from the credit union the whole time until these guys kickoff and what's the chance of six executives dying all at once?"

"Jesus," Agent Gillis said.

"Yeah," Kent says. "Jesus is right. Go on."

"Okay," Traian said. "This time the boys in Detroit get anxious and don't wait quite as long to call the hit. They have a French-Canadian button named Reggie Jacques come down to Florida, go into the plane hangar at night and rig something up that will make the plane stall out mid-air. I don't know how he knew how to do it cause he's just a button for the family up there. Sheet long as your right arm, but nothing that indicates he would know anything about sabotaging a private plane. Reggie goes the night before the four guys are flying out, does what he needs to, leaves and then hits a bar and gets popped driving back to the hotel for DUI. Put him in County and start poking around—this guy with the accent driving around Tampa with a bag of tools in the back seat and lit up like an M-80. Tells the patrol cops that he'll show them what resisting arrest looks like where he's from if they feel like a trip to the fucking morgue. They get him booked and turns out that he's got outstanding warrants in Toledo and Madison, Wisconsin. So they decide to let him sleep it off before they send someone in to ask him what he's been up to on his vacation."Traian looks around the table, over at Agent Gillis and another guy who is sitting next to him, clone outfit and nursing his beer glass. *Wrap it up,* he thinks, everyone still watching.

"The execs get in the plane the next morning. Golf bags, brief cases, and travel stuff in the back. Climb out over Tampa Bay and it just dies. No 'May Day, May Day.' Just drops like a rock into the water. All over the front of the Tribune the next morning. Pictures of the four guys, the widows and kids left behind, speculations on what happened to the plane. Allen reads the story and now he's sure of what's going on, but he's got nowhere to go. Just has to wait until Detroit calls to collect, but he also knows Puget is gonna balk, right? No one is that stupid, and the way this has all gone down, they're gonna think he's in on it. Which he is, because he's greedy. And he knows it's gonna be a hard story to sell.

"Couple days go by and the phone starts ringing from Detroit. The intern, Regina, keeps telling them that Allen is not there, Allen standing in the doorway chewing on his fingernails. The last call they get is from a hotel in Tampa and the guy says that they are on their way over to the office to talk with Allen about the money that he owes them. Intern hangs up and tells Allen this and he splits. Goes home to pack and get out of town, make plans later. The guys from Detroit show up and when Allen's not there, they get rough with Regina who gives up her boss's address pretty quick. Now these two guys go over to Allen's house, turn it upside down, but no Allen. In the meantime, Regina is spooked and calls the Tampa PD and gives the desk sergeant the whole story—the insurance scam, Allen, the guys from Detroit who threatened to put her head through a glass wall in the office if she did not spill the address. This intern talks to Tampa PD for twenty minutes and the sergeant hangs up and calls our office and says, "You know that plane that went down in the bay, yea? Well guess what.'"

"What about the other people in the office?" Director Haskins said.

"Which office?"

"Jame's office. It was an agency, right? There had to be more people there."

"Oh yea," Traian said. "Plenty of them, but when we questioned them, they were oblivious. Allen kept this whole insurance product to himself. Had not rolled it out to other agents yet. I guess he was having too much fun making money."

"Until he wasn't." the Director said.

"Exactly," Traian said. Saw that Suzie had fallen asleep with her head on the table and Kent was gone. He looked at the rest of them.

"Did I do that," he said and pointed at the sleeping woman.

"Never mind her," Agent Gillis said. "Tell us how it ended."

"Yes," Kim said. Sleepy looking. Promising expression if he would hurry up and get her home.

·

How it ended was that Traian listened to everything the sergeant had to say and then spent the next few weeks tying all the pieces together. Jacques got pinned for the plane after security at the hangar called the Tampa Police. Airport security had the guy on closed circuit breaking into the hangar at two in the morning. Tampa PD runs it up the chain.

Traian was the lead investigator, sending out law enforcement to track down Allen James who they found in Dahlonega in a rented cabin in the woods. Georgia trooper ran the plates on his red Mercedes while he was getting gas. They brought him back to Florida and after several hours of interrogation, they let him go home with a warning to stick around. Believed him when he explained how he had been caught in the middle and that he would testify against the two guys out of Detroit. Left a patrol car out front with directions for the uniforms to pay attention. People not fucking around about killing witnesses.

Traian flipped Jacques in the same room where he'd talked with Allen, telling him that if he did not cooperate he was going to do the whole stretch for a quadruple homicide, not to mention what they charged him with for tampering with an airplane that could just have easily gone down overtop a crowded beach full of tourists and their kids. Traian and Jacques watched the security tape together. Traian said, "That sure looks like you Reggie." Reggie coming out of the hangar with his bag of tools, looking left and right and then getting into his rental and driving out of the camera's view. He was wrapping up the confession when a good-looking black woman from his office named Angie knocked and then opened the door and asked Traian to step out with her. He got up, patted Jacques on the back as he walked behind him, and went out in the hall, closing the door with a gentle click.

"DC called," Angie said.

"And?"

"They want it. They got the two guys from Detroit office now. Both of them singing about the credit union board and the front. It goes all the way up and they want to take the lead. Said for you to write up your report and send it there way. I'm sorry, Traian."

"Well, shit." he said, hands on hips, looking down the empty hall, bright with the overhead fluorescents. The whole place needing a coat of paint.

<h1 style="text-align:center">7.</h1>

ABOUT THE TIME THAT CLARENCE WARREN REACHED the medical examiner's office, waiting to load Mildred Parsons in the back, leaning against the shiny Cadillac hearse, smoking, Rollie pulled into the rutted drive of his house that doubled as the Tri-State Crematory. Bed of the truck loaded down with the bags of lime. The tires still inflated, *thank Christ*. Grass in the yard ratty brown, patches of the red Georgia clay like skin grafts dotting the slope of the hill that ran down to the road. The house seeming to lean on its foundation on a knoll of rock and clay. Water eroding both sides of the driveway, making ditches.

Rollie came from a long line of black Mays in Noble, reaching all the way back to a white man from North Carolina who had settled a small jog down the road in Lafayette, Georgia. Arrived just in time for the civil war, giving his surname to the slaves he brought along with him. Rollie's ancestors had built Mr. May's house and now it was a historic place to visit.

"Field Nigger Ingenuity," Rollie had said to Shawna one day when they were driving past the plantation. Big porch and columns, stone walls around the perimeter, kitchen built in the basement so the help could carry the food upstairs to the dining room. Stark white in the light of the day. Felt haunted at night, antebellum ghosts in the rocking chairs looking out over the expanse of the fields. Shawna had looked cross at him when he made the comment. Then looked at the cars parked in the gravel lot and the old white men and women toting cameras around their neck on cheap plastic straps, reading the iron plaques telling how Mr. May had been a pillar of the community in his time. Even started a school and a successful textile business.

"No need to use that word," she had said.

"What, *nigger*?"

"That one," she said, glaring across the bench seat at her husband.

"Well, it's still standing ain't it? That's craftsmanship. Ingenuity. And what you think that they called us back then? Still call us now when we got our backs turned?"

"Doesn't matter," she said. "You don't need to use it. Makes you sound ignorant as them."

He supposed she was right, but still admired the strength and feel the house gave off, even if it was only a stopping place for twentieth-century Confederates reliving their *war of northern aggression*. Called it that when they were together like it made the whole thing justified and their loss something to be memorialized. Stopped at the May house and then on up the road in their RVs to see the battlefield at Chickamauga where the rebels knocked a hole in the Union army only to be worked over like rented mules at the battles of Lookout Mountain and Missionary Ridge. Rollie's namesake had left the house in LaFayette before the Union troops showed up, then came home after. The bluecoats had occupied the May place while the fighting was going on, riding horses up into the parlor, getting blood on the floors and the walls. Troops sleeping and dying in the rooms. Lot of yelling and foul smells. That's about all Rollie knew. May had let the slaves go after emancipation and they had all stayed around, settling in Noble, his relatives moving into established positions in the slowly emerging black community, living in shacks alongside broken down white farmers and eroding households mean with drink and latent hatred. Rifles and sighted glances when they crossed paths in town. Profanity spilling in drunken encounters, black folk reticent and eager to get out of the way. His family had been there ever since. All that blood and history just down the road like it happened the day before yesterday, a community gathering with muskets and cannonballs, and limbs lying all over the place like they'd been knocked loose in a storm.

Rollie looked around the yard, saw Shawna's car gone and counted himself lucky for once. Wondered where the kids were, then set it aside. In addition to the house he observed several more peeling paint buildings on the property. There was the main building that housed the cremation retort, the only structure made of cinder block, two maintenance buildings that were full of junk dating back twenty years, gravel pads for the tractor and the hearse that he used to go pick up bodies for the smaller funeral homes that did not have their own transportation. The vehicles hunched in the shadows, sunlight coming through the back side and casting a weak orange glow like the dark space was lit behind with embers. Behind the cleared yard for the house and the buildings was a semicircle of pine trees that stood like craggy sentries rimming the dense woods beyond. The yard sloping up slightly so the trees seemed to tower above their actual height, brooding over everything that he and Shawna owned. Further back into the brush was a stagnant pond with a few picnic tables set up along the edge of the scummy water where they sometimes hosted family reunions. Rollie and his oldest son Levi had dug a pit back behind one of the picnic tables and placed an old pipe rail cattle gate over the exposed opening so they could roast a pig, smoke hovering over the water like mist from something ancient and ritualistic.

Rollie let the tail gate down and began pulling the lime bags out of the back of the truck. One by one he carried them up to the closest storage building, kicking the door open and setting them down on the concrete floor, far enough into the opening so he could come in and out without having to move them a second time. He got the last bag from the bed, dropped it on the ground and pulled a shovel out that had been buried beneath all the sacks of lime. He closed the tail gate, leaned the shovel against the truck, then took the last bag up the slope and around the side of the storage building and dumped it into a rusted wheelbarrow. Then he went back down and got the shovel and returned to the wheelbarrow, dropped the shovel on top of the lime bag and began rolling the creaking thing with worn wooden handles up the path that led through a break in the pine trees. As he went up the narrow path, the birds overhead stopped their chirping, as if they were watching and judging his progress. The sun was still hot in the windless trees and he stopped to wipe the sweat out of his eyes, then went on. He crested the hill and then started down a slope. Flies found him out and now it was not just the sweat, but the biting insects that were feeding on his skin, coming in sideways, like fat black drops of rain, bouncing off his slick forearms and neck, so that he had to stop two more times before he finally dropped the handles of the wheelbarrow and looked down on the bodies stacked there at the base of a Chestnut tree. They were three high. An older woman who looked to be about seventy-five; a white man in his mid-twenties, rail thin with sunken features and bleached looking skin. Looked like an OD. And another woman at the top of the stack, this one about forty-five by her face and decent figure, almost peaceful with pronounced cheekbones and closed eyes that Rollie could feel stdy-ing him from behind the lids. He tried to remember what had killed each of them. Usually the funeral home drivers made small talk about the dead people in the back of their vehicles. Young guys, and really old guys. No one in between he had noticed ever since he started Tris-State. Always a little nervous. Always smoking or dancing around, unsure of what to do with their feet. Typically he'd offer them a drink from the bottles that he kept under the kitchen sink. Jack Daniels, or maybe George Dickel. They would stand out in the barren yard, chatting about the ride there. If they were new to the job, they wanted to talk more. Asking about how it all worked. Saying they were glad to have that dead body out of the back, wanting to head home to wherever they came from, but not before they settled their nerves. The old men—the old white men—looked like they might be dropping themselves off, and never wanted to take a drink with Rollie. Probably had their own pint underneath the seat. Sad old fuckers with dented skulls and eyes full-up with cataracts and distrust. Wearing cheap black suits and monkey caps that fit them like kids playing dress-up. Not happy about leaving white folks with a black man out in the middle of the North Georgia pine woods, fixing to cart some old white woman off to be burned up and sent back in a shoe box with her name taped over the top. They would open the back, wait for him to help them pull out the coffin and then cart the box up to the retort building. Both of them grunting under the weight, then back out the door, down to the car and their headlights backing down the drive onto the two lane that would take them out of Noble and onto the state highway, sipping something bitter and oaky on their way to park the hearse in some town where people were literally dying to leave.

Rollie took up the shovel, then put it back down. He went around the wheelbarrow and kicked at the dead leaves and pine needles, exposing wet earth. He looked up into the trees and thought about how he would square all of this. Not just with Shawna, but with whomever was up there watching him, a stare as piercing as the yellow sun, mixing with white heat so that it shimmered in waves. He dropped the shovel then, and went back down the path, into the yard, and then up the steps of the house and into the kitchen. He turned on the faucet and rinsed his face, then unbuttoned his shirt and splashed the water on his bare chest. Opened a cabinet and pulled out a mason jar. Opened the cabinet under the sink and brought out the bottle of Dickel and filled half the jar, put the bottle back behind the can of Comet, and drank a third of the liquor standing in the quiet room. He carried the jar back up the path to where the shovel and the wheelbarrow were waiting for him, birds still quiet overhead, the leaves loud and revealing beneath his heavy boots, strides purposeful, the liquor steeling him a little, feeling grateful and vindicated. The bag of lime limp and rumpled in the rusted bucket of the wheelbarrow. Creases in the plastic. He drank the rest of the Dickel and tossed the jar onto the ground. He bent to pick up the shovel and smelled them, just beginning to turn. Said out loud, "You could stop this now." Then he breathed deep, raised the shovel handle over his head with both hands, and brought the head down into the dirt, which gave freely under the force.

He was almost through. Had dug a shallow hole, long enough and deep enough to hold all three of the bodies, dumped the lime over them and pushed the dirt back in place, when he heard the engine behind him, coming up his drive, daylight still there, but fading quickly like it was running out of steam. He tossed the shovel back into the wheelbarrow and turned it around and went up the rise and then back down, emerging into the yard to see the hearse idling in front of the house. A black Cadillac it looked like. Shadows over the windshield so he could not make out the driver inside. Thinking hard about what he had been doing minutes before. The nice looking woman's head resting on the shoulder of the old woman like they were sleeping in the hole. The driver had not turned off the Caddie's engine, and Rollie could feel the paranoia creeping up his throat like the way it felt when he was getting a summer cold.

He dropped the handles of the wheelbarrow and came down to where the Cadillac waited for him, loud with the AC running, windows tinted black and mirroring the buildings and woods surrounding them. He stood. Breathing shallow, hands at his side, the digging fresh in his mind and beneath his nails where he had touched the loose top soil. The sound of the bodies, muted and soft, going into the hole. The woods silent as their family BBQ smoke over the pond water. The door opened and a large black man climbed out, head bent for clearance, and then standing at his full height, looking around the yard like he was not sure if he was in the right place. Could have been his son, standing on the sidelines waiting for the kicking team to come off the field.

"This Tri-State?" the man said, looking at Rollie, a grin on his face. Rollie could hear music coming out of the open cab of the hearse. Sounded like Sam Cooke. Live though, not the crooning studio shit. Something about a handkerchief swinging.

"Yes sir," Rollie said. "You found it alright."

The man grinned wider. "I guess you into privacy, huh?"

"Dead don't seem to care," Rollie said, and then thought about how that might sound. "But yeah, we out here alright. You looking for me?"

The man tilted his head, amused. "Not me," he said. "But Mrs. Parsons here," he turned and motioned at the back of hearse, "She need you, I guess." Sam Cooke loud now, yelling at the people in the audience. Clarence saw that it was distracting Rollie, and he reached in and switched off the car. Stood up, took the pack of cigarettes out of his shirt pocket and offered one to Rollie who shook his head. Lit the smoke and looked around the yard of the Tri-State Crematory.

Said, "This your place, I guess? I ain't never been out here before. Holy Family usually uses some place over in Birmingham, but that motherfucker Tyler Arnold I work for is cheap like you would not believe. Bit of a grammar coach too. Don't like smoking in the hearse, even when I got to come two hours to drop off a body. Anyway, it's a job. What you gonna do. You like it way out here?"

"I'm Rollie. Rollie May."

Clarence held in the smoke and then laughed. Broke himself up. "Shit, I'm sorry, man. I get off by myself too long and I start talking like people aren't around. I'm Clarence Warren. I'm supposed to drop off Mrs. Parsons here for cremation. Mr. Arnold says that he talked with someone yesterday afternoon about scheduling it. That sound right to you?"

Rollie relaxed. "Yeah, that sounds right. Let me go get the book. Your man probably talked to my wife, Shawna. Come on up to the porch and I'll get you taken care of." He turned and walked toward the house, did not wait to see if Clarence was following him, thinking about the bodies in the freshly dug hole. Thinking he was in the clear. He went onto the porch and through the screen door, found the leather book next to the phone on the wall in the kitchen then started back outside, went back for the Dickel and two of the mason jars, remembering the one he left out in the woods, making a note to go back for it later. Clarence was sitting in one of the rocking chairs when he came back outside, watching the man's eyes looking at the bottle in his hand, holding the jars by their lips with the same hand. Thought, *Okay, just be cool* and set everything down on a small table. Held up the bottle.

"That's right, yes sir, thank you much," Clarence said. Rollie poured, handed one of the jars over, then sat down and they sipped the whiskey in silence, Rollie's mind like startled birds. Clarence's head right where he rocked, smiling, and thinking he would drive back to Chattanooga and get himself a hotel over off the Lookout Valley exit. Maybe wander out later and see what was walking around. Truck stop not far up the road. Maybe slide over there and see if one of those girls working the lot wanted to sleep in a clean bed in a motel. Drink the man's whisky first. Drive back in the dark, slow, watching for deer in the road, then find the Howard Johnson's and check in. Call Mr. Arnold and tell him he was too sleepy to drive back that night. Be home in the morning. *Christ,* he thought. *Fucking Tyler Arnold.*

"Say, my man," Clarence said, feeling the whiskey on his teeth and in the back of his throat. "How long you been in the cremation business? Me, I've been in the funeral business awhile. Got into it after I did a stretch in prison. Been kinda clean since, but always wonder when I do this taxiing around for dead people, why the folks I drop them off with got into the business. You know what I'm saying—some spooky shit when you think about it, you know?"

Rollie sipped from the jar. Half-listening. Then took up a memory, seeing it in front of him like an old photograph or a wilted playing card.

"Well," he said, "my Daddy made headstones around here for

a long time. Got to where he was one of the best in the state and cause he was located near Georgia, Alabama, and Tennessee, he took on a lot of work. Both white and black parlors all over the place. I don't think most of the white owners even knew that a colored man was chiseling their relatives' markers. Least I don't think they knew back then on account of white folks never like black folks messing with their remains. You feel me? Anyway, he got big and still wasn't making no money cause he couldn't make the stones fast enough, so he bought that retort over there." He pointed at the building where the broken retort was housed. "Brought me up in the business. Been doing that ever since he died."

"A what?" Clarence said, putting down his jar and looking at Rollie in the half-light.

"Retort."

"How come they call it that?"

"Not sure," Rollie said, looking at the hearse in the yard, thinking about this woman Parsons in the back. Wondering why this man on his porch was not in any kind of hurry. Asking questions. "Has something to do with the indirect heat. See, back in the day, they used coal and wood and they did not want to get the ashes mixed up together, so this word 'retort' means the ashes stayed apart. 'Least that's the way that I understand it. Probably more to it, I guess. Never really thought about it."

"Huh," Clarence said. "That's it?"

Rollie did not answer his question. "Might be time to get this lady out of the back of the hearse, you think?"

"I don't see any of us is in a hurry. You?"

"Well," Rollie said, standing. "My wife gonna be home soon and got our son with her. Best not to be moving bodies around the yard at night if I can help it."

"He don't know about the *retort?*"

Rolli stood up and moved off the porch, no longer liking the company. Wanting to go inside and wash up. Thinking about where he was going to put Mrs. Parsons after this man Clarence went back to Gadsden in his Holy Family hearse. His son Matt's bike leaning against the broken lattice work hanging from rusted nails covering the empty space beneath the raised porch. Bell on the handlebar. Boy not old enough to know much of anything. Soft spoken and sweet like his mother was when Rollie met her. *His good child*, he thought, looking back to the porch with no light on. The big man just a large shadow up above him, the jar in his hand. The jar still out in the woods, little bit of liquor puddled in the bottom. Not-too-long dead in the ground and no ashes to send back. People calling for delivery updates, talking about schedules and loved ones making their own phone calls trying to make plans for moving on.

"Alright," Clarence said, getting up and stretching his arms above his head. Exaggerated like he was put out with the short visit, wanting more of the Dickel sitting on the small table. Plenty left. Man being stingy with his time and his liquor.

"Alright. Where we putting her?"

8.

THERE WAS A PROCESSING ROOM IN THE RETORT BUILD-
ing, and Rollie went around back of the hearse with Clarence and
took Mrs. Parson's body out of the Cadillac, the old woman in a
bio-degradable box that funeral directors sent to Tri-State since
neither the box nor the body were coming back for any kind of
burial service. They lifted the box out, Rollie in the back holding
the weight while Clarence got a hand hold, then walking up the
yard's short slope to the rear door of the building that opened into
a simple, cheaply paneled room with stained concrete floors and
built-in benches running along both sides of the wall, wide enough
to hold the makeshift coffins. No windows, the air still and heavily
perfumed with stagnant smells of trapped smoke and other things.
Clarence had sworn under his breath most of the walk up, talking
about getting mud on his shoes and almost breaking his neck for
the stones protruding in the dark.

Clarence said, "Goddamn, man. You ever think about hitting
the floor and walls of this place with some bleach or something?"

Rollie guided the box over to one of the benches and set his end
down, holding it to make sure Clarence had a chance to rest the
other end.

Clarence looked around the small room and then at Rollie.

"This some spooky shit in here, man. Out in the middle of
nowhere Georgia. House and family about a stone's throw from
a cremation building. Fucking woods all around you. Goddamn
bugs and wolves and shit roaming around out there like Dracula's
haunted forest. Jesus, man. How you do this? I mean, I know I
drive a hearse, but I got a degree of separation. Even a real window

"

between me and the deceased folk in the back. I mean, I go home at the end of the day. Put my feet up in a two-bedroom apartment and watch television. Think about something besides dead people, you know. You out here like you communing with them. Getting to know each other. 'Hey, Mrs. Parsons. We gonna go eat. You sit tight.' Shit."

•

Now Rollie stood like a man who did not recognize where he was, looking out at the yard in the brilliant morning sunlight, the leaves across the street looking like they were ready to turn. Waiting on his wife, daughter and youngest son to join him so they could cram in Shawna's car and drive up to Chattanooga to watch his son play football against Wofford College, a team out of Spartanburg, South Carolina with a decent running game. Enough that his son Levi would need to be on top of his game as a sophomore linebacker who was still intent on making a career of it. Clarence, this man who had driven the hearse from Gadsden, had begged another drink of the Dickel and had nursed it on the same porch where he stood now, single bulb turned on now to illuminate the dilapidated wood planks, making small talk and comments about the funeral business. Shawna had come home in the full dark with their son Matt, and then Caroline had pulled in not far behind her, getting out of the car, dressed in her blue jeans and tight white blouse that gently draped over her smooth coffee-colored skin, seeing Clarence in the dim light, and Clarence seeing her. Rollie watching the smile on his lips, like something predatory, obviously sexual and leering. Rollie introducing Clarence to Shawna because she had taken the order for Mrs. Parsons, but wanting to avoid introducing his daughter Caroline, who paused intentionally on the porch. Looking the big Alabama man over like he had been mail ordered to Noble, just for her. Stuck out her hand and said her name. then asked him about who he was, looking too intent, posture cocked, and brown eyes playfully slitted. Touching her hair. Rollie had given her a look. Stout father peering over the shoulder of the suitor, studying the girl, his daughter, like she was something out of their collective reach. *Get inside.* And she had seen the look and followed her mother and brother into the house to help start dinner. Carry on with the routine ending of the day like normal. Rollie thinking about the box in the retort building, working over the comment about bleach. *Probably not a bad idea.*

He had seen Clarence to the hearse, told him to come back on Monday to pick up the cremations, or they could ship them back to Gadsden, his choice. Clarence said he would pick them up. Was going to stay in Chattanooga for the weekend. See what kind of action was there. Rollie told him to call before he came then had gone back in to wait on the dinner. Shawna looking at him over the steam of the pots, telling Matt to go do his homework, Caroline leafing through a magazine, wanting to ask more about this man Clarence. Tease him some. They ate together, Rollie trying to be natural. Cool about what he was hiding behind. Then clearing the plates and laughing. Talking about the football game in the morning and warning Caroline not to be late. His daughter left and Shawna went to the back of the house to help Matt with some math, and Rollie had gone out onto the porch and saw that the bottle was there. Looked hard at it. Started down the steps and went back for the Dickel and took it with him up the slope where Mrs. Parsons was waiting in the box. He went past the retort building and stopped in front of one of the shed building openings and looked into the dark until his eyes fixed on the over-sized moving dolly leaning against one of the walls. He set the bottle down and went in to retrieve it, talking to himself while he was clothed in the blackness and had to stop halfway inside to let his eyes readjust. Then he went on and touched the cold metal of the dolly and pulled it free from the wall and rolled it out behind him, sensing the heaviness of his intention like a rolling nausea. He looked to the porch and into the window of the kitchen to make sure no one was watching, then he unlocked the door to the retort building, opened it and pulled the dolly in behind him. He emerged ten minutes later with the box on the dolly and pushed it in front of him up the worn path and was almost to the trees when he realized that he did not have a shovel. He tried to stand the weighted dolly upright, but it wanted to fall back down the hill, so he laid it down and returned to where he had taken the dolly, almost kicking over the bottle of Dickel as he got close to the entrance.

He thought about going back into the chilled blackness of the shed, and paused, hearing the night bugs louder than ever. He bent over and picked up the liquor and returned to the dolly and let his fingers run along the crease of the box lid, and feeling a gap, he wrenched it open, nestling the bottle inside in the crook of Mrs. Parsons' arm, and then pushed on up the hill till he was under the cover of the trees. When he was far beyond the faint lights of the house, he steered the dolly down a side path that led to the lake. Thinking he was safely away from where anyone might see him fumbling around in the dark, he dropped the dolly flat to the ground once again and pried open the lid all the way. The old woman, limbs bent at awkward angles from being hit by the car, looked back at him with lids closed, a spidery wisp of white hair and dressed in what looked like an outfit that white women wore to church. He pulled the Dickel free from its temporary resting place, unstopped the bottle cork and drank deeply. When he had let the whiskey settle, burning warm in his stomach, he set it down and tilted the box over so that the body rolled out onto the ground. He could see the still water through a break in the pine trees and he swallowed hard. He took Mrs. Parsons under the arms and dragged her a few feet away from the dolly and the box and leaned her against a large tree trunk, thinking again of the buried faces speckled with dirt, then averting his glance away from the old woman who was rigid so that he had to force a sitting position to keep her upright. Feeling the resistance of her skeletal frame, unyielding as if in defiance. Legs jutted out from the trunk of the tree, and back leaned against the bark like she was napping beneath the canopy. Good shoes and unblemished church outfit. Comfortably alone in the woods as if she had chosen to remain that way. Wanted not to be found. He studied the scene. Imagined it discovered and then dismissed the ideas because no one came this far out here. Never. Did not question his family's sustained position in the Noble community. He carried the box away from the tree trunk, dragging it behind him, the lid with its exposed nails tossed haphazardly inside, and went to the edge of the pond. He took up several handfuls of pine needles and laid them in the box, then went into his pocket for the Zippo lighter he kept there. He unclasped the lighter and let the flame crackle over the pine needles, allowing himself to smile at the irony of burning this flimsy repository, then stepped away and watched the flames lick over the side, the dead woman with eyes closed in eternal rest, watching him from midway up the bank. When the box had burned itself down, he kicked at it with his boot and sent the ashes into the shallow water where it hissed, and the small parcels floated into the algae coated shallows. He drank again from the bottle and then walked slowly back to the house, smelling of sweat, sour mash, and wood smoke.

·

"Daddy?"

"Daddy?" Rollie turned on the porch to see his son standing in the doorway, an oversized football jersey swallowing his small frame, draping down to his knobby knees, a pair of Nikes on his feet. His hair freshly cut, and a smile stretching across his face like it was stuck. Small little head and eyes like his sister's. Nothing mean about him. A perfect third child.

"When we going to see Levi, Daddy?"

Rollie turned and looked at the boy. "Your Momma and your sister still in there messing with their hair?"

"Uh-huh. But they said they was almost ready to go. Momma got all the stuff for the tailgate party ready. Said we was going to see Robbie Lewis' family before we went into the game."

"Is that right?"

"Uh-huh. And me and him . . ."

"He and I. You know better than that."

"He and I are gonna get to go down on the field and stay with his daddy during the game cause his daddy is helping security for the Mocs. Get to go out on the field and everything."

"You excited about that?"

"Yes sir."

"Then I'm excited for you too."

"You think Levi is gonna do good . . ."

"Well," Rollie said gently.

"Well. You think Levi is gonna do well."

"I do," Rollie said. "I do indeed. He's a good football player. You like football?"

The boy nodded. Mocked breaking a tackle, made a circle on the porch then ran back in the house yelling for his mother and sister to move it along. Rollie was looking back across the empty yard, not wanting to look toward the woods.

"Well," Shawna said behind him.

"I don't want to talk about it now," he said.

"I'm sure you don't. Not something I like to ponder either, but I think that you might have forgotten something."

"What's that?"

"The cremains."

"What about them?"

"Rollie," she said, even tone now that meant turn around and look at me when I'm talking to you.

"What?"

"You need to change that shirt before we go. And then you need to think about what you are gonna send back to these funeral homes if we're not . . . if we're not going to . . . "

"Uh—huh," he said. "I thought about that. Just had not gotten around to telling you how."

Then Caroline and Matt were yelling behind them in the house and Shawna started to touch her husband, but then pulled her hand back. "Come inside and change that shirt, and put on some decent shoes. Then you can help me get some of this food into a cooler so we can leave."

Rollie paused, looked up the hill and noticed a pile of cinder blocks that he had stacked alongside one of the buildings. Not sure why he had kept them in the first place but noticing them now. Roughly stacked, some of them broken and jagged. Weeds coming up through the holes. Would come apart easy and crumble with a sledge. Maybe mix them with some dried cement. Could work.

"Rollie, can you please." Edge in her voice, somewhere back in the house.

"I'm coming," he said, opening the screen door. "I'm coming, dammit."

•

Hi Lewis stood in his driveway, looking at all the things that his wife insisted on taking to the football game tail gate. The trunk of his cruiser was not going to hold it all so he would have to put some in the back seat with Robbie. Probably the card table would need to go back there, he thought.

"We going in the cruiser?" Sherry was coming out the back door, dressed like she was in one of the sororities. Nice tight jeans, a pair of boots, but wearing a sweater that looked three sizes too big for her, hiding all of the best parts. Her pretty face atop some thick collar of wool like she was a longshore worker or a model for LL Bean. Even her tight can of an ass hiding under all of that. A sloppily wrapped present that nobody got to open. Just wonder what was inside all that scratchy material.

"You wearing that sweater?"

"What's wrong with the sweater?"

"Nothing, Honey."

"You know," she said.

"I do. Yes, we are taking the cruiser. It will make it easier to get a spot in front of the stadium. Course we can take yours if you want to hump all this stuff around the parking lot."

"Keep it up, Sheriff," she said and went past him to put a stack of blankets in the trunk. She went back inside to collect Robbie and then they came out and got in the cruiser and traveled up the state highway to Chattanooga, coming into the city through St. Elmo with its streets lined with the old factory homes that had belonged to the bleachery mill workers back in the day. The neighborhood going to seed now, sidewalks buckled with tree roots and yards that were unkempt. Porches lilting over darkened windows and roofs that were slinking to one side or the other. Half-rotted homes on dismissed urban lots. Peeling paint and neglect everywhere.

Sherry said, "We ought to buy up one of these places and fix it up. They have nice lots and we could put Robbie in school up here and go out to eat somewhere besides that Noble Diner every now and then. Maybe visit a library. It would be nice, don't you think?"

"What's wrong with the Noble Diner?" Hi said, looking at three black teenagers standing on the corner looking back across the road at him. Eyeing the cop car with suspicion, a little adversarial. Hi wondering what they might be up to, not coming or going. Just lingering. Wondered if they lived around here. Turned away from them and looked up at the traffic light, sitting too long on red.

"Oh nothing," she said, "if you like diabetes with your sweet tea."

He let that go along with the prospect of being hemmed into a neighborhood, punched the cruiser and came out of Georgia and into Tennessee, heading up Broad Street toward downtown.

"What do you want to live up here for, anyway? Traffic and crime and everything that comes along with it. Noble's fine by me, and Robbie has friends there in school, and what about your teaching jobs? Hell, I have not seen a decent tree in six miles."

"It was just a thought," she said and then got quiet, looking out the window. Then she said, "There, Hi Lewis. A bunch of trees."

Hi looked to where she was pointing and snorted.

They pulled into the stadium parking lot and Robbie spotted Shawna May's Toyota parked along the curb. Probably waiting for them to arrive. Hi pulled adjacent and Sherry put down the window, Shawna smiling back at her. Rollie in the passenger seat and their daughter and Matt May sitting in the back.

"Follow me," Hi said and moved the cruiser forward, driving alongside the stadium, people not yet inside, then found the emergency vehicle turn-off and pulled in straight, the Toyota parking on his right side. They all got out, Matt May holding a football and asking Robbie if he wanted to throw.

"Can we go in and throw behind the end zone Dad?" Robbie said.

Hi glanced at Rollie who was getting things out of the trunk of their car.

"Don't matter to me, Hi," he said. "You the one in charge of security."

Hi nodded. "Give me a second," he said to the boys, and walked toward a door that led to the offices beneath the stadium, seeing Caroline out of the corner of his eye, noticing her sweater and how it was painted over her. He went through the door and found the head of the security detail sitting on a folding chair drinking a bottle of Coke and smoking a cigarette.

"Hal," he said, extending his hand. The man looked up from the chair.

"Sheriff Lewis. Thank you for filling in today. I was going to put you on the Tennessee side if that's not going to give you too much heartburn being a Georgia boy like you are."

"Only football game I care about today, Hal, is kicking off in Athens this afternoon. I think we might be able to make the second half, so you put me where you need me."

"We got an hour yet," Hal said. "Enjoy your family, and meet me back here a few minutes before they come on the field."

Hi started to turn, then looked back. "Hey, I gotta a couple of boys out in the parking lot that want to throw a football. You mind if they toss it around back behind the end zone. I'll make sure that they know to stay off the field. That be okay?"

"Sure," Hal said. "Send them on."

•

The parking lot was beginning to fill up when Hi came out. He looked at the two boys waiting on him and pointed to the entrance and they ran past him and disappeared into the darkened corridor and were out of sight. The cars pulling in were finding spaces and people were unloading chairs, coolers, and Tupperware, placing them on fold-up tables. The air was crisp, and the energy level was light and contagious in the sunshine, kids running around and yelling, their parents opening cans of beer or pouring Bloody Mary cocktails out of Thermos jugs. Men in khaki pants and button up shirts standing above their seated spouses, holding their cans of Coors and talking about their jobs and UTC's running game. Showing off for each other, reciting stats or making predictions about the market and the economy. Leaning back into the coolers and taking another can out, the first one gone in less than five minutes.

Rollie, Shawna, and Sherry had set up their tables and were unpacking snacks, chips and nuts, some potato salad that Shawna was famous for, fried chicken that the Mays had picked up in a bucket from the KFC on Broad Street. A tub of slaw Sherry had made.

Rollie met Hi walking back to the cruiser and the Toyota. Stuck out his hand and grinned.

"Nice day for this," he said.

Hi shook. "It is. Your boy starting?"

"Yes Sir. Linebacker. They let our boys out on the field?"

Hi nodded, touched his tan campaign hat. "Guess you could say that the job has its advantages now and again."

"Job gonna keep you from having something to drink?"

"I won't tell if you won't." Rollie grinned. The two men walked to the rear of the cars and Rollie took a fresh bottle of Dickel out of the trunk and showed it to Hi, inclined his head instead of asking.

"Better stick to beer for now," Hi said, and Rollie nodded.

"Understand that," he said.

•

How the Mays knew the Lewis family was through the Walker County school system. Shawna an administrator and Sherry a substitute teacher, trying to get on full time. Was supposed to take over a third grade class the coming fall. The two women fell in together through education, and found that they liked each other's company outside of the classroom and the dusty admin building where Shawna had her office. They talked food, and husbands and kids. Even talked about Sherry not being able to have more than one, Shawna telling her that there were days when she wished she did not have any.

Said, "Caroline is gonna be the death of me. She's out of the house now, but I wonder sometimes if she learned anything growing up. We raised her to think, but damn if she'll do it willingly."

"I don't know," Sherry had said. "I feel like one more would have been good. I think Hi wanted another one. Me. I'm not sure half the time."

"Uh-huh. Noble will do that to you—all these fucking woods and silence and the same old redneck folks walking around all the time." Cutting Sherry a glance that apologized, *not you.* "You got babies in the house and sometimes all you can hear is them crying like they was being murdered. It's hard. Lord it's hard."

Sherry said, "I come from a big family. Over in Dade County. Poor. God we were poor. But that did not stop my Daddy from getting Momma pregnant. Seemed like every full moon she'd turnup pregnant. Daddy worked a county job that did not pay shit—pardon the French—and we're all living in a trailer on the side of the mountain eating whatever we could shoot out of the trees. It's like something out of a book the more I think about it. I have to compose myself to name all my brothers and sisters. I met Hi working in a grocery store. He was a stock boy and I was a cashier. He told me he was going to get me out of that trailer and he went into law enforcement and came over to the house the day he got on with the sheriff's department. Pulled up in a cruiser and told me to pack my stuff and come with him. Daddy didn't care for him. Not because he was Hi, but because he was with the law and that did not sit well with Daddy. I didn't care what he thought. We left and moved into an apartment and got married. The poverty situation was not much better, but Hi was working steady and bringing home a decent paycheck, and I was taking classes to get my teaching certificate. Even thought I might run for school board. Maybe politics." She laughed. "They were pretty good times. But you know, I was not gone six weeks and my mother died while she was washing dishes. Cancer. Ate her like drain cleaner. Daddy didn't have the money to bury her, so he just went out in the woods and dug a hole. Put up this flimsy wooden cross. My brother called me and told me she was dead and I drive up there to that filthy trailer and asked Daddy what he had done with her and he walked me down in the woods and said 'Here she is, Sherry.'"

"Em?" Shawna said.

"But you know what?'

"What?"

"At least she got out." Shawna sat back on the couch. They were talking in the teacher's lounge in the elementary school where Sherry was substituting that day. Green shag carpet. A coffee maker on a scuffed table in the corner by a stand-alone sink that looked like it belonged in the janitor's closet. Stacks of yellow glass ashtrays next to the coffee maker. The room claustrophobic with stale smoke and hints of donuts someone had brought in that morning. A pack of playing cards on the coffee table in front of the couch. Sherry pulling at her skirt, thinking that she might have said too much.

"I think about that," Shawna said.

"About what?"

"Getting out."

•

Rollie joined Hi on the sidelines with the young boys after kick-off. Rollie's son Levi on the kick return team, then going in to play defense after Wofford ran the ball back to their own forty-yard line. First snap and Levi May came through a gap in the line and put the Wofford quarterback down hard, Rollie's son standing up as quickly as he fell and back across the line of scrimmage, wound tight and alert. Looking back at the offense. Ready to pounce again. Hi touched Rollie's shoulder.

"That's a good way to start, right there," he said.

"Yeah, he's got some instinct for sure. Gets it from his Momma, I think."

"I can see that."

"You can, huh?"

"Well," Hi said.

Rollie gave him a look and then let it turn into a soft grin. "You know, it's true though. I played till I got hurt and then I was always working for my father, breaking rocks, you know. Making head stones. I guess I'm awful proud of him, but I can't take credit for plays like that. His mother is the one who taught him to go after what he wanted. Rode him all through high school about going to college. Told him that if playing football got him a degree then he needed to be the best football player on the field, and I reckon he took that to heart. Looks like it today, anyway."

"It certainly does," Hi said. "Just ask the Wofford quarterback. He have any idea what he wants to do when he gets out of school? I mean, he's obviously got talent, but I'm not sure they're paying that much attention at UTC. No offense."

"Naw, you right about that. We talked to him about it, but he says he can't decide yet. He's got some time. Hell, maybe he can come work for you, Sheriff."

"I hope he has higher ambitions than working for the Walker County Sheriff's department," Hi said.

Rollie started to say something else, but stopped. Thinking of Pine trees lining the lake, quiet as an empty church. Stillness in the air, shallow gulps of air and sweat cold and pasty under a Long John shirt. Shovels and empty bottles of liquor lying flat on the ground. Thinking about how hard it would be to dig into that red clay chert once the winter set in, rain and sleet covering everything like translucent skin. Black birds up in leafless trees making their accusations. Watching him move across the ground like he was lost prey. *Maybe not law enforcement,* Rollie thought and watched the game.

UTC won on an option play in the fourth quarter. The half back rolling out to the right and taking the ball neatly into the corner of the end zone. Rollie's son had three sacks and so many tackles such that Rollie lost count by half-time. After the game was over, Hi walked the team's coach out on to mid-field to shake hands with the Wofford coach and came back to find Levi talking with his father on the sidelines, Caroline and a group of girls hanging back against the wall on the track that encircled the field. The girlfriends all making eyes at Levi. Big linebacker all grins, standing three inches shorter than his Daddy. Giving Caroline a hard time about her sweaty brother in his grass-stained uniform. The boy looked younger than he was, Hi was thinking as he made his way over. Short, but built like a fire truck. His head shaved close to the scalp and a grin that mimicked his father's bright on his face, the far sky's violet light casting long shadows on the field. The stands mostly empty. The wives and the smaller boys packing things into their cars out in the parking lot. The women tipsy from drinking in the stands. Pouring Mimosas out of a steel thermos. Blankets over their laps. Laughing too loud and forgetting there was a football game going on in front of them. Talking about school politics. Hi walked up and stood a respectable distance from the father and son, making small talk about the game. The son dropping his head with that grin. His body jerky and still amped-up from the game and the hitting. Feet restless. The rest of the team was heading to the locker room. Hi waited, then heard one of the players yell Levi's name and Rollie patted his boy on the shoulder pad and told him to go catch-up.

Hi stood where he was, said, "That's gotta feel good," watching Levi wave his helmet and run toward the player who had called out to him. The two of them colliding and then running together toward the dark hole that led under the stadium.

"Yeah, it does," Rollie said. "It sure does." Then he turned and looked at Caroline. "I suppose you plan on spending the night on the town, girl?"

Caroline straightened, looked at her father with an innocent face, then looked at the girls and they all broke into laughter.

"See this man, here," Rollie said, pointing at Hi, standing straight in his uniform, watching the cluster of black women looking back at him. "Don't make this man put you in jail for driving around drunk."

"Sheriff Lewis don't have any jurisdiction in Chattanooga."

Rollie cut a glance at Hi who shrugged. "Girl, you better mind how you talk."

Hi thought and considered walking to the cruiser to help get it packed for the ride back to Noble. *Let Rollie handle this.*

"Yes, Sir," Caroline said. Then they were gone down the track toward a large group of young people waiting around, trying to decide what to do with their buzz.

"What are you gonna do?" Rollie said.

Hi watched them go. "Beats me," he said. "She's right though. I have no jurisdiction here."

9.

IF LEVI MAY HAD HEARD THE STORY ONCE, HE'D HEARD it a thousand times. How his family had been a part of the Noble community for generations, going all the way back to some white man who'd brought them into Georgia on wagons and then stood around with a whip and a bunch of redneck boys like the ones who lived down the hall in the dorm. Demanded that this wagonload of slaves build a house from the ground up. Everywhere he went in Noble, that story followed him like it was some hungry dog, let out of the car on the highway. *There goes Levi May. You know his family built that white man's plantation home over on the highway?* Fuck that. He'd decided before he was out of high school that playing the easy-going slavery relic was not for him. Not that he was ashamed of what his Daddy had built with Tri-State, and not because he thought his mother was anything less than a panther in administrative clothing, but he wanted to build something beyond all of that routine glad-handing and barely disguised subservience. Wanted to feel like the world was willing to give him his own shot at self-resilience. And on a playing field that was not littered with pine trees, red clay, and myopic men and women who had given up on something better, even if they were not aware that they had done it.

Football had been a natural path out of Noble. A straight fly-pattern up through the valley and into Chattanooga which he knew was no more exotic than *Noble*, just more buildings and homeless wandering the sidewalks. But it had a university and Levi knew that if he wanted to explore something more interesting than shovel heads, urns, or a filthy push broom in the retort building, it was an education that was going to get him there. He had seen the way that the funeral home directors had tried continuously to manipulate his mother and father with their velvety talk and hints about the state licensure and how by looking the other way they were doing the Mays and Tri-State a favor.

"Shit," Rollie had said, driving down to Rome, Georgia in his old pick-up, Levi on the seat beside him, not more than ten or eleven – Levi thinking about this as he was taking off his uniform in the locker room after the game. Noise all over the place. Teammates talking about going out after the game. Get some strange. Drink pitchers of beer at the Brass Register and Yesterday's down on Georgia Avenue and Patton Parkway.

"Boy, you take this woman we're going to pick-up now," his father said, looking through the filthy windshield glass, the truck laboring to make sixty miles an hour. Traffic on seventy-five coming by them on the left like a cluster of disturbed wasps buzzing toward the capital city.

"See, the man up here running this funeral home, he knows that the son of this woman we're going to pick up wants her to be cremated. Okay, fine. But see, now this funeral home director can't sell her son one of these fancy caskets that he has all polished and shining in the front room when you walk into the place. So, the son says 'No, no, my mother wants to be cremated.' So this man Jenkins who runs this funeral home up here in Rome, he says, 'Well, we want to respect your late mother's wishes, but I have to tell you that cremation can be expensive as well.' Son says, 'More expensive than one of these goddamn coffins?' And then Jenkins says, real cool like, 'We don't refer to them in that manner.'" And now Rollie broke up driving the truck, imitating the white man Jenkins and Levi laughing with him as they pulled off the highway. Levi relieved that they were leaving the traffic behind. Watching the fields open up in front of him. Floyd County looking a lot like Noble just off the interstate.

"See, I charge Jenkins a fee for coming to get this body and for cremating the remains and then I got to send the remains back down here, and so I'm charging him for all this, but it ain't shit compared to what Jenkins in gonna charge this woman's son, just to spite him for not buying a coffin. And here we are doing all the work. And they tell me they's doing me a favor. You believe that?"

Levi believed it. He pulled on a pair of jeans and a clean white shirt he'd left hanging in the locker and went out the door and down the dimly lit corridor and out into the parking lot where the team was allowed to park before the games. No bus ride home this time. He felt good. Breathing easy. The wind picking up a bit, but not real cold yet. Might have brought a jacket from the dorm if he'd thought about it. Checked his watch. Early yet, and then he caught sight of two of the other players walking in the direction of the bars and he yelled for them to wait-up, jogging over the black top, forgetting about Jenkins and spite and his father's old truck that was still parked in the yard back in Noble. Dad making deliveries and barely skimming off the white man's fat profit margin. The boys waiting on him at the corner, telling him to hurry up. Should have brought a jacket. He came to where they were standing, rubbing his arms to warm them up.

"Shit, Levi. You cold?"

He shook his head. Boy named Tyrell looking him over, then looking at his own outfit. Nice collared shirt, leather jacket. New shoes, white as a supernova in the gathering dark.

"I got one back in my car, you want it?" The other boy looking at him now, wearing a hooded sweatshirt, Freshman kid that Levi did not know except for the sidelines. Quiet. Nice kid.

"I'm alright," Levi said. "Let's get going." They walked up to Market Street, turned left, made their way up a few more blocks then cut up to Georgia Avenue and they could see the crowd moving around in a cluster outside the bars. Music loud inside, spilling out when the doors opened and closed. Tyrell held back, stepped beneath a torn awning overtop a dark storefront window. Lit a joint, sucked in deep on the smoke and blew out the cloud. Levi and the freshman turned around, came back.

"Y'all want to hit this?" Tyrell said. Levi took the joint and put the moist paper between his lips. Pinched the end and handed it over to the freshman who examined it then toked as well, coughing so that the other boys laughed.

"You okay, now," Levi said and took the joint back, skipping Tyrell who was grinning up the street. There had been the weed and the booze in high school when he had been the star of the show. Had to keep it cool then. Rollie not going to say much with his hidden bottles around the place, but Shawna not caring for any of it, especially with his little brother around. Would give him the look over breakfast when he came in late, up early the next morning to help his Dad, smelling of beer and body odor while he ate his eggs and sausage, Shawna slamming pans on the stove top. Caroline giggling at him before she left home to live on her own. Now it was easy, leaning against the large window of the store, thinking about the game and his unchecked aggression. Sleeping now like it was hibernating till the next week. *Always there though*, he thought to himself. *Gotta keep it close.* They passed the joint a couple more circles then started toward the crowd, feeling loose, happy to be out of uniform and into another character. The freshman diffident from the weed, Levi grabbing his arm and whispering something encouraging. Brotherly. They ran into the crowd and the three of them dispersed, talking to the other players, eyeing the cheerleaders who were eyeing them cautiously, like cats on windowsills. Tyrell laughing louder than the rest, being physical with the other boys. Levi turned and looked to see the freshman talking with one of the girls, her stomach showing tight and brown, her limbs like they were caught in a steady breeze. Levi nodded and went inside to find a beer.

The band on the stage was a ragged group of white kids, torn jeans, boots and guitars turned up so nobody could hear one another. Drummer having a seizure behind the kit, the singer with a straight sweaty mop draped over his eyes. Getting into it. Four girls in the front row showing their appreciation. Levi made his way over to the bar and ordered three draughts. Turned around to watch the band as he waited. White boy music. Some amped up cover song he had heard ten times before in this same place under the same circumstances, but could not recall the name. *The Romantics, maybe?*

"That's what I like about you." He turned and saw Caroline standing at his shoulder, singing along. The bartender yelled at him and he turned around to pay for the beers.

"You gonna buy your sister a drink?"

Levi handed her one of the beers and called back to the bartender, but had to wait.

"You the one with a job," he yelled at her. Crowd now singing along to the Romantics song.

"Yeah, but you are the football star," she said and sipped the beer. "Besides, I think I'm gonna go back and get a job with Daddy. He said the other day that they needed a bookkeeper besides Momma doing it on the weekend. She's got too much going on, you know? And I hate my job now. Working for those old men and women accountants, talking about tax codes and shit in the depression."

Levi laughed and then nodded, turned again to the bar to get that fourth beer. Said, "You ain't gonna like working for Daddy."

She punched him on the arm. He could tell she'd already had a few drinks. All light and airy, eyes a little glassy, always moving around like she was anxious. Never liked standing in one spot.

"Why you say that?"

Now the band was playing the Ramones. Levi knew this one. Liked how it built on itself. Lyrics kinda stupid, but catchy. "Cause, I just do. He's an asshole to work for." She sipped at the beer, watching something across the bar. "To you maybe. I'm his little girl."

"I gotta take these beers out to my boys," he said.

"Alright." Absent minded.

He went past her then turned around.

"Find me if you need someone to walk you home."

She waived him off and he went through the bouncing crowd, trying not to spill the beers as he moved sideways through the bodies, then out the door to find Tyrell and the freshman back across the street under the ripped awning, this time with two girls. Levi checked to see that the bouncer was looking in the other direction and then crossed after them.

 ·

Rollie opened the bottle of Dickel and took down a glass. Set it softly on the kitchen counter. He poured two fingers.

"You want to have one of these with me?" He did not look over his shoulder. Watched the liquor's smooth and shimmering surface in the short glass.

"I guess," Shawna said.

He had asked because she was still finishing her wine cooler on the way home from the football game. In a good mood. Talking about how well Levi had played and about school and how she really thought Sherry was a friend. Everything that was easy to go on about and he had driven home ten feet off the bumper of Hi's cruiser, feeling okay to be behind the wheel with the Walker County Sheriff escorting them. Matt was spending the night with the Lewises, and he and Shawna were alone for the first time in a long time. Alone with the goodness of the day and the bodies that were outside in the woods. He took down a second glass and poured a shot into it.

"You want water with it?"

"A splash," she said, her voice softer now. The house unusually quiet, a small space heater humming in the corner of the kitchen. Rollie turned on the faucet, letting a trickle of water into the glass, hating to dilute the liquor but feeling optimistic. Knowing it was the residual effect of the booze he'd had that day, wanting to hold onto the buzz. Maybe get her into bed and make love before they fell asleep. Maybe sleep late. He set the glass down in front of her and took his seat across the table, pushing the chair back. Being cool like when they had first met each other. Casual. Letting his looks speak for him. He sipped and put his glass down."Levi did look good today."

"Uh-huh. He seems real happy at school."

"Yeah, gotta a lot of things going his way."

"He does," she said. Paused and tasted the liquor. Grimaced. Then took a full sip.

"And what about us, Rollie?"

"How you mean?"

"You know what I mean." Looking across the table at him now, feeling him out. Searching for how he was going to play this second conversation.

He drank, held the glass on his stomach. Met her stare. "You mean about the business?"

"Yeah," she said. "About the business, Rollie."

"I told you that it was just till I got this retort fixed up. Then we can go back to how things was."

"Were? How things were?"

"Right."

"But I got a feeling that you don't intend to go back to how things were."

He looked past the table and toward the kitchen window, panes black, not giving anything back. "What makes you say that?"

"I can just tell how you think. It's the money, right? We don't get that retort fixed and you move those bodies out in the woods, spread lime to hide them. Then you don't have any expense in any of it. You just collect them and what—what are you going to send back."

"Hold on," he said, scooting the chair into the table. "Who said

I was thinking about anything like that?"

"Well aren't you?" He stood and started toward the counter with the bottle.

"You need more of that to talk about this?" He ignored her and brought the bottle back to the table.

He said, "You know how much money these funeral homes charge people for a cremation?"

She shook her head.

"Well, see, it varies. But usually they mark them up to where they are charging more than a thousand dollars. Sometimes as much as twenty-five-hundred. And what do we charge for all that we do to provide our service. Five-hundred dollars?" She nodded.

"Okay," he said. "So they making all that money and Tri-State is carrying all the load, making nothing but profit for them and us barely getting by month to month. I don't know about you, Shawna, but that don't sit well with me. Not for this business and not for the welfare of this family we are raising."

She looked at her glass, picked it up and drank the rest of the Dickel. Reached over and pulled the bottle toward her. Poured.

"We're doing alright," she said.

Rollie looked at her until she raised her eyes. Said, "Okay, maybe we are doing alright, but not what we should be doing. Hell, I can't even afford to get the damn retort fixed, and when I was talking to one of the funeral directors last month, he said they was talking about making us get a license with the state to run the business. Gonna add even more expense and we still carrying all of this by ourselves."

"We could just raise the price."

"Yeah, and they gonna find some other niggers to do it cheap for them."

"I told you about that word in this house," she said.

"Okay. But you know I'm right. Them funeral home owners don't care what comes back in that box. They gonna dump it into some urn that costs even more money for the family and you think they are gonna call and say 'Rollie, we making money hand over fist down here in Alabama. You want us to send some up your way?'"

She laughed at the thought. Knew he was right. She understood the accounting better than he did. "I was in the church the other day. Thinking about all of this, and I don't know how to reconcile something like this with God."

"Jesus," Rollie said.

"That's right," she said. "Jesus. Suppose he was sitting here and you told him about this idea you are having about leaving bodies lying around in the woods so you can stick it to a bunch of white funeral home directors. 'Jesus, hang with me here, brother, cause this is gonna sound crazy as hell, but I have this plan . . . '"

"This ain't got nothing to do with Jesus," he said.

"No?"

"Hell no, Shawna. Listen here. Ain't there something in the Bible about leaving the body behind and celebrating the soul in eternity and all of that?"

"You know there is."

"Okay, well then, I guess we're just making some cash off the bodies that Jesus and God want left behind in the first place. It's like that saying about ashes to ashes and dust to dust. We're just returning the bodies to the earth rather than making ashes out of them. Seems the same thing to me, and we can maybe get out from underneath the bank in the process."

"You hear what you are saying?"

"Do *you* hear what I'm saying, woman?"

She paused, drank. "What about leaving these bodies around like that—I mean, we get all kinds of bodies here and it's not like, I mean, I mean, have you thought any of that through?"

"Shawna, ain't nobody coming up on this property. Not past the house and the buildings anyway. We got woods all around us. We just gotta be smart about it. Can't leave any signs of anything not being normal, see? Just move them around the property and use the lime and dig some holes if we need to. We got the pond."

"The pond?"

"Well, maybe not the pond, but you see what I'm saying. We just gotta be smart. And you're smart enough for the both of us, Shawna. And if we get to where it's a problem, then we can always go back to the way it was, and if we can make enough doing this new way, then we can maybe set aside some money and get out of here one day. Live someplace else."

"Leave Noble?"

"Why the hell not. What has Noble ever done for us aside from bringing dead folks to our front door?"

"Ashes to ashes," she said, looking at her empty glass.

"That's right," he said, smiling. "Cashing out ashes. Now you seeing it."

•

His head was starting to hurt. The beer no longer having the effect and the weed wearing off, making him sleepy and ready for the metal bed frame and limp mattress in the dorm room. The freshman had disappeared, and Tyrell had a cheerleader over near her car. The girl leaned back against the driver's door, Tyrell moving around her like he was waiting on the ball to snap. Levi coughed, walked toward the door of the bar, rubbing his arms again. Feeling the late night cold. He went in. Saw that the band was packing up their gear. The drummer and what he thought was the lead singer over by the bar, laughing, pulling on their cigarettes. It had been a good show. He scanned the lit-up signs on the walls looking for the restrooms. No neon, but a sign with arrows pointing toward a cased opening in the back right corner. He started that way, then stopped. He could not be sure, but it looked like Caroline was talking to a large man. Big shoulders and head. Animated face looming over the top of his sister like a storm cloud. He stepped around a table and moved to his left, keeping his eye on them, trying to see Caroline's profile without being noticed. An annoying big brother flanking her dark suitor.

He moved further left and went behind a column and hid his face. Ducking into the bathroom alcove. He stepped into the men's and pissed in the urinal. Stopped at the sink and ran some cold water and splashed it on his face. Looked at the cracked mirror and thought it over, drying his face with his shirt. Went back out into the barroom and stood behind the man she was talking to. So big that Caroline almost did not see him standing there, so that he stepped out to the side and waited on her to says something.

She said, "Levi, this is Clarence." Waiving her drink at the man. Built like something from a history book. Nice clothes. Levi could smell cologne. The man—Clarence—turned and looked down at him. Reached back around for his drink and then addressed Levi by turning fully in his direction. Caroline sipping the last of her drink through one of those red cocktail straws. Clarence stepped back, looked him over.

"The football player," he said, grinning. Extending his hand. "Clarence Warren. Up for the night from Gadsden. It's good to meet you, brother. Caroline been talking about how you played out there today." *Good to meet you, brother,* Levi thought. Man how that got tiresome.

"Oh yea," Levi said.

"Yea," Clarence said. "Said you was good."

"You didn't catch the game?" Levi said.

"Naw man. I'm not much on sports. Had other things occupying my youth, you know. Not so big on chasing balls around and piling up on other brothers. But you know, it's alright. Sounds like you got it going on though."

"Clarence is in the funeral business," Caroline said. "He dropped a body off at Tri-State. You believe that? Small world, big brother."

"Well, I don't know that I'm in the business like that. I drive the car all over the place for this little dick head man named Tyler Arnold back in Alabama. He run the place. I'm more like a delivery man."

"I see. You waiting on cremations to take back?"

"What's that?"

"You know. The remains."

"Aw yea, right," Clarence said, nodding. Looked away and saw the bartender and yelled down the wooden expanse. "Let me get another one of these." Then looking at Caroline. "You want another one, girl?" She nodded. Clarence said, "Make it two." Then again. "How about you, Levi? You want something man?"

"I'm good. Was just getting ready to head back to the dorm."

"The dorm?" Clarence said.

"He's in school, Clarence, remember?"

"Aw yeah, shit. Right. The dorm. Okay, well . . . "

"You good, Sis?" She looked at him, smiled in a way that should have been for Clarence.

"Alright, I'm out."

"Bye," Caroline said. Clarence reached down the bar and took up the new drinks and waved them both at Levi.

Said, "Be good, big brother."

10.

ELLIS CARVER SAT ON THE EDGE OF TANYA'S DESK. Wearing his tan uniform, boots muddy and his hat sitting beside him. Tanya was behind the desk, done up for a Tuesday. Lots of eyeliner, a pink blouse that looked like it was made out of parachute material, and a skirt that seemed to cut off her circulation at the waist. Feet jammed into heels like overpacked canoes. She had a fan going in the corner. A habit that she had whether it was cold or hot. Said the office smelled stale if the air was not moving.

Hi tended to agree. He came in the front door of the office and put his own hat on a rack near the front window and took a seat on a couch that they had salvaged from the fire house down the street, the arms thread bare and the pattern more like a hallucination. He looked closer at Ellis' boots, caked with field mud.

"You get your cruiser stuck somewhere," he said, pointing at the boots.

"No Sir," the deputy said, standing up and adjusting his gun belt. "Was telling Tanya that it's been just about the craziest morning I've ever had. You want me to start the story over?"

"There coffee made?"

"Yes, Sheriff," Tanya said. "You want me to get you a cup?"

"Would you be a dear and do that for me?"

"I sure will," she said and had to force her way out of the old metal swivel chair, springs squawking with the relief.

"Thank you." He looked around the office, then at the wall clock. Said, "It's just now ten, Ellis. How could you have that kind of morning already?"

Ellis walked into the center of the room. Sunlight came through the dusty blinds and Hi could see the motes working their way around with the fan's intermittent passing. And he could smell the deputy.

"What you been into son?"

"Well Sheriff," he said.

"Hold on. Let her bring the coffee back. I gotta feeling this is going to take a minute."

"Oh right," Ellis said and stood waiting, looking a little lost. Tanya came back in, the mug so full that she had to take small steps to keep from spilling it.

"Strong, hot, and black, Sheriff. Just how you like it."

He took the cup and held it gingerly. Watched her walk back behind the desk and replace herself in the chair. He nodded at Ellis to continue.

•

What happened was a fire was called into the station just after sunrise. The caller was a man named Blevins who lived on Long Branch Lane, way out in the county. His neighbor, he explained, had a bonfire going and he was burning all of his animals in it.

"So Tanya hands me the phone and I say, 'He's doing what?' and then Blevins starts explaining that there's black smoke all over the hillside and so I said 'Why don't you call the fire department, Blevins?' and he says cause there's nothing burning except livestock, and so I told him I would be right there and then I asked whose livestock was on fire and he said it's the Dunns' place, just down the way from his farm."

"Tim Dunn?" Hi said.

"That's him."

"Okay. Go ahead."

"Tim Dunn took me to the prom," Tanya said. "Little Tim I mean. Not his daddy." She giggled, and Hi sipped from the mug.

Ellis said, "They used to call him 'Tiny' in high school. You know. Like the book."

"Yea," Tanya said. "Like the midget in the Christmas book. Ratchet or something."

"Ellis," Hi said.

The deputy startled. "So anyhow, I drive out there and I'm coming along the creek road and I can see the smoke a couple miles out and I thought, Jesus that's a lot of smoke, and I pushed the cruiser faster and I come in the gate of the farm and sure enough there's a fire roaring out in the middle of one of his pastures and him, Tim I mean, and his three boys are standing out there watching it. And I can see right off that there's animals in the fire and I'm thinking, Good God, what has he done. Anyway, I walk up to Tim and I ask him what's going on. He says, 'Blevins call you?' and I told him yes, but that you could see the smoke from all the way down by the creek road and that it would only have been a matter of time before someone called it in, not to say anything about the smell, and so I ask him again what's going on and he looks at those three boys and says, 'Tell him.'"

"Was there any trouble?"

"No, no trouble. Not unless you are one of the Dunn boys, I guess."

"Go ahead, tell him the rest," Tanya said. She was drinking a fountain drink from the Seven-eleven down the street. Using a paper towel for a coaster.

"So the older one—one who took you to the prom," Ellis said, pointing at Tanya. "Tiny or whatever. Anyway, he tells me that one of his brothers left the gate open on the corn crib. Oh, and when you asked about there being any trouble. I guess there was a little trouble cause they started yelling at each other and looked like they was gonna fight, but I handled it."

"Good," Hi said. "

"Right. So after everyone quieted down some, Tiny says again how the gate got left open and all of the sheep in the pasture come into the corn crib and they ate everything that was in there. Every last kernel. And I didn't know this, but a sheep doesn't have the sense to stop eating and so when they ate-up a week's worth of corn, they made themselves so sick that their stomachs burst."

"What?" Hi said, sitting the coffee cup down on the side table.

"Yep, burst," Ellis said.

Tanya said, "You want some coffee too Ellis?"

He shook his head. "So yea. The Dunns were down at some 4-H function or something like that and when they got home late last night, all the sheep were dead or almost dead, and big Tim had to get a rifle and shoot all of them to make sure. How you like that?"

Hi shook his head. Took up the mug again and looked at Tanya over the rim. "And so, he was burning the bodies after he shot the sheep."

"That's right. First thing this morning. But I have not even got to the craziest part."

"This is just nuts, here" Tanya said. "Damn if it ain't."

"What's nuts?" Hi said.

"Well, since them sheep killed themselves eating all that corn, we were just standing there and Tiny got done telling me what happened when—well, I guess the fire got hot enough and all of that corn . . . "

"Started to pop," Hi said.

"Damn, how did you know that Sheriff? That's right. It started to pop, and I jumped thinking someone was taking shots at us out there in the pasture and then big Tim said it was just the corn cooking in their stomachs and I tried not to laugh, but man it was something else. Like someone had thrown an entire box of fireworks in the flames. And every time a bunch of the kernels would explode, we all kinda hopped in place. Anyway, I told him to keep an eye on the fire and not to use that rifle on any of those boys. That it was just an accident, but he didn't care much for that so I came on back and was finishing up telling Tanya about all of it when you walked in. You ever heard anything like that, Sheriff?"

Hi shook his head, then looked back at the deputy's boots. "Go back there to the janitor's mop sink and wipe off that mud before you get in my car. I stopped in to get gas at Patel's this morning on the ride in, and he says that Delbert and some of those other homeless boys been back around the store making trouble. We're gonna go visit that camp they got in the woods." Hi walked past them and through a cased opening that led back to the interior offices and the four cells that they had in the building. Ellis started to follow, then turned and looked at Tanya. Closed his fist and then thrust it open like an explosion. She giggled into her hand and Ellis smiled. Proud to have been at the center of it all.

Hi and Ellis drove along the state highway. The trees were beginning to shed their color and the empty land looked abandoned and desolate through the car window. Ellis talked about the sheep and Hi thought about how nice his wife looked before heading out to meet Shawna and her family at their church. She had asked him to come along but he had begged off for work, not wanting to be confined to a pew, but feeling guilty not going with her. He often felt guilty for being away as often as he had been, but with the department being as small as it was, there really was no alternative. She understood, but he could tell that she wished he were around more often, even telling him that he was missing Robbie growing up. That might have been a stretch, but he knew that the choices he made would have consequences if he did not pay attention to them and the subject preoccupied him more than it ought to. They drove on and came to Mr. Patel's market and gas station, and like he was seeing it for the first time, Hi saw how run down and sad the place looked. People passing through would look at their gas needle pointing empty and tell themselves that they could make it to LaFayette on what was left in the tank.

He pulled in, Ellis still talking, and he parked on the side of the building near the ice machine where they had confronted Delbert

Weir a few weeks before.

"Why we going in here?" Ellis said. "We taking them some more snacks?"

Hi put the car in park. "I thought we would walk into whatever they have for a camp," he said. "Just want to get an idea of how they come and go. Patel is not the most caring of individuals, but he has a right to keep them from loitering. You all natured out from your journey this morning?"

"No Sir. Just wondering is all." Mr. Patel was in the window behind his checkout counter, watching them through the glass. Hi waved, but Patel did not wave back. They pulled jackets from the back seat and went around the side of the building and up the worn foot path that made a straight shot into the woods, crested a small rise, then led down to the bottom land. They walked in single file and when Ellis began talking again, Hi turned around and looked at him.

"What?"

"Just maybe, talk a little less?"

Ellis nodded and they went on, the path becoming poorly defined beneath the fallen leaves, their footfalls loud in the undergrowth. The land leveled out and they walked side by side along the creek that was moving at a decent pace. Hi pointed out the empty beer cans and bits of trash strewn along the way.

"Looks like we are on the right track."

"Yea," Ellis said. "Old Delbert has been living back in these woods since I was a kid. We would come back here with our BB guns. You know, playing army and shit like that. We were out here one time and I was hiding behind this downed tree and I raised up cause I thought I heard one of my buddies coming through the woods and it was some woman walking around in a pair of jean shorts and a bikini top. No shoes. Looked like she crawled out of a beaver dam. Her skin was all muddy and . . . "

"Ellis, will you please."

"Right," he said. They went along another ten minutes and Hi stopped.

"You smell that?" Ellis shook his head.

"You don't smell that? Smoke?"

"Hell Sheriff, I've smelled like smoke since sunrise."

"How could I forget. Follow me." They turned off the flat land and walked up to their left to come down into the camp instead of straight on. They used the trees to climb, then went ahead again, and in a few more minutes, they could see the clearing below them. Two, maybe three figures moving through the trees. They started down the slope, making plenty of noise and when Hi saw the figures stop and look up, he called down to them.

"Delbert. It's Hi Lewis with the Sheriff's department. Don't you do something stupid like run. Tell those boys with you to stay put." Ellis put his hand on his service pistol and Hi shook his head.

"Just stand out to the side of me. I'll talk to them." The men were ragged and thin. The camp itself was nothing more than a couple tents, a circle of stones for the fire that was burning, a five gallon bucket half full of water, cans and bottles of spent alcohol, and a pile of cut wood, an ancient axe stuck in a chopping stump. Hi looked the three of them over.

"This it?"

"Is this what?" a stringy black-haired man in an undershirt said.

"Is this all of you?"

"We was just getting ready for church," Delbert said adjusting the baseball cap on his head and the other man, bald and missing most of his front teeth laughed through a phlegmy cough.

He said, "Yeah, we was just getting ready to go to church, Sheriff."

"That so," Hi said, watching them all together. Drunks living near a water source and pestering Mr. Patel's patrons for spare change.

"Hey now," Ellis said and Hi turned around. The deputy was reaching down to pet a mongrel dog that had come down the slope after them. Missing an eye. Its tail wagging and mouth open.

"That's Baxter," Delbert said. "He's mine."

"Hello Baxter," Ellis said, patting the dog's head. "You're a good dog, aren't you."

"Delbert, Mr. Patel says you been back at his store bothering people."

"I never," Delbert said.

"We never did it," the black-haired man echoed. "He hates white men, by God. I was in the service."

"Well gentlemen," Hi said, "considering you're in the bag about ninety percent of the time, I'm inclined to take Mr. Patel's word over yours. I'm sure that you can understand that."

"That fucker," the bald man said to no one in particular.

Hi ignored him. What was the point. "Mr. Patel can be a difficult man. I'll give you that. But I warned you Delbert. Deputy Carver and I warned you the last time that you were over there, drinking that filthy Ice House beer and camping out near the gas pumps. You told me that you'd not be back."

"Well," Delbert said.

"Did you buy something when you went back this last time, Delbert?"

The man looked at his dog.

"Never mind that. It's not important. See, what is important is what I'm going to tell the three of you next. The County Commission is not real keen on this homeless camp situation, and they keep after me about running you out. Now, the County Commission is not big on taking field trips into the woods looking for alcoholics and stray dogs. But when you piss off Chamber of Commerce members like Mr. Patel, well then it comes back to my office and I have to deal with it. See where I'm going with this?"

The men nodded. They understood and were thinking about where they would go next if the Sheriff scuttled their camp.

Hi was about to say something else when the dog shot in front of him, holding what looked like a light blue night shirt in its teeth.

Growling and running in circles.

"Baxter!" Delbert tried to catch the dog. It darted away from him and ran into Ellis who took the cloth from the dog's mouth, the animal sitting on it haunches, whining up at the deputy.

"What is that?" Hi said. Ellis turned the cloth over in his hands until he found the hole in the neck. He turned his head as he read what was stamped inside.

"Property of Coroner's Office," he said.

"What's a coroner?" the bald man said, scratching an armpit.

"Dog comes back with all kinds of things from the woods," Delbert said. "I can't keep up. Hard enough to keep him fed.

"We gonna have to move?" the black-haired man said, pulling a rumpled pack of cigarettes from his filthy pants.

"Let me see that," Hi said, holding out his hand to the deputy. Looked it over then held it to his side. Said, "And where would I move you too," looking them over and feeling the agitation of booking them all for vagrancy only to have to pick them up again further down the road. He looked at the gown and snorted a laugh. The dog next to the deputy, tongue and tail wagging.

"Delbert," he said.

"Yes Sir?"

"Goddamit, listen to me this time old man."

11.

"WILSON?"

"What?"

"Wilson."

"I said *what*."

"A man of my station. A man of the cloth that is, does not answer to *what*."

Wilson came into the vestry and saw Reverend Righteous standing in the middle of the room. Short, heavyset. Nice suit on. No tie. Shirt's top button undone. Silk pocket square. Gold around his neck and wrist. Watch as big as an overturned tea cup. Sweating on his forehead like always.

"Nothing holy about that suit. Looks like you been back down to Atlanta, preaching at the Cheetah. You look like you need a glass of water, and maybe another blow job."

The Reverend turned and looked at the custodian, studying his slovenly appearance. Haircut like a BLA soldier from the mid-seventies in New York where he had done some time as an understudy after he got out of school in a small college upstate. Long way from South Georgia where he grew up in a cabin the size of a VW Bug with a father that knew how to make and beat kids with tremendous efficiency. Not that Wilson would know anything about his past, or the BLA from the PTA. Or how to get to New York if he took a bus.

"Remind me again, Wilson, why I keep you employed in this house of God—this beacon of hope in our black community..."

"Hell" Wilson said, cutting him off. "Save all that slippery bullshit for the folks filling up the nave, dressed-up in their Sunday outfits and carting around ball-busting kids. You keep me around here cause I know where you keep your bottles and how I watch the parking lot when you've got—what you call 'em, Jezebels—back here polishing your chalice. You gonna have a heart attack fucking around with those young women. They gonna put the spirit in you alright. I gonna come in here and find you slumped over and drooling on your shoes. And you got some nice shoes, Reverend. House of God my black ass. Shit you pulling on these people would turn them white."

The Reverend opened a closet door and took out one of the robes hanging inside. He shook it out and removed it from the hangar and looked at Wilson with what might have been a grin and frown at the same time. Man could put on a look.

"What I do in my private life is no concern of yours, Wilson."

"Uh-huh," Wilson said, then added, "Less you fuck up."

"That's enough." He took off the suit jacket and hung it on the hangar and hooked it back in the closet. Shut the door and picked up the robe and pulled it over his head.

Said from beneath the robe, "If it's not too much of an inconvenience, would you mind cleaning the communion cups and platters for the service? They are filthy. I looked at them when I came in."

"My cousin says they pass out grape juice in those little Dixie cups where he goes to church over in St. Elmo. How come we can't use those and some crackers out the sleeve for these people. We too good for that, or you got something going with the Brass polish company?"

"What I have is taste," the Reverend said, pushing down the wrinkles in the robe. "Now, if it's not too much trouble, please take care of those things. I'm going into my office to think on the sermon before the first service starts."

"Want me to bring you some Excedrin?" Wilson waited, the man turning his back to walk to his office.

Heard him say over his shoulder, "That would be nice. And

maybe a cup of coffee how I like it."

"Right," Wilson said. "You want a splash or you want your half and half so you floating through the sermon?"

"Half and half," Reverend Righteous said, and he closed the office door, frosted glass rattling in the frame.

•

Wilson walked to the kitchen, went down the galley and stopped in front of the commercial range. He bent over and pulled out the drawer in the bottom and took out a fifth of Early Times. He placed the bottle on the counter next to one of the stove eyes and reached into a cabinet to take down two juice glasses. He filled each of them half-full with the liquor and then put the bottle back. Then went to the Bunn and topped off the Early Times with cold coffee from the pot. Wilson not sure if the pot had been made that morning or was a day old. Didn't matter. The Reverend would take it down like spring water. Been back down to the strip clubs in Atlanta and had swamped his head with liquor and expensive pussy. Sweating in his robes out front of the congregation. Too much Early and he'd pitch around the pulpit like a blind man in a dark cave. Had seen it before and it was not easy to disguise. The one glass would do. He opened another cabinet and found the plastic bottle of Excedrin and put it in his pocket. Then he picked up the juice glasses and walked out of the kitchen and went to the office where the man was recuperating before the big show. He used his body to push the door open. Came inside and placed the glasses on the big wooden desk, the man sitting in his tall office chair behind it, rubbing his eyes with his right hand. Stomach huge creased in the chair like he was.

"You look like shit, man."

The Reverend snaked a hand out and slid one of the glasses toward him. Wilson took a seat in the chair across the desk then stood back up to pull the Excedrin out of his pants pocket. He started to hand the bottle over, but opened it instead and shook out three of the chalky pills and laid those on the desk.

Said, "How long you down there?"

"Down where?"

"C'mon man. I ain't seen you at the church since your last sermon back a week ago. You been down there all this time?"

The Reverend took a drink of the liquor. Sat back in the chair and belched. Seemed like something came up with it the way his face contorted. He shook his head. "I had to drive down to Valdosta."

"Valdosta? What the fuck kinda thing you into in *Valdosta*."

The Reverend shook his head again, sipped from the juice glass. "My mother lives there in an apartment with her sister. She's sick. Probably not gonna make it much longer. That's what her doctor says. I went down to see if there was anything that I could do to assist her. Left her some money. She says that she's seeing my father again."

"Your father live there too—in that apartment in Valdosta?"

"No," the Reverend said.. "He's been dead for going on ten years."

"And your mother been seeing him, even though he's dead?"

"That's right."

"She gone crazy?" Wilson held the glass in front of him. Looked at the man across the desk. His boss. Big influence in Noble, Georgia.

The Reverend finished off the liquor and looked at Wilson, who put his own glass on the table and pushed it across. The Reverend nodded thanks, took it up and sat back. Man could put away his liquor. Look you in the eye and transform right there in front of you. Spooky.

"My mother is a decent woman," he said. "Gave birth to eleven children. I could not tell you where most of them are these days. My father. Well, my father was a brutal man. Worked odd jobs in saw mills or on farms. You get south of Atlanta and there's not much going on down that way. Handful of rich whites running farms that used to be called plantations not too long ago. Never could get over losing all of that free nigger labor. Made my father an angry and dangerous man. He took it out on us kids, but mostly he beat my mother for all of his short-comings. He was a terror."

"But he's dead now." Wilson said this as much to himself. Picturing this woman he'd never seen lying in a bed and waking up to a sawmill worker standing over her, eyeing her in her bed clothes.

"Yes, but much like the story of Lazarus, his hateful and violent ways were resurrected in our minds. His children ran. I ran. My mother did not, and she is succumbing to his haunting torture."

Wilson looked around the small office, embarrassed. Watched the Reverend drink down the last of the liquor, putting the glass on the desk with a thump. Then spotting the Excedrin, he picked them up and ate them dry.

"Yeah, but you didn't get like this spending time with your sick mother," he said. "You expect me to believe that you sweating like that and your color all washed out is cause of grief and a mean-as-fuck Daddy? You had to come back through your playground down there. You must have had quite the lay-around, Reverend."

"I have to compose my thoughts, Wilson. Take these glasses and go make sure that there is nothing needed in the church. Tell any of the deacons that are here that I'm canceling our lunch meeting today and that if they are available, we can meet tomorrow or Tuesday morning for breakfast." He made another face and Wilson could see the paste of the aspirin on his tongue. He took the glasses and went out, hearing the Reverend doing some of his voice exercises. Warming up for the audience of believers.

•

Shawna waited on the steps of the church so she could walk in with the Lewises and her son. She knew that this would not be the most comfortable setting for them, especially Hi, if he came, who was a sheriff after all, and had probably arrested some of the congregants over the years. The church was a literal sanctuary for many of the black folks in Noble, and Hi Lewis sitting in a pew might make them uneasy. Wonder why she was sitting with them and what he was up to.

She watched the parking lot begin to fill up and then saw Sherry pull in. Looked like it was just her and the kids in the car. *That was good*, Shawna thought and allowed herself to relax a little. She could always playoff Sherry being there with both of them being in the school system. She waited until they parked and then went down the stairs and stood in front of the car. Sherry waved at her through the windshield and then they were all out in the cold air, the white woman looking around the parking lot at the black faces and trying to look at ease. Shawna went to her and took her arm, thanking her for having the kids over for the night. They made small talk walking to the church steps and they had to tell the boys to calm down as they went inside, Robbie looking around now, realizing how they stuck out, moving in closer to his mother. Shawna led them down the aisle and went into the pew where she and Rollie sat every Sunday with Matt. Levi and Caroline not making it back for services much anymore. Rollie not there this morning because he had stayed up after she went to bed, finishing the bottle. Stunk next to her that morning like he'd rolled in a baby pool of the booze. Not even pretending to protest when she told him to keep his ass in bed. Shameful.

They sat down together and Shawna talked about the church and the history that she knew. Then about school and the game the day before. Then the organ piped up and everyone got quiet and waited on the procession. Sherry looked like she was sitting in a movie theater, eyes wide and expectant. They watched the choir taking their seats and then the organ hit a long note and they stood and began singing and the congregation was on its feet and singing along without a prompt. In an instant the entire hall was alive with motion and energy and the singing became more fervent. They went from the first hymn into the next, Shawna caught up in the emotion of it, not seeing Sherry, helpless without the words. Then as if summoned by the rousing music, the Reverend Righteous emerged from a side door and made his way in front of the pulpit, his Bible with him, clapping it against his free hand, both raised above his head in supplication, the voices almost raucous, and as it reached a feverish crescendo, dying back until the room was silent again and all eyes were on the Reverend who was pacing back and forth as if in consultation with himself. They rested together. The choir director taking his seat. The careful shuffle of the congregants awaiting what would come next. Heads inclined forward and mouths tightly closed.

"My people," he said. "My good and honest people who have come here today to be with one another in praise and celebration of our Lord Jesus Christ. The son of God almighty who looks down upon us, whether we are searching for him or not. God, who looks upon you and sees the goodness that is in all of your hearts, even when we try and hide that goodness from his all seeing, all knowing eyes. We have come here out of divine faith and it is through this faith that I want to speak with you, my brothers and sisters, today, for I have a message from God and His only son Jesus that I would like to share with you in generosity and love. Praise God. Praise the righteousness of God and His son. Do you hear what I'm saying to you? Praise God!"

"Praise God," Shawna heard herself say.

"I must be losing my hearing in this old age of mine."

"Praise God," they said in unison. Shawna looked at Sherry and smiled.

"You okay?" Sherry nodded and touched the top of her son's head.

"Yes," she said quietly.

The Reverend stopped moving and stood facing the congregation. The room had grown hotter, the windows steamed over with the heat barricading the cold outside. Men and women pulling out of their jackets, eyes fixed on the man up front. Everything tense but under control.

"Now, normally, brothers and sisters, in this morning service, I like to read from my Bible." Here Reverend Righteous raised the Bible above his head and took on a solemn pose. "But this morning, I want to talk about where I've been this past week since last we came together in praise of Jesus and the Holy Father. Praise God."

"Praise God," they said. In the back of the church, Wilson leaned against the wall. He'd taken the glasses back to the kitchen and washed them out in the sink. Then he had upended the bottle and taken two long pulls. Started to put it back and decided on a third. Now he felt the liquor smooth in his belly and he watched his boss working the room.

"That's right, brothers and sisters, I was on a journey this week. A journey to reach out and comfort the sick—a woman who has been a disciple of Christ her whole life. A repentant, God-loving woman who has been stricken down by a demon you all know as cancer." A slow murmur through the pews.

Wilson said just under his breath, "Fuck, he's gonna tell it."

"And this woman, this woman who lived in poverty all her days. This woman who was laid low at the hands of a man who beat her and treated her like a dog in the yard. This woman who raised many children, only to see them move away and leave her in the squalor that was her home and her life. This woman held to her faith as Mary held to the rock in front of the tomb, awaiting the resurrection and life to come. This woman, brothers and sisters, was my own, sweet mother."

The trickle of whispers grew stronger.

"And as she waited for her eternal reward. As she waited patiently as Job waited and was confused by what he believed to be God's wrath, so did my mother. Because after all that she had endured— after the suffering that held her in a cloak of darkness for all her years, she was given a disease for which there is no cure."

Now affirmations and spoken words drifted up and Wilson felt the liquor turn sour in his stomach.

"That's right. That's right. She was told that she must wait longer still. And so I went to her. I got in my fine automobile and I drove through the cities and towns of Tennessee and Georgia, where sin hides and awaits every opportunity to spring upon us. Where the glorious are subdued and made lame by the sinners of this world. But did I hesitate in their path?"

"No," came the resounding response.

"Uh-huh," said Wilson.

"I did not, brothers and sisters. I prayed and steered away from the shallow and the cunning devils and I drove and drove until I came to where my mother was laid-up in her bed. And I took my dear Aunt's hand who had been with my mother to comfort her in her time of need, and I asked my aunt, I said 'Aunt Louisa, how is my mother fairing?' And do you know what she told me?"

"Praise Jesus," said a woman in the first pew.

"No," the Reverend said, raising his hand, starting to move now. Getting up a rhythm. The choir taking notice. Sensing they might be called on.

"No. She said, 'James. Your Momma is dying. She is dying, but she is strong and ready. She is ready, James, and she is waiting for you in that bed and wants to see her son and tell him that she is not afraid because God has blessed her in baptism and in the blood of our Lord Jesus. She is ready for you as she is ready for God.' And I said, let me through to her, Aunt Louisa, and went down the hall to the room and I looked inside and I saw that the cancer had taken my mother's earthly form, but that her spirit was a bright candle of salvation and I went to her bedside and I went down on my knees and I tried to be strong as she was, but the tears came into my eyes." He stopped in front of them again, tears on his cheeks, his heart hammering.

Said, "Oh, brothers and sisters, how I felt the love when she took my face in her hands and pulled me to her and smiled. 'I am not afraid son,' she said. 'And you should not be either. Because you are a man of God, and I am your mother, who raised you to be a man of God, and he will see that I have done right by him and in turn, he will do right by me. So stand, son. Stand strong and pray over me for this body is merely a vessel that will be consecrated in holy earth when I am gone from this mortal world. And from that consecrated burial, my soul will rise up and be in song with a choir of angels.'" He looked at the choir leader and nodded his head.

"I will be in song with a choir of angels!"

They began to stand. Wilson felt the momentum. Straitened up. Ready to clap. Now they were moving like a synchronized wave.

"Tell me now, brothers and sisters, are you afraid to leave behind your body and release your soul unto God!"

They were not and the organist dropped the first chords like a hammer and the hymn came out of the choir in sweat and hot breath, and the Reverend turned his back on all of them while they sang, and Wilson eaten up with the emotion of it all, slipped through the door and went back to the kitchen to make sure that there was enough in the bottle under the stove in case the Reverend wanted to repeat the performance at the next service.

•

Shawna and Sherry came out of the church together. The cold air as welcoming as a swimming pool in August sun. The white woman looked shaken, but the smile on her face seemed positively amused.

"Never seen anything like that over at the Episcopal church?" Shawna said and giggled a little.

I've never seen anything like that anywhere," Sherry said.

"Well, did you like it?"

Sherry turned to her. "Yes, I did. I mean, I would be lying to you if I said this was the most comfortable thing I've ever done. But I thought it was...exhilarating, I guess would be the best word. I mean that, Shawna. I really do."

Shawna nodded her head. The two boys had taken the football out of the back of the Lewises' car and were throwing it around on the far side of the parking lot.

"I don't like how we have to tip-toe around things like this," Sherry said.

"How you mean?" Shawna said.

"I mean, I guess I don't like the way that black and white people are always talking like we are learning each other's language for the first time. It just seems to take the authenticity out of relationships. You know?"

"I do," Shawna said. "But it is different. For us I mean. This place has a different history for us than it does for you. I don't mean that to be ugly. But it's the truth."

"I know," Sherry said and pulled her coat around her. "I wish it were not that way." She tugged her watch out from under the cuff of her coat. Looked at Shawna. "I gotta run," she said.

"Okay," Shawna said. "Thank you for coming."

Sherry was turning to go to her car. Collect her son and drive back to her house. "Thank you for having me," she said. "I hope I can come back again." Then she was making her way through the parked cars and calling for Robbie. Shawna started to follow.

"Hey!" She turned. Wilson was coming down the steps.

"What the fuck you doing bringing that sheriff's wife around here? She's fine and all that, I mean, but damn. She got an earful today. Probably put wire taps under the pews. Help her husband catch some spooks when they ain't suspecting anything but a blessing and a pat on they nappy heads. What you been up to, Shawna? Where Rollie at?"

"Wilson."

"What's that, Mrs. May?"

"Never mind," and she started to the car.

"Hey, you ask your husband about me getting some work over there at your place? I gotta sick mother I gotta see down in Florida." Then he broke up and walked to the side of the church to smoke in the shadow.

12.

SHAWNA HAD GONE TO CHURCH. MOVING AROUND THE bedroom, making lots of noise. Slamming the dresser drawers and banging shit around in the bathroom. Sliding dresses around on their hangers in the small closet. All put out and him lying there with his head beneath the wheel of a cement mixer. Stomach like the bottom of a drainage ditch. *Hell with that,* he thought and then pulled his legs up to his chest like he expected something to reach from beneath the worn box springs and drag him under. He'd lost track of how many he had put in the woods. He would wait for her to go see the Reverend and then he'd get dressed, heat up the coffee that she would have let get cold to make his morning harder, then maybe put a little dribble of Dickel in there to take the harshness out of the daylight and then he'd go reconcile his inventory and start thinking about how he was going to send back something that they would accept. He was sitting up in the bed when Shawna came back in. Dressed. Looked real nice, but not smiling at him. He could smell the perfume he had bought for her last Christmas. Violet something or other.

"I'll pray for us today."

He looked at her, his shirt off and the hair on his chest going grey. Muscles starting to lose some definition, but a big man even if it was a small bed. His feet hanging over the end.

"You mean you're gonna pray for me."

"Naw, Rollie. For us. For all of us."

He listened for her car to start and then he put his feet on the floor, rubbing the top of his head, trying to shake out the cobwebs. He went into the bathroom and forced himself into a cold shower.

Hollered at the sting of the sulphur-smelling water. Made himself take it until he could feel the blood starting to move then climbed out, toweled off and pulled on a pair of jeans and a t-shirt and went downstairs with a pair of wool socks in his hand. He turned on the coffee pot and found another half-empty bottle of liquor under the sink, in the back behind the sink cleanser and a single rubber glove. Set the bottle on the counter and waited for the coffee to warm up. Took a pull out of the bottle. Tired of waiting.

Said out loud to the empty kitchen, "What you gonna do, Rollie? Ain't got the money to keep things running like they's supposed to. Got a boy in college. Got a daughter wants to come home and work. Another boy ain't old enough to know the difference you play it right. Goddamn funeral directors making money and sending you these bodies so you can make less money. And what for?" The coffee maker beeped and he took down a mug and poured the sludgy liquid. Picked up the bottle and unscrewed the cap, still holding the mug. Turned it up and poured the Dickel in. Screwed the cap back on. Stood and looked out the kitchen window, thinking about his Daddy and the headstone business. The buildings out there. Each one a mess inside, weeds climbing up the peeling paint walls. Seeing the cinder block pile again and making a note to get the sledge out of the far shed for later.

He drank the first cup of coffee, then poured the little bit remaining into the mug and filled the rest with the Dickel. Sat down at the kitchen table. His thinking moving from his Daddy to Shawna. Sitting in church, praying for them both. That shifty preacher up there talking Bible verses and sticking his hand out. They were all sticking their hand out the best that he could tell. White or black, it did not matter. It was all green as far as they were concerned and as long as you put something in their palm, they left you alone. Left you alone to keep doing what they needed you to do. Either taking the money directly, or through a back door like Reverend Righteous—running that offering plate down to Atlanta and spending those oily dollars on whores and only God knew what else. Shawna handing it over. His neighbors hollering like he had in the cold shower. *Save me Lord.* What a load of bullshit. Stunk to high heaven. He yanked on the wool socks and stood up too quick, feeling the booze working in him. Getting back to a normal he did not trust. He took his Carhartt jacket off a peg just inside the front door and pulled it on. Went outside holding the mug and put his feet into his unlaced boots then went down the porch steps slowly. Took a long sip and knew that the day was on its way to ruin, and the sun barely up.

He found the wheelbarrow and put several bags of the lime into it and nestled the coffee cup into a corner and started up the path that led back to the woods. Stopped and returned to the house and then reemerged with the bottle tucked in his coat pocket. The cap poking out. He took the barrow's handles and started into the woods. Everything still as he went save for the squeaky wheel that sounded angry in the morning silence. There had been four if he remembered correctly. The three that he had covered up and the old woman that was resting against the tree. But Shawna had taken a couple calls on Friday and he knew there would be more coming and he figured he could go dig some of the holes and be ahead of things when they showed up. He was half-way to the pond where the lady from Alabama was when he thought about the shovel and he had to go back for that. Staggering a bit now and knowing that he had drunk too much of the liquor and that he would need to do this quickly and get to the house and shower. Warm and long this time. Park himself in his chair and wait for Shawna to come home with Matt. Wondering if the other kids would be there for her Sunday dinner, but not really caring as long as he wasn't digging when his wife and young son got back. It was only one hole and he felt good enough to get that done. Doze in the chair. Watch the Falcons play on the TV and try and help out if Shawna needed something. If she was still out of sorts then she would leave him alone and he could lay off the booze for the afternoon and be right come dinner time. Start fresh on Monday.

When he saw the body he could tell from a distance that something had disturbed it. The old woman was still propped against the tree, but she was leaning now, like someone had tried to wake her up and realized that she was dead and had not bothered to put her upright again. Whatever had gotten to her had torn the gown that she was wearing when that man Clarence had dropped her off and he felt something shift in his gut and he staggered off the trail and had to take hold of a skinny poplar to stay on his feet. The wheelbarrow was heavy now and the liquor in the coffee mug had sloshed out. He took the bottle from his coat pocket and took a drink. Then he pushed down toward the pond and picked up the shovel and looked around for a clear patch of dirt to dig the hole. He found a spot behind where she was propped and kicked the fallen leaves out of the way until he saw the earth. Then he put the nose of the shovel into the ground and began to dig. The woods around him swirled a little with the exertion, and each time he took a break to suck in the cold air, he could see the old woman legs extended out from the tree, shoeless and veiny. Like misshapen dough coursed through with purple. The torn gown hanging off her shoulder, the other side also torn, exposing an old breast that sagged like an empty hot water bottle against her thin skin and pronounced rib cage. Her arms, partially hidden, bent at crooked angles from the collision with the car. Everything inside of her old frame broken and mangled. He was glad she was looking in the opposite direction of the hole he dug. Intolerant and furious at the blasphemy of the scene.

When it was what he hoped was deep enough, he dropped the shovel and went back to the wheelbarrow for a sack of the lime. He carried it to the hole, not looking at the body, and then returned for a second bag. As he was pulling it free, he felt something in his back give and he almost dropped it. He stood, breathing hard and watching the pond, thinking about pulling his legs away from the edge of the bed while Shawna was getting dressed. Thinking now that something beneath the still water might break the surface. Smile at him and come ashore to see what he was up to. Dripping with pond scum and lumbering like a drunkard. Arms outstretched. Wanting an embrace. He got a grip on the second bag, shuffled it back to the hole. Then pulled the liquor out of the coat pocket, steeling himself for what came next, realizing in the splintered sunlight that he could stop all of this now and go back to doing it straight. Go back to what his Daddy had called an *honest living that even white folks can't disrespect.* Then seeing the smirk on the hearsedrivers' faces when they rolled into the yard and dumped the bodies off. Dictating when they would need the cremains back. Not asking about how Levi was doing up at the college, knocking the shit out of the back field, or how Shawna was getting along. Just putting the car in park, unloading their dead charge, and pulling out as fast as they had arrived. Looking around the place with disdain and indifference.

The cold was starting to be chased away by the Dickel and he was having trouble keeping his thoughts in order. He looked at the pond and then back at the woman from Alabama's legs, jutted out in front of the tree. He snorted and blew snot out of his nose and wiped his hand on his jeans, then went around the side of the tree and stared down at the body that had been violated by some indiscreet animal moving around in the dark. He thought again about Shawna praying for them all and reached down and took the corpse under the arms and dragged it toward the hole. What he had dug was too short and he put the body in with the head at one end and the broken arms not quite fitting the narrow width. The legs lopsided, and the gown hitched to expose her female parts. He cursed and bent to pick up the shovel, feeling the same twinge that he had felt when picking up the lime bag, suddenly a scream in outrage, dropping him to the ground next to the partially buried old woman, his mouth open wide but silent with the pain. He saw the sun overhead, a muted white burning through his slitted eyes. Posture bent on the ground and the seized-up pain in his back like a tight coil. He put his right arm behind him to push himself up and it buckled beneath his wait. Said *Son-of-a-bitch*, and laid back down in the damp leaves, the dead woman beside him, halfway in the hole, impatient for him to finish-up.

·

Clarence had said, "How 'bout we get out of here and go someplace quiet." Caroline's brother was gone and the bartender was chasing them all out, telling them to go home.

"Alright," the girl said and turned around without asking anything more.

Clarence finished what was left of his drink and followed her out to the street. Deserted now in the cold, early morning air. He took her by the hand and turned them down the street to where he had parked. She was leaning in to him against the wind. They came down to Georgia Avenue and turned right and went up half a block and stopped at the hearse.

She looked at him. Thought he was kidding. "This where you're thinking about having some quiet conversation, Clarence?"

He unlocked the door. "I had to come down and drop someone off at your family's place. You think I brought her down in my convertible? Besides, once you up front, you don't know that you're in a hearse less you look behind the curtain. It's a nice ride otherwise. Good stereo and sits heavy on the road. Handles good."

She looked at the hearse and then back at Clarence. Not sure about this. Maybe not the hearse. She'd been around plenty of them. But the going home with this man driving a hearse. Seemed like maybe it was a big black warning sitting there on the curb.

"C'mon, Baby," he said and opened the passenger door. Made an exaggerated bow. "C'mon." She stepped off the curb and into the front seat, Clarence closing the door as soon as her legs were clear. Came around the front of the car, finding the ignition key. Got in beside her and started it up. Blues music in the speakers.

"That's right, now," he said. "Enough of that skinny white boy shit. Banging on guitars and yelling at everybody. Dig on this," and he turned up the volume and pulled the car onto the avenue and turned at the next light, heading downhill, crossing Market and then a left onto Broad. Then right on Main and onto 24 heading west.

Caroline listened to the music. Some old man she knew nothing about. All sounding the same to her. Young black girl wanting out of Noble and all the old south bullshit that came along with it. Clarence was alright, though. Fine looking man that seemed to know his way around a good time. She'd be okay. They were coming around a big bend in the Tennessee River and she could see the lights of the mental asylum campus that the state had built back in the sixties. Looked just like that movie with Jack Nicholson in it—whole place not making any apologies for what it was. Scramble of low red brick buildings along the banks of the powerful river. All the people inside dressed in pajamas never seeing anything of it. Flood lights giving off a mean orange glow and reflecting off the tall fencing.

"You know what that is?" Clarence turned down the radio, looked out the passenger window.

"No."

"That's Moccasin Bend. It's a state asylum. We get bodies out of there sometimes. Scary as shit when they drive up. Don't know who they bringing with them."

"Uh-huh.

•

They lay in the bed. No clothes. The sheets a tangled mess. Caroline's body a rich caramel color with curves like rich hillsides. Clarence propped on his elbow beside her, a finger tracing her spine up and down. She smiled up at him.

"That was real good," she said.

"Told you, girl." They were quiet, and Clarence got up and went to the small sink in the hotel room. Smelled like it had been closed up after a flood. He washed his face and went back to the low dresser and poured drinks into the short glasses off the cheap tray. Came back to her side of the bed and handed her the glass.

She took it and set it on the nightstand. "I think I've had enough."

He picked up her glass and poured the liquor into his own and went back to his side of the bed. Propped up a pillow and leaned against headboard, looking at her bare ass. Smiled into the dimness. Just a little light coming through from the bathroom. He could not see her face.

"You like working in the funeral business?"

He sipped, thinking about it. "It's alright. Not bad. Get to work on my own most of the time. Nobody giving me a hard time 'cept Mr. Arnold and I can handle him okay. Might be something in it for me long term I play things right, you know. People always gonna die and they don't want their bodies lying 'round the house. Gotta take 'em somewhere and someone gotta drive them wherever that is. You make a business out of a demand that everyone in the world gonna need someday, and you never run out of customers willing to pay you for your service. Your Daddy never tell you that?"

"No," she said. "But he doesn't talk all that much about work. But I'm thinking about asking him for a job. Later on I mean. Not right now. Keeping the books or something like that. My Momma does it now, but I bet she'll be happy to give it up if I ask her. She'd like me around more anyway. Give her more time to work at the school building. Be at the church more often."

"Your Momma religious?"

"I guess. She likes being at the church anyway."

"Yeah, well, I don't know much about all that. I come up different. Never really had a family like you got."

"That make you sad? Not having a family?"

He sipped again, tasting the liquor on his lips. Could not decide how to answer.

She turned to look at him, pulling up the sheet over her exposed breasts. Saw his face. Working through the question. "I upset you?"

"Naw, Baby. I was just thinking about how to answer. I guess I miss some things about my family. But I never felt like they had my back, you know. Had to come up on my own and then I had to go away for some time because I was young and stupid and didn't know any better."

"You mean jail?"

"Yeah." Got it out there quick. See how she felt about being naked next to a con. Want to go home right then.

"What for?"

"I beat a man who hurt someone I loved a lot. He was Alabama white. So."

"So they put you in jail."

"Uh-huh."

"But you're done with that now. I can tell."

"How can you tell?"

She giggled. "You know."

He reached over and set the glass down. Turned back, leaned over and kissed her upturned face.

She kissed him back, lips apart. Pulled away quick. "But you're done with that." Said it without asking the question. Telling him so he would not have to think about it.

"Uh-huh. I'm done with that."

"That's good." She burrowed into his chest. Felt him pull her body closer to his. Outside the light was beginning to come into the sky. He could just see it through a gap in the shade. Howard Johnson's parking lot half full of cars when they got there. Could see the hearse parked in front of the door.

She sensed him preoccupied. Looked up. "What's the matter?"

"Nothing," he said, still looking through the dimly lit gap.

13.

TYLER BENNETT ARNOLD IV WAS IN HIS OFFICE AT THE Holy Family Funeral Home, seated behind a hulking oak desk that had stood in the same place for four generations of Arnold men, each one a director of the family's burial service empire in Gadsden, Alabama. Tyler's father, Big Tyler, had passed away ten years before, his portrait hanging in the hallway leading to the back offices, alongside his grandfather and great grandfather, all three men seated in a leather wingback chair and glaring out from the canvas as if their professions denoted ambassadorships to a world beyond the living. As best Tyler knew, the men had considered their roles imperative, austere in their stewardship of the white community's dearly departed. Tyler himself found the job tedious and lacking in almost every way. He had known in his youth that his destiny would lead him to the desk he now sat behind, but there had been a time, before he acquiesced to his professional fate, when he had dreamt of a life in the theater—far from Alabama and this redneck town where hunting and football passed for intellectual stimulation. He had dreamt of New York, or even London, where his artistic propensities would be recognized and revered. Write-ups in the New York Times with lavish reviews that praised his aristocratic presence on the stage. His command of the great works, spilling from his mouth like manna from the theatrical heavens. His father had chastised his ambitions as blatantly homosexual and an embarrassment to the family's heritage. And after four years at the state university in Tuscaloosa, sniffing around the periphery of the theater department like a lean and starving stray, he had given up the idea of international flamboyance and fame in exchange for the comforts of brown liquor, drugs, and undecided young undergraduate men who were as equally torn and lazy about their sexuality and inheritance as Tyler was. He had arrived back in Gadsden with herpes and a general contempt for all of humanity, and found himself working for his father, catering the eternal repose of the dead in button down Oxfords, blue blazers, pleated khakis and soft leather loafers.

Now he sat at the desk wearing a thin, light blue slip he had pilfered from a young woman who had died from some rare heart disease during a pageant rehearsal. His bare ass and legs sticking slightly to the wooden seat of the swivel banker's chair, legs crossed so that the slip exposed some of his hairy white thigh. On the sparsely littered desktop was a yellow legal pad with a list of names. Beside that, an ashtray made in the shape of an upturned hand, holding the brown butts of the four or five clove cigarettes he had smoked while he made the list earlier in the morning. Next to the ashtray was an invoice from Tri-State Crematory. The total a ridiculously low cost for the incineration services. On the credenza behind him was a silver serving tray with a bottle of bourbon and a crystal lowball glass. Across the wooden floor, a grandfather clock ticked noisily. 9:06.

He let his fingers play along the lace collar of the slip, spun in the chair, refilled the glass, spun back to face the desk, lit a clove and exhaled the fruit-cake-smelling smoke through his narrow nose, his balding head sprinkled with perspiration, like irritating dew that made your socks damp all day. He held the cigarette off to the side and ran a manicured finger down the list of names on the legal pad. Clarence would be back in an hour or so, and he wanted to make some phone calls before his return, not to mention showering and dressing in his public attire. He opened the desk drawer and retrieved the pen he had used earlier to make the list. Then he went name by name and noted the state where the men were located. He opened the drawer again and pulled out an address book, embossed with his initials on the leather cover. He flipped to the A's and found the name he was looking for, then pulled the phone from the corner of the desk and dialed the number. A woman's pleasant voice answered on the second ring.

"Eternal Bliss," she said.

"Yes," Tyler said. "This is Tyler Arnold in Gadsden, Alabama."

"Okay," the woman said.

"I'd like to speak with Mr. Arnault, please."

"Hold on," and he heard the receiver dropped on something solid. He waited, smoking the clove, brushing quickly at his lap when some of the ash fell onto the slip.

"This is Gene Arnault."

"Gene!"

"Yes, this is Gene."

"Gene, it's me. Tyler Arnold. In Alabama." The line was quiet. "Gene?"

"Tyler," he said. "Oh, yes, Tyler. How are you?"

"I'm fine Gene. It almost sounded as if you did not remember me."

"Well, certainly not that, but it's been awhile Tyler and of course the last time we saw one another..." Tyler stubbed out the cigarette. Panicky.

"Yes, that was?"

"Atlanta, Tyler. In midtown. We, well, I mean you were. Well, you were quite drunk and I had to make it clear that. Well, Tyler, you know."

He stood from the swivel chair, his bare legs making a peeling sound as he rose. His scrotum trapped like chewed gum between his legs. The nightclub in Atlanta suddenly clear as his crystal glass. He frowned at the list on the desk, disbelieving. There had been a lot of drinking. Funeral directors from all over the Southeast. They had started in a restaurant and gone club to club after that and then, he had—that's right, he had gone to the restroom with Gene and that's when he'd thought that maybe Gene was up for something else entirely and Tyler had offered...

"Tyler, are you there? I have to say this is somewhat of a surprise given the last, ummm, conversation that we had. How can I help you?"

Tyler picked out a spot on the wall next to the funeral home license hanging in its cheap black frame. Focused and purposeful. "Yes, Gene, I'm here, and let me say that I profusely apologize for any awkwardness in Atlanta. I was, as you said, quite drunk, and of course I meant no offense if I came across as forward. I've since cut back on my alcohol intake and regret any infelicitous behavior..."

"Infelicitous?"

"Inappropriate."

"Yes, I know what *infelicitous* means, Tyler. I suppose I categorized the evening more severely."

Tyler walked around the side of the desk, pulling the slip down and wishing he had not stubbed out the clove. He reached for the crystal glass and held the phone away from his ear. Took a gulp. *Get this back on track,* he thought. "Regardless of that evening, Gene, the reason that I'm calling is business-oriented. I'm calling to find out where you send your bodies to be cremated?"

"Why?"

Tyler set the glass down and collected his thoughts. He had learned by watching his father that there was always more money to be made when it came to people in the midst of sorrow. They were not concerned with costs, unless they were poor, and those people were a waste of time anyway. They came in with their hat in their hands, looking for discounts in the literal wake of their dead relatives and if Gene thought that an offer of a blow job in midtown Atlanta was offensive, try telling an impoverished, three-tooth-widow that all she could afford was a coffee can to bury her dead husband in during her greatest hour of need.

"Because," Tyler said. "I've been going back through the invoices for our cremation services. We use a rinky-dink outfit in Noble,

Georgia and to say that they are a bargain is to insult K-Mart. We don't use them all that often, but when I went back and looked at the accounting, what they are charging is almost equivalent to the cost of gas to get down there and back. It's obscene how low this is and I was thinking that if we pushed more and more business in their direction, then we could all increase our margins by at least ten to fifteen percent." The line was quiet.

Gene said, "I'm listening."

"I've made a list of the funeral directors that I know in the region. Tri-State serves exactly that: three states. Georgia, Alabama, and Tennessee. If we collectively send them all of our business, and they do not know any better than to raise their rates, then we can all increase our retail pricing for clients and they will never know the difference. Do you follow me? These hayseeds in Noble don't understand the dynamic of the model, and we can take advantage of that if we build a consensus. But it will not work if only a few of us participate. It takes volume so that our pricing model mirrors other funeral homes in the three states. We set the market rate and the service provider keeps our costs at a minimum. The relatives never see their invoice, and we never have to disclose how absurd the costs are. And the folks in Noble, they think they have hit the jackpot because they'll have bodies showing up as if they were receiving a school bus tour of their facility. I've gone and looked at the books and they have not adjusted the pricing for years. The company goes back forever and they are still billing like the bodies were coming in on a wagon bed." He was breathing hard. Pacing the room. Did not notice that he had picked the glass back up and was sauntering in front of the desk in the slip, hands flitting like a new bird. Not waiting for Gene to respond. Laying it down like mortar over a layer of new brick. Feeling the strength of his idea hardening into fruition.

"And if they did catch on—which I doubt they ever will— we'll have enough market share to buy them and that's even better cause then we can cut costs even further and demand whatever it is that we want to charge. You following me, Gene? What-ever-we-want-to charge!"

"Okay," Gene said. Cautious and still thinking about Tyler from back in midtown Atlanta. Breath stale with booze and tongue thick with whatever pills they had been taking. He had written him off for good. Knew his Daddy before he died, and had never cared for him either. But this made sense. Made good business sense, and Gene was willing to push past being forced into the bank of sinks with Tyler whispering his solicitations through gritted teeth.

"Who else you have on your list?"

Tyler stopped moving. Sat down on the desk, thinking about Clarence and knowing that he had to make more calls before lunch. "I've got a full list on my desk," he said, slurping the last of the bourbon and not caring whether Gene heard this time or not. Forgetting about the apologetic tone that he'd taken at the beginning of the call. "Don't concern yourself with that, Gene. I just need to know if you are in."

"I'll look at our books as well," he said. "We've sent bodies down there. But we send a lot of bodies out of Eternal Bliss."

Tyler smiled. "You look at your books, Gene, and you let me know. I think you are gonna be surprised." He put the glass down and shook a clove loose from the pack on the desk. He was sweating under his arms and he realized that he was going to have to send Clarence on an errand when he got back so he could make all of his calls. He gripped the phone receiver tighter.

"Gene?"

"Yes?"

"What was the name of that club?"

"Which club is that, Tyler?"

"The one with the nice men's room, Gene."

The line was quiet again and Tyler leaned over the desk and hung up the phone. He stood in the office, feeling the rough beat of his heart and for the first time since he was a young man, his father sneering at him and resentful of passing along the family legacy to his fairy son, his mother dressed for church in the kitchen, studying her hands and picking at a run in her stockings, he felt something like ambition blowing cool and invigorating up the open front of the slip. He turned the legal pad around so that he would not have to read it upside down and reached for the receiver to make the next call.

He went through half of the list, calling the directors one by one. No small talk this time. No anecdotal charades. Just outlining the fiscal benefits. Take advantage of those simple people down in Noble. Never knew what they were missing before, why would they recognize it now? Smoked five more cloves and quaffed a good half of the bottle of bourbon before he ambled out of the office in the powder blue slip, perspiration heavier now with the liquor and the cigarettes. Feeling some accomplishment but needing to reset. He went down the corridor of framed Arnold men, intentionally looking away as he passed under their somber countenance. Up a small flight of narrow stairs that led to a simple apartment above the offices. He unlocked the door and stepped into the dimly lit room. Not even Clarence was allowed in the apartment. It was a haven of his behavior patterns and persuasions, neat and organized, with movie posters on the walls, some scented candles, a stack of clean towels on the bedside table and several dressed mannequins standing in the corners. Flirty off-white things with hands in animated gestures, clothed in elaborate dresses, hats and spangled jewelry. He stood just inside the door and looked them over, nodded as if to greet them, then removed the slip and tossed it on the single bed before walking naked past the windows that looked down to the street. Plantation blinds vented down so he could see out but the street could not see in. Liked the depravity of it. Naked and stark white body like one of the mannequins peering out on the day with their dead eyes and carved faces. He went into the bathroom to shower. Stood in front of the mirror chewing a handful of Tums, waiting on the water to heat up. Rinsed them with the brown bottle of Listerine, spat in the sink, then stepped into the tub.

He was drying off, his clothes laid out on the bed, when he heard the chime downstairs. Clarence coming back. Would be useless the rest of the day after staying out. Would have gone out and no doubt brought a whore back to the hotel, the two of them drinking cheap liquor and smoking menthols. The room smelling like the inside of a minty fireplace when they left. Clarence was as predictable as the sun in the West. He dressed. Tossed the slip into a hamper in the corner and went back to the office. Refreshed. He called for Clarence but got no answer. He sat behind the desk and made the rest of the calls from the list of names on the legal pad. Then tallied the results. Almost all of them, three-states-worth of funeral directors, had been open to flooding Tri-State with their bodies. Cut their costs in half, pick up twice as much for cremation services and pocket the rest. He smiled, opening the address book again. Went down the M's and found May. He picked up the receiver and dialed the number.

"Hello." A child's voice.

"Hello," Tyler said. Voice calm. Approachable. "Is this the Tri-State Crematory?"

"Uh-huh."

"And you are?"

"Matt," the boy said."

"Matt May," Tyler said, thinking it comical. "Matt. May I . . . " He stopped. "Oh, see what I did there?"

"Uh-huh."

"Can I speak with your father. Roland, I believe." The boy dropped the receiver and Tyler could hear adults talking close by. Then the receiver was snatched up.

"This is Rollie May. Can I help you?"

Tyler cleared his throat. "Mr. May, this is Tyler Arnold in

Gadsden, Alabama. Director at Holy Family?"

"Yes sir. Your man was here couple days back. There a problem?"

"Not that I'm aware of," Tyler said. "Clarence just got in and I have not had a chance to speak with him, but seeing how we have done business before and it has always gone well, I don't anticipate anything being wrong."

Rollie said, "Can you hold on for a minute. I need to change phones." The receiver banged again and then another line picked up and Rollie yelled for the first receiver to be hung up."

"Sorry about that," he said, sounding out of breath. "We got the whole family coming for supper this afternoon. Gonna be noisy in the kitchen, you know."

"Oh yes," Tyler said. "I understand."

"So what can I do for the Holy Family?"

Tyler lit a clove. Wanted this to come out just right. Said, "Well Mr. May . . . "

"Everyone 'round here calls me Rollie."

"Well, Rollie. I wanted to talk with you about a business proposition. A venture if you will. I hope I'm not interrupting you. Is now a good time to discuss something?"

"Business is business. Don't reckon it cares what hour of the day or day of the week it is. What's on your mind?"

Tyler smiled broadly, then went into the pitch. Spooling it out piece by piece, just like he had in his head. Thinking, *this is too easy*, listening to the man on the other end of the phone agree and then agree again. Not pushing. Turning things over in his head, thinking about money. Asking questions that were meant to confirm what Tyler had just told him. Not quite disbelieving. Would get quiet and Tyler would slow down, thinking maybe the to-good-to-be-true thought was waking up in Rollie May's head, and then moving faster when he told him to 'go ahead.'

Tyler said, "Is all of this making sense to you, Rollie."

"Yes, Sir."

"And this sounds like something that you might like to pursue—to be partners with us on this thing?"

"Yes Sir. It does."

"And do you have any questions for me?" Tyler waited. Could almost see the man's bedroom in his mind. Big black man sitting on the edge of the double bed. Head thick with arithmetic. Space cramped and his wife's dressing table jammed-up in a corner. Man thinking about getting ahead for his family. Man walking into this like he picked a winning lottery ticket.

Said, "Well, I guess I only have one question that I can think of right now."

"And what might that be?" Tyler said, stubbing out his clove in the upturned hand that was full of butts. Ready to be off the call. Smug with what he would take back to the other directors. Said, "Go ahead Mr. May."

Rollie said, "How many bodies we talking about?"

14.

RICKY TATE WAS WAITING IN FRONT OF TURNER'S FEED and Seed when Lester Peacock parked his Citation in an angled spot in front of the store. Took his time climbing out of the car, a Hardee's bag in one hand and an insulated cup of coffee in the other. Tate watched the car rock back to its full height as the clerk loosed himself. Put the coffee on the hood and glanced over his shoulder at the mechanic.

"Early ain't ya?" Tate said.

"I closed yesterday, and opened yesterday, and the same the day before and the day before that. Pardon me, *Warden*, if I slept in a little this morning."

Tate took a cigarette out of his coverall pocket and lit it, watching the small fat man waddle over to the curb, give a half-hearted hop, and then amble down the sidewalk toward the front entrance, the door flanked on either side by large bay windows. A sandwich board out front with discounts scrawled in chalk. "Jesus Christ, Lester. I should have just gone to the auto parts store."

"That would make sense being that you are a mechanic and we service the farming community here. But you're two fucking cheap to drive up to the highway and take a right, I reckon."

He handed Tate the Hardees bag and took a ring of keys out of his pocket. "There's an extra biscuit in there, Mr. Prompt, if you care to have one. Lisa called in sick this morning and I'd already been to the drive-through."

Tate opened the bag and smelled the scent of warm biscuit wrapped in the wax paper. Tossed the cigarette into the road. "Well. I guess I could eat something. You got any orange juice?"

Lester got the door unlocked and pulled it open wide. "Mind you don't trip going in through the dark. It would be a shame if you were to fall and hit your head."

The discourse between the two men was a regular occurrence, Tate coming in for small things that he needed around the shop, the clerk appreciative of the conversation, farmers being taciturn men who seemed to be constantly preoccupied. Tate walked a few steps inside and set the bag down on the check-out counter. Behind him, Lester flipped the light switches, the overhead fluorescents blinking on in sequence over the rows of merchandise until the room looked like an operating theater. Tate took out his biscuit and unwrapped it, smelled again and then began eating over the counter. Lester punched a key on the register and looked in at the cash drawers. Nothing changed since the night before. He reached over and pulled the bag toward him and fished out his biscuit and a short envelope of hash rounds. They ate in silence.

Lester said through a mouth of food, "How's Bee getting along?"

The mechanic chewed. "Tolerable. Arthritis is bad in the cold weather. Warms up some and it eases off. She's like a Copperhead in the winter. Can't seem to say much of anything without getting her coiled up."

"People don't need arthritis for you to set them off. Cold weather or not. You got the nursing instincts of a black fly."

Tate smiled, teeth mustard yellow.

"See," Lester said and laughed.

"Yea, I guess. Thanks for the biscuit."

"Thank Lisa."

"Thanks Lisa." Lester finished his biscuit and offered the hash rounds to Tate who shook his head.

Lester said, "Go grab a coke or something in the back, I gotta do inventory this morning." The mechanic rolled the wrapper up into a ball and dropped it in the sack. Started a hand for the coverall pocket.

"Don't light that in here. Boss will have a fit."

Tate walked to the back of the store, paused and lit his cigarette. Took a can of Coke out of the stand-alone cooler. Opened it and drank. Then walked down the aisle until he reached the one he needed and turned to his left. Lester was still behind the register, slumped over, looking for the inventory ledger book.

"You got any hose back here?"

"Aisle nine."

"I'm in aisle nine."

"Then you're looking at all of the hose we got."

Tate picked through the cardboard boxes until he found one that could be cut into the lengths he needed.

Lester yelled, "I told you not to light that goddamn cigarette in here Ricky."

"Why, your boss can smell it from the golf course?"

"That ain't the point. You find what you need?"

"Yeah. Can I get one of these cut down shorter?"

"That tractor hose not going to work for you, Ricky?"

"Working on a hearse," Tate said.

Tate came out of the aisle, tasting the residue of the biscuit in his mouth, flicking ash onto the concrete floor and rubbing it out with his boot before Lester could see. He weaved through some of the displays and came back to the counter. Put the hose down and went to the front door, opened it and flipped the butt out onto the sidewalk. Lester was making notes in the ledger book. Running a stubby finger down the line items and marking where he needed to place orders.

"Yea, a hearse," Tate said again. "Coming up here from somewhere around Huntsville. I think that's what the guy told me. Bringing a body to be cremated. Towed him in off the highway yesterday afternoon. Sheriff's deputy called it in."

Lester looked up. "That fella Ellis? The one whose kinda soft in his reasoning?"

"Yep. That's the one. Driver just slept on the couch in the shop. I told him I'd take him up to the roadside motel but he said he could not leave the body alone with anyone but the people who are going to cremate it."

"Sweet Jesus. There's a body in it?"

"Well, Lester. Who you think they're carting around in the back of those things?"

Lester waived a hand at the mechanic and went back to his ledger book.

"You gonna cut this down for me or not? All I got at the shop is a pair of loppers and that won't help when it comes to fitting it tight. I fuck that up every time." Lester extended a hand without looking up and took the length of black hose into a room behind the check-out counter. Yelled for how long it needed to be. Tate yelled back and the clerk came out with three pieces the same length and tossed them on the counter.

"I'm gonna get back," Tate said. "That boy on the couch is about done with Noble." Lester nodded, leaning over the ledger again. Something about the talk of the hearse had him curious. The mechanic went out, the door chime and the smell of his cigarette lingering. Lester looked at one column and double checked his order marks. Flipped the page and ran his finger down until he came to LIME. His eyes glanced right and he clucked his tongue beneath the hum of the overhead lights. One bag left. And he had ordered fifteen just a month before. Typically Turner's did not go through that much lime in three months. He bent over and reached down for the accounts book and pulled it free. Opened it overtop of the ledger and flipped to the M's. Ran his finger down to May and looked right. Clucked his tongue again seeing the big black man standing there making an order. Lester saying, 'What you need all this lime for?'

He closed the ledger and stood up to stretch his back. Looking out at the empty space, he thought about how much he was going to miss looking at Lisa's ass when she was stocking shelves. He took the empty Hardee's bag and threw it in the trash can behind him. Tate had a dead body in the back of a hearse in his garage with some guy wearing a driver's cap waking up on the couch. Lester imagining the man rubbing his eyes and saying, "Did you get the hose?"

•

Shawna said, "What are you working on?"

Rollie looked up from the open notebook that his wife used to track the accounts for Tri-State, her neat columns of numbers and notations starting to get hazy in his vision. Not understanding them fully. Debit here. Credit there. He was not a numbers man, and they both knew it. He was a salesman. Made the introductions and convinced funeral directors of the services he provided. Not an accountant who had to make columns reconcile at the end of the page. Shawna was no accountant either, but she understood business. Did not let the details make her flustered and angry the way that they did him. She was cool. One of the reasons that he had watched her in the early days. She caught him looking, but let it play out until she saw the opening and took it. Him playing football and her thinking about college. Slinky thing in conservative clothes, hauling around books while the rest of the kids were trying to figure out ways to ditch class and get high. He was lucky and tried not to let his head get big when she asked him why he never spoke to her in class. Knew it would embarrass his big ass. This smart girl asking questions and expecting an answer. Black girl in Noble and tired of playing an assigned role. All that bullshit she saw through like a thin white sheet.

"Hey," he said.

"What you looking at in my accounting book, Mr. May?"

"Aww," he said, pushing the chair back from the table. "Just trying to make sense of all this."

"And," she said.

"And what?"

"How we coming?"

"Alright, best I can tell."

"Not the book," she said. She had a glass of tea. Opened the freezer door and pulled out the ice tray and cracked out the cubes. "How we coming with the corpses in the woods project?"

"Why you gotta talk like that?"

She dropped a few cubes in the glass. "Sorry? Did you have a more refined name for what's going on out there?"

"You know what I'm trying to do here, Shawna. We talked about this."

"We did," she said, sitting across from him. Their kitchen table a conference room for the business. "We did and you said that it was a temporary thing. I have to be in this community everyday, Rollie. School. The church. People at the super market. You think Matt can't see there's no smoke in that retort? How long before he asks about that? Caroline coming to work here next week."

"I got it under control, and..."

"Nigger," she said, banging the glass of tea on the table top.

His eyes shot up, knowing.

"That's right," she said. "Nigger, what you mean dumping bodies out in the woods. White folk from good white families laying out in the muck, and you getting paid all the while. How'd you like it I call some of the boys down at the sawmill to come over tomorrow night and hang your black ass from the tallest tree we can find?"

"You need to stop that talk."

"Uh-huh. Okay for you to use that word, but not me? Too proper because I'm educated? *Because* I'm educated I know that there's no good way out of this for us. This is Noble, Georgia, Rollie. Just because the Klan don't parade anymore does not mean that they've changed their way of thinking, folded up their sheets and stacked them in the motherfuckin' linen closet. And they find out that their

Ma-Maw is out there in her Sunday dress rotting in the swamp, they gonna understand? Cause of money trouble? I see what we're bringing in, and I see you biding your time, but I don't think that you are waiting on…" She stopped.

"What do you care about white folks and their dead people?" Rollie said, his temper rising. Feeling the blood hot in his head. "I'm trying to get us ahead out here in this place and I got to do what I got to do. I don't need any mouth out of you or anyone else. I'm tired of being looked at like I'm some dumbass cotton picker from back in the day when my people was building plantation homes and getting whipped for *sassing Master*. It ain't right. Never has been right. You know that. Them bodies out there," he pointed toward the woods, "they dead people. Don't know whether they are in an urn above the fireplace or in the roots of an Oak tree. What the hell do they care?"

She slowed herself, letting him talk.

"Shawna, I know we got to do something about this, but I ain't worried about them people at school or the church or the super market. I'm worried about our kids, Shawna. Our kids and getting them out of this place." Sat back. Knew she would have a hard time arguing with that.

"Uh-huh," she said. "Our kids is right. And how are you going to explain this to our daughter? How are you going to explain…" The phone rang loud in the kitchen. They looked at each other and Shawna sighed. "You get that. I don't have the energy to talk to anybody about dead people right now. We got everyone coming over here for dinner today."

Tyler Arnold had been on the other end of that line, and Rollie had switched phones to talk to the man so he could be private about it. Listened to the *business proposition* as Arnold had called it. Squinting at the phone, trying to block out the conversation with Shawna, hearing about all those directors using him for cremation services. Had danced from one foot to the other asking how many bodies was he talking about and hearing the estimated number, he'd sat down on the bed, Shawna in the shower with the bathroom door closed, getting ready for the family. He hung up the phone and whistled lightly, looking around the room, wanting to go into the bathroom and tell his bookkeeper that things were about to change. Change forever but decided to wait until the next morning. Talk at the kitchen table and make her see how it could all work. How he'd done the right thing afterall.

The phone call with Tyler Arnold had been three years prior, and the bodies had come just like he said they would. Rollie running all over three states retrieving them and bringing them back, stacking them around the place like cords of wood. Forgetting one here and there, and using some of the out-buildings when the weather got cold. Closing the door behind him thinking the rooms were getting kinda crowded. Shawna no longer asking too many questions. Walked to the car with more purpose, keeping her eyes trained forward. Holding Matt's hand and getting him in the back seat. Older kids coming and going, Rollie not sure what they knew and what they did not know and afraid to ask. Rollie now looking out the window of the kitchen, spring coming into bloom and the retort like a bleak and forsaken artifact, dormant among all of the budding color. He turned away from the window and heard Shawna talking to Matt in the back of the house. Something about homework and picking up his clothes for the thousandth time. He smiled to himself, and turned to go back out to the truck when he felt something shift in his chest and then a tightening up his left arm. His face strained against the pressure and his eyes bulged. He put his hand out to steady himself on the table, the room blurring out of focus and then he was on his back, two chairs toppled beside him. He tried to turn on his side to get up, but he was pinned. *By what?*

God, he thought and looked up into the lamp that hung below the ceiling fan, full of bugs and grime. He closed his eyes and had to try and register the face leaning over his own. *Was it real, or like out in the woods, when they got laid down, staring back up at him in question and, and, how many were there?*

"Rollie!" Screaming at him. "Rollie baby, what happened? What happened?" She was tugging at him, the boy in the doorway. *Was he crying?* "Rollie, speak to me."

"Looking back up at me from the ground, Shawna," he sputtered. Numbing-up. "Shame is what it was. I see it now. Hovering. Shame. They want to shame me."

15.

"THE WORST? OH, I DON'T KNOW THAT THERE IS EVER really a worst in this line of work." Assistant Director Cindy Carlisle was standing in the GBI break-room, pouring coffee from the Bunn that was on the counter. Traian Thomas was seated at a chair with his own mug on the white Formica tabletop. Steam swirling up from the refill the assistant director had poured him a minute before. She was putting the pot back and realized there was not enough for the next person and she took down the filters and the can of Maxwell House from a cupboard and began making a new pot.

"See, I got to where my rationale for some of the things that we've investigated was to prevent them from happening again. You know, proactive law enforcement. Something that everyone talks about, but rarely executes. But I guess coming from white collar crime, the murders are still alluring?"

Traian put down his mug. "No, I don't think that is the word that I would use. I mean, I've been here several years now. The grittier stuff has become pretty familiar. I guess I was just wondering . . . " He stopped. Thinking how to proceed. It had been an innocent question. Even a rookie question. 'What's the worst case you've worked?' And now it had turned into a conversation that also included him. He liked the assistant director. Thought she was cute and put together. Smart and not intimidated by the mostly male office. Was just making conversation, reporting to her for several years, and just now realizing that she was not much on small talk.

"You're wondering about Williams?"

He smiled. Nodded. Caught.

"Uh-huh. Haskins hasn't gone through all of that with you? His intentions are in the right place, but he seems just a little too proud of our involvement, if you know what I mean. It was a TV show by the time it was over. Then of course it *was* TV."

"He has talked about it. But more like how much stress it put on the department. How it impacted morale. That kind of thing."

"It did that," she said. Coming back over now to sit down. "And then some. Those three years just about broke every law enforcement official in the entire region. Metro. County. This office. Feds in Washington, even. It's different, you know. When its children I mean. We were consumed by it."

"Hey, I don't mean to drag something up that makes you uncomfortable."

She said, "Shit, after that it would take a lot to make me uncomfortable. I don't mind discussing it. Professionally I mean. I been on dates where guys find out I'm with the Bureau and they want to know about all the details, and *what was he like* and *how come you didn't just shoot the motherfucker.* That kind of thing. But with a colleague, I got no problems talking about it. Those agents who were with us then that tried to keep it to themselves—a lot of them are gone. Some left the profession altogether and some just wanted out of the city. Could not move around it anymore and think of anything other than bodies being found in the woods or in some vacant lot. Good agents too. They just kept running into the same brick walls and got tired of the way it made them feel. I don't blame them. A lot of them had families to go home to. Wives wanting to take their kids out of school for fear they might be murdered on the way home. You read those initial reports from every case and the kid was on their way to do some errand or something simple like that. Not out running drugs or stealing cars. They were kids. I think the youngest was about seven."

"Jesus," Traian said.

"Yeah. I think there were three murders in '79. They were warming up. Then around twelve in '80. Then by '81 was when it all became so confusing because we were finding the bodies of victims who'd been reported missing for more than a year. So, we had the killings happening in real time and the bodies of those already reported showing up in the woods and empty buildings. All over the fucking place."

"They?" he said. She looked at him. "You said *they* were getting warmed up."

"Oh, sure. He was not working alone. I don't know what sick degenerate or degenerates he had working with him, but he was not by himself all the time. Those kids went through a lot more than being strangled. The being strangled was probably the most merciful of the whole thing. Williams may have been the planner and lead psychotic, but he had help. Then you had all those pseudo-militants out in the sticks who we were looking into. KKK hoping for a race war. All that low-rent white trash bullshit with entitled trailer hicks looking to resurrect the Confederacy. It was a lot. But you asked."

"I did," he said.

She paused. Considered her coffee mug. Said, "Then I'll tell you. Of all of them, there were two who stand out the most. Don't ask me why because I can't tell you with any specific reason. The first was a boy who had gone to the grocery store and never came home. They found him at an abandoned elementary school. Some janitor reported it. We looked at him pretty hard. The janitor. I worked that one. October of '79 I think it was. Beautiful fall day. You know how autumn can be down here. Leaves finally turn and the sky is that immaculate color of blue. It was a day like that and we got called in because there had already been a couple kids reported missing and the local guys were getting anxious about it. It was early for GBI, but we're as much an extension of the locals as we are for the Federal. Anyway, I went out by myself and they already had the scene marked off and with the school being closed for a while, the whole place just had this really bad feel to it. Out there on its own. Parking lots full of weeds. Nothing making any noise. No lights on. No people coming or going. Just felt wrong. I parked over by the cop cars and started in and I guess it was just coincidence or maybe some kind of sign, but there was this young patrolman there, standing off by himself at the corner of the building and he had his back turned to me as I was going toward the door where the body was and he turned around and I could see that he had been crying. He wiped his eyes, made a big show that he had not been, but it was all over his face and when I got inside that building I could see what would have made him need to be by himself. The child was nine years old. Had been hit in the head a couple of times and then strangled to death. He was in the same pair of shorts that he had on when he left the house and the expression on his face in that shadowy room—the sun going down outside and the cold starting to creep in so that they had to bring in some heaters and lights so we could work the scene. It was that expression that had gotten to the cop outside. Got to me the same way. *Abandonment.*

"And you know, weird as it sounds, it was not the death of a child that tore at me. I had seen that before. It was that desolate space and the cruelty of what must have been his last moments. That and he had a piece of industrial tape stuck to his shorts, and when I saw that, I knew that there was nothing random about it, and that it was not ending there."

Traian stood up and walked over to the Bunn and switched on the brewer. Cindy had forgotten it.

"Sorry," she said.

He did not say anything. Came back to the table.

"So, Yusuf was the first. For me. The other one who clings is Angel Lenair. She was the first female. She was 12. She went missing in the spring of '80. March. They found her a week after her disappearance. Someone had put panties that did not belong to her in her mouth and her hands were tied with electrical cord. I guess that one does not require a lot of explanation, does it?"

Traian shook his head. Stood again and took their mugs over to the coffee machine and filled them. "You take anything in yours?"

"No." She took the offered cup and sipped. "God, it's hard thinking about all of that now."

"Then let's not," Traian said.

She looked over the rim of the mug. Grateful. Eyes at the ready. "What does Haskins have you on right now?"

"Not a lot," he said. "We just wrapped up our work in that Statesboro thing with the Mayor and the school board. You hear about that?"

"I did," she said.

"Anyway, that's done and I'm kinda waiting on what comes next."

She laughed and got up to leave. "Careful, Agent Thomas. Being idle around here can lead to some pretty shitty assignments. And I should know, because I hand them out. You need to look busy." He gave her a thumbs up. She went out the door and then came back in.

"You know the worst thing about all of that?"

"I can't imagine," he said.

"It's the not knowing. Not knowing the whole of it. How big it was in scope. We had so many gaps in our thinking, and that's what keeps me up. We knew the who, the what, the how, the when—just not the why. And not knowing that *why* is what they never tell you about the job when you sign-up. That you might get saddled with a case you might solve. Get a conviction even, and maybe it's a confession. But if they don't tell you *why*, it all seems like so much lost time." She paused. "Makes me feel old just thinking about it."

Traian watched the assistant director cross back in front of the break room door once she rounded the cubicles, not looking his way. Thought, *My God, how would I have handled something like that?* The idea of it being so overwhelming he found it hard to breathe. It had been all over the world. He had known about it when he was down in Florida. Watching TV with Kim in their apartment. Her even saying that she hoped he did not get transferred to Georgia. *Was that right? Had she said that, or had he imagined it?* Either way, it had outshone anything that he had ever been involved in, and probably anything that was coming. *The Atlanta Child Murders*. That's the name they gave it, like it was a sitcom or something banal as that. Scared the shit out of every parent in the country.

His job in Statesboro had been a glorified embezzlement case with a crooked Mayor screwing one of the school board members and the two of them stealing budget money. It would never had reached his office if they had stayed put in Statesboro, but the Sheriff, who was up for re-election, wanted to make a bid deal out it and insisted that they be charged at the federal level for using the money out of state for lavish vacations in the Bahamas. After two days in Statesboro, Traian thought that the Sheriff was being a hard-on because he'd been left out of the scam, but rather than push that issue, he had spent another three days in their shabby department building, drinking luke warm coffee and confirming what was and what was not a federal case to the prosecutor who seemed almost as bored as he was.

But those murders. Lack of motive and consequence still fresh and raw, made fraud look like jaywalking. Traian looked at the people coming and going in the office—some of them around while a monster was loose in the their city, snatching and killing children. Their job to stop it. Breathing it day and night. Made him think about conversations with Kim about having kids. *Jesus, this world to welcome them into.*

·

He waited another forty-five minutes and left the office. Went out to the parking lot and got in the car and thought about a liquor store where he could stop on the way home and pick up some champagne. Maybe some flowers at a super market. Kim had been talking about their anniversary all week. Started the car and worked his way though traffic. Stopped at a liquor store called Abe's in a run-down strip center. Picked up the most expensive bottle of champagne that they had and asked the clerk if there was someplace close he could buy some flowers. Skinny black guy working the register. Looked up and smiled with some gold in his front teeth.

"Alright! You gotta date, man?"

Traian nodded. "My wife," he said. "It's our anniversary."

"No shit," the clerk said, putting the bottle in a plain brown bag, then handing it across the counter. "Gonna get you some here, right?"

Traian smiled. "Not unless I can get some flowers to go with it. You Abe?"

"Naw man, I'm Dargin. Abe's dead. Tell you what though. You go down about three blocks there's a cemetery on your right. People all the time putting flowers in there. You pull off and slip inside, you can maybe find a nice bouquet for your lady. How that sound?" he cackled, moving his arms above his head.

"You serious?"

"Are you?"

"About what?" Traian said, holding the bottle.

"Getting some pussy brother."

"Easy," Traian said. Then, "Give me a pack of those Winstons too."

"Okay, okay. Sorry about the disrespect. It's your wife and all."

"It is. About the flowers, Dargin?"

"Yeah, man. Go past the cemetery like I was talking about. There's a pace called May's further down. She a friend of my aunt. Tell her I sent you and she'll lay off the poison ivy in the arrangement. You dig?" He looked over his shoulder at the clock. "She be open another fifteen minutes."

"Thanks," Traian said.

"Uh-huh," the clerk said and looked back at the magazine he had been reading, spread open on the counter.

Traian went out the door, the bell going off behind him and stood for a minute in the parking lot and thought about his parents in Ohio. Retired now and probably at home in the living room, talking about the Federal Reserve or the college's new dean. That place where it had been so safe and uneventful. He watched the Atlanta traffic moving along the access road that paralleled the interstate and the violent nature of the speeding cars and the people inside them moving in so many directions all at once. He gripped the bottle of champagne against his ribs and fished the cigarettes out of his jacket pocket and tore off the plastic and paper tab and shook one loose. With the Winston in his mouth, he went over and dropped the bottle through the open window of his car and leaned in to punch the dash lighter. When it popped he pulled it free and stuck the cigarette into the coil, breathing the smoke in. He leaned against the car and thought about Kim and their life there. It would be hard to convince her to move away from this. There were opportunities here that she could not get elsewhere. At least not in someplace like rural Ohio. And why should she want to leave, just when things were lining up her way. She had come along willingly. Supportively. And she had worked hard to achieve this while all he had done was to merely transfer into the same role in a different city. A lateral move they called it and the idea of it had started to upset his digestion. But it was not the city's fault. He knew that. It was not the city's reflux. It was his and not because of the interaction, but for lack of it. If he was to be an agent, didn't he need to feel some gratification for the work that he was doing. If not, wasn't it just an *academic* exercise. A task-oriented job that just about anyone could perform. Hell, look at Gillis. The man was average on his best day and nobody seemed to notice. That was not what he was looking for. He knew that for certain.

He pulled on the Winston and checked his mood. He could pontificate himself out of a really nice evening with this woman he loved and admired and wanted to support. Or he could get in the car and drive home. Climb in the elevator and take it up to their floor and rather than use his key, he could knock and when she asked who it was, he could tell her and wait for her to open it up and see that he had remembered, maybe even surpassed an expectation. And wouldn't that be fine—to hold her and kiss her and feel the natural way that they fit together. He tossed the half-smoked Winston into the parking lot in front of Abe's and got the car started, hoping he could make the flower shop and skip the grave robbing.

•

They got Rollie to the hospital in Chattanooga in time. Shawna drove him instead of waiting on the ambulance. Matt in the front seat with a bag of Reese's Pieces to keep him calm, her husband slumped in the back where she had dragged him into the car, head against the window and spittle running into his grey and black beard. Eyes closed, breathing shallow. She had left a note on the front steps telling Caroline and Levi where they had gone. *Gone to hospital in Chatt. Come. East 3rd street. Momma. I got Matt.* They had arrived half an hour later. Rollie somewhere in the back with people scurrying around like there was a fire. Still not conscious when they rolled him through the doors. They all sat together in the waiting room anxious and fidgeting for a report from the doctor. Shawna had taken a chair by the window, looking down at third street. Ambulances pulling into the emergency room turn-around. Sky looking like tarnished tin. Not far from where Levi went to school. Just up the street from the practice field that was down along the Tennessee River. Close to graduating, and Caroline coming to work with them after changing her mind a dozen times over the last couple years. Shawna's breath hitched. Rollie would wake up. She knew that he would. But he would not be able to work like he had been working. Taking in all those orders from the funeral homes. Steady as the current of the river. All those souls piling up in the woods and nobody but her and Rollie knowing that anything was any different than how it had been before. Harder and harder to hide it. Harder still to believe she had not put a stop to it. Now pinned to the wall with only her kids to help see their way forward. She would have to come clean on all of it. Not only come clean, but she would have to recruit them into what she and Rollie had been doing all this time. Because now they had taken it so far that they could not talk their way out of it with the police or the state of *fucking* Georgia. And God only knew what the relatives of these dead people would do if they had any idea what the Mays had done with their loved ones. Just trying to think objectively about how out-of-hand it had gotten made her want to put a chair through the upstairs hospital window and follow it out. And Sweet Jesus now her only place to turn was Levi and Caroline or they would lose everything that they had earned, including custody of Matt. Matt who had not asked a lot of questions and had believed them when they told him that the retort had a new filter on it and no longer made the smoke. What a load of shit to tell a child. Especially one as sweet and believing as Matt. Had watched him like a hawk outside to keep him away from the woods for fear he'd be struck deaf and dumb at what he found out there. She looked at her three kids and swallowed hard. They would wait until they knew how Rollie was doing and then she would take them some place and talk it through. *Mercy,* she thought.

"Shawna?"

She looked up expecting a doctor in blue or green scrubs. Come to tell her that Rollie was dead. "Hi?" she said.

"Hey, what's going on?" He stepped into the waiting room and went over and spoke to the kids and then turned back to her.

"It's Rollie," she said. "We think he had a heart attack. We have not seen the doctor yet, but it looked like that's what happened."

Hi Lewis sat down next to her, taking off his hat and holding it. Still listening. *Like a cop,* she thought. *Listening instead of talking.*

"We were at the house and he just fell over in the kitchen. I drove him here. We were supposed to be having a big dinner tonight with all the kids and I don't know, he just…"

"Hey now," he said, reaching for her hand and looking across the bare room at the children who were staring into empty space. Matt's head on Caroline's shoulder. Levi looking stunned.

"Hey now, it's gonna be okay. He's a strong man. You know that." She nodded. Tears coming now as he touched her.

"Okay. Let me see if I can find something out for you." He stood and went around the corner and was gone for five minutes, then came back. Stood looking at all of them. Face tired like he was processing what he'd found out. Then he woke himself up realizing that he was keeping them from it. Went looking for someone to talk to. Getting into his official role. Came back fifteen minutes later.

"He's out of the woods," he said, hands smoothing the brim of his hat. "I spoke to the nurse. He's in intensive care, but he's gonna be okay. Probably be there for several days. Doctor should be out any minute."

"But he's alive?" Caroline said.

"Yes, very much so," Hi said.

"Oh thank God," Caroline said and walked over to her mother.

Hi looked at Levi. "You okay, son?"

"Yes Sir," he said. "I was not even there when it happened."

"Hi?"

"Yes, Shawna."

"How come you're here? Everything alright with you and Sherry? And Robbie?"

"Yes, yes. Sorry. I was working a traffic accident and had to escort the ambulance here. I was getting ready to leave when I saw you. Everything is fine with me. Not so much the driver of the car, but we'll see."

"Thanks for checking on Daddy." Levi said.

Hi looked at his watch, then realized that he had done it in full view and tried to slide it up under his sleeve.

"You go on," Shawna said.

"I was going to pick up something for Sherry and Robbie on the way home, but I can wait if you want me to stay."

"No, Hi. You go home and tell Sherry I will call her when we get back to Noble. But I do have a favor to ask."

"Shoot. You want me to pick up some food for y'all and bring it up here while you wait?"

"No, thank you, but would you mind taking Matt with you tonight? It's gonna be a long one I'm afraid and he has school tomorrow. Thought maybe he could ride in with Robbie?"

"Of course." He looked over and motioned for Matt to come with him. The boy stood and walked toward Lewis and then veered off to his mother who pulled him close to her and whispered something into his ear.

Matt looked up to her face and smiled. Said, "Okay Momma."

"You ready buddy?" Hi said.

"Yes," Matt said. Hi looked at the Mays and took Matt by the shoulders and walked him to the elevators.

Shawna waited until the doors closed. Said, "I have some things that I need to talk with you both about. Not a good time, I know, but the more that I think about it, I'm not sure there is ever gonna be a good time to go through all this mess. Let's wait for the doctor to come out and then we'll go someplace and get something to eat."

"What mess?" Caroline said, and Shawna was about to answer when the doctor came into the waiting room, pulling off his green scrub mask.

16.

SHAWNA SAID TO THE TGI FRIDAYS WAITRESS WITH THE red shirt, suspenders and large plastic promotional buttons, "Gin martini. Lots of olives." Caroline looked at Levi, eyebrows raised. Her brother returned the look.

"Coke for me, please," he said.

"I'll have a glass of white wine," Caroline said. The waitress wrote down the orders, stood looking at Caroline.

"I need some ID, honey. I'm sure you're of age, but you look awful young. My manager makes us card just about everyone these days. Says we can get fined if we serve underage kids. They come in here all the time trying to buy alcohol, you know." Caroline opened her purse and pulled her driver's license free. Handed it across the table. The Fridays waitress read it and handed it back. "You keep looking young like that and I don't guess you'll have any problem finding a husband."

Caroline flashed her a smile. *A winning smile,* Shawna thought. *Her Daddy's smile.* They waited for the their drinks to come back. Shawna nervous. Pretending to read the menu for the third time. Levi looking out the window at the parking lot. Pop music played over their heads, jaunty something-or-other that made Shawna think of kids' toy jingles on the television set. The waitress came back and asked them if they wanted to order something to eat.

"We're gonna wait a bit, if it's okay." Shawna said, and put the menu down.

"Sure, suit yourself," and she was walking down the aisle of blood red booths, stopping at the last one to check on a family of five or six. Kids making a racket, food and napkins littering the floor.

"""

Shawna sipped the martini. Closed her eyes and let the gin work for a second. Then took another sip and sat the glass down with a small *clink*.

"So," she said. "The good news is that your father is going to live. I was not certain that was going to be the case when we brought him in. He's a strong man, but that was a mean heart attack. I think it wanted to kill him."

"Momma," Levi said.

"Hush," she said. "I got a lot to get through and you're gonna have a whole bunch of questions along the way, but you got to let me get through it first. You hear? I have prayed and prayed that this day would never come, but God, as you both know, has a funny way of listening to our prayers. Okay?"

They both nodded, wondering how there could be much more than they had already heard in the waiting room of the hospital. Shawna sipped and Caroline mimicked her. Levi had his hands in his lap, wanting a drink too but afraid to order in front of his mother. Crammed into the booth. Use the poster board fake ID he'd made with some friends in the dorm. Not sure that it would matter watching his mother steel herself with the gin. He had caught her looking at him while the doctor talked about the severity of the attack, the challenges of the operation. The blockage and the likelihood that Rollie would be in a wheelchair for some time after he got out of the intensive care unit—months he had said. Maybe longer. Hard to tell with what the lack of oxygen had done to his brain and some of his limbs. No, he would not be awake that night. That was when Shawna had told them to come with her, looking sideways at Levi. Not with questioning or concern, but with assessment.

"So, he's gonna live. But he's gonna have a long road to his recovery and that means that I'm gonna need your help. I can take care of your father. I been taking care of him for as long as we've been married. I'll need your help with the business. Caroline already helps out with the books some, but I'm gonna turn a lot more of that over to her now. With all this." She waved her hand and like cheap magic, the waitress came over. Appearing out of nowhere. Maybe wiping down tables and thinking about tips.

"Another?"

"No." Then, "Yes, please. When you have time."

"Momma, I can do that," Caroline said. "That's not a big deal."

"I know," she said. "I know you can, But it's not you who is going to have to make an adjustment," and now her eyes were back on Levi.

"Son, I'm going to need you to come home from school for a little while. And before you say anything, let me tell you that your father and I have never been more proud of you. You have made your grades. You have played football and made a name for yourself. You have accomplished so much since you went away, and I know that you have a lot more aspirations that you want to realize. You are young and powerful and a beautiful black man. You make us so, so, proud and you've made your community proud. But right now, I need you to be home. Running Tri-State is too much physical labor for me to handle, and Matt is too young to be doing that kind of work. You have been around it all of your life so it wont scare you like it would little Matt." Now he forced an interruption.

"Momma, I don't have to quit school to keep up with that. I know that you've gotten more and more work since Daddy made those connections with the other funeral homes and stuff, but I can come and go and take care of that and still keep school. Even if I have to commute, I don't have to give everything up. Not football. I mean, I have a real chance with that. I could turn that into something, I think. Maybe get out of here for good." He thought about the reality of that idea, not sure which way to turn it in his mind so that it felt real and not simply imagined. The threat of losing the idea itself made his underarms start to sweat and he looked over the booth and tried to think of the best way to expand it. Make it stick with his mother.

"Get you and Daddy and Caroline and Matt out of here, too. You wanted me to go to college. Wanted Caroline to go to college so she could make something of herself. And she has. Just like I want to. But it's not just me and Caroline that need to get out, but all of us. Noble never cared about us. You always told me that. And now you're saying..."

She let him go on. Understood that what had been her dream for so many years was now his dream. Fully adopted and recognized and secure in his mind. Realistic even, and he would fight for that. She had expected that. Some part of her had even hoped that he would fight hard for it and that she would have the negotiation in her to make him see things her way. Make him believe that he could go back after Rollie made a recovery. Except Rollie was not going to make a recovery. She felt that in her pulse. The heart attack was not about cholesterol or some other earthly shit. It was divine intervention. And now she had to decide between the immediate hell of state or possibly federal prison and the potential of burning in the eternal fire of the Devil's forked-tongued deception as Reverend Righteous put it. Sipping the last of the gin, her constitution was choosing the latter, thinking, *at least we can gamble that he's wrong about all of that.*

"Nothing that you have said is wrong, Levi. Nothing. And like I told you earlier..."

"Would y'all like to place your dinner order?" She was back in her suspenders, fresh martini for Shawna and a big smile for the kids, too tight in the booth and startled. Shawna's nerves jangling like a charm bracelet.

Caroline said, "Can you bring us a couple orders of the pot stickers and some of the mozzarella sticks?"

"Uh-huh. Sure. Anything else?"

Caroline had not even read the menu. Had remembered the appetizers from the time that she and Clarence had come there before the Lookouts baseball game. *When had that been?* Clarence called but he had not been back in several weeks. She missed him. Missed his confidence and easy way with people and with her. He might be helpful right now. Her mind drifting to the account books. Had wondered how they had been keeping up. Orders coming in left and right. Shawna just shaking her head and Rollie somewhere out in the woods instead of wandering in and out of the buildings like she remembered when they were kids. Rollie waving them away. Telling them to go inside and play while he was working. Caroline coming and picking up the ledgers now, taking them back to her small apartment. Working out the columns at a small table in her eat-in kitchen. So many orders.

"No. I mean, yes. I will take another glass of wine, please." Gone back down the row again, stopping where the family had been sitting and shaking her head. Another mess and probably had left the change he had in his pocket. All those mouths to feed.

"Look," Shawna said, picking up the fresh drink. Needing to get the worst of it out before the gin made her less sharp. Emotional. She could not be emotional in TGI Fridays explaining what she and Rollie had been doing with the bodies that were supposed to be cremated and sent back to the funeral homes. She could not be iffy on the subject of cement dust in urns instead of ash and small particles of bone. She was asking her son to leave school and her daughter to keep the books on a business that was so wrought with illegal ramifications that she had to be able to tell it straight. Like practicing for an investigation. She took a breath, Caroline and Levi across from her. Suspended

Shawna said, "You remember a long time back when the retort broke?"

Caroline thinking *Jesus, what now.*

•

Alan Shanks felt like he did some of his best thinking after two or three beers. His father had always said that life in general was easier to stomach after two or three beers, and while Alan's father rarely stopped after two or three beers, his son thought that there was some logic in the old man's thinking. He had been dead for a decade as best he could remember. He and his mother had spread his ashes in a sand trap at his favorite public course, standing on the lip of the bunker in the fading light, the flag on the far green limp in the breezeless evening. His mother saying a few choice words about the endless amount of time her husband had wasted there. Alan looking down the rutted fairway with tears in his eyes. His Dad had been a soft-spoken man and Alan could not help but wonder if maybe he'd chosen an absurd handicap, type two diabetes, and a constant buzz over his mother's relentless nagging and criticism. Lay it up, chip it to the hole and then putt-out.

Now he was sitting in a near-empty bar called Dusty's, relaxing at the end of his shift driving a propane truck for North Georgia Gas. Watching Missy stock the beer cooler. Hank Williams Jr. on the jukebox, too loud in the quiet space. He sipped from his Miller and called down the bar for another. Missy could not hear him over the racket, so he waited till the song was over and something softer from Dolly Parton came on and he tried again.

"Another one of these, if you please," he said.

She brought the beer and looked him over. "How was work, Alan?"

He tilted his head back and forth. "Okay, I guess."

"You still seeing Danielle?"

He shook his head. Then took a heavy breath, leaned into it. "No. She said she had higher aspirations than marrying a truck driver that sold gassy air."

"Sounds stuck up to me. I only knew her from all that karaoke singing she did in here. Liked to run us out of business. Sounded like a cat in a blender."

"Well," he said.

"Uh-huh. I can tell you're in one of your moods. You got that look like someone took your winning lottery ticket. I'll let you contemplate your near fortune while I finish stocking up. Holler if you need another."

He nodded. Tried to give a well-meaning smile and went back to thinking about what he had seen at the May place earlier that morning. The scene had spiked the fillings in his back molars, and because it had been one of his first stops on his route, he'd had all day to contemplate it if that's what you called it. *Contemplating it*. Sitting alone at the bar, he thought it was more like a waking nightmare. The yard in disarray. The kids things laying on their sides. The rickety looking porch. The tall pines around the house making it impossible to see what was back behind them. Rusted machine parts up against the side of the house and piles of debris, rotted wood, and blocks. The unsettled feeling that he got, like maybe he was coming down with something. He took a long sip of the beer and walked himself through how he might process all of it going forward. Not process *what* he thought he'd seen. That was plain enough. But what he might do or not do about it.

Alan had only been on the property a couple times before that morning. He remembered that other drivers had complained about having to make deliveries to Tri-State. Said the place gave them the creeps. One of them said that he felt like someone was watching him. The old man had been okay. Friendly enough. The kid though. Something was off about him. Alan sipped the beer and walked back through it. Getting it straight in his head.

He'd come up the driveway, waiting in the cab of the truck. Thinking that the diesel engine would alert someone that he was there. After about five minutes, he'd gotten out and looked around for where they kept the tanks. He had walked up between two of the buildings and seen more piles of trash. More machine junk and weeds encroaching on the yard. He kept his eye out for snakes. A piece of equipment that he thought was a woodchipper over by one of the trees. Pile of chips and what looked like pebbles about five feet from the chute. A broken down swing set, stacked, the pipes fuzzy with the rust. He came around the corner of the building on his right and stopped. Stretched in front of him was a frayed blue tarp, stretched to its corners, lumps beneath it in a random pattern, and sticking out from beneath the side closest to where he stood, three naked feet. Speckled with splashed mud, but stark white in the sun. One foot further out than the rest, black hair running up the ankle. The other two belonging to the same person. He could tell because the toes were all painted the same pinkish color.

"What you thinking about so hard, Alan?"

He looked up and saw Missy and it was then that he realized how bad he missed having Danielle around. She could be mean. Talked down to him like he was a kid struggling with simple math. But she would get over being mean and try and help him work through things. Like the time he had almost quit the propane route to be an assistant baseball coach at the high school. She had torn a piece of paper off a rough looking legal pad and drawn two columns and worked out the pros and cons. Then circled the salaries and pointed the pen at him and told him that the only consideration that he needed to give that decision was the difference between those two numbers. She had clicked the pen on her teeth while she watched him work it out. Given him the same look when she had told him she wanted something more out of their relationship. Was that sympathy or pity?

"Nothing much. Just something that I saw today at work."

"Oh yea, what was that?"

He was going to tell her. Substitute Missy for Danielle when the door of the bar banged open and a silhouette appeared in front of the white light from the outside.

"Y'all listening to that honkytonk bullshit in here again?"

"Maybe," Missy said. "What's it to you?"

"Cause I don't like drinking to no hillbilly hymns. You know what I'm saying girl. I like the gospel stuff myself. Been over to the church. Had to bum a ride out here. You gonna hook a man up with some bumpy face?" The door swung closed on its own and the shadow walked into the bar.

"Who is that?" Alan whispered.

"Just Wilson," she said, kinda smirking. Turned to the counter of bottles and started looking for one to pour.

"Bumpy face?" Alan said, not realizing he was speaking out loud.

"Seagrams, brother," Wilson said and clapped Alan on the back. "What you drinking? Apple juice?"

Alan laughed. Said, "No."

"I can see man. From the bottle. I was just fucking with you." He turned and looked at Missy. Said, "Girl you want to go home with me after your shift and I'll give you a back rub. Put some lotion on it. Clear kind that don't make all that mess. What they call that?"

She put the drink on the bar. "Wilson, Jesus."

"That's right," he said. "I been over to the church listening to the Reverend go on about Jesus, meanwhile he can't quit sniffing and pawing at his nose like he had some kind of bug go up it. Only it ain't no bug, you know what I'm saying? That man gets in his Cadillac. Drives down to Atlanta. On a Friday afternoon. Gets some Jezebel to suck his dick. Lays around some apartment all afternoon then goes out to the clubs at night, spending altar money like his congregants are all living in Beverly fucking Hills. Then he come rolling home like a dog that's all fucked-out and says...you know how he does, clears his throat, you know, puts that deep voice on like he's the sex DJ, and says, 'Er, Wilson...'" But he could not finish. Cracking himself up. Limbs all moving in different directions. Stopped long enough to sip the Seagrams. Smiled at Missy. "You want to come home with me, girl?" Missy had been watching Wilson and his act, thinking that despite all the bullshit he was not a bad looking man. No prospects unless you compared him to Alan and then it got kinda muddy because it seemed like most of the men she knew had one wheel in the ditch. Bouncing along the highway like teenagers thick with beer. Her in the passenger seat thinking *what next?*

"No, Wilson. Not tonight. Y'all go on. I got work to do. Go sit in the back and get to know one another. I see that you're getting low, I'll bring another one over." Paused, then said, "One of you has money, right?"

They took their drinks and found a table in the back. Dark and secluded like they were working through a plan. Wilson making his way over to the jukebox and taking some change out of his pocket, picking out some songs that were familiar to Alan, but he could not name the artist. Marvin Gaye maybe. Wilson shuffling back to the table over the concrete floor of the bar, singing. Sat down heavy in the chair. Rattling the ice in his glass.

"What's it about?" he said.

"How do you mean?" Alan said. Nervous for no particular reason. Trying to get easy with the beer and the music. This black man who did not seem to observe boundaries like most of the older black men that Alan knew. They were timid. Not asking so many direct questions. This cat laughing all the time. Seeming to have something smart to say before Alan had finished his thought. Tired of the old rules.

"Don't mean nothing special. Just making conversation. What's your name again? Anthony?"

"Alan."

"Alan, right. How come you're in here all alone anyway?"

"I don't know," Alan said. "How come you are? All alone, I mean."

"I'm not. I'm with you and Missy, man."

"Oh," Alan said. "I guess that's right."

"You kinda funny, ain't you. You drunk or something?"

Alan looked for Missy, waving the empty beer bottle. Looked back at Wilson. Said, "Well, I've had a weird day, if you want to know the truth."

"Sure I do. Tell me all about your weird day. What do you do?"

"Huh?"

"You slow, Alan?"

"No. I'm not. What do you do, Wilson?"

"Custodian over at the church," Wilson said. "Not that white church your folks probably go to. The one..."

"I know the one," Alan said. Missy dropped off two more drinks. Came out of nowhere. Put them down and wrote something on a pad walking in the other direction. Nice looking ass. Better than Danielle's.

"Yeah, you do. Old nigger church, right. Where we hoot and holler at the Lord. Talk about salvation and the promised land and then have a big picnic afterwards. Fried chicken and all that?"

"I didn't call it that," Alan said.

"I know." Wilson sipped the fresh drink. "I called it that cause *that's what it is.* Listen, you ever got Missy in bed?"

"No."

"Me either. But that don't mean I'm not gonna try. You watch me work this. Got the music changed now. Make a big difference. Gotta make my move before the Dukes of Hazzard crowd shows up. So anyway, you were saying?"

"I don't know, man. Just one of those days."

"Help if I tell you something first. Break the ice?"

"What are we doing here?" Alan said.

"Okay. So listen. You know this church where I work? There's a graveyard back behind it. Been there a long time. Ever since white people had us working without pay. You know what I'm saying?"

"I think so," Alan said.

"He thinks so," Wilson said and cackled in that shrill way that made Alan think of bad brakes.

"So I was down there with a weed eater a couple days ago. Clearing out around the headstones like Reverend Righteous likes. Wants to keep the place clean. Honoring the memory of those who died in the service of God or some shit like that. I'm down there smelling like two-cycle engine oil and slave sweat and the fucking thing starts choking out. I pull the cord. Nothing. Pull it again. Nothing. Pull it again?"

"Nothing," Alan said and smiled. "You flooded it."

"That's right. I flooded that motherfucker. So I sit down on one of the bigger headstones to let it settle out like you're supposed to when it gets flooded. I think I put too much oil in the mix on account of all the blue smoke, see. And I'm sitting there on the headstone and I got this little pinner joint that I rolled up that morning cause I knew I was goin' to be outside and would need some relief and I look down toward this creek that runs along the back and I see this little girl standing down there just inside where all of these trees are clustered and I have to shake my head cause there was no little girl down there before and I'm thinking maybe something wrong with my head and I look again and she's still standing there, in this white dress with mud all over it and she's just looking up the hill at me and I turn around and glance back at the church, cause I'm thinkn' somebody has decided to fuck around with Wilson, and when I look back down that way, she's gone. Gone man."

"Well somebody—some little girl was playing out in the woods and she saw you and got spooked."

"Ha ha, man. I see what you did there. *Spooked.* But see, it was like. No, it felt like maybe that girl had climbed out of her grave or something. Mad at all of the noise I was making or something like that. She had this look on her face like she was wondering why I was disturbing her. In what they call a period costume or some shit like that. Weird like she was there and was not there at the same time. Like a ghost or maybe—hold on, my aunt called them something like taints, or haints—fuck I don't know. You dig what I'm saying?"

Alan could dig it. Could see the little girl in his own mind and now he wondered how it could be possible to have the day that he'd had and the things that he had seen on the May place turning over in his head. That he could run into this man who he had never met and now was telling him about dead people above the ground. The two of them talking like old friends, Alan drawn to the man's up and down cadence and shifty grin.

He said, "How far is that church from Tri-State?"

"The Crematory. One Shawna May owns with her husband?"

"That's right," Alan said.

"Shawna May is a fine piece of church-going-ass, man."

"How far?" Alan said. Pulse ticking up. "Couple miles maybe?"

"Sure. About that."

"Okay," Alan said. "Jesus."

"You said it man. Jesus and slave ghosts. Goddamn crazy around these parts. I never had nothing happen like that. You the first person I told. People start getting funny you tell them you see children down by the creek crawling out of the mud. Mad at the weed eater." He sipped the last of his drink. "Now you tell me about your weird day."

Alan swallowed air that smelled faintly of bleach and stale beer. Said, "So, I'm not sure if this is anything, but..."

"Hold on, man. Just hang tight. Any story starts like that and we need to get fresh drinks. Sounds like a conspiracy, you know. Sounds like the way the Reverend starts a story. All apologetic and then you find out all the bad shit he's been up to. 'Now Wilson, I'm not proud of this,' and all that throw-them-off-the-scent bullshit. This sounds good, man. Let me get Missy over here with some more bumpy face. You want another apple juice, Alan?"

17.

SHERRY LEWIS STOOD IN THE KITCHEN LOOKING AT HER son eating his cereal before school. His head drooped over the bowl, shoveling in the flakes and splashing milk all over the wood grain table top. Hi was pouring his coffee, starched and ready for work. Monday morning and he was relieved that he could spend most of it in the office, processing paperwork on a couple of drunks that he'd booked over the weekend and spend the rest of the time reorganizing the storage room with Ellis and Tanya. Boxes of files left by the previous sheriff had overtaken one half of the closed off space and the rest was a mismatch of everything from ammunition to cleaning supplies. He turned with his cup and looked at the boy. He had been over to the Mays house the whole weekend, playing outside and had come home Sunday afternoon exhausted and happy. Hi looked at Sherry.

"I'll drop him at school."

"That's silly. I have to be there anyway."

"Yeah but we can ride around a bit. You know, speeding and running the lights." Robbie looked up.

"Really, Dad?"

"No, but I will take you to school and you can tell me all about your adventure this weekend and how things are going in class. That sound good?"

"Eh," the boy said and went back to the cereal. His long hair threatening to dip into the stained milk.

"It was good of Shawna to go to bat for you like she did," Hi said. "You're liking the job and it seems to suit you. I guess I'm right in assuming that?"

"Yes," Sherry said. "She's been great to me and I've told her as much. That and Robbie and Matt seem to be really good friends. Isn't that right Robbie?"

"Uh-huh."

"Yes Mam," Hi said.

"Yes Mam."

"How's Rollie," Hi said. Turning his back to his son and dumping the rest of the coffee in the sink. Sherry shook her head.

"Levi is home and Caroline is helping. They seem to be getting along. But I can tell that Shawna is stressed out. I guess I would be too. Not having you here to take care of us." She winked. Being coy. Hi smiled.

"He's in a chair, you know. Having a lot of trouble talking and Shawna says he wheels out to the front porch and just stares up into the woods. She says the worst part is she can't tell what he's thinking, you know? What he wants to tell her. She said it's like having him there and not having him there at the same time. She just seems, well, distracted. Maybe it's running the business and working at school and everything piling up at once. Hard to say. I've told her that we're here for them if they need us."

"That's good of you," he said. See you later." He kissed the top of her head. Turned back to Robbie.

"Let's go, kid." The boy dropped his spoon and slid from beneath the table. Ran through the kitchen to get his shoes.

"Tell him I will meet him outside," Hi said. Walked toward the table to get the bowl and spoon.

"Leave it," Sherry said. "I'm going to pick up the house before I head into school. Throw in some laundry anyway. You go on. See you tonight."

•

Sherry Lee Lewis, before she met her husband Hi, had thought that she was destined for great things. She had grown up in a trailer home with a sense of self that was uncanny for a child her age. Her mother stayed pregnant like there was something in the well water. Kids before and after her with no more identity than the maze of identical trees clinging to the sloped mountain terrain of poverty-soaked Dade County. Her daddy working for the country street department when he wasn't laying out for one reason or another. Her mother's pear shape wobbling around the tiny trailer, dodging kids like she was crossing a stream over protruding stones. Sherry could just see things differently than other people could. Had the ability to push aside the parts of conversations that had little relevance and observe the true nature of who she was talking to. Not judgmental or dismissive. Just honest and consistent. She might say to her mother, "I'm not sure I like Evan. He seems like he might be mean on the inside." Her mother looking at her, probing sometimes, but mostly guarded wondering how a seven-year-old could see that her little brother had malcontent written all over his smudged little face. Mean rodent eyes, the boy had tried to set the trailer on fire one winter morning not long after Sherry made the comment. All of them sleeping inside like sardines.

So she could read people and she knew it. And because her intuition was keen, she thought that she could swing that toward ambition. Demonstrate her ability to lead through the understanding of others. Find a career that was stimulating and paid well. It was not impossible, and for a while she went looking for the gate that opened onto that path. She took some college courses after high school. Got involved in some local political campaigns. Even thought about running for school board. Working her way up the political ladder. Who knew. These were the things that were in her orbit when her mother got sick. Cancer that was not going away, and with her older brothers and sisters living elsewhere, she stayed around to help her dad. And she remembered thinking that this would permanently derail her. Talking with her mother while they sat in cheap lawn chairs out in the yard. Her body disintegrating in front of her, wrapped in blankets despite the warm day, Mom looking at her through hollowed-out eyes that told the whole story. Hair receding with her dignity. Intuitive or not, Sherry could see how that was going to end, and it was during that time, when the fissures in her confidence began to give under the strain, that she reconsidered what she really wanted. It was the compassion of those transparent conversations with her mother. The glass of Jack Daniels she would have with her father at the kitchen table after a particularly bad day. The cleaning out of closets and the insufferable smell of illness that lemon disinfectant only intensified. It was the plainness of the back yard. The simple, cramped kitchen. The board games stacked in the hall closet. The merciful death at the end that they all wanted. It was a *family* that she desired. A family that she could craft into its own being. A husband that she respected and respected her. And children who would be free-thinking, thoughtful and at ease with the world around them. Not timid or anxious, but driven and curious. And when she had met Hi, she did not have to give that a lot of thought. He was rough around the edges and she was not crazy about law enforcement, but realized her apprehensions in that regard were clichés. And how much trouble was there to encounter in Walker County Georgia? As she walked to the back of the house to her son's room, she realized that the only disappointment she really had was being told that Robbie was going to be the only child. A cruel thing given her mother's fertility. It was her and not Hi, and he had been kind through all of it. Even professing how perfect the three of them would be. She'd already thought of that, but hearing him say it in his deep and assertive voice, she had embraced the idea. The *adventure* as Hi called it. And now that Shawna had helped her get the teaching job, Noble no longer seemed so bad. As her mother had always told her, there was a lot more to be thankful for than there was to regret. She had laughed that off then. Not so amusing now.

She came into her son's room and stopped in the doorway to survey. Clothes, toys, and the backpack he had taken with him to play at Matt May's. She picked up the clothes, piled them in the middle of the floor, started to make the bed and thought maybe there was a lesson in leaving it a mess and went and opened the backpack. A wet t-shirt, some socks, a rolled-up comic book. A water gun. Her fingers touched something smooth and hard, and she took the other items out and let them drop on the floor, not seeing what was still inside with the room dark. Then she reached in to dig out whatever Robbie had collected in the woods and brought home. She pulled it free and immediately dropped it at once and stood staring, her hands over her mouth. Not sure if she was going to scream or not.

She was frantic on the phone. Tanya telling her to slow down, that she would get Hi. She could see him getting out of his cruiser in the parking lot. On his way in now, she said. Hold on. Then Hi was on the line, sounding distracted.

"Slow down," he said. "You found what?"

"A skull, Hi. A human skull. In his backpack for Christ's sake."

"Are you sure it's human?"

"Jesus, Hi. Of course I'm sure it's human."

"Okay, okay. Calm down."

"Oh," she said. "Sure. Nothing to get rattled about."

"You know what I mean."

"Hi!"

"Okay, Sherry. I hear you. Did you touch it?" Silence. He could see her standing in the kitchen, phone clamped to her ear. That look she got sometimes when they were in bed together and he knew her mind was somewhere else.

"Yes, of course you did. You had to take it out of the backpack. Let me think for a second."

She waited.

"Okay. Go get a pillowcase. A clean one. Then get a rubber glove from under the sink and put it—put the skull in the pillowcase, and either me or Ellis will be there to pick it up."

"Don't send Ellis, Hi."

"Why?"

"Because," she said. "Because this was in our son's backpack. You need to come get this because you are going to have to go from here to his school and find out why the fuck he has a human skull in his room. I don't think that Ellis needs to be the one to do that. Do you?"

"Probably not," he said. When he hung up, he asked Tanya where the deputy was and told her to get him on the radio. When he came on Hi told Ellis that he needed to go pick something up from Sherry. He thought about not telling Deputy Carver what was in the pillowcase and then thought better of it. It took a minute to pull Ellis out of his dismay and then amped up excitement.

"It's a murder, isn't it Sheriff."

"I doubt it," Hi said. "It's probably some Cherokee's skull."

"Huh," Ellis said.

"Bring it back to the station, Ellis, and we'll ship it off to the medical examiner's office. But be sure and tell Sherry that I'm on my way over to the school. You get that? Be sure and tell Sherry that I'm on my way to Robbie's school. She's gonna be pissed that I sent you to pick this up, but she'll understand if she knows I'm going to the school. 10-4?"

"On your way to the school," Ellis repeated. "Got it."

And then it was just Hi and Tanya in the quiet front office.

"Wow," Tanya said. "A murder." Bemused and looking out the window. Hair piled up on her head. Smelling like hairspray and cigarettes. Hi was not listening. Already moving toward the door he'd just come in, trying to think through interrogating his kid. Wondering if he had time to get coffee at Patel's market on the way.

•

Hi said, "Can you please call Robbie Lewis and Matt May up to the office?" The principal, a short toadstool of a woman with a wavy blouse and black slacks that were too tight looked at him.

"You mean your son, Robbie? That Robbie Lewis?" Hi nodded. Put his coffee cup on her desk then removed it, wiping at the moisture it had left in a ring.

"Yes Mam," he said.

"Is he. Are they in some kind of trouble, Sheriff?"

"No," he said and was about to explain, but thought better of it. "I just need to talk with them about something that happened over the weekend. It will not take long, but I'd like to use the break room or an office to speak with them in private. I'll make it quick."

"Okay," she said. "Let me get them."

She left him alone and went to the front reception to have the boys called out of class. Hi thinking that he might like to have a beer. Heard his son's name called over the intercom and then Matt May's. "Okay," he said out loud. The principal came back in and escorted him to an interior door that led to a windowless conference room about the size of a storage closet. Musty with mustard brown walls. Fake flowers on a cheap credenza. He went in and took a seat at the table. Sat to the side instead of the head, thinking it would feel more casual. The principal stood in the doorway, trying not to ask any more questions. Then she turned and he heard the muted voices of the boys and could tell they were nervous.

She said, "Robbie, Matt, Sheriff Lewis . . . I mean Robbie's Dad needs to speak with you boys for a minute. He said you are not in any trouble so it's okay." She led them in, Robbie looking lost and Matt May somewhat relieved. Maybe glad to be out of class.

"Hey Robbie," Hi said. "Hey Matt. You boys take a seat. I need to ask you a couple questions." Robbie sat first, not returning the greeting, watching his father carefully.

Said, "Is Mom okay?"

"Yes son. She's fine."

"My Dad okay?" Matt said.

"Yes. He's fine son. Have a seat."

They sat and Hi decided that he would stand. "Boys. I need to ask you about what was in Robbie's backpack."

They were quiet.

"You know what I'm talking about?" Hi said.

Short hesitation, then a joint recognition.

"The skull," Matt said and looked excitedly at his friend.

"Yeah, we found a skull, Dad."

Hi noticed that the principal was still in the doorway. She was staring back at him. Unsure of what to do with her hands. Fidgeting.

"That's right," Hi said sensing some relief. "Can you tell me where you found it?"

18.

DEPUTY ELLIS CARVER WAS TALKING TO HIMSELF AS much as he was to Hi. They were pulling into Patel's market, Hi for the second time that morning.

"I don't know, Sheriff. It did not look all that old to me. Not that I know a lot about bones. Seemed kinda clean, you know? Like maybe it was . . . fresh."

"Fresh, Ellis?"

"I don't know Sheriff. I guess if it had been a Cherokee skull like you said, it would have been more busted up. Old looking. Like something in a movie, maybe. It's hard to say. Like this one time me and my cousin who lives over near the Ocoee River. Up there around Cleveland, Tennessee. We were out hunting in the woods. This is when we were little kids. Just shooting .22's at squirrels and rabbits and such. Anyway, we found this old bone in the woods along the river there and we thought it belonged to some escaped convict or something. We took it back and my Uncle Joseph said it wasn't anything but a deer leg. This seems a lot different than that, don't it?"

"Yes," said Hi.

"And Robbie and his friend. What's his name?"

"Matt May."

"Right. They said they found it down near that creek. Where Delbert and them other boys were camping. Huh. I don't know." Then he said, "Wait a minute Sheriff."

"Uh-huh," Hi said. Putting the cruiser in park. Looking at his deputy. Not being able to help smiling.

"That coroner's office garment," Ellis said.

"Now you're getting it," Hi said. "Let's go."

•

The Sheriff and the deputy went past the ice machine where Hi and Ellis had talked with Delbert Weir the last time and then up the beaten dirt path that led through the weedy patches behind Patel's market. It had been cloudy all the way over in the cruiser and now a thin rain, nagging, had started to fall. They went up the small embankment and into the woods. Lewis checked his watch. It was ten-thirty in the morning. Once in the woods, he stopped and turned to look at Deputy Carver.

"No whistling or singing, okay? I don't want to give them a heads-up that we are coming. I don't know how Robbie and Matt got this far from the May's place and maybe this will all lead to nothing but two kids playing in the woods and finding a skull from someone whose long dead and ceased to care. But given what we know about that medical examiner's gown and now this, I don't want to give them any notice that I'm coming to ask them a bunch of questions. I doubt that Delbert Weir is wrapped up in anything like homicide, but that guy he had with him the last time we were out here—he didn't seem right to me. And who knows who else wandered in here since then."

"I know all that, Sheriff," Carver said, looking hurt. Holding onto his gun belt as if to emphasize that he too was an officer of the law and understood the dynamics of surprise interrogations.

"I know that you know all this Ellis. But sometimes you get a little distracted is all that I'm trying to tell you. This is a little different than burning sheep. You get what I'm saying?"

"That was something though, Sheriff."

Hi nodded and pointed in the direction of the path. "It certainly was," he said. "You keep to this upper path and I'll walk down along the creek."

They split apart and made their way toward where the homeless camp had been. The rain was now steady, bigger drops that came through the canopy, covering their steps over patches of dead leaves and starting to soak into their clothes. The interior of the woods was shadowy and Hi felt more and more uneasy the closer he got to the clearing where the men had been camping. It was not the men themselves, but the events of the day so far and how they had brought him back here. He kept seeing Robbie across the table from him in the small office at the school. Non-reactive to the fact that he'd brought home a human skull in his backpack. Matt May even less so. Both of them like that guy in the movies who was always digging around in the desert and pulling up biblical artifacts, fighting the Germans. They were boys after all and ignorant about most things. But then so was he. And certainly Ellis Carver was. He looked up the rise to the Deputy and motioned for him to stop. From where he stood, he could see into the camp. There were three men moving around. Looked like they were trying to get things out of the rain which was coming down heavier with the clearing open to the sky. They would be preoccupied and Hi wanted to take advantage of that as best he could. How old was Delbert Weir? Eighty? Eight-five? The other men he had no idea. The key was to get to Delbert and see what he knew. Drag them all in if he had to, but Delbert seemed to be the one in charge. He looked up the rise again and was ready to tell Deputy Carver to move forward when he saw the dog moving quickly along the slope, tail wagging and Carver sinking to his knees to pet the animal and then as if it had been written that way, Carver said "Hey Baxter," and each of the men in the camp turned in the deputy's direction.

Hi moved along the creek quickly and all of their heads swung in his direction and he called out for them to stop moving. They did not. Each moving in another direction and Hi, running now, came into the open area of the camp and saw that they had built something beneath a make-shift lean-to, the ground strewn with plastic jugs, tubing, and stained towels. A couple propane tanks. And the smell, strong with ammonia. Hi touched the handle on his revolver and glanced up at Ellis and motioned for him to pull his gun. He wondered why he had not brought along a shotgun now that they were looking at a cook camp in the rain in the middle of the woods with three suspects who may or may not have killed someone running in opposite directions. The dog was barking and jumping on the deputy who was trying to make his way down the hill. Hi caught sight of the stringy black haired man trying to climb up the bank to the upper path that ran along the ridge line and he whistled at Carver to follow him. The man was naked from the waist up and had nothing in his hands. Hi scanned the camp and saw Delbert Weir holding something to his chest and running toward a tent directly across from him and he moved in that direction, glancing up the slope to check on Carver and to his right, along the creek for the third man he'd seen.

"Delbert," he yelled. "Stop Goddamit. Don't make me chase you down."

"Sheriff," Delbert yelled over his shoulder. Frantic. But that was it. Hi saw the third man. He looked younger and was splashing into the creek and moving toward the other bank. Younger and not planning on stopping because Hi told him to.

"Sheriff," Carver called. "I got this one. Coming down with him." Hi went after the younger man yelling at Delbert as he went past.

"You stay right fucking there, Delbert Weir." Weir was holding what looked like a musical instrument. A mandolin maybe. Hi went past and turned down to the creek as the other man was reaching up for a tree root to pull himself out of the shallow water that was muddy and churning with the rain and his scrambling feet. The man was not wearing a shirt either and had on what looked like cut-off blue jean shorts and maybe sneakers. He could not have weighed one-hundred-forty pounds and rather than walk around with wet feet, Hi stopped at the bank and called over. Said, "Stop right there."

The man kept pulling on the root.

Hi said, "Stop right there, or I'm going to pull this gun and shoot you right in your skinny ass."

The man stopped.

"Good," Hi said. The man turned and Hi thought maybe one-thirty-five at best. And not a man, but a kid. His eyes and face were sunken in, but there was enough youth in him that Hi could see that the damage was from the speed they'd been cooking and not age or some genetic something-or-other. His legs looked like a colt's coming back across the creek and Hi thought he might fall over.

"Good God, son," he said. Some pity in his voice. "Come out of that creek and come back here and sit down." The kid said nothing. Just clambered up the bank and went past Hi. Walked into the camp. Not looking at Delbert or the other man that Carver had brought down the slope. Hi glanced around and shook his head. All of them standing in the cold rain in the middle of the woods.

"Christ almighty," he said. "I guess we're gonna have to walk them out of here. I'm not going to do this standing in the god-damn rain."

"What about the dog?" Carver asked, looking down at Baxter who sat expectantly at his feet, tail wagging. "We can't just leave him out here by himself."

•

They marched the men out of the woods in single file. The dog following them up the path. When they got to the convenience store parking lot, Hi sent Ellis back to the station with the direction to borrow a truck from the street department. The rain had settled in rather than move on. All of them soaked through, standing beneath the awning in front of the market, Mr. Patel inside looking anxiously out the window at them. All three of them shivering a little.

Hi went in and got another cup of coffee and stood dripping in front of the counter. The men outside with their back to the large window. Delbert holding his mandolin that he had refused to leave behind in the weather. Hi giving in just to move things along. The skinny kid had started to shake on the walk out and he was holding his arms over his chest. In bad shape. Needing something that would not be cured with a dry cell and a cup of soup.

"Why are they out in the woods?" Patel said.

"I don't know," Hi said. "They're a sad lot aren't they."

"Yes," Patel said. "Bad for business. Scare the customers."

Hi nodded. "Bad for a lot of reasons," he said. Sipped the coffee. "You ever see them selling drugs out here?"

Patel thought about it. "Don't know. Mostly I think that they ask for money. Scare the customers. I tell them to leave and they just come back. Bad for business."

"So you said. You've never seen them selling anything to the customers?"

"Don't know," Patel said. "You take them to jail now?"

Hi saw the county truck pull into the parking lot and slide up along the building. He finished the coffee and tossed the empty cup in the garbage can and went out to load everyone up for the ride back to the station.

There was a single shower in the cell block. He had the men strip and get clean. Gave them orange jumpsuits to wear, explaining that they were not being charged with anything. Just getting them dry and warm before they sat down to talk. The man with the stringy black hair had not spoken until then.

"This is bullshit," he said, taking off his wet pants. "I want my phone call."

Hi smiled. "And who you going to call exactly?"

The man continued to undress.

"I did not get your name," Hi said to him, ignoring the fact that the man had not been wearing underwear. Standing naked before him. The shower running hot behind him. Steam moving along the ceiling.

"Blackie," the man said.

"No shit," Hi said. "How come they call you that?"

"On account it's my name."

"Your name is Blackie? Your Christian name is Blackie?"

"Ain't nothing Christian about it. It's just my name. You mind if I get in that shower. My privates are hanging loose here."

Hi stepped aside. "By all means, Blackie."

•

When they were all showered and in dry clothes, Hi had Ellis put them in different rooms to sit while he got his thoughts together. They had gone out to the camp because of the skull the boys had found not far from where the vagrants had setup shop. He had not counted on the make-shift drug kitchen, but that would be easy enough to handle. He had them on that without a lot of police work. But he did not want to confuse the speed with the remains of a human body, and he wanted to either tie the two together or keep them distinct. Drugs and Walker County were an on-going problem. One that was only going to get worse. Murder was not a common problem. The occasional domestic fight that went too far. A stabbing that bled faster than the EMS could drive. Observing the men from the walk out of the woods and in the station, nothing about them gave him any sign that they were the killing type. They were more like hermits that had stumbled their way into a side business that was keeping them in their vices. For all he knew, the kid was doing that on his own. The other two either not caring or afraid to tell him no. Ellis came into his office and set the pillowcase on his desk. The skull made a soft *thunk* when it hit the wooden surface.

"Glad we hadn't shipped this off yet," he said.

Hi looked at the small shape beneath his wife's clean linen. "Yeah. I'm gonna start with the kid," Hi said. "See if this rattles him at all."

"You think he knows something about it?"

"I have no idea, but he's looking at some real time for the cooking he's been doing. We'll have to go back out there and get someone from the state to come down and verify what he's been up to, but I'd bet my house he's making speed out there and given his condition, I don't see him giving us much resistance on admitting it."

"You want me to talk with Delbert and Blackie while you do that."

"Yeah, I do," Hi said. "But not about that." He pointed at the pillowcase on his desk. "Just go in there and chat them up. Get them some coffee. Ask Delbert what kinda music he likes to play on his fiddle."

"Mandolin, Sheriff."

"Mandolin. I don't care what you talk about. Just let me catch them off guard with this." He picked up the pillowcase and stood up from behind the desk, handing the skull over as he went by Ellis.

"What do you want me to talk with the Blackie fella about?"

Hi turned in the doorway. "Hell, Ellis, I don't know. Just make conversation. After I'm in with this kid for about ten minutes, bring that skull in and put it on the table between the two of us and then leave. Real casual." He tried to walk out again.

"Hey Sheriff?"

"Yes, Ellis."

"You think maybe I could keep Baxter when this is over?"

•

The kid's name turned out to be Luke and he was from a small town called Blackshear, way south of where he was sitting now. Hi listened to the vague details, the kid shivering despite the warm shower. Eyes cagey and roaming everywhere. Not so concerned about the lawman in front of him as he was about his failing condition.

"If I remember correctly, there was a union troop prison camp in Blackshear. You ever visit that? I think there was a memorial or something like that. My father was a big Civil War buff and every time we'd go anywhere, if there was a memorial we'd drive fifty miles out of the way to look at a plaque in the ground that told us what we knew before we got there. You ever see that one in Blackshear?"

"No."

"Well, that's fine. I don't think it amounts to much. How did you get way up here, son?" Hi speaking to the kid like he might have been a family friend. Watching him and thinking about Robbie at the same time.

"I don't know."

"You must have some idea of how you got from there to here, Luke. Drugs you been cooking bring you north?"

Now he looked at Hi directly, but did not say anything.

"I know what you've been up to out there with your buddies Blackie and Delbert. They seem a little old for a kid like you to be hanging out with, but I'm gonna guess they aren't too judgmental about your habits. Maybe even chip in now and then. You the chemist in the outfit?"

Luke said, "I don't know."

"Look," Hi said. "This strategy you're using with the 'I don't knows' and all that—it may seem the smart play now, but I've got you pretty much dead to rights on the cooking part, which as you may or may not know is a helluva lot worse than the using part. If I turn you over to the county prosecutor's office, it will take her about seven minutes to build a case that will put you in a state lock-up for a whole bunch of years. Now, not to sound preachy or act like a father that you never had, but judging from the way you're looking right now, real time does not look like it would agree with you."

Luke said, "I'm not sure about any of this."

"No, I can see that's probably true," Hi said. He sipped the last of his coffee and was about to go for more when his deputy knocked lightly on the door and pushed it open.

"Sheriff. You wanted me to bring this in?"

"Uh-huh. Just put that on the desk here between Luke and me, if you would please." Then said, "Ellis, if you would, please go back in that evidence closet and make sure that we have that gown bagged from the last time we were out at this camp of theirs. I want to make sure that we address that with the other two."

"Okay, Sheriff."

He went out and Hi turned to look at Luke who seemed to have stopped shivering for the moment. Hi reached out and took the pillowcase and placed it in his lap.

"I'm gonna show you something, Luke. And I want you to think long and hard before you answer anything I ask. Cause cooking speed in the woods down from Patel's store is not good. Not good at all. But if you had anything to do with what's in this case. Well, then we're talking worse."

Luke did not seem impressed or worried with the speech. Hi pulled the skull from the pillowcase and set it on the table in front of Luke. Said nothing. Just watched the boy to see if there was a reaction.

"What's that?" he said, chewing on a thumbnail as he said it. Came out garbled.

Hi said, "What?"

"Right," Luke said. "What's that?"

Hi stared at the boy. "It's a human skull, son."

"I know that," Luke said.

"Can you tell me anything about it?"

"About skulls?"

"This was found by two boys playing in the woods not far from your camp. A while back we found a coroner's gown out there and did not think that much about it until this turned up."

Luke took his hand out of his mouth and said, "And now you think that them boys might have been playing with dead bodies? Or do you think that a dead person got up and walked out of the coroner's office, jogged to the woods, took off their gown and then removed their head and hid it?"

Hi almost laughed. "That's good," he said. "But I don't know if the two things are connected or not. That's why I went out there to speak with you boys and what I found as a result turned this conversation from a simple inquiry to an interrogation that now has real consequences for all three of you."

Luke said, "Do you think it might be the headless horsemen out there in the woods?"

Hi smiled, then put the skull back in the pillowcase and stood. "I'm going to put you in a cell now, Luke, and charge you with drug manufacturing with intent to sell. You're gonna be here a couple days before a hearing, but we'll feed you and keep you warm and look forward to more of your witty humor. In the meantime, I'm gonna send some real smart scientist types to your camp to pick through your cook-kit so we can back up my suspicions with evidence. If you think of anything that I might need to know you just ask the duty officer and I'll come back for a visit."

·

Blackie said, "That's Delbert's." Pointed at the skull. "Can I have a cigarette?"

Hi stuck his head out the door and yelled for Tanya to bring Blackie a cigarette and an ashtray. Turned back.

"How do you know that?"

"On account that he had it in the camp with us."

"Had it in the camp?"

"Yeah, sure. Well wait. I mean to say is that Baxter was always bringing things into the camp like that."

"Bones?"

"Uh-huh," Blackie said.

Tanya came into the room with the cigarette and ash tray. Said, "I brought a lighter too."

Hi kept looking at Blackie, then turned and said, "Tanya, will you go down to where Deputy Carver is talking with Mr. Weir and bring both of them back here, please."

"Mr. Weir," Blackie said and laughed. "Come here, Mr. Weir."

"So, Blackie. The dog brings bones into camp. Human bones. And you didn't think anything of that?"

"Well sure I thought something of it. But what the hell was I gonna do. Call the fucking cops? We were cooking speed out there, man."

This time Hi laughed.

"See, Delbert, er, Mr. Weir, he thought that Baxter had found some old, abandoned graveyard from back in Union aggression times or something and was just digging up shallow graves. Course he didn't know that was true, but we all thought it sounded good and so when the dog would bring something into camp, we'd just chuck the thing back in the woods and you know, just do our thing."

Carver brought Delbert into the room then and Hi gave a summary of what Blackie had said.

"That's about right," Delbert said. "But I never cooked any of that speed shit. Blackie can attest to that. I told him that shit would get us in trouble and that we ought to stick to being homeless drunks and not fuck around with some felony bullshit. But here we are." He glared at Blackie. "Had to have your say. Big deal man. Jesus."

"But you did not think anything about the human remains that the dog kept bringing into camp?" Carver said. Catching up and not quite believing it all.

Hi stood over in the corner with his arms crossed. Watching it rain through the cramped office window. Then looking at the skull in front of Delbert Weir and Blackie.

"Well I don't know exactly how to answer that Deputy," Delbert said. "See I figured that Baxter had gotten into something he shouldn't have an us being who we are, we'd get blamed for it, so I just decided to let nature take its course and throw them bones back to the woods. You know that saying about being out of sight and out of mind?"

"Yes," Carver said.

"Well, there you go," Delbert said.

"Yep, there you go," Blackie repeated. Smoking another of Tanya's cigarettes. Room smelling like mildew and tobacco.

"What about the coroner's gown?" Hi said. The two men looked at each other.

"Beats me," Delbert said.

"Me too," Blackie said. "I'm not much for women's clothes."

"Well, that make three of us," Hi said and walked out of the room to call the medical examiner in Atlanta to let him know he'd be driving something up in the morning. He got the assistant and left a message. Then went back down the hall and told Ellis to get a few men from the EMS unit to meet them at the camp to help police-up the speed kitchen and see if they could find the bones that Weir had tossed back into the woods like he might have been playing fetch with Baxter.

19.

ZEUS HAD THREE DAUGHTERS THAT SCULPTOR ANTONIO Canova portrayed in his work, the Three Graces. The girls were known as the Charities. There names were Euphrosyne, Aglaea, and Thalia. They were said to embody youth and beauty, mirth, and elegance and looking upon their gracious forms, one was inclined to believe it. Or at least the state medical examiner, Dr. Richard Wendell, Dick to his friends and contemporaries, thought them the epitome of all those things. Not quite the same as the real thing, of course, but as close as it could get with inanimate objects. He had bought a small marble version of the sculpture when he and his wife had gone to Europe the previous summer, telling her that it reminded him of their three girls. She had looked at him in the way that she often looked at him when the topic was about females and then asked if it was their skimpy robes or bare asses that made him think of the children. Or, was it his newly found passion for Neoclassical sculpture? He had ignored the question, taken the statue back to the hotel and carried it home in his travel bag where it now sat on a credenza next to a picture of himself with Jack Nicklaus and Arnold Palmer at Augusta, the tops of the brilliantly white women's heads just below his framed diplomas. Faces smiling like they were sharing an inside joke.

Not long after he returned from Europe, his long-time administrative assistant, Ruth, announced her plans to retire. She was in her late sixties and moved like one of the large planters that his wife kept full of flowers on their back patio in Buckhead. She even smelled like flowers that had been too long in stale water. Her breath, despite the cinnamon gum she liked to chew, was foul and when she took dictation across the desk from him, he could smell it as if something was wrong with the building's pipes. She told him that she was moving back to Macon to live with her sister and Dick had to constrain the urge to ask her if she needed help packing. But despite his insolent tendencies, he had not risen to his position as the state medical examiner for lack of diplomacy. He had wished her well and inquired about her replacement with feigned regret that she would no longer be working in the office. Ruth, who thought Dick Wendell was a lecherous cur whose ego was surpassed only be his propensity for infidelity, told her boss that she had already identified a replacement and that she was certain that the new girl would clear human resources with no problem. She had chosen the replacement as a final revenge against Dick's wife who was the only person that Ruth disliked more than her soon to be ex-boss. Mrs. Wendell had treated her like a 1950's sitcom maid for as long as she could remember. Asking her to make hair appointments, lunch reservations, tennis engagements, and countless arrangements for the three little twits that were either cheerleading at their private high school or looking for a husband at the university in Athens. Ruth had lost track of their ages and secretly wished venereal diseases on all three of them followed by costly divorces and problems with alcohol or maybe pills. The young woman that Ruth had selected for her job was named Gina Ross, a hot-blooded thoroughbred that seemed smart enough to handle the mind-numbing work, and striking enough to make Dick fidget with his crotch and bump into walls on the way to the bathroom.

"Her name is Gina Ross, Dr. Wendell. A fine young nursing student that wants to move into administration. I think you will like her very much."

"Well, Ruth," he said, studying something on his desk, "It will certainly be impossible to replace you, but if you say so, I'm sure you are right."

"Oh, Dr. Wendell. I'm certain you will get along fine."

"Uh-huh," he said.

Ruth got up from the chair across the desk for the last time and went back to her own desk outside of his office to pack her things in an empty Smirnoff box she'd gotten at the liquor store. She put her personal items neatly inside, picked up the box and started toward the elevator lobby. She had already said goodbye to everyone in the office that she cared to say goodbye to. She waited on the elevator and when it arrived, she stopped before getting on, then went back to her desk and set the box on the edge, a framed picture of her late husband peeking over the rim as if watching what she would do next.

What she did next was to take out a sheet of paper from a lower drawer so she could leave a note for Gina Ross. She had already received word that the girl had been hired, but she had not told Dick that. She wanted it all to be a surprise. She thought for a second about what to write and realizing that it would take days to say everything she might want to say, she wrote: *Watch your ass honey cause you can bet Dick will.* She put the note in the top drawer of the desk, picked up the liquor box, and left. She had several stops to make before heading to Macon and she wanted to beat the traffic out of Atlanta. Hopefully for good.

The next morning when Dick met Gina Ross, he forgot all about the Charities, Zeus, Neoclassical sculpture, his wife and even his own daughters. She glided into his office like she was on high heeled ice skates, stood poised in front of his desk and offered a slim, ringless left hand as introduction. He took it clumsily, looked at her blouse and skirt and tried to imagine her in a nurse's uniform and then tried to imagine her with nothing. She asked him if he wanted coffee—she was on her way to get some from the break room. He did not answer immediately and when she asked again, he sputtered that, yes, he would like some coffee. He watched her walk out with a look of disbelief. Thought about sending Ruth a gift in Macon. "Sweet Jesus," he said, and swiveled the chair around, his eyes falling on the miniature statue. He laughed out loud and patted his knees before swinging back around to face the office door.

She returned with the coffee and set a mug on the desk in front of him. Sat down where Ruth used to sit and waited for him to speak. Here he was at a loss for words as if he were the one being evaluated. Cleared his throat and pushed his chair closer to the desk. Moved the coffee out of the way and swiped at the already clean surface of the green leather blotter.

"So, Gina," he said. "Where are you from?"

"Lakeland, Florida, originally," she said. "But I've been here in Atlanta for several years. I was going to nursing school but decided that I liked the idea of working toward hospital administration better. That's the plan anyway."

"Interesting," he said.

She nodded and smiled.

He said, "And why here—I mean the medical examiner's office?"

She shrugged. "I don't know. Sounded kinda fun. You know, dead bodies and crime and all that."

"Right," he said. "We get a lot of those."

"Yep," she said.

"So," he said and was thinking how best to talk more about his background when the phone at Gina's new desk rang through the open door of the office. She turned her head and looked in the direction of the sound and then back at Dick.

"I guess I need to get that," she said and laughed a little. "Dr. Wendell's office," she chirped and hopped out of the seat, spinning on her high-heeled skates.

"Sweet Jesus," he said again and jotted a note to have Gina find a forwarding address for Ruth.

She came back in the office but did not sit down. Dick sat in observation, a wooden smile on his face. Trying to look cool. Reminding himself that he was the boss and that if this was going anywhere, he would need to take things slow.

"There is a Sheriff named Hi Lewis in the front office here to see you," she said.

"Hi?"

"Yes. Hi Lewis. A sheriff."

"Hi as in 'Hello?'" he said.

"That's what they said. He's in the lobby. Waiting to see you."

"What kind of name is Hi?"

She shrugged. Thin shoulders. Adorable.

"Did they say what he wants?"

"No, Dr. Wendell. Just that he's here to see you."

"Where is he a sheriff?"

Gina just looked at him.

"Never mind," Dick said. "I guess go out and get him." He posed this more like a question hoping that she might come around to his thinking. An unannounced sheriff dropping in on the state medical examiner. Shouldn't that require an appointment? But she remained still. Waiting on what, exactly, he could not say.

"Okay then," he said.

"Okay?"

"Yes, Gina. Go get Sheriff Lewis please."

"Oh, right," she said. He watched her walk out. Disappointed at the interruption. She would need some breaking in. Ruth would never have let the intrusion go this far. But then, Ruth did not look like something the Greeks would have sculpted.

He waited behind the desk, looking out the open office door trying to catch a glimpse of Sheriff Hi Lewis. Then he heard the two of them talking. This stranger and the new girl. Gina laughing at something the visitor said. He fiddled with a pen on the desk, pretending to be engaged. When he looked up a tall lawman in his uniform stood in front of him, holding what looked like some kind of linen in his right hand, something bulging in the bottom. He leaned back in the chair. Looked over the man's shoulder and showed his teeth. The man waited to be formally recognized and decided to make his own introduction.

Said, "Dr. Wendell, I'm Sheriff Hi Lewis from Walker County." He held the linen that was hiding the object in his left hand and reached across the desk with his right. Wendell took it.

"Nice to meet you Sheriff Lewis," he said. "Did you have an appointment?"

"No. I left a couple messages and never heard back. It's somewhat urgent, I guess, so I drove down from Noble this morning hoping I could get in to see you. Or someone in your office."

"Noble?"

"Yes Sir. Noble, Georgia. It's outside of Chattanooga, Tennessee."

"Ah yes. Walker County."

"That's right."

"And you said you left a couple messages?"

"I did."

"Well, the new girl, Gina. You met her on the way in. She replaced my old secretary, Ruth. I'm afraid your messages may have gotten lost in the transition."

"Okay," Lewis said.

"You met Gina, of course." Fishing now.

"Yes."

"And?"

"And what?" Lewis said. Dick held the man's gaze a moment. Then leaned back in the chair. Assuming his in-control tone and posture.

"Never mind. Please have a seat. Seeing that you drove all the way down here, I'm sure that you have something more pressing to discuss?" Hi sat down, placing the linen on the desk between the two of them. All business.

He said, "We've found some remains in the woods and I have some suspicions about them. There are a lot of mounds in and around Noble. Indian mounds. The Cherokee were abundant in North Georgia and it's not uncommon for someone to discover artifacts from that time. But this seems different somehow. That and we found an article of clothing that came from a coroner's office in close proximity. Both of them were near a homeless camp that I've let slide because until now they were really no more than a nuisance to the community. But we looked a little closer and we found out they were into drugs and now I need to either connect these items to a crime or write it off as a . . . "

"Coincidence," Dick Wendell said, finishing the sentence for the sheriff. Then, amused, said "And you have brought the remains here in what looks like a pillow case? Surely not."

Hi shifted in his chair, knowing before he walked in that this would be the reaction to what he knew was amateur forensics. Feeling the disbelieving, local hick condescension in the medical examiner's expression.

"I could have had this moved to a lab in Chattanooga, but if it is a crime, then they would be out of my jurisdiction, and I'd just end up here anyway. I left the messages hoping to get some direction, but as I said, they were not returned and so I drove them myself. I know how it looks, believe me. But we don't have any resources in Noble. This seemed to be the fastest way to get an answer."

Dr. Wendell reached across the desk and picked up the pillow case, holding it aloft. Looking at Hi with a slim smile. "And here it is." He hefted it a couple times then stood up and walked around the side of the desk. "Come with me, Sheriff." He went out of the office, Hi following like he was in trouble. Wendell stopping at Gina's desk telling her that they were going to the lab on the third floor and that he would be back before lunch. They waited in silence for the elevator. Rode the car down a floor and then walked down a sterile corridor until they reached a double glass door that had State Forensic Lab in black letters across one of the panels. Wendell pushed the door open and went inside. Turned left and walked in front of a cluster of cubicles and then through another door into a large open room where men in women in lab coats were moving around a maze of steel tables. Hi saw several bodies under sheets toward the back of the room. Wendell zig-zagged through the maze and stopped in front of a desk where a petite woman was writing something in a notebook. He stood in front of the desk, Hi a few feet behind him, waiting. The woman looked up and put her pen down.

"Hello Allison," Wendell said.

"Dr. Wendell," she said.

"This is Sheriff Lewis from Walker County. He's brought you something to examine." Allison looked past her boss and gave Hi a once over. Wendell put the pillowcase on her desk and stepped back.

"Before I tell you anything about why we're here, I'd like for you to quickly assess what's inside that linen."

Allison stood now, wondering if there was some kind of joke underway. Hi said nothing. She picked up the case then set it back down on the desk. She opened a drawer and took out some rubber gloves and put them on. Then she reached into the case and brought out the skull. The three of them looked at it together.

Allison said, "Am I missing something here?"

Wendell shrugged.

"It's a skull," she said.

"Correct," Wendell said.

"Again, am I missing something?"

Hi stepped around Wendell. Tired of it. "I'm trying to determine how old this is," he said. "It may or may not be connected to a crime in my jurisdiction and I needed a professional opinion. I would go into how ridiculous this all seems, but it's not that interesting and I don't want to waste any more of your time than I have to. Can you tell me how old you think it might be?"

Now she smiled at him. Appreciating the candor and the shared understanding of Dick Wendell's self-importance. Allison looked at the skull, turning it over and peering into the eye sockets. Running her small hands over the surface.

She said, "Give me a second."

•

When she came back she placed the skull on top of the pillow-case. Hi had remained standing. Wendell had left him alone and was across the room talking to a tall man with thick black glasses. Wendell laughing and doing something exaggerated with his hands. The tall man motionless in front of him, his arms crossed in front of his chest. Hi imagined that Wendell was talking about the new girl. Giving the guy the details about how he had lucked out. What a catch. Just wait till you see her.

"It's not old," Allison said. "Or, it's not artifact old, if that's what you were thinking. I would say that whomever this was died within the last couple of years. See here?" She pointed to several parts of the bone where nicks were evident.

"Something has been at this post-mortem," she said. "Most likely an animal of some kind, is my guess. The body was probably left out in the weather and then the animals found it. But the structure of the skull itself is still very much intact which is why I know it's recent. If it was an older remain, there would be more natural deterioration."

"The suspects that we talked to said that a dog brought it into their camp. They're homeless. Living along a creek in the woods."

"There you go," Allison said. Intrigued now. "These marks could be from that dog, or really anything else in the woods. Coyotes, a fox. Any predatory animal. And of course the birds and insects before that would have been at it too, although they would not have damaged the bone like the teeth of something larger."

"Any indication about cause of death?" Hi said.

"Not from this," she said. "Or I should say, whatever killed her was not due to head trauma."

"Her?" Hi said.

"Yes," Allison said. "It's a female remain."

"Oh," Hi said. The one time living person hitting closer to home.

"I'll keep it here," she said. "Open a file and see if we can find out who she was. That okay with you? We can leave him out of it." She motioned at Wendell still talking to the tall man. "He'll only get in the way."

Hi smiled, liking this spunky lady. Knowing Wendell for who he was. Not afraid to make the comment. "I understand," he said and turned to go.

"Sheriff," she said.

He stopped and faced her.

"Yes M'am?"

"No other remains found, correct?"

"That's correct."

She picked the skull up. Looked at it. Dramatic. Like a movie. Hi thought she could pull it off. Some thriller where the lab tech catches a killer. Maybe falls for the cop.

"Weather and animals separated the head from the body," she said. Looked at him.

"Okay."

"Well, I mention that because in all likelihood, the rest of her is still out there somewhere."

•

He left Allison and walked past Wendell. He heard the medical examiner laugh again and saw the man in the glasses look toward Allison's desk. Trying to get a read on things. The top medical guy down here making house calls and small talk. Chatting up the help for Christ's sake. Wendell joining him now, adjusting the knot in his tie. Running a hand past his temple to smooth his hair.

"I'll show myself out," Hi said. "Sorry about the protocol—coming in unannounced. We don't get much in the way of forensics in Walker County. Most of our bodies are in one piece when we show-up."

"Yes, well, I'm sure that Allison can sort you out."

"She seems like she knows what she's doing," Hi said.

"We try to hire people who know what they're doing, Sheriff Lewis. It's rather important. work we do here.

"Yea," Hi said, waiting for the car to drop. "I can see that."

Wendell sniffed.

Hi said, "I'm curious though."

"About what?" Wendell said.

"Well, you seem to have all these people in here working for you."

"What of it?"

"Nothing really, only I was just curious to know what it is that you do? I mean, what is it that you actually do every day?" The elevator arrived and Hi could see Wendell smirking. He stepped back to let the medical examiner into the car.

"I'll get the next one, Sheriff. Back to my office. To work." Hi stepped into the car and punched the lobby button. Stopped the door from closing and stuck his head out. Hat on now.

"I hope your new girl works out for you, Dick. She's a looker, alright. I wouldn't mind leaving more messages with her. Let you know next time I'm coming." He smiled. Ducked back in, doors closing behind him.

20.

LEVI MAY SAT ON THE FRONT PORCH OF HIS FAMILY home and looked out at the crematory grounds, then looked beyond the buildings and up into the woods. Drinking a cup of coffee. Waiting on his sister to come out and talk to him. Shawna had gone into work and Matt was at school. He needed to get things clear in his mind and Caroline was good for that. Shot him straight. Settled him down. There was a new hearse in the gravel drive. He tried to keep it clean. Had bought it not long after the night their mother had told them about the new plan for taking care of the bodies. His father inside watching TV. Mindless and wearing adult diapers. Talking gibberish and shaking like he was always cold. Hands moving around like he was plugged into something. The hearse had been Caroline's idea. She said something about it when they got back to the hospital. Making sense explaining that if they were going to sneak around all of this, they could not have people driving up to the house and poking around. Could go pick up the bodies same as they could be driven down to Noble. Call it an added service. Improve customer loyalty and all that. Levi looking at her in the waiting room. Just the two of them. Mesmerized at her processing what they had been told. Not scared of it. Just handling things as they were given her. He needed more of that for himself.

She was still dating that man Clarence from over in Alabama. Levi wondered if Clarence might know something about what they had going here at Tri-State. Was he cool about it? Into Caroline and not really caring knowing about the money they were bringing in? Thinking he might cash in if he played it right. Fucking his sister. Get rich down the line.

"Whatcha thinking about?" Caroline came out on the porch with her own coffee. Sat down next to Levi on the step, blowing the steam off the cup. Fall weather hinting around in the breeze. Levi did not look at her.

He said, "You know. Just things."

"What things?"

"How we gonna pull this off?"

"What you mean?" she said. Sipping at the coffee.

"What do you mean, 'What you mean?'"

She sighed. Looked at him like she didn't want to go through all of it again, but would if she had to.

"I know you got a lot on you, Levi. But we all have a lot on us. Me, you, Momma, Daddy. We can't be making ourselves out to feel guilty about a decision that we never made. A decision that was not even Daddy's to make the way I understand it." She put her mug down, turned to him and waited until he was looking into her face.

"Those men that run those funeral parlors? You think that they care one way or another how we handle our business in this little operation we have here? Or do you think that they're just as happy to turn the other direction and wait on an urn to come back. You think they are any better than us for what we're doing? They are complicit as hell, Levi. And us? We're keeping up with the orders and sending back the product that they turn around and charge those folks for. They don't ask any questions. Just hand out bills. Think they are duping their clients and us. We just figured out to turn it around on them—sending back sealed up boxes that weigh and look like ashes." She paused, picked up the mug and sipped from it.

"I know what you are thinking and I'm not gonna argue that any of this is right. That it's all above board and moral. But honestly, who gives a fuck?"

He gave her a startled look. "Those people who think they got their relatives back home, *fuck*, Caroline?"

"Yeah," she said. "They might. But what they don't know don't hurt them any, does it? They're not going to go sifting through those remains and start snooping around about how this does not look like my grandfather. They are gonna grieve and move on. And you think that the funeral crooks are going to give them any reason to think anything's wrong? Hell no. They in this up to their necks. They're shipping bodies down to some small Crematory—an unlicensed Crematory—in Noble, Georgia and nobody is inquiring about our practice. It's business as usual for them. So, we take their business and keep things cool."

"What do you mean unlicensed?"

"I did some research on it. Asked around."

"Research on what? And who are you talking to about it? Clarence?"

She looked at him. "What I talk about with Clarence is none of your business."

"It's my business if you're talking about Tri-State."

"Okay," she said. "You're right. But no, it's not Clarence. When I took over doing most of the books, I asked Momma if we had any paperwork we needed to keep up with and she said that there was not much. Mostly tax stuff, you know. Anyway, I called up to the department of health and pretended to be inquiring about what you needed to get into the funeral business and if you wanted to get into the body disposal business."

"You called the country health department asking questions like that?"

"No, I called the department in Forsyth County. I ain't stupid."

"And?" he said, nervous now. Not liking phone calls and questions about the business.

"And, we don't even have to have a license to do what we are doing. So we got the funeral homes who they do license, not paying any attention to what we're doing and we're unlicensed because we don't need one to operate, so nobody is paying attention to us at all. We might as well be one of their vendors cutting the grass or something like that."

"Don't need a license?" he said.

"We don't," she said. "If we were starting this business now we would have to apply for one but since it's as old as it is we get *grandfathered* in."

"What does that mean?"

"It means that they ain't paying any attention to us, Levi."

"Yeah, but we got this body problem."

"True. That's true. But as long as we keep them out of sight and deal with them in a way that don't invite any attention, we're gonna be fine."

He sighed, stood up, then turned to face her on the porch steps. Stepped closer and leaned over. "Caroline, between what Daddy done and what I've been doing, there's a lot of bodies up in those woods. Hell, there's a body from Opp, Alabama in the back of that hearse right now. I get home last night and think, *man, I need to get that out of there and taken care of,* and then I'm thinking *what's the rush?* We got almost as many dead people lying around here as we got trees. Just leave it back there for now. There's two of them up there right now still in their hospital gowns with ID badges on their wrists. Jesus. I mean, what the fuck?"

She stood up and her brother stepped back. She took his hand. "Levi," she said. "We are in this now. What are you going to do? Call someone out here to work on the retort and when they say that they can tell that it ain't been working for awhile and ask you what you been doing with bodies in the meantime?"

He grimaced. Had not thought that far ahead. Could see that he was more trapped than he even realized. He took his hand back.

"That reminds me," he said.

"What?"

"Propane man," he said and looked at the retort. "I got to get rid of those tanks he's dropping off. All of them full and stacked back there. He usually takes the empty ones with him but I told him that we're slow so I don't need as much as we normally do. Name is Alan. Alan Shanks. Works for the propane company." Levi looked at the ground. "I think he might have seen some bodies the last time he was up here. Stacked up."

"What?" Caroline said. Aggressive. "What do you mean, you think he saw?"

"I don't know," Levi said.

"You don't know? That's the kind of silly shit that gets us caught, Levi."

"I know. I know, Caroline. That's why I said something. Fuck."

"Uh-huh. He say anything?"

"Naw. Just looking around and I forgot they was back there. They was under a tarp, but might have had some limbs sticking out. It's what I'm trying to tell you. Those motherfuckers are all over the place."

Caroline wished she had a cigarette. The pack laying inside next to the ledger book. Accounts still needing to be reconciled.

"Goddamn," she said.

"Hey," he said.

"Hey what, Levi?"

"Nothing."

"He did not say anything about it? Just went on after he dropped off the tanks?"

"That's right."

"So we're fine, then?" she said. "He's not gonna think anything about it. Just that you're sloppy and stupid."

"Easy girl," he said.

She looked at her brother and then at the hearse. "You gotta get that body out of the back of that hearse before Matt goes in there wanting to play like he does. And we gotta tell him to keep out of the woods until you get some digging done."

"I know," Levi said. Then, "You got your cigarettes?"

She did not answer. Went inside to get them. Left Levi standing in the yard, thinking about Alan Shanks and the propane tanks and the best way to empty them so he could return them. Make Shanks think that they were used up. Burning bodies. Then thinking about shallow graves. He was going to need a machine and more lime to manage that.

21.

ALAN SHANKS SAT ON A FOLDING CHAIR IN HIS TRAILER, the soft hinge broken and door flapping against the cheap siding, making a racket. Alan looked out into the patchy yard that gave way to his neighbor Betty's trailer. Betty had been in the park almost twenty years and new everything about everything. Alan sat thinking. Rainy day in North Georgia. Wind gusting and the light turning green outside. Man on the radio talking about tornadoes and then going back to classic rock music. Bad Company talking about shooting stars. He stood and went to the small fridge he had sitting on the kitchen counter and took out another Miller and twisted off the top. It had been a couple weeks since his conversation with Wilson and he could not get the May place off his mind. Kept seeing the legs poking out from beneath the tarp. The place like an abandoned movie set. Alan did not know much about the funeral business but knew something about the sanctity of life after death and he was pretty sure that leaving bodies out in the yard in the rain, under a battered tarp, was not part of the program. The office had not gotten a call from Tri-State since he had been there last and when his boss asked him about making another delivery to the Mays, he had felt something like dishonesty in his voice. Telling him that they had not ordered any more, but not telling him about the bodies. Trying to convince himself that he had not seen what he had seen. And then listening to his boss telling him to go up and check to see if maybe they had forgotten to place their order. Alan had said that it was not like the Mays to miss asking for new tanks and his boss saying that you did not make a living in the propane business guessing what people needed or when they needed it. You had to force it on them. Fill it whenever possible.

Alan sipped on his Miller and put it down on the small table next to his pack of cigarettes. He had quit smoking when Danielle was still in the picture, but with her gone it had taken all of two hours to start back again. He had been willing to give up just about anything for her. Now he felt like he was living moment to moment and the smokes helped that along—moving time forward, the watch hands seeming to pin him like they had not before.

He'd gone up to the Mays after the lecture about good sales strategy was over, pulling up their drive in his truck and had not even put it in park when Levi May had come out, grinning. Something off though. He could see the itchy nature on his face through the dirty windshield. They had looked at each other like that. Truck idling and cycling diesel, the two of them trying to read the other. Drinking the fifth bottle of Miller, Alan realized then that what had kept him in the truck was fear. He was opening the door when Levi crossed the space from the porch to the truck and almost closed the door on Alan's foot.

"Hey now," he said. "How come you're up here?"

Alan looked at the large black man through his open window, eyes looking down at Levi's hand on the door, then back into the man's face. Young looking. Smile still there, but cagey.

Alan said, "The boss asked me to come by and see if you needed to order more tanks or fill-up. Said that you did not call one in and just wanted me to check and see if maybe you forgot."

Levi glanced away from the truck. Up toward the buildings. The sister Caroline came out on the porch, watching them in the yard. Alan wondered about the old man. Always pleasant. Asking about what was new. How he was getting along. The kids were not like that. Almost resentful, but Alan could not figure out why he was in the middle of whatever had shifted.

"Naw, we good," Levi said. Then, "But I got some tanks for you to take back for the credit. Hold on. They around the back." He let go of the door and walked toward his sister, strong athletic stride, walking on the balls of his feet, then disappearing around the side of the house. Caroline on the front porch still looking at Alan like he was someone she did not recognize. Parked in their yard, maybe lost out in the middle of the sticks. Pine trees and red clay dirt everywhere. Alan opened the truck door and stepped into the yard.

"Miss Caroline," he said and waved.

Her posture softened when he called her name, and she came down to where he stood. Slender hand outstretched. Fluid and exotic looking. Wearing a nice dress. Out of place in front of the busted looking house and the shabby buildings. He swallowed.

"Hey Alan," she said. "Levi getting the empty tanks for you?"

He nodded.

"Good," she said. "We have plenty right now. Business has been kinda slow, I guess. But probably need to place an order for next week."

Alan nodded again, eyes moving from her face to other points around the yard. He could not see around the corners of the buildings further up the rise. Place where the legs had been sticking out from beneath the tarp. Then Levi came around the side of the house carrying three grey oversize tanks.

Alan said, "What about the big one in the back. The stationary one. Do I need to fill that one for you?" Feeling his boss looking over his shoulder. Encouraging him to sell something. Not knowing about what he had seen or what he thought he might see again.

"Naw," Levi said, setting the tanks clanking on the ground. "You know my sister?"

"Uh-huh," Alan said. "You need some help with the rest of the empties?" Not liking the conversation or the siblings coming out to meet him in the yard like dogs that were uneasy. Levi glanced at Caroline and grinned again. These two in on something.

"Sure, Alan," he said and they went toward the house together, Caroline turning her head over her shoulder to watch them walk up the yard, Alan behind Levi, keeping pace. The two men came around the corner of the house and Alan stopped, staring at the empty tanks lined up along the bare block of the foundation. A dozen at least. Wondering how he could have not taken any of these back before now. Turned around and looked toward the buildings, not seeing anything out of place.

"Levi?" he said.

"Yeah?"

"How come you have not turned any of these in for credit before now? I guess I didn't know how much we'd delivered. Rollie was always sending me back with empties and I was filling up the stationary tank every other month. How slow are things, man?"

Levi, bending over to pick up a tank, looking back at him with that careful grin. "Ah, man. You know. Just forgot, I guess. It'll pick back up. Just a slow time for the dead I reckon." Laughed and handed one of the empty tanks over to Alan who took it tentatively. Holding it like a strange baby. Afraid to let it go but wanting someone to take it from him at the same time. Levi handed him another tank and he turned to go back to his truck. Levi moving the tanks away from the house. Now Alan seeing the hearse for the first time. Parked between the narrow slit of open space between two of the buildings a good twenty yards off. Holding the bulky tanks by their handles and looking and walking at the same time. Then stopping and peering hard at the hearse. The gray light overhead muted and seeming to mimic the stillness of the woods. Like something draped over top of them. Then he turned to face the hearse and made himself concentrate. A coffin halfway out of the back. Balanced. The heavy side still in the vehicle, and beside the back rear tire, something laying crumpled on the ground. Heaped on itself and indistinguishable among the tall weeds and that distance. *Maybe blankets*, Alan thought and then he heard Levi behind him and he continued walking toward his truck. Caroline no longer in the yard. The road empty below the driveway. Just him and Levi

May outside now, Alan thinking he would have to go back and help with the rest of the tanks. Pretend he did not see what was up near the edge of the woods. He thought how much pretending he'd been doing. He went to the back of the truck and opened the rear doors. Stepped in and secured his two tanks in a cage that was bolted to the interior panel to keep them from moving around. Some full and some empty. The other side of the truck having the coiled hoses that could be used to fill the big stationary tanks. The inside of the truck went dark and Alan turned around and saw Levi's shape in the open doors. Handing in the empties and for a second Alan felt stupid for letting himself get trapped like that. But then Levi was gone out of the opening and he stepped down into the yard and followed him around the rear of the house to help with the rest. Not looking up to his right as he passed the view of the hearse and whatever was on the ground beside it.

Levi said, "Hey Alan. You know where to rent big equipment?"

Alan picked up a tank. Said, "How you mean Levi? Like a dozier or something like that?"

"I guess," Levi said. Both of them walking back to the gas truck now. "I got some work I need to do out near the pond and I just need something to clear some of the scrub out, do some digging. You know."

"Well, you could always get something rented at Turner's. They got Bobcats and maybe a skid steer. Something like that."

Levi handed his tank into the back of the truck to be locked in the cage next to the others. "I think I probably need something bigger than a Bobcat," he said. Like he was thinking it through out loud.

•

Now Alan stared out the open door of the trailer. Watching the rain come down harder, blowing in sheets with the wind gusts that were coming up through the valley floor in the shadow of

Lookout Mountain. The mountain hidden in soupy fog. He drained the Miller and went and got another one. Came back to the same spot, thinking that this was the pattern of his day. Tossing an idea around in his head like one of his Dad's old golf balls he sometimes found lying around under the couch or on a shelf in the laundry room. Tees scattered around it. His mother yelling about things fucking up the washing machine and the dryer.

The idea that Alan was tossing around had to do with his father's sister Eunice who worked for the GBI as a secretary. She had been there for as long as Alan could remember. Answering phones. She always had good stories to tell on the rare occasion that he saw her. Maybe an Easter dinner or at Christmas when she came home to see his Dad and her parents. Staying away from Alan's mother because she had not cared for her. Always ragging Alan's Dad and acting like the world owed her a favor. Eunice, in her sharp clothes and hair done-up. Talking about criminals and the men she was dating in Atlanta. Smoking long cigarettes and drinking with the men. But cocktails that had to be mixed properly. Not the cans of beer. Alan stood and went to a dresser in the rear of the trailer. Yanked on the top drawer that stuck with moisture and pulled out a worn address book that had belonged to his Dad. Came back to the table and set the book down next to the sweating can of beer. Lit a cigarette and opened the book and found a number for Eunice with *work* scrawled next to it in his old man's handwriting. The whole thing was becoming emotional and Alan took a minute to breathe deep. Getting his nerve up to make the call. The phone was on the floor next to the table. Long cord snaking to an outlet in the kitchen. He leaned over and put the phone on the table and picked up the receiver. Then dialed the number before he lost his nerve. It rang only once and he couldn't believe it when he heard Eunice's voice on the other line. Like it had been the right decision all along. Her just waiting on him somewhere in a big office with important people coming and going.

He said, "Aunt Eunice?" Then a pause.

"Alan?" she said and he leaned back in the metal chair and exhaled the smoke out of his nose. Rain starting to slightly pool just inside the door of the trailer on the tattered brown carpet.

"Yes Mam," he said. "It's me. You got a minute?"

22.

After high school, Tanya had married a boy named Russ Garrett, a defensive back for the Lafayette football team. She had been a cheerleader and had fallen in love watching him run over people on the field, standing over top of them in barbaric conquest, taunting them. Telling them to try and come around his side of the line again. He dared them. She had found that masculinity sexy and gave herself over in the front seat of his Ford F-150 behind the gymnasium building one Tuesday night when they were both seniors. They had a scare that she was pregnant a month later and decided when she finally got her period in algebra class that it was a sign that they should get married after school. Russ telling her that he loved her and she telling Russ that she loved him too.

They moved into a small rental house outside of Noble, and her husband took a job in Ricky Tate's body shop, learning how to fix cars. Tanya picking up odd jobs here and there, mostly filling in at a dollar store off the state highway. Checking people out buying canned goods and cheap toys. They had got along okay until Russ got fired for fighting with one of the other mechanics and took up drinking as a full-time occupation. She had tried to rekindle her attraction to him but found that his lack of motivation was not only a function of his general laziness, but also a symptom of his mental simplicity. A year in and his stupidity got mean. She had come home from a shift and he had pressed her about where she had been and if she was sleeping around on him. Paranoid and blustering in the small kitchen. Tanya pushed up against the counter near the sink, not sure how to respond. Then scared when he threw a bottle into the wall and stumbled out into the front room where she could hear the football game playing. Russ talking to himself as he went. That had been the first warning. A week later the same thing happened, only this time he had met her coming in from the driveway and had started to ask a question and slapped her before she got it all the way out. She was on her knees in the driveway when he reached down to pull her up by her hair and she fought back, kicking and punching blindly, her hands hitting bulk that had turned into an undefined mass of flesh and muscle. Russ hit her again and she went down hard, falling backwards, bouncing her head on the concrete. Russ coming in for more when she heard a man's harsh bark behind her and brakes locking up. She could not see who it was and when she started to get up someone pushed her gently back down and told her to hold tight. That an EMS unit was on the way. Told her that she might have a concussion and to take it easy. She could not see the man's face, just the dark outline and what appeared to be a broad brimmed hat. She looked to her left and saw Russ on his stomach in the weedy grass of their lawn. Handcuffed. Looking at her with a dazed expression she could barely make out save the faint light from the porch bulb that was uncovered to the right of the front door.

"It's over," the voice said. "It's over." And Tanya closed her eyes and tried to make her head stop buzzing.

·

Now Tanya picked up the phone and said, "Walker County Sheriff's Department. How can I help you?"

A man's voice spoke back. Very even. Smooth almost. Said, "This is Special Agent Traian Thomas with the Georgian Bureau of Investigations. How are you this morning?"

"I'm fine," Tanya said.

"That's good," Thomas said. "I wonder if you can connect me

with Sheriff Lewis. Hi Lewis I have here?"

"Yes Sir," she said. Feeling excited now with this GBI man on the phone.

"You mind if I ask you something?"

"No," she said.

"What kind of name is Hi? That a nickname or something like that?"

Tanya paused and thought about Russ Garrett hog tied in the yard and smiled.

"You know, I've never thought to ask," she said.

•

Sheriff Lewis was thinking about what the doctor in the coroner's office had told him about the remains being a woman. Making it more personal now. More urgent. They had gone out and searched the area around the homeless camp and come up with nothing. His deputy walking around with the dog, Baxter, insisting that if the dog brought the skull into camp, that he might be able to take them to the rest of the body. Hi obliging him thinking that maybe it was not the worst idea. They had gotten nowhere with Delbert, Blackie and the kid, Luke, and after keeping them for a few days, he cut Blackie and Delbert loose telling them that if he had to talk with them again about being up at Patel's asking for money of if he got even a whiff that they were involved in the drugs, that he would run them on a straight line from the woods to a cell. No questions asked. The kid he kept, letting him sweat out the speed in his system at the hospital and then charging him with intent. Luke cooling his heels in the back of the station, waiting on trial tomorrow morning. The prosecutor on the same page as Hi. Hit him with it and get him the fuck out of Walker County.

•

He was turning things over in his mind when Tanya buzzed him and said there was a man on the line from the GBI that needed to talk with him. He told her to send it through. Pulled the lever on his chair that allowed it to recline and picked up the receiver when it rang.

"This is Sheriff Lewis."

"Sheriff, this is Traian Thomas with the GBI. How are you?"

"I'm fine, Agent Thomas."

"Good to hear. How are things up in Walker County?"

"Oh," Hi said. "About like you'd expect."

"And what would I expect?"

Hi took the phone from his ear and looked at it. "How can I help you, agent?"

"I'm sorry," Thomas said. "That came out wrong. I just don't know much about where you are. Been up to Chattanooga once. Been a while though."

"Well," Hi said. "We're like any other little hick town in Georgia. Just trying to keep up with you sophisticated folks in the capital. It's hard work, but we manage to get along. Somehow." Silence now. Hi waiting to see if this line of talk would continue or if the GBI man would get to the point.

"I'll start over," Thomas said.

"You go right ahead."

Thomas said, "We got a call about a Crematory in your area. Woman in our office named Eunice Shanks took it. Seems she has a nephew up there that runs propane for North Georgia Gas."

"Okay."

"The nephew. Man named Alan Shanks. You know him?"

"I do not," Hi said. "Believe there are number of people living here that I don't know personally, nor am I related to them."

"Okay," Thomas said, ignoring the sarcasm. Thinking, *Jesus.*

Hi heard him flipping pages.

"The place is called Tri-State. Run by a family named May. You know it?"

Hi let his chair come back straight. Leaned into the desk on his elbows. "I do," he said. Flat. Waiting before he said anything more. Thomas had asked if he knew Tri-State. Not the Mays.

"And the family?"

"What about them?"

"Do you know the family, Sheriff?" Thomas said.

"Yes," Hi said.

"And?"

"And what?" Hi said. Still leaning forward. Intent. "You have not told me what this call was about. The call from this Shanks." He heard pages turning again.

"Alan Shanks told his aunt, Eunice, who I mentioned earlier, that he had seen bodies unattended on the property. More than once. And that the last time he was there, the owners . . . Hold on. Their names are Levi and Caroline May. That the owners were acting strangely. Like maybe they were hiding something from him. I told Eunice that it did not sound to me like something that warranted investigation by the GBI, but that I would look into it for her. So that's what I'm doing now. By calling you. Looking into it."

"Looking into it," Hi repeated.

"That's right," Traian said. "Any light you can shed on this?"

Hi said, "No." Needing to be assertive now. "I know the Mays personally. Pretty well-respected family in Noble. Their mother Shawna works in the school system in Walker County. My wife actually works with her. She's a teacher. The husband, Rollie, had a stroke a while back and is pretty much incapacitated now. Wheelchair bound to be specific. His son Levi left school to come home and run the place for his dad. I think Caroline keeps the books. Sad story really. They're good people."

"I see," Traian said. Not shuffling his notes now. Listening to Hi.

"This Shanks fella. What did he say that he saw exactly?"

"I'll get to that in a second," Traian said. "Did you know that they are operating a Crematory without a license?"

"How would I have known that?" Hi said.

Traian paused. "Is there some kind of problem, Sheriff?"

"What?" Hi said. "A problem?"

"It's just that I feel like I'm trying to drag this out of you."

Hi sat back again. Feeling the tone shift.

"I'm not trying to step into your backyard here, Sheriff. I'm respecting your position, otherwise, I would not have bothered to call. I'd be in your front office. In one of my blue suits that you local boys like to make fun of."

"I see," Hi said.

"So, you did not know about the license which I understand, but that's not really a black and white issue either because they—the Mays—come in through somewhat of a loophole in state governance. It's only been recently that crematories had to retain licensure. And the fact that licensure is overseen by the state could warrant our involvement. Since they are not licensed it means that they are not inspected by the state's Funeral Home regulatory office which in turn means that no one is really paying attention to what they're doing or how they are doing whatever it is that they are doing, or in the case of this call, potentially not doing. Clear as mud. Now, to simplify, I'm not interested in making this more than it has to be. For all I know . . . "

Hi cut him off. "They *are* cremating bodies on the property," he said. "And I'm going to guess that what Mr. Shanks saw was a part of the process that people don't normally see and it spooked him. Understandable. I'm not crazy about being around dead people myself and I'm in law enforcement. But to save you the time, I'm more than happy to pay them a visit and make sure that everything is okay up there. Does that sound good to you?" Hi in control now. Wanting to be off the phone. He could picture the agent on the other end thinking it through.

"You there?"

"I'm here," Traian said. "That sounds fine and if it's not too much trouble I would appreciate a call back. Just to close the loop, you know. I can give you my direct line . . . "

"I'll find it," Hi said. "That it?"

"For now," Traian said and Hi hung up.

He sat at the desk and thought, *well fuck Rollie.* Stood up and went out into the front office looking for Ellis. Tanya was hanging up the phone.

"Who was that?" Hi said, looking through the window at the street and low, two-story buildings that made up almost half of the downtown area. Nice day outside. Clear blue and a little wind. His cruiser parked in front, needing a wash.

"That was that guy from the GBI," she said.

Hi turned. "Again?"

"He said you hung up before he could leave his number."

Hi laughed. "Alright. You know where Ellis has gotten to?"

"No," she said. "He was going over to the body shop but I have not heard from him this morning."

"Why does he need to go to the body shop?"

"Something about his fender."

"What's wrong with his fender?"

Tanya pretended to look at some papers on her desk.

"Tanya?"

"Yes?"

"What's wrong with his fender."

"He caught it on one of those concrete poles in the back that keep you from running into the dumpster pad," she said. "But he asked me not to tell you that because he's real embarrassed about it."

Hi laughed again. "I've got some things to do out of the office. Radio me when you hear from him. We'll pretend that I don't know about the fender."

"Thanks Sheriff." Then, "Hey Sheriff?"

"Yes Mam," he said.

"Can I ask you a sorta personal question?"

"Well now, Tanya."

"Oh, nothing like that," she said. Getting red in the face.

Hi could see the cheerleader in that look. The innocent look before she started getting knocked around her front yard.

"Go ahead Honey."

"Well," she said. Deliberate. "I was wondering. What kinda name is Hi anyway?"

23.

TO GET TO THE CHEETAH LOUNGE, REVEREND RIGHTEOUS would take I-75 south out of Chattanooga, to Techwood Drive to Spring Street. Almost a straight shot. It took just over two hours if he did not hit traffic. He had a self-imposed rule that there was no drinking or drugs on either the trip down or on the trip back. The trip back being a bit more challenging because he was always in need of some relief after a night out with the girls who danced in the club. The girls and the men who came to watch them. All of them hitting the booze hard. Inhibitions soaked and gone entirely before ten o'clock. Like boys sneaking beer after the ball game. Scared of the girls, but intrigued and then fiercely lusting. Sometimes he would stay the night with one of the women who he'd come to know. The older ones who were not pulling in the large tips and had become friends over the years. Some of them single mothers making money to take care of kids. Decent girls who needed his kindness and special brand of salvation. The Reverend felt strongly that despite their profession, these girls were children of God just the same and were deserving of his comforts as much as the men and women in his congregation back in Noble. And he had always felt that the sinners needed his attention more than the devout. Even if that attention was carnal in nature and not in line with the doctrine of the Christian church. Who was he to judge?

Still, he knew that his actions would be frowned upon and could even put his livelihood in jeopardy and so he kept his missions close to the vest. Only Wilson really knew what he was up to, but Wilson had his own transgressions against the Lord as well as the law and felt obliged to keep a secret. He had a good gig at the church and the two men took comfort in their mutual understanding of one another. It almost felt like the relationship was ordained by a higher power. Both them spreading their wings when no one was looking.

Late afternoon, after leaving the church, he had gone home, showered and chosen a dark tan suit, a starched white shirt and gold cuff links. Unbuttoned the top of the shirt and looked himself over in the full-length mirror on the back of his bedroom door. Studied the open neck of the shirt. Not liking the grey hair that poked out disobediently, he had gone back to the closet and chosen a gold tie and cinched it up. Went back to the mirror and nodded his approval. He checked his wallet for the cash he'd taken out of the strong box in the bottom drawer of his desk in the church office and counted the five-hundred dollars he had crammed inside. He would replace it when he got back. Went out to the Cadillac that was covered beneath a tarp under the carport and guided the white sedan through Noble and onto the state highway that led out of town. He took 24 East to 75 South and stepped hard on the pedal, bringing the Caddie up to a smooth eighty. Set the cruise control. Dialed in a soul station. Listened until the advertisements came on, then switched it off and thought about the sermon he would give on Sunday. He needed something with fire in it. Had seen them nodding off lately. Something to make them take notice. Loop it into one of the gospels, sure, but that's not what got them stirred up. What worked was shoving plight down their throats. Turning their misfortunes and dissatisfaction into pledges to the church. Believing that through their benevolence to God, they were seeing their way through to a promised land. A salvation that was awaiting them once their penance on Earth was finally paid. A flowery garden path populated with lambs on which their children could walk. A strengthened faith that would carry them like babes through a forest of white wolves and devils. That would make them stand and avow themselves. Would make them pull bills out of their purses and place them in the offering plates without hesitation. Would entrust themselves to him. Reverend Righteous. A resolute man of God. A man who was divinely intervening on their behalf. *Thank you Jesus, yes.* He took the exit as the sun was turning buttery in the western sky. Easiness coming on. He turned on Spring Street and then into the Cheetah parking lot. Filling up on a Friday night. Checked his reflection in the visor mirror. Got out and locked the car. Moving toward the entrance with a groove. Steady and cool. Adopting a less reverent persona.

He recognized the man at the front door. Ricky. Or Terry. Shane maybe. Something Georgia cracker anyway. Man eyeing him as he came in under the awning. The Reverend stopped. Strip of carpet a bright red. Worn in a couple spots with stains that looked like rain had sat on it. Needed to be vacuumed.

"There a cover tonight?" he said. Smiling big. Staying on the step so his eyes were even with the bouncer.

"No," the man said. He had a toothpick in his mouth. Moving it around. Not bothering to take it out when he spoke.

"You mind if I go inside?" Reverend Righteous said.

The man stood straight. Had been leaning against the wall next to the door. Dressed in black. Short haircut and beady eyes. Looked like one of those redneck boys back in Noble. Barely able to walk straight for the chip they carried around on their shoulder. Everyone keeping them away from a better life.

"No," the bouncer said.

Reverend Righteous stepped down and looked the man over. Chuckled and clapped his hands.

"What's your name, son?" he said.

"Brandon. But mostly people call me Rottie."

"Like the dog? Why they call you that? You like howling, pissing on things?"

"No, that's not why."

"You kinda short on vocabulary, ain't ya son?"

The bouncer bristled. Changed his posture.

Reverend Righteous said, "Tell you what Brandon. I'd like to go inside here and look at some tits and have some drinks. Maybe get a blowjob before I head home. I was trying to be friendly this being a strip club and all of us here to have a good time. But see, I can tell by the way that you carry yourself that you either ain't fond of negroes in this establishment or maybe you just bored and mad that you got to stay outside while I sit girls in my lap. Cup their ass with my black paws. Either way, Brandon, you think maybe you could do your job and open that fucking door?"

Brandon took a step forward and the door came open behind him. A short man in a black suit stepped onto the carpet.

"Brandon, T.J. needs help with a delivery out back." Then he stopped. Saw Reverend Righteous there and went around the bouncer with his hand out.

"Well now, look what the Lord has seen fit to bring us."

Reverend Righteous took the man's hand. Both of them smiling. Old friends.

"Reggie, it's good to see you. My man."

Reggie turned and looked at Brandon. Said, "What the hell are you still standing here for, Brandon. Go help Bobby with those kegs they're unloading in the back."

"That's Rottie," Reverend Righteous said.

"Who's Rottie?"

"This man here," pointing at the bouncer.

"Shit," Reggie said. "He tell you that?"

"Uh-huh."

"Well, okay." Both of them looking at the bouncer now. The man uncomfortable.

"He told me that, but you know, I don't think he likes colored folks all that much."

"Is that so." Reggie said, "You giving this man here shit, son?"

"No, I was just . . ."

"You was just being your same old redneck ass is what. Go help

T.J. before I fire your dumbass right here and now. Do it on principle of being a shit-kicking hick I was ignorant enough to let work the front door." Turned back to Revered Righteous. Said, "You come inside with me, Reverend. I got a table you gonna like right up at the front. Got some new girls working that gonna send your night into overdrive."

·

The two men went inside the Cheetah together. Reggie explaining that Brandon was a nephew of one of the owners and had not been a choice for employment but a mandate.

"Most of the time they don't get involved with the help. Know what I mean? This time they called in a favor only it was not really a favor for me. You dig?"

"I dig," Reverend Righteous said, looking around the floor and seeing girls up on stage swinging from poles in muted red light. Other colored lights swirling and the man on the PA system talking them up. Talking about one of blonds being from Tallahassee and putting herself through college so all of them needed to tip her nice. That kind of chatter.

"Listen," Reggie said. Having to talk loud over the music that seemed to be testing the building's structure. Some pop band. Real bouncy sounding. "I got this table up front, like I said, but see them there," he pointed over to a stage on the far-right side of the large room.

"Yeah, I see them."

"They a bunch of funeral directors from around the Southeast. They all came in together and getting all kinds of fucked up. I had to send one of the bouncers over twice now. Tell them to quit touching the girls. They getting nervous and all. I told them if they wanted to touch something then they had to pay more for that. Be more discreet."

"Okay," Reverend Righteous said. "You got another table?"

"Sure, but not that close. You go on over and I'll get Martha to bring you a cocktail. You don't like it there, we'll move you. That work?"

"That'll work. Appreciate you Reggie."

"Shit. I feel better having a man of the cloth around. Like having the Big Boss looking after the business."

He left and Reverend Righteous walked toward the table. The girl on the stage was a tall black woman who must have been new. He did not recognize her. Knew most of them by name. The table was a two top to the left of the funeral directors. Not more than a few feet between them. He moved through the room and stood next to his table watching the girl, skin glistening like she had washed in Canola oil, jet black with legs that were so long it made it hard to see where they stopped. From the hips up like a smooth, hilly topography with wonders to discover over each curve and dip. The DJ faded out the pop band and slid in a bluesy number that took the tempo out of her dance, making her adjust. Reverend Righteous sat down, glancing from the girl who had noticed him taking his seat, and looking over the large group of men in sport coats and Oxford shirts. Khaki pants and alligator loafers. Holding their drinks and yelling up at the stage. A couple of them sitting behind the ones standing. Heads bent close and talking. When he looked back at the stage, the girl was squatting on its edge, a clever and confident balance. Big brown eyes hovering above him. Knees almost in his face. Knowing grin. Darkened corridor that led to the thong she was wearing. Nothing on up top. Predatory posture that got his blood running.

"Here you are," Martha said from behind him. Martha no longer dancing but still fine to look at. She placed the Scotch on the table with a napkin along with her tray and gave him a warm hug when he stood to meet her.

"Where you been stranger? Tending your flock?"

"That's right."

"And now you down here sinning in the big city?"

He smiled. "I came to see you."

"We know that's bullshit," she said. "I got to run. We're backing up at the bar. I'll come see you later."

"Okay girl," he said and turned around to retrieve the drink. Dancer moved off. Her back to him across the stage. He sat back down to watch the show. Get into it before he picked one out for the additional pay experience.

"She's something, right?" He put down his glass. Thought, *Jesus, again?*

A short man standing over him from the Funeral Directors Group. Wandered over to make conversation. His shirt was unbuttoned, and his face sweaty. Hair like he'd gotten out of the shower. Eyes gone all pupil.

"Looks like one of those Zulu women in Africa, you know? Could be chasing down zebras if she weren't on that stage. Holding a spear or something. Christ she's exotic."

Reverend Righteous looked away from the man, then back again. Said, "Spears?"

The man did not appear to be paying attention, but answered.

"Hey, I didn't mean nothing by it man. Just, you know, she's so exotic looking and all of that." Amped up and moving shakily to the music.

Reverend Righteous waved him off.

"Whatever you say man. I'm just here for the show."

"Yeah, me too. My name's Tyler. Tyler Arnold. You gotta name?"

"Yeah."

"What is it?"

"James."

"Hey, nice to meet you James. You mind if I sit down?" Took the seat without waiting.

"Look man," Reverend Righteous said.

"We're down here on a convention. We do it every year. Sometimes more than once. We're all in the funeral business." Pointed at the group behind him. Then got up quick and came back, holding his glass. "This your first time at the Cheetah? I ask that cause you're by yourself and it's kind-of a party scene in here. You know, guys hanging out looking at these exotic girls. Partying, you know? We usually hit a couple clubs. They say the ones in Dallas are better, but fuck that."

"No," Reverend Righteous said. "It's not my first time."

"Okay," Tyler said. "You're not a cop, are you James?" The question hung there, the man looking at Reverend Righteous with that unhinged expression. More than the booze working him. Been putting powder up his nose all night. "You gotta tell me, you know. Least that's what I heard. I ask you if you're a cop and you gotta tell me straight. Otherwise it's entrapment."

"And what would I be trapping, Tyler Arnold?"

"First you gotta say."

"Say what?"

"If you're a cop."

"I'm not a cop." On the stage the Zulu woman was climbing up the pole and sticking one long leg out over the open air, then pulsating her whole body with the guitar riffs, then hopping off in a graceful pounce onto all fours, making her way toward Reverend Righteous and Tyler like a starved cat.

"That's good. See, we been partying, like I said, and maybe more than booze is all and I didn't want to be doing something that might get us in trouble."

Reverend Righteous sat back, keeping an eye on the stalking Zulu woman and reaching for his wallet. Would need to get change for one of the hundreds. He said, "What y'all been doing that might get you into trouble?"

•

It was coke, cut-in with a little speed. Medical grade stuff one of the other funeral directors scored from a doctor in Bowling Green. Brought it down to Atlanta in his overnight bag and now had it out on a table in the back of a private room that they had secured so they could be alone with girls and geeked-up at the same time. Reverend Righteous sat in one of the overstuffed chairs pinching the underside of his nose and blinking in the light. His head like an overheated wall plug. Eyes protruding. Taking in the ass that was not three feet from his face. The Zulu. Back dancing privately for him. Tyler Arnold in the next chair making strange noises and whistling like he was having trouble breathing.

Reverend Righteous said, "Goddamn Son, you got to quit that shit. You fucking up this girl's dance." Tyler looked at the girl and then threw his head back on the red cushion of the chair and howled at the ceiling. Then the other men were howling and Reverend Righteous sat up, moving the girl out of the way and went over to the table, picked up the spoon next to the baggie and stuck a pile of white powder into his wide nostril. A door to the outside corridor opened and one of the bouncers stuck his head in the room. Looked at the scene and motioned for the girls to come out. The four men stopped and watched them leave.

"Y'all got about an hour till you got to go home," the bouncer said. "These girls got to work tomorrow and we got to close this down."

"C'mon man," the director from Kentucky said. Reverend Righteous thought his name was Bradley or some shit like that. "We paid for this party."

"You did. For two hours. Girls stay for the two hours and Reggie said I should give you another hour on the house without the girls since you been such nice customers. But I got to get these women to bed. Understand?"

"We understand," Tyler said, looking at Bradley.

"That's good," the bouncer said, moving out of the way to let the naked woman out into the hall. "I'll be back in an hour. Don't leave nothing illegal in here. Health inspector pops in now and then." He closed the door and one of the men turned the volume down on the speaker knob. Music being pumped in from a control room somewhere else in the building. Tyler went over to the table and snorted some of the powder and went back to his chair. Took the bottle of J&B and poured some into his cocktail glass. Tilted the bottle at Reverend Righteous who had sat back down and he nodded. Tyler poured. The two other men sat down at the table. Worn out and stoned.

"So, James," Tyler said, said, sipping his drink. One leg draped over the other. Hair a mess and skin white as a toilet tank. "You're a preacher."

"Reverend."

"Preacher. Reverend. What's the difference."

"Preacher stands around on the street or goes from place to place in an old wagon with a mule teaching the gospel. I got a church. More sophisticated."

"I see," Tyler said. Words slurring so it came out *sthleee.*

"Uh-huh. That's right. I have a flock, see. I am pointing my people to the Lord and they come willingly. Not forced. I am like a guiding light to a world of paradise in the clouds."

"No shit," said Bradley.

"You know," said Tyler, "We are in the same business, you and me."

"How's that," Reverend Righteous said.

"Well. I collect bodies. Prepare them for the afterlife. Deliver them in a nice new box or urn. And then you take it from there. Once I hand them over. I take care of the physical remains and your job is to take care of the spiritual ones. Right?"

Reverend Righteous said, "Cept you making money on your end. Can't sell something you can't touch."

Tyler nodded. Approving.

"That's true," said Bradley. He picked up his drink from the table and finished it and looked at the fourth man in the room. "Oh shit.

We lost Bobby." The man named Bobby was passed out in his chair. Head slumped. No shirt. Breathing shallow and fast. Thin arms and patches of grey hair on his chest. Stains on his khaki pants.

"He'll be fine," Tyler said. "We have another hour. Let him sleep, Bradley."

Reverend Righteous laughed and reached for the Scotch bottle.

"Something funny?" Bradley said.

"Yeah," Reverend Righteous said. "Y'all got some honkey fucking names. Tyler. Bradley. Bobby. Where's Blake at?"

"Blake?" Bradley said.

"He's mocking you," Tyler said. Then, "But you are right. We do make money. Lots of it." Raised his glass at Bradley and they toasted across the room. "Quite a bit more since we made our arrangement." He smiled and looked at Reverend Righteous. "Where is this church of yours, James?"

"You wouldn't know it," Reverend Righteous said. Thinking about his ride down that morning. Putting some fire into the Sunday sermon. Burn like this Scotch going down, but spreading warmth and love once it was in the stomach. Not itchy like the coke. Smooth like a message aged in a barrel.

"Try me."

"Place called Noble, Georgia. It's outside of Chattanooga."

Tyler sitting up now. Trying to focus his eyes, shot out with black pupils. Glancing over at Bradley who had gone back to the baggie on the table.

"Where did you say?"

"Noble. Georgia."

Now Tyler was standing over him, holding his drink, but attentive. Bradley at the table, spoon paused just below his nose. Bobby still sleeping.

"Are you fucking with me, James?"

"Why you standing over me like that, man?"

"Noble, Georgia? Are you fucking with us, James?"

"Man, I don't know what's wrong with you white boy, but you better back away from me. I'm about to get unholy."

Tyler backed away. Took in a deep breath.

"You told me you weren't a cop. You been shoving powder up your nose all night just like the rest of us. Then you tell me this about where your church is. Tell me you are from Noble. Tell me all of this and then—and then you act cool about it. Like we don't know about Noble. Like we aren't sending our bodies down there for cremation. Talking about making money. Talking about us making money and you saving souls and letting on that you're just a preacher down here at the strip club getting his rocks off like the rest of us. James?" His voice high now. Whiney and a rasp in his breath.

"I'm a Reverend, Tyler. I told you."

"Reverend my Alabama ass," Tyler said.

"Reverend my ass," Bradley said. Now Reverend Righteous stood up. Coke and speed working his heart. Skin going clammy and then hot. Balance like a table with one short leg. Bradley standing up. All of them unsteady and swaying like something in a fun house.

Reverend Righteous said, "Man, what you carrying on about? You asked where I was tending my flock and I told you and now you act like Noble's something special." Paused, then thought out loud, "What you mean sending bodies down to Noble. Where to? Tri-State?"

Tyler sat back in the chair and stared. The walls covered in what looked like soft yellow fur to deaden the sound. All the colors in the room mismatched and chaotic. Mirrors on the ceiling and the light playing around in the glass. He looked at Bradley and then picked up the J&B and poured. Collected himself and turned in his chair.

"I'm going to ask you again."

"Ain't no need to ask that cop question again, Tyler. That shit is bordering on insulting."

"Alright," Tyler said. "Alright. You have to understand that you being from there is a mighty big coincidence. We have an arrangement with Tri-State Crematory and let's say for the sake of polite conversation that it's not something that we want to publicize. It's something that we want to be careful about. It's not illegal per se, but at the same time, it's not entirely above board. You follow me?"

"Uh-huh," Reverend Righteous said. "But let me guess, if you don't mind. You found this place in North Georgia. Owned by a black family been around there for a couple generations. And you got together with all your funeral home motherfuckers and sent them all your work so you could get a big break on the pricing, and then you get back the ashes and mark them up by seventy percent. That sound right? I'm guessing you know. But it sounds to me like you defensive about this cause you taking that margin and sticking it to people on your end. Taking advantage of my people in the bargain. How am I doing so far?"

"Remarkably well," Tyler said. "But it's north of seventy percent and we call them cremains. Not ashes, Reverend."

·

They went back to the Scotch and the powder and when they were escorted out of the Cheetah by the bouncer, the man Bobby being held on his feet by Bradley, Reverend Righteous and Tyler put the two other men in a cab and tottered off down the street to a dive bar that was open all night. They sat on stools and Tyler, in a manic state, told the Reverend everything about the body dump at Tri-State. Mentioned nothing about the Mays, sticking instead to the massive profits he was accumulating marking up the remains and passing them along to the bereaved families that were his clients. Grandmothers. A kid here and there. Someone's sister who'd died of leukemia. All of them marks for the scam. Reverend Righteous listened to the story, nodding along, trying to concentrate but failing the longer they sat there. Not being able to snort the powder, the liquor taking its toll until he finally got up and told Tyler he was going back to get his car. He walked to the empty parking lot at the Cheetah alone. Got in the front seat of the Caddie and went to sleep for three hours. Woken up by the same bouncer telling him to go the fuck home.

He stopped for gas before getting back onto 75 and then fought nausea and a headache that felt like a prairie fire in his head all the way back to Noble. He parked the Caddie under the carport and went inside his house and took the hottest shower he could stand. Took six aspirin and put on some pajamas. Then he called Wilson.

"I need you to pick me up something to eat and bring a bottle over here," he said into the phone.

"What's wrong with you?" Wilson said. "You been on one of your mission trips?"

"Please Wilson," he said. His voice raspy.

"Alright then," Wilson said and they hung up. Reverend Righteous went into his living room and sat down on the large couch and thought about the Mays and the sermon that he had to give the next morning. Would need the whiskey to loosen up his thinking. Get the words unstuck. They were pooling up in his mind like a stopped-up drain, floating and drifting around in a dirty basin. He could see Tyler on the stool next to him, going on about the funeral business and how the people meant nothing to him except lines in a financial statement. *The cast-off husks of humans,* he called them. Thought that was clever. Looking at Reverend Righteous for some affirmation. Not getting it and then jumping in again with both feet. Bartender watching them out of the corner of his eye. Everyone in the place a degenerate. Came with the job.

Wilson knocked on the door and when he opened it, the custodian stepped back, holding a sack from a BBQ place out on the highway and a brown bag that had the bottle in it.

"Goddamn," Wilson said, looking him over. "You all kinds of fucked-up this time, ain't you."

He stepped away from the door and Wilson followed him into

the kitchen. Put the parcels on the island and went over to the cabinets. Took out two glasses. Came back and opened the bottle of Jim Beam and poured out two slugs. Handed the glass over to his boss.

"You look like you been fucking around with a sleepy tiger. Hey, but like they say, the Lord works in mysterious ways. Only, nothing mysterious about this here, right? This here is the devil smiling at you. Only he ain't smiling now. Shit."

"Wilson." Then back to the couch, the custodian coming in and standing in the living room.

"You want to watch the football game or something?"

"I have to work on my sermon for the morning." Wilson shifted from one foot to the other.

Then he said, "You mind if I stick around and watch it? The place where I'm staying ain't got a TV set. I'll just catch the game and get you drinks and that kind of servant shit. You work on channeling God's voice and preaching about the right way to live. That be alright with you?" Reverend Righteous did not answer. Sipped from the glass and then started to the back of the house where he had a desk. Pajamas hanging off him. Shoulders slumped and shuffling in bare feet.

"Hey." Wilson calling him from another room. "Where you keep your remote control, tiger man?"

24.

CLARENCE SAID, "LET ME CALL YOU BACK GIRL. SOUNDS like Tyler just come in the front door. He'll be talking a lot. Hungover as a Thanksgiving Uncle. Asking how things went while he was gone to Atlanta playing dress-up." He hung up the phone and listened for his boss coming down the hall toward the office. Clarence coming from behind the desk where he'd been on the phone. Talking to his girl in Georgia hill country. Thinking about how things might be moving from sex to serious. Not sure how he felt about that.

"Clarence? Where are you?"

He did not answer. Waited for the short man to step into the door of the office. See who he was talking to first. The fastidious little shit or the playboy, home from the big city with scorched sinuses and a bumpy heart.

"There you are," he said, leaning against the jamb of the door.

Clarence waited. Man wearing an undershirt he'd sweat through. Suit pants and loafers with no socks. A Goodwill outfit.

"Well?" Tyler said.

"Well what?"

"How are things?"

"Things here are just fine, Mr. Arnold." Waited on him to say something else. Tyler not looking at him. Staring at something on the far wall.

Then said from far off, "Aren't you going to ask how the convention in Atlanta went?" Clarence paused. Trying to play it straight. Wondering how long he wanted the conversation to last. Gave in.

"How was your trip?"

"Oh, you know," Tyler said. "About like you would expect. Worked some. Played some." Then he giggled like he did when he was coming back from his drug fog. Probably been back into whatever he'd been taking while he was gone. Keeping himself up for the ride home. The speed or maybe some pill that the quack from Kentucky gave him. Clarence signing for nondescript brown packages coming from Bowling Green now and then. Tyler coming out of his office in the late afternoon like he was filled with helium. Brown paper from the package on the floor like the man had torn into it looking for an antidote.

"Gene was not there. Shame." Tyler had come into the office now. Sat down in one of the old wing back chairs his grandaddy had bought. Slumped down. Bones out of sorts and fatigue setting in.

"Well," Clarence said.

"Well." Tyler yawned and waved a hand at the room. "Gene does not like to be seen in the places where we go." Then said, "No matter," and giggled again. Recollecting. "He's a cold fish, Gene. Never one to trust people. Never one to—let go. Laisser partir as our French friends say."

"You speak French?" Clarence said.

"No," Tyler said. "But I'm..."

"Uh-huh."

"So Gene was absent. But the rest of us were not. We were very much present." He started to nod off. Then, "Oh, but I met the most delightful colored man while we were there. He was with us in the Cheetah and then later he and I had a wonderful conversation at some hell-hole of a bar down the street. One of those places that's open all night."

"Colored man," Clarence said. "You mean like an Uncle Tom?"

"God, Clarence. So gauche."

More French, Mr. Arnold in a real state performing for him now. Scratching at an armpit. Even smelled his hand after. Looked like he was good for the embalming table.

"What did you and this negro man talk about? Y'all discuss reparations and injustice? The plight of my people in the land of cotton?" Arnold was falling asleep again and Clarence started to leave.

Speaking with his eyes closed, Tyler said, "It was just remarkable, Clarence. We, well, this man. A Reverend to be specific. Was from this town outside of Chattanooga. Charming and had quite the appetite for the woman and the powder, you see. He was not a preacher, but a reverend. He was quite clear on that. Had a church in Noble."

Clarence startled, then listening. Went over to the bar on the hutch and poured two fingers in one of the crystal glasses and brought it back over to Tyler. The man pasted to the chair. Clarence not sure he was hearing this correctly. Wondering if Tyler had been listening in on his calls. Tracking him when he went down there to see his Georgia Girl. He handed the drink to Tyler who took it without looking up at him. Smiled and sipped at it. Smiled and snuggled into the chair.

"Was it Wilde that said irony was wasted on the stupid?"

"Yes," Clarence said. Wanting the man to move on. "You said Noble?"

"No, Wilde," Tyler said.

"The reverend," Clarence said. "Was he from Noble, Georgia?"

"How did you know?" Tyler said, seeming to perk up a little, then settling back.

Clarence went to the hutch. All of this feeling wrong. Too much at once.

"He was a reverend from Noble, Georgia. That is correct. Reverend Righteous if you can believe it. Reverend Righteous with a penchant for whores and cocaine. And so much fun. I have to say."

Clarence thinking now that maybe it was coincidence all along.

"But," Tyler said. "Do you know what else is in Noble, Georgia?"

Clarence said, "Yeah. I carried a body down there a while back."

"That's right," Tyler said, semi-lucid, looking from behind the wing of the chair at Clarence standing in the middle of the room. "That's right, you have. But just the once, correct?"

"Yeah," Clarence said.

"To Tri-Sate, right?"

"You know that's right. What are you trying to say?"

Tyler sipped the drink and adjusted himself in the chair. Dark read leather. Cracked and making noise when he shifted his bony frame.

"Well, Clarence. I'm saying that while you may have only been once, I have been shipping bodies down there as fast as they come into the coroner's office. As fast as they come in and for a profit you would not believe. Those ignorant sharecroppers at Tri-State Crematory in Noble, Georgia, home of Reverend Righteous, and God knows what else, are making me and the rest of the funeral directors in Dixie rich. One corpse at a time."

"Bullshit," Clarence said. Flat and even. "I drive the fucking hearse around here. I ain't driving back and forth to Noble no five times a week."

Tyler Arnold sat up abruptly and smiled at his hearse driver. Looked sideways at the man. "Not the ones we burn Clarence. Just those in the box. You just drive the ones who go into a box they buy off the showroom floor. Death is a good, good business, Clarence. You should know that by now. And when you smell a mark as green and ignorant as Rollie May's family in that seedy, kudzu choked landscape they call North Georgia. Well, you pounce."

"The fuck you say," Clarence said.

"The fuck I say, Clarence. I even confessed it all to a reverend. If you can believe that." Clarence believed it but could not figure how it was happening without him knowing. Had been doing a lot around the Holy Family facility lately. Had even been thinking about cleaning up the parking lot islands. Doing some driving, but not down to Noble. Just around town with coffins riding around in the back. That part making sense. Thinking again now, watching

Tyler drift off. Wondering if he cared or what it all meant. The man too proud of himself. Considering why he was cut out of it.

"They pick up the bodies and we up-charge the families, see, Clarence? We make the profit and they do the work. And it all comes back in a neat little box. They hand over a check and we hand over the mortal remains. Or the cremains as they are called in the parlance of their profession."

Clarence said, "I don't see any boxes coming back here like that."

"No," Tyler said. "I don't have them shipped back here."

"Where you shipping them to, then?"

"Oh, that should not concern you. Let's just say I'd rather not leave a trail leading back to Holy Family's door. It's more of a delivery service. Something like the underground railroad, you might say. Very hush-hush."

"Who you dealing with down there?"

"Down where," Tyler said.

"Noble. Who you working with down there?"

"What's his name," Tyler said.

"Who," Clarence said.

"Young colored man, now. His Daddy is ill. Big boy, the son. Looks like he might have played some football. He was the one we worked the deal with. The Daddy, I mean." The hand holding his glass started to droop. Some bourbon left. Then he said, "Levi. His name is Levi May."

Clarence let the glass fall on the rug beneath the chair. Finished his own drink and went out of the office thinking about calling Caroline back. Find out what the fuck was going on with all this cremains business.

25.

THEY CAME OUT OF TOWN AND TOOK BACK ROADS OVER
to the scatter of houses and a few cheap commercial buildings that made up Noble. Everything spread out and run down. Aside from what had been built, everything else was desolate woods and red clay. Big patchy shadows the further you looked into the trees—cooler back there when it was hot out. Lots of bugs and ticks. He wondered what kept him. The mountain always somewhere over your shoulder. Hi turned off onto a road barely wide enough for two cars to pass and then they were going past the black church and coming up on the Mays' driveway. The white cruiser's engine loud in the quiet. Ellis singing to himself. Not entirely sure what they were up to. Hi okay with that. He pulled into the drive and put the car in park.

"What are we doing here, Sheriff?" Hi looked up at the dilapidated house and checked it against the new-looking hearse parked alongside.

"Not exactly sure," he said and then they both got out and came around the front, standing side by side. Beyond the hearse, Hi could see an oversize black van parked in front of the hearse. Surveyed the yard, thinking about the propane salesman, Shanks, being there before him. Seeing something that got him rattled enough to call an aunt with the GBI. Thinking about Rollie somewhere in the darkness of the house. It was a Wednesday morning. Just then ten when he looked at his watch. Shawna and Robbie's friend Matt at school. He walked around the side of the house and saw an ancient VW parked back there. Would have been Caroline's he guessed. No sign of the pick-up that Rollie drove. Ellis behind him, waiting on instructions. He came around to the porch and climbed the steps and then knocked on the screen door and called inside. Announcing himself. More like the friend he was than the Sheriff. No authority in his voice. Waited on a response and then he heard the truck's engine and saw it turn into the drive. Braking hard to avoid running into the back of the cruiser. Ellis jumped and spun around and then the screen door was opening and Caroline was behind him. All of them stacking up in front of the house.

"Ellis," Hi said and the deputy looked up at him where he stood on the porch above him. Hi threw him the keys. "Let Levi in. We've got him blocked." Hi turned back around to speak to Caroline. Took off his hat.

Said, "Hey there, Caroline. How are you?"

She looked confused, peeking around his shoulder to watch Ellis pull the cruiser up into the drive and then moving it to the side to let her brother pull forward.

"I'm fine Mr. Lewis. How are you?"

"I'm good," he said.

"How come y'all's out here?"

Hi smiled at her. Beautiful girl. Helping out her mother and father. Could be on the cover of one of those magazines Sherry liked to read.

"You want to come in and see Daddy," she said.

"Sure do," he said, then heard the door of the truck open and Ellis saying something to Levi. The man wearing a white t-shirt, jeans and some heavy boots. "But before I do, I need to talk with you and your brother about something. Shawna is not home is she?"

"No Sir," she said. "She's at the school admin building this morning."

"I thought she might be," he said. "C'mon down here with me a minute."

"Okay," she said and followed him off the porch to where Levi and Ellis were talking in the yard.

Hi thinking about the best way to ask them his questions. Deciding to play it straight and to the point. Leave out the call with the GBI, but ask about the gas man. They stood together in a circle. Ellis not talking now and the May kids watching Hi. Alert and nervous. Hi saw it in the way they carried themselves. Eyes moving around. Hands in pockets. The shuffle of anxious children.

He said, "I'm sorry to barge in on you like this. I would have called first but we were out and I thought I'd just drop by. Everything going okay out here? The business doing okay? I know it's a lot to handle."

"We doing okay," Levi said. "You come to see Daddy, Sheriff Lewis?"

"Well, I would like to see your father before I go, but that's not why I came."

"Oh," said Levi. "How come you came then?"

Ellis looking at him too. Wondering the same thing.

"Well," Hi said adjusting his hat. Trying to be casual. "I got a call about how some things are being handled out here."

"Call about what?" Caroline said.

"Call was about some bodies being left out in the open." They were quiet. Hi said, "You guys get regular delivery of propane for the facilities out here?"

"Yes sir," Levi said. "For the retort over there." He pointed over his shoulder at the cinder block building. "We use the gas for the cremations, you know."

"The *retort*?" Ellis said.

"It's what they call a building that disposes of bodies," Caroline said. "We use the propane to burn them, like Levi said. We got behind on the bill a while back, but I got that paid up. That what this is about?"

"No," Hi said and then paused. Intentionally, letting them talk more if they were going to. Maybe answer his next question without having to ask it. Then said, "No, not about a bill. It was about the disposal of the bodies themselves. The propane delivery man made a call about something he saw on more than one occasion that he thought was strange."

"Strange how?" Levi said. "Cause you know, this place can creep some folks out, us doing what we do. Daddy had to run kids off the property every now and then cause they wanted to see dead people." He laughed and looked at Ellis. "That kind of thing. That it?"

Hi looked at Rollie's son a long moment and then over at the daughter. Trying to see who was doing most of the thinking now that they were in charge. Could tell that Caroline was listening instead of talking. Wanted them to come out and say something that she could respond to.

"Dead people out in the woods could make anybody a bit jumpy," Ellis said, looking up at the buildings. Still not sure what they were doing in the Mays' yard.

"Sure," Hi said. "But the reason this man was calling was because on more than one delivery he said he saw bodies laying around the place like maybe they were not being taken care of properly. Like they had been left outside instead of processed like they were supposed to."

"He said that? Alan said that?" Caroline said.

"Alan?" Hi said.

"Alan," Caroline said. "He's the one who usually brings the deliveries out here. Funny white man. Kinda shy. That who called you?"

"I'm not really in a position to tell you about the details, but let's just say that he was pretty convinced that something was not right. Anything that I just told you sound true?"

Levi said, "No sir. Not sure what he's talking about. I go and get most of the bodies these days. Used to be—the way Daddy ran it—people bringing the bodies to us and sometimes they still do that, but now we go and collect them and bring them back, so we seeing the bodies from the time they go in the hearse or in the van that I rent sometimes to collect more than one, and then I bring them back here. Not sure what he means cause we get them turned around in a couple days—depending on how busy we are—and then we run the cremains back to where they came from."

"I see," Hi said, looking at Levi.

"There's something else," Caroline said.

Hi and Ellis looked at her. Casual cop demeanor.

"What would that be?" Hi said.

"He drinks. If it's that man Alan who made the call, he drinks. I smell it on him when he's here."

"He drinks?" Ellis said, thinking out loud. Hi gave him a look.

"Maybe so," Hi said, "but I doubt he's hallucinating while he's on the job. What can you tell me about what he said that he saw," then rethinking, "better still, is there any truth in what I'm asking you?"

The Mays were quiet. Hi waited, then said, "You mind if Deputy Carver and I take a quick look around? It's just a formality to say that I checked up on things and that I found nothing wrong and that maybe this call was unnecessary. Maybe it was a misunderstanding and we can close the door on this. That be okay?"

Levi said, "Where are you wanting to go?"

"Just take a look around, Levi. No place special. That be okay with you?"

"Sheriff," Caroline said. Using his title now and not his name like she had when he had come to the door. Her thinking he was there to check in on Rollie. She said, "We're having some trouble, see. With keeping up with all of these funeral homes. They sending us a lot of bodies. Daddy is sick and can't help us all that much and Momma is working a lot. And we've been getting behind some."

"I understand," Hi said. "I can understand that."

"Right," Caroline said. "And, well, a few times when we get behind we back up on the orders and we have to—we have to kinda stack them up while we're waiting on the ones ahead of them in line to get done, you know. Levi is working as hard and as fast as he can, but you know, he's doing most of this himself and I guess what I'm saying is that this man who called you, Alan, I saw him the other day when he was here with a delivery and taking the empty ones back with him and I could tell that he thought that something was wrong cause he kept looking up there and I knew that we had some bodies waiting to be burned and I had told Levi that we needed to keep them in one of the barns so that they would not be out in the open like that, but he was busy with something else and he forgot. We forgot. I forgot too, and that's what he saw I'm thinking and I'm embarrassed about that cause I know that Daddy would never have wanted that to happen, but it did and now I'm telling you cause you're the Sheriff but you also know our family and..."

Hi stopped her. "Okay," he said. "It's okay Caroline. That makes sense and we can leave it there for now." The girl was starting to cry and Hi put an arm around her. "What happened with your Daddy is hard and what he left you kids I imagine is a tough business, even though you've been around it all of your life. Let me make a suggestion." He left his arm around Caroline and addressed Levi. "Make sure that you keep any bodies that have not been burned out of sight so this does not come up again. Maybe get some kind of cooler or something that you can use for storage. I don't know a damn thing about this business but keeping them cold is how they handle it in the coroner's office so it should work for you. If you can't afford it, save up for one and then you will have someplace to handle the overflow."

Ellis was looking at him like he was dreaming. The absurdity of the conversation written all over his face.

"I'll handle the gas company and will explain that I have been up here and that whatever they think they saw was simply part of the process that they are not necessarily meant to see. You focus on the work. Does all of that make sense?" Hi thinking that none of this would fly with Traian Thomas. He would have to put him off some other way. Not sure of that now, but Caroline crying had softened his investigative impulse. Thomas would already be moving around the buildings. Playing things by the book. Not knowing about Rollie and their kids being friends and all of those things that mattered to Hi and would not hold much water with a stranger working in the Atlanta bureau of the GBI.

"Yes Sir," she said. Levi nodding, taking the advice seriously.

"Are there any bodies up there now?"

"No Sir," Levi said. "We caught up."

"Okay, good," Hi said. He squeezed Caroline's shoulder and she moved away from him. He shook Levi's hand and told Ellis he was going into the house to say hello to Rollie. Told him he would be right back.

Caroline said, "Let me get y'all some coffee or some tea. Y'all want something to drink?" She went up the slope to the house, Hi following her, Levi walking back to his vehicle. Ellis leaned against the side of the cruiser and waited for the coffee Caroline said that she would bring out. Levi pulled his truck forward and Ellis could see stacked bags of something in the bed and what looked like ten to fifteen cinder blocks, the truck groaning on its springs and crawling up the side of the house and then out of sight. He felt the warm sun on his face and thought, *Jesus on a crutch, this is a fucked up little place*. Levi came down the slope with a flat head shovel and gave Ellis a small wave and then went into the building they had called the retort and closed the door behind him. Ellis hitched up his pants and pulled at his boxer shorts bunching in his crotch, trying to think of something more pleasant than dead people stacked and waiting to be burned-up.

•

They were back in the cruiser and accelerating onto the small two-lane road, not talking with the windows down, tires humming. Hi driving with his hat on the seat, Ellis looking out the window, watching the pines filing by, deep ditches lining the sides of the road, sprouting weeds with puddled, stagnant water in their bottoms, full of bugs, frogs and snakes.

Ellis said, "Sheriff, I don't guess I was expecting that."

"Expecting what?"

Ellis looked across the seat, Hi staring ahead, one hand lazy on the wheel and the other in his lap. Ellis picked at something underneath his fingernail.

"You're wondering why I did not fill you in on what we were going over there to discuss?"

"That," the deputy said.

"I've known Rollie May since we were kids," Hi said. "He's a good man and his family has been a part of this community for a long time. Go back generations in Noble. I guess I wanted to give them the benefit of the doubt. Those kids got thrown into the deep end of the pool when it comes to running a business like that and I guess I felt a little guilty not checking in on them and just thought that— hell, Ellis, I don't know what I thought. That call I said I got from the gas company was not really from the gas company. Well, it was in a round-about way, I suppose. It started with them like I told the Mays, but it came to me through the GBI. This Alan Shanks fella has an aunt or something like that working in the Atlanta bureau and he called it in to her and an agent called me checking up on it as a favor to the aunt. You know as much as I know at this point."

"And you believe them?"

"Who?" Hi said. "The feds in Atlanta?"

"No. Levi and Caroline. About getting behind and all that." He paused, then said, "They did not want us looking around up there by those buildings. Least it seemed like they did not want us looking around. I mean..."

"I know what you mean," Hi said, slowing down to break at a four-way-stop. Nobody at the intersection. "When I was inside the house, their old man, Rollie, was sitting in a wheelchair in the living room and probably could not tell you what year we were living in.

Didn't even recognize me. Or if he did, could not put the words together to say anything. Smelled like he needed his diaper changed. Breaks your heart. It really does. They say that they're doing the best that they can and I'm inclined to believe it for now."

"What about the GBI?"

"What about the GBI?" Hi said.

"Well, you think they are going to be inclined to believe them?"

Hi turned right and exhaled. Looked over at the deputy and gave him a meek smile.

"I don't know, Ellis," he said. "I guess we'll find out soon enough."

"I guess," Ellis said. "Hope they ain't hiding something is all." Then he said, "Are you gonna tell them that we were over to their place—I mean, are you supposed to be reporting back?"

Hi did not answer the question, although he'd been thinking about how to handle it since they left the May's driveway. It needed some closure, but he was not sure of the best way to deliver that. He knew he was being territorial, but was justifying it in his mind at the same time. This was his jurisdiction and these were his people he'd taken an oath to protect. Did that or did that not apply to keeping the GBI at a distance. He had not figured that far.

"Whatever they've done, they know we're aware, so hopefully this is the end of it." Then he said, "Speaking of hiding something," and then stopped. Tried to keep his expression even.

"Aww shit, Sheriff," Ellis said. "Tanya tell you about the fender?"

Hi laughed and reached over and patted his deputy on the shoulder.

"I can keep a secret if you can," he said, watching the road.

26.

TRAIAN SAT IN THE LARGE GBI CONFERENCE ROOM, HIS feet on the long, cheap table, looking out at the gray sky that hung over Atlanta. Dressed in jeans, a t-shirt and worn Red Wing boots. A Braves cap on his head. Waiting on the directors, Randy Gillis and Eunice Shanks to join him. His day off, thinking about taking a trip up to Chattanooga that afternoon with Kim. Do some hiking and eat some soul food on the south side of the city. Maybe *See Rock City*. Hook up with Gillis on Monday and nose around Noble and see what they could find out. Thinking about his conversation with the Walker County Sheriff, Hi never calling him back to tell him everything was okay with the May family and their supposed misconduct. Something about their conversation had stuck with him. Nothing that the Sheriff had said, specifically, but the defensive tone. Beyond one cop interfering with another one. Something about the tone had been—*personal.* It was that and he needed a case. Even one that might start small and atypical for the bureau. He felt a lack of productivity and it was making him anxious. Kim had called him out on it. Traian drinking orange juice in their kitchen a couple mornings before. Kim asking him what was wrong and when he could not put a finger on it, she had broken it down and clarified it for him. Had said, "You're bored and when you're bored, everyone has to suffer." She had smiled but she meant it and he had gone to work and asked for the meeting, not giving a lot of detail.

He heard the swish of the heavy glass door behind him and he took his feet off the table and turned to see all of them coming into the room at the same time. Haskins looking at his attire and then taking a chair at the head, the others taking seats across from him, holding legal pads and pens. Traian feeling like a suspect about to go through a rough patch of questioning.

"You been working in the yard, Agent Thomas?" Haskins said. leaning back in the chair. Traian looked himself over.

"What makes you say that, Sir?"

"What's this about?" Carlisle talking now. Looking over at Eunice Shanks who had been in the conference room only a handful of times to set up a coffee maker and dry off bottles of water from the break room fridge. Maybe leave a basket of fruit or a tray of pastries.

Traian said, "We fielded a call. Wait, Eunice fielded a call from a relative."

"We know about that," Carlisle said, still looking at Eunice and then back to Traian. "I asked her to brief me before we came in and I have briefed the Director. I don't know what Agent Gillis knows, but you can proceed as if we are all up to speed."

"Alright," Traian said.

"Where or what is a Noble, Georgia," Haskins said, checking a note on his pad, "and why would we even care at this particu-lar moment?"

"Well, Sir."

"Hold on," Haskins told Traian. "Eunice, do you know any-thing more about this than you've already told Agent Thomas and Director Carlisle?"

"No Sir," she said.

"Anything we need to know," he looked at the pad. "About Alan?"

"How do you mean?" Eunice said.

"Well, I mean do you know him to be a reputable person. Is he a drug addict? Does he make up stories when you are all together at Thanksgiving? Does he have an unnatural fascination with the dead?"

Eunice looked at her lap. "None of those things, Sir."

"Well then, you are free to go back to your desk while we interro-gate Agent Thomas here to find out why he has called a meeting to discuss a Crematory in a town that no one knows a whole lot about. That be okay with you?" Eunice stood and went toward the glass door. Then stopped before she exited and looked back at the room.

"Alan is not a liar, if that's what you mean. If he saw something like he said that he did, then he saw it. That's about all I have to add."

"Thank you for that," Haskins said, looking at Traian.

"That was a bit harsh, don't you think?" Carlisle said when Eunice was out of the room.

"Perhaps," he said. "Now, Agent Thomas. Your turn."

He leaned into the table and told them what he thought. Walking them through the conversation with Hi Lewis and the apprehension that he had detected in his voice. His lack of follow-up after he had told him that he would get back in touch. Said, "I can't be certain, and there is nothing but a third party witness to go on, but I've got a gut feeling that maybe there is more to this. I don't know what that might be, but if they are not taking care of bodies down there the way that they are supposed to, then it's a crime that would likely be a state level infraction and not a county matter. And even if it was a county matter, I don't think that we are getting the full story from the sheriff in Walker County. And I can't make sense of why anyone operating a Crematory would be doing anything other than their job unless there's a motivation not to. And a motivation not to leads to money, which leads to fraud, which leads to other parties that may be involved and all I want to do is go up there and see for myself. I need Agent Gillis to help with the investigation and if we find out that there is nothing there, then we come home and I go to work on another case. Simple as that."

"Simple as that?" Haskins said.

"Simple as that," Traian said.

"How big of an operation do they have?" Carlisle said

"It's my understanding that they service at least three states for cremation services."

"That would be federal," she said. "If money is involved like you said, then you might be looking at federal violations and that would justify our involvement."

"Possibly," Traian said.

"But we have nothing to go on except what this Alan Shanks told us?" Haskins said.

"That's correct," Traian said. "But, I don't see how we can ignore it when I'm not getting anything back from the locals."

"Have you tried this Sheriff Lewis back again?"

"Yes Sir."

"And?"

"And he seems to be a lot of places except his office. I can't get a call back and I can't get anything out of his department."

"That's odd," Gillis said.

Traian nodded at him. "I think so."

Haskins said, "Gillis, you got time to do this?"

"Yes Sir."

"Okay, Agent Thomas. Go scratch your itch. But do it quickly. I can't spare two agents out of the office wandering around the woods of North Georgia chasing hunches and speculative witnesses. Cooperate with law enforcement in Walker County, but you can run over them if you have to. Report everything back to Director Carlisle and she can keep me updated."

"Yes Sir," Traian said.

"And one more thing."

"Yes Sir?"

"You need to wear something with a collar on it when you come into this office. You think that you can handle that?"

Traian stood, thought *Jesus Christ*. Then said, "I think so."

Gillis caught him in the hall on the way to the elevator.

"What time you leaving?" he said, Traian punching the down arrow on the silver panel.

"I'm taking Kim for the weekend and she's gonna take the car back here. I'll just ride back with you on Monday. That's okay?"

"Sure," Gillis said. "You really think there's something to look into?"

"I don't know. I told you everything I was thinking back there with Haskins."

"Christ," Gillis said. "Could be anything, you know. Bunch of crackers down there fucking around in the woods. Kinda spooks me thinking about it."

"How much you know about it?"

"Not much," Gillis said.

Traian glanced at his watch and the elevator arrived. He stepped into the open door and held it from closing. Looked at Gillis. "Why don't you come up on Sunday and bring your wife. We'll go out to lunch and then we can send the girls home late afternoon and I'll fill you in on what I'm thinking we need to do. Get an early start on Monday. I got a nice place downtown. Supposed to be haunted. Hit the road early and shake some people up before they get their second cup of coffee. Sound good to you?" Gillis nodded and Traian stepped into the elevator. The doors closing, Gillis stepped in to stop them.

"Haunted. How do you mean haunted," he said. "My wife ain't gonna like that."

"Then you can protect her, Agent Gillis. I'll cover you if we run into anything supernatural."

"When's Kim coming?"

"She's riding up with me on Saturday. She wants to get out of Atlanta. You can bring Ellie up then as well, if you want. But either way we can send the girls back in my car and you can bring your state-issued. Let Georgia pay for the gas."

27.

KIM THOMAS STOOD ON THE CORNER OF MLK AND Chestnut waiting for the valet to bring the car. Traian and Randy Gillis bringing the bags out the side entrance. Gillis' wife Ellie with them. All of them except Kim a little drunk from a long lunch and hitting a few bars before heading back to the hotel. Girls asking about the case in Noble. Traian telling them some of the details and all of them talking about funerals that they had been to with open caskets and how they agreed cremation was better. Talking about where they would like to be scattered when the time came. Dampening the mood slightly and then asking for the last check before walking back to the hotel, no longer as a group, but coupled and walking slowly. Talking privately.

"You want to go back inside and get a couple of coffee," Traian said. Kim looking through her purse for some singles to give the valet. "Ellie gonna drive you crazy on the ride home?"

"She's sweet," Kim said. "She'll be asleep before we pass Dalton."

"And you, you wide awake?"

"Yes, Officer."

"Not tired out from last night?"

"Oh," she said. "The three Bloody Mary's have elevated your sense of sexual prowess I see. How will I make it alone in our big empty bed?"

He kissed her and then pulled her to him and held her there. The car pulling up to the curb and Randy taking the two small travel bags around to the side and putting them in the back seat. Ellie talking to herself on the sidewalk, looking for a stick of gum.

Gillis walked Ellie to the car and helped her into the passenger seat. Gave Kim a look over the top of the car as she watched him close the door on his wife, then walk back toward the hotel entrance. Traian stood in the street.

"Don't go to the bar, you two."

"How do you mean?" Traian said, watching Gillis walk into the hotel, the automated doors closing behind him.

"I don't know," she said. "There's just something about all of this that does not feel right."

"I get it," Traian said.

"Just be careful."

"I will," he said. "I'm always careful."

She started to duck into the driver's seat, then stood back up. "This time, it feels like another kind of agenda. Maybe a perspective that you have not considered."

"Are you sure that you are okay to drive?" he said.

"It has nothing to do with that. It's just. I don't know. Somehow different."

"How do you mean?" he said.

Kim said, "If I knew what I meant, I would say it," then went into the car and put the window down before pulling off. "I know that you have dealt with a lot, Traian. This just feels like a new—a different kind of thing. Everything about it feels unsettling. Tell me I'm being paranoid."

"You're being paranoid," he said and let her pull into the street and watched until she made the turn that would take her out of town.

•

Monday morning. Traian sat by himself in the restaurant in the bottom of the hotel. Big bay windows open to the street. Morning traffic coming in heavy. Backing up at the lights with a thin rain starting to fall. Red brakes and horns all over the place. People forcing their way into the cross walk. He picked up his water glass and opened a headache powder and poured it in, then drank it down trying not to taste the bitter aspirin. He had met Agent Gillis in the bar after the girls had left, ordered a few beers and then ate sitting on the stools, talking through the case and then other things until late, the place almost empty. Gillis asking about the woman who had been killed in 311, the bartender going through the story, bored and ready to go home.

The bartender said, "Word is that she was a prostitute and that the maids found her in the bathtub with her head almost cut off. Her lover supposedly did it. Caught her running around on him. That sort of thing. This was a ways back."

"They catch him?" Gillis said.

"I don't know," the bartender said. "Most people just want to know what happens in the room when the lights go out."

"What happens?" Traian said.

"Beats me, fellas. You want anything else? I got to close-up."

Now he saw Gillis standing next to a bank of phones in the lobby. Traian took a breath and looked at the newspaper they had left outside his door and started to read a column by some local reporter named Chambliss. Something about local crime hurting tourism and the need to revitalize the downtown area. Picture of the guy next to his by-line, smiling. He pushed it aside when Gillis sat down.

"You visited by any headless women?" Gillis asked, putting his napkin in his lap, scooting the chair under the table.

"If I was, she was kind enough to let me sleep."

Gillis said, "It's a nice old hotel. Old, but nice. Sits right down here in the middle of everything. Got all this dark wood paneling and classy decor—just feels historic, like it's always been here. Big mirrors all over the place. I keep passing myself in the hall. Rest of downtown looks like someone went out for cigarettes and never came back. But this place has managed to hang on. Good for them."

They ordered more coffee and breakfast, and Traian sat back in his chair. Headache starting to fade.

"So what are we doing here, really?" Gillis said.

"I was thinking about that," Traian said. Put down his cup in the saucer and leaned into the table. "See, I went over all of this with Haskins and it's just one of those things that I feel like needs a closer look. This Shanks guy, I ran him down to a trailer just outside of LaFayette and we have to start there, and then we'll follow what he gives us and then we'll either go to the next spot where it makes sense to dig around, or we'll drop in on Sheriff Lewis and find out why he has not seen it necessary to call back and fill us in on what he found out at the May place. I want to be out front on this and say with confidence that there's absolutely nothing to investigate here. But it's kinda like this headless woman in 311. Chances are that's all made up bullshit to add some character to the place, you know? But sometimes it's more fun to follow the story than the facts. You with me?"

"Sure. But that's not gonna hold up in any courtroom or with a prosecutor's office. But hey, I like a good scare now and then."

Traian said, "You have to find out the facts. But maybe—shit, I don't know. I'm not sure what I mean. Just that I want to chase this one to ground. Feels like something that needs to be done. Maybe I'm just bored with everything right now. I keep going back to the thing in Tampa and this is the same kind of feeling, right? Call it intuition."

"Whatever you say," Gillis said, and the waiter brought their food, the commuter traffic starting to thin out, the rain picking up. Traian forcing down a plate of eggs and a couple English muffins. Gillis pushing his plate away after a couple bites. Balling up his napkin and tossing it on the table.

"And if it's nothing?"

"Then we go home," Traian said.

They were in Gillis' car. Took Broad Street to Tennessee Avenue over to 17 and then out 193, stopping in some place called Flinstone for directions, guy behind the counter at the Phillips telling them that Noble was hard to define, but knew where Edith's trailer park was. Said he had some friends living in there.

Gillis said, "You know Alan Shanks?"

Clerk said, "Who?"

•

They got lost once more and finally found the entrance to Edith's. Some sad landscape at the foot of a cinder block entrance, white paint peeling off the block, *Edith's* in loopy cursive at an angle. *No Credit* in smaller letters, partially hidden by weeds. They pulled the Mercury into the rutted drive and Traian read the numbers as they went by the different trailers. They stopped at twelve and sat looking at Shank's home. A woman walking a dog came up the row and stopped next to the car. Gillis put his window down.

"Who you here to arrest?" she said.

"Pardon me?" Gillis said. Looked over at Traian who was smiling.

"I think she might have made us for cops," he said.

"It's the car," she said, the dog whining up at her. "Might as well have Miranda on the license plate. You after Alan?"

Traian said, "That's clever. Miranda."

Gillis said, "Should we be after Alan?"

The woman snorted and went around the back of the car and down the row toward the front, the dog lagging behind her, then turned up toward the front office building and went in the side, the aluminum door making a loud slap on the tricky hinge.

"I think that might have been Edith," Traian said, still smiling.

Alan opened the door of his trailer holding a mug of something. He looked at the two agents in the idling car, gave them a wave and went back into the dark.

The first thing Alan said to the agents was, "I wish I had never made that goddamned phone call. I should have left well enough alone. Now I got feds in my living area. As if I needed more head-aches around here, you know?"

"Alan," Traian said.

"Yea."

"You smell like you might have been drinking."

"It's probably the septic tank you're smelling. There's always a problem with the septic tanks. Edith's too cheap to have them cleaned out."

"I don't think so," Traian said.

"So, what? I'm not allowed to drink in my trailer? Why, cause it's morning?"

Gillis laughed. Said, "We're not here to pass judgment on you Alan. We're not those kind of guys. But we are here to get a state-ment from you. About the call that you made to your aunt and if you've been drinking then that might compromise the statement. That make sense? After we're gone, you can brush your teeth with it if you like."

"I guess," Alan said. "But like I said on the phone, I've already told you everything that I know. Don't see why we need to go through all of that again."

"We just want to hear it in person," Traian said, paused then pointed at Alan. "If whatever you have in that mug is not straight coffee, you mind setting it down till we're done?"

Alan put the mug down on a stack of magazines and leaned back into the plaid couch, cushion showing through in one of the arms.

"Go ahead," he said, trying to look relaxed.

Traian said, "Let's go back to the beginning if you don't mind. You were on the May property—have been on the May property a number of times with your job. Do I have that right?"

"Yep," Alan said.

"Okay, good. So, you're on the property delivering propane. Pretty normal job, but something about it is wrong. Wrong enough to think about it when you leave. Can you tell us what bothered you?"

"Well," Alan said. "Let me say first that I never had any kind of problem with the Mays. I figured it was tough on Levi and his sister when their dad got sick and all. Taking over that business and what-not. I mean, it's a pretty shitty line of work if you ask me, but then, so is hauling propane around all day. You smell like a pilot light when you get home. Anyway, I was up there a while back. After Mr. May, Rollie I mean, got sick, and I noticed that they had some bodies up near where the retort is."

"The retort?" Gillis said.

"Yeah, that's what they call the building and the mechanics that burn the bodies at really hell-hot temps. A *retort*. I didn't know that either till I started making deliveries up there. So." He stopped. Then said, "Well, I think they were bodies. What I actually saw was just limbs sticking out from underneath this tarp that was stretched out like you would do if you were letting it dry, you know. Or raking leaves onto it. Anyway. I think these feet were still connected to the bodies because there were all these humps underneath that tarp keeping it from laying flat. Or *lying* flat. My mother used to ride me about that. Fuck if I know why. You mind if I put on some coffee?"

"It's your home, Alan," Traian said. "Long as we keep it to coffee."

"Alright." He got up off the couch and walked between the two agents, Gillis and Traian exchanging a look as he went past. Then following him with their eyes into the small kitchen. Alan pulling a can of Folgers down from the cupboard and spooning coffee into a white filter.

"Y'all want some too?"

"We're fine," Traian said. "But keep talking while you make the coffee."

"Right," Alan said. "So, they got these feet and legs and maybe bodies up there and Levi sees me looking at them but he don't say nothing about it that time and I figure they're just not up on all of the procedures or something like that and I let it go and drop off more tanks and get back in the truck and keep on my route."

Traian said, "You said that they used a lot of gas, or they used to use a lot of gas. What do you mean by that? Were they ordering gas and not using it—then ordering more? And you didn't notice, just kept making the deliveries?"

"Look man. It's none of my business how people use or don't use the propane. I get an order sheet, load the truck, deliver the tanks, or maybe just fill the tanks with the hose, leave a ticket and then I leave. I don't stand around and ask how they like the way the fuel burns or if they decided to use a tarp instead of burning people like they are supposed to. Standing out in the woods with that big motherfucker Levi May. What am I gonna say? 'This seems awful strange Levi, you being in the cremation business and me delivering all this and there's these full tanks around back.' Jesus guys I don't know. They order it and we deliver. I called you didn't I. What else you want?"

"So it wasn't the gas orders that made you suspicious?" Gillis said.

Alan looked at the agent. Turned on the coffee pot, came over and sat down heavy on the couch. Sighed.

"No man. What got my attention was dead people laying or *lying* around, under a tarp, in the woods when they were supposed to be in a cremation chamber. I mean, look, if I had been there and seen them unloading a hearse or someone carrying a body inside, that would have been normal. Right? Creepy as fuck, you know, but all part of the process. These dead people were up there and didn't look to me like anyone was paying attention to much of anything. It was like, 'well, we got this new shipment of bodies in, what you reckon we ought to do with them?' and then someone's like, 'just put them up there on the hill next to the retort and we'll see about that later.' I mean, shit. Levi acting all cool about it and his sister too, but I could tell. Cause, you know, I mean they saw me looking sideways and I guess it finally clicked like maybe they was not doing such a good job with disposing of these bodies and all that. And you know, I mean, the reason I think I really called was on account that those bodies up there—those were people's relatives and loved ones. And I got to thinking about that and I said to myself, I said, 'Alan, that's not right and you know it. What if that was your Daddy up there in the woods?' and then I got to thinking if they're not burning those bodies, just what in the hell are they putting in those brass pots that go back to the funeral home?"

The Mr. Coffee chirped and all three men were quiet. Alan stood. "You sure you don't want some coffee?"

Gillis said, "I'll take a cup," looking at Traian who was off in his own head, looking around the trailer. Taking everything in.

"By brass pots, you mean urns?" Traian said.

"Yeah, that's it. *Urns.*"

"And the bodies you saw, were they the only ones, up near the retort?"

Alan got down two mugs and poured out the coffee and brought one of the mugs over to Gillis and handed it to him. Then went back to the kitchen and turned around to face them.

"Well, I might've seen another one. I couldn't tell for sure. They have a hearse up there and I thought maybe there was something—someone, a body maybe, on the ground next to it. Just like it rolled out the back. I can't say for sure on that one cause Levi and his sister were there with me and I was not going to walk over and get a closer look. You know what I mean? Someone who would leave a body there, up next to the house and all. That's not a person I want to spend a lot of time with."

"Okay," Traian said.

Alan said, "To tell the truth, something about the whole place felt wrong to me. I mean there was shit scattered all over the yard and the place just looked like it was going to hell. I don't know about any more bodies—the ones that I seen was enough or you wouldn't be sitting here making me drink straight coffee on my day off."

Traian said, "We're sorry about that, Alan. But you know, it's like you said about people's loved ones. We just want to understand what may or may not be going on and we have to ask a lot of questions before we can make any decisions. We appreciate your help."

"Uh-huh," Alan said and picked up his coffee mug. "You got any more questions for me?"

"Just one more for now," Traian said. "If you needed supplies or tools or tarps or equipment—I mean outside of the propane—where would you go around here for things like that?"

Alan sipped the coffee and made a bitter face. "Turner's would be my guess," he said.

"Turner's?" Gillis said.

"Feed and seed store," Alan said. "Y'all being detective types, I'm sure you can find it."

•

They were back in the Mercury, moving slow up the row of trailers and coming even with the office building with Edith inside. Talking to her dog.

Gillis said, "Why that last question? I think I know, but what made you ask it?"

"I'm working through this as I go. Makes sense to me to track down the Mays through the places that they frequent as it relates to their business. I was hoping that we would get more out of Shanks. He's obviously spooked but I don't know that there's enough there to warrant us questioning May yet. I'd like to have some corroboration. Plus, Shanks being half in the bag does not do a lot for his credibility. For all we know he was crocked on the job."

"You mean someone else seeing what Shanks saw? The corroboration?"

"No. Someone witnessing something that supports what Alan said he saw or believes that he saw. Anything that supports getting rid of bodies without cremating them. It's a long-shot, I know. But it's only one degree of separation away from May's business. We'll go by this Turner's place and ask some questions, then we'll go see Hi Lewis and find out why his phone is out of order."

Lester Peacock was on his phone when they came in. Two guys in suits standing in the feed and seed store walking up and down the aisles, one of them picking up a hammer and then putting it back on the rack. Lester telling the caller he would get back with them.

He said, "Help you gentlemen?"

The one who had picked up the hammer held back and Traian approached the counter, going into his coat pocket for his ID, Lester putting on reading glasses and leaning past the cash register to look at the badge.

Said, "Whoa, just like the movies."

Traian put the ID back and explained why they were there. Asking Lester if he knew Alan Shanks, Lester saying he vaguely knew him. Had seen him at the bar from time to time. That was about it.

Traian said, "What about Levi or Caroline May?"

"Sure," Lester said. Hands on the counter and watching over Traian's shoulder at the other suit who was looking back at him. Lester thinking black sunglasses would have completed the outfit. "I know Levi. He's in here all the time. Knew his Daddy better. Rollie. But he had a stroke or something like that and his son took over. Heard the old man got mind trouble too. Probably all of them fumes he breathed. Nice enough people."

"You mind if we ask what Levi May buys when he is in here?" Traian said.

"Well," Lester said.

"You own this store?" Gillis said, Lester looking up.

"No."

"Then maybe we need to talk to the owner?" Gillis said.

"I can't just give out information like that," Lester said.

"Can't or won't?" Gillis said.

A pause and then Lester said, "Hold on."

Traian turned around and motioned for Gillis to back off.

"Sorry," Traian said, turning back to Lester. "He's wound kinda tight."

"I'll say." Lester not sure how the conversation turned so quick.

"We're looking into something, and we need your help. You don't have to comply and this might be the last time you see either of us. Or, we might be back in a more official capacity. It's hard to say with investigations in their early stages."

Lester said, "Investigations?"

"We can call it information gathering," Traian said. "If that sounds less ominous."

"Less what?" Lester said.

"I'm going to guess you keep a ledger," Traian said. "Accounts payable, that sort of thing. Probably tied to an inventory register?"

"Yeah," Lester said.

"Well, what Agent Gillis and I would like to see is what you've been selling to the May family. And because I can tell that all of this makes you nervous, I'll assure you now that we're not looking at you as we gather this information. Not yet anyway. And if you cooperate, we'll make sure to take note of that as we move forward. If you don't want to cooperate, then we'll leave you alone. But I can tell you that when we get back in our car, Agent Gillis is going to say to me that he wonders why the clerk at Turner's was acting cagey about opening his books. If there's nothing to hide, why won't he just open the books? That kind of thing."

Lester clucked his tongue and then reached under the counter and brought out the ledger books and dropped them in front of Traian. He pointed at them.

"Lime," he said. "Levi buys a lot of lime from us. So did his Daddy. But it's more and more lately. It's none of my business, but . . ."

"But what?" Traian said.

"Buuuut," Lester said. "It's a lot of it and it don't make much sense is all. That and he's been renting a Bobcat from the machine lot and was asking me about how much one would cost if he was to buy one for himself instead of renting it."

"Why don't those things make sense?" Traian said.

"Well, because if the Mays were in the construction business, buying lime for mixing would be pretty normal. But if you were in construction and needed it then most likely you wouldn't be buying bags of it from here. You would buy it in bulk. Have it delivered to the site. The Bobcat's a pretty normal rental, but most people needing that are just clearing land or doing some light grading."

"And why is any of that strange when it comes to Levi May?" Traian connecting it now, but wanting Lester to say it.

"Because the Mays are in the burning bodies, not covering them up business."

"Covering them up?" Gillis said.

"Well," Lester said, seeing the line of questioning now. Like he and Traian were sharing a joke. The other guy in the dark.

"And before now, you never thought to tell anyone about this?"

"It's none of my business," Lester said.

"And Mr. May. Levi. Did you ever ask him why he needed that much lime?"

"I asked," Lester said.

"And," Gillis said, stepping up to the counter.

"Never got an answer. Listen, we don't make a habit of harassing our customers. People around here don't care much for people nosing around like that. That don't sit well with us rural folk. You poke around where you're not invited and you're asking to be on the wrong end of a shotgun. You understand what I'm saying? Sure, a man buying a lot of lime in the body business seemed off. And I asked him and he didn't feel like answering me. I left it at that. No law against buying lime the last time I checked." Cleared his throat. "I just sold it to him. I don't want any trouble if he's up to something out there in the woods." Paused, then said, "I think that's all I have to say."

They had Lester walk them through the ledgers and took down some notes. Traian pointed at a line item next to May's name.

"What's this," he said. "What does CB stand for?"

`Lester turned the book around so he could read it. Took his glasses off and pushed the book back around.

"Cinder block," he said.

•

Deputy Ellis Carver was sitting at his small desk in the back office of the Sheriff's department, thinking about Tim Dunn's sheep and how messed up that whole thing had been. Then there was the trip that he and Sheriff Lewis had made to the May place and that had been bizarre too. Ellis not knowing why they were there in the first place. Sheriff Lewis seeming conflicted and uncharacteristically unsure of himself. Normally cool about everything. Playing everything close and not wanting to talk about it.

Ellis had spent his whole life in and around LaFayette, Georgia and there had been a time when he thought that all he wanted to do was get out. He'd even thought about the military, going so far as to visit the Marine recruiting station which was nothing more than a one room office on West Villanow Street. Some kid maybe a little older than him behind the desk, not really promoting the armed services. A couple torn posters on the wall. Dingy carpet on the floor. The kid in uniform looking bored. Told Ellis that he should try and get on at the Sheriff's department and skip all that basic training shit. Told him there were a lot less tasking ways to carry a gun for a living if that was what he was after. Ellis said that he did not care so much about carrying a gun. Just wanted out of LaFayette. Marine recruiter said that Paris Island made LaFayette look like the garden of Eden and Ellis left the office more confused than when he had gone in. Standing out on the sidewalk in July heat, trying to picture LaFayette as something like paradise.

Now he was sitting at his desk thinking about the black smoke in the Dunns' pasture. Watching it curl overhead and just hang there, the stench of the burning wool and then the cooking meat enough to make him want to go home and take a shower. Eat plants for the rest of his life like the Seventh Day Adventists up near Cleveland, Tennessee. He was allowing his thoughts to wander around when the chime in the front office sounded and he had to get up and see who had come in. Tanya's day off. No one in the holding cells. Glad for the distraction.

Traian and Gillis stood in the front room looking unimpressed. Ellis came through the door and stood behind Tanya's desk and waited for them to say something.

"Good morning," Traian said.

"Morning," Ellis said, realizing he had left his hat on his desk and feeling less like a deputy without it. "Help you?"

"Looks like you'll have to. This place is pretty quiet."

Ellis nodded. "Today it is," he said. "Sometimes it gets a little hectic."

"We're not here to make it hectic. We're here to see Sheriff Lewis."

"Well, I hope you did not make a special trip. Looks like you might have made a special trip, being dressed like that. Sheriff Lewis is not here today."

"Is that so," Traian said.

"That is so," Ellis said and gave a short laugh. "Something I can do for you?"

"We think we probably need to speak directly with the Sheriff on this one. We're with the GBI. I'm Agent Thomas and this is Agent Gillis."

"Hi," Ellis said.

"Hi," Gillis said.

"Where is the Sheriff, deputy . . . "

"Carver. Ellis Carver. He's taking a couple days off. He called in yesterday afternoon and told me and Tanya to hold down the fort.

Said he was going to take some R and R. That's how he put it. R and R. Rest and Relaxation."

"And he left you in charge?" Gillis said.

"Well, me and Tanya, I guess. But she's off today." Thinking how the place might look to these men. He said, "What does the GBI need with Sheriff Lewis?"

Traian said, "I'm just going to leave my card. We're staying up in Chattanooga at the Reed House. Can you give him the name? I can write it on the back and they can ring me in the room."

"He's not here," Ellis said. "The Reed House. That the one that's haunted?" Gillis smiled.

"I know he's not here," Traian said, taking a pen from Tanya's desk and scratching the name of the hotel on the back of the card then handing the card to Deputy Carver. "If he calls in, you can give him the message then. That work for you?"

Ellis looked the card over. "Sure," he said. Read the back of the card.

"You won't forget—it's important," Gillis said.

"I guess I can handle it," Ellis said. Not caring for the way that the men were studying him. Seemed hesitant to leave.

"Anything else I can do for you?" he said.

"No," Traian said. "Just make sure that he gets that." They turned to leave and Ellis watched them go through the door and then stand out on the street talking to each other. He looked again at the card and thought that maybe he ought to call Sheriff Lewis at home to deliver the message.

28.

REVEREND RIGHTEOUS WAITED ON THE FRONT STEPS for Shawna, dressed in one of his tan suits with no tie. He needed a cigarette but did not want Shawna to smell it on him. Needed to be clean for this.

He stood in the early morning light and listened to the quiet. He had caught Shawna on her way out the door on Sunday, telling him she did not have time to come by the church before work, but when he told her it was important, she said she would come. He heard a car engine coming up the road and then she was turning into the lot. He could see her through the windshield. Looked nice. Her hair done-up. Looked like she was wearing a dress with flowers on it. Small and pretty behind the wheel. She parked and when she got out and saw him waiting, she frowned. She came up the cracked sidewalk and started up the stairs.

She said, "What's wrong?"

"Let's go inside, Shawna," he said and opened the door for her to pass into the church.

They went down the aisle on the left side of the pews and when they got to the front, he stopped her by touching her shoulder and motioned for her to sit. She put her purse down on the pew and sat.

"What's going on, Reverend?" Looking up at him until he sat beside her.

"Shawna, you know that you are an important member of this church. You and Rollie and your family. You are like my own. You are my own in the eyes of God and his son Jesus. And we are all his children..."

"What's wrong," she said. This time no patience but irritation in her voice. Demanding.

"You want it like that?"

"Like that," she said.

"Alright," he said. "How much you know about the funeral side of your business? I mean, how much you know about these people you working with from out of town?"

"I know that that's how we stay in business. They provide the bodies and we provide the service."

"Right, but you are not answering the question."

"I don't understand your question and I'm not sure why you would be the one to ask it even if I did. You know I've been working this business with Rollie and now the kids."

"Sister," he said.

"Uh-uh," Shawna said. "Don't start that flock shit now. You tell me what you're up to here." Both of them sitting straight, not leaning into the back of the pew. On guard. Jesus up on the cross like a mannequin in a b-rated horror show. Eyes closed. Preoccupied.

"I ain't up to nothing woman," he said, now irritated at her impatience with his gentle approach. Always the way with the women. Till you told them how deep in the shit they were. Right up to their chin. "I called you because I'm watching out for you."

"How's that?" she said.

"For one, you can start by answering the question I asked you: How well you know these motherfuckers in the funeral business? The ones been overloading you with bodies?" Jesus overlooking that indiscretion. Still sleeping.

"Overloading?" she said "What are you talking about, *overloading*?"

"Shawna," he said and risked touching her shoulder. Less heat in her eyes now. "I don't know if you think you're working something on your end, but these men running these funeral homes sure as hell working something on theirs and if you get caught up in that, then you Mays will be the first to get popped. You hear me? They ain't going down when they can let a bunch of ignorant niggers in

Noble take the fall for them. Why you think they picked you in the first place?"

"Who you calling *ignorant*?"

"You know what I mean, Shawna. C'mon."

"How you know anything about this? Who you been talking to?"

"It don't matter, Shawna, does it? I know their side of the story. Just got to trust me on that. And you want to tell me your side of the story, that's alright cause you know I'll keep it in confidence cause we on the same team. We in the same *flock* you just dismissed like you left the congregation last week to visit the rabbi. Like you ain't washed in this same colored-blood. Listen here, you make light of that if you want, but you know as well as I do that this church here cares more about you than any white man and his lawyers ever will. I'm just telling you that you got to get your house in order if it ain't already. You hear me?"

"I hear you," she said. Thought about what she wanted to do next. Trusting the information and the source, but shaky about it. Wondering what Levi and Caroline knew and whether the funeral men knew what they had been up to in return. Wondered how long it would be before some lawman came sniffing around the property. All this information from the Reverend.

"You want to tell me anything?"

She shook her head. Could not see how spreading it out any further would be beneficial. Then stopped short. Looked at him thoughtfully. "Who we talking about, Reverend—the funeral people taking advantage?" He sighed. Being friends again.

He said, "Best I can tell? All of them, girl. All of them in on this."

29.

SHERRY LEWIS WAS MAKING SANDWICHES IN THE kitchen for Hi and Robbie. A ham and cheese for Robbie and turkey for Hi. Wrapping them in cling wrap and then putting them inside of a small Igloo cooler. Bag of chips, a couple of cokes and two cans of Coors for Hi. Robbie was in his room getting ready. Hi out in the garage putting the rods and tackle boxes in the car. She closed the lid of the cooler and set it on the kitchen table and then crossed the kitchen to answer the phone. Ellis on the other end telling her that he needed to talk with Sheriff Lewis and Sherry telling him that unless it was urgent, and Ellis interrupting her before she got the rest of the sentence out saying that *yes*, he thought it was urgent enough.

Hi said, "Ellis?"

"Sheriff. I'm awful sorry to bother you and all, but..."

"Go ahead Ellis."

"Sheriff, a couple GBI agents was just into the office wanting to talk to you."

"You tell them I was out?"

"I did. Yes Sir. But, well they seemed kinda bothered."

"Bothered how?"

"I don't know. Just bothered."

"What did they want?"

"Talk to you."

"I know that much, Ellis," he said. Looking at Robbie standing in the door of the kitchen. T-shirt, jeans and a Braves baseball cap pulled low. Sherry looking at him from over near the sink.

"Wouldn't say, Sheriff. One of them left his card for you with their hotel up in Chattanooga on the back."

"What's the name on the card?"

"Looks like *Train Thomas*.»

"It Traian," Hi said.

"Okay," Ellis said. "Traian."

"What's the hotel?" Ellis gave him the name.

"How long ago did they leave?"

"Ten minutes maybe."

Hi said, "Thanks Ellis. You did the right thing." Hung up and looked at Sherry.

"I got to make a phone call, and then we're going. Don't look at me like that. I'm not going to spoil anybody's day." He called the hotel and left a message for Agent Thomas. What he said was, "Tell him I will meet him at the Pickle Barrel at eight tonight. Tell him, just him at the meeting. Got that?" Put the phone back in the cradle motioned for Robbie to get moving.

"What's going on?" Sherry said.

"We're going fishing," he said.

•

Traian stood outside the Pickle Barrel. A scaled attempt at the Flat Iron building in New York. Sitting on Market Street like a stained brick pie wedge. Car traffic downtown almost non-existent. The clerk at the hotel that gave him Sheriff Lewis' message telling him that it was the college watering hole. Kinda a hippie joint that was hard to maneuver once you were inside. Good rooftop bar. The college being the same one Levi May had gone to before going home to run the family business. Traian had checked up on it. Football player showing promise.

He decided to wait inside. Went in an ordered a draft from the girl pulling the taps without a bra and a Grateful Dead t-shirt. Looked like she needed to wash her hair. She put the flat beer on the bar top and went back to a guy sitting near the end, smoking one cigarette after another. Into what he was telling her. Maybe an ex pleading his case. The door opened behind him, and he turned on the stool to see Lewis wearing jeans and t-shirt. Ball cap on his head that read *Lookouts*. Seemed at home there. Traian standing out like the Fed he was in suit pants and a rumpled dress shirt. Sleeves rolled up to his elbows.

Lewis said, "Let's go upstairs. Bring your beer. They'll run a tab." They went up a narrow spiral staircase, only wide enough for one person, Traian wondering how a waitress came up the wrought iron steps with a tray full of beer glasses. Lewis went between a few tables and outside to a two-top and sat down. Motioned for Traian to do the same.

"I understand that I may have interrupted your day off," Traian said. "I'm sorry about that."

"Not sorry enough to let it wait till I got back in the office on Monday, though."

"You're a sheriff. You normally let holidays get in the way of an investigation?"

"That what you're running now—an investigation? In Walker County?"

Traian sat. Said, "You going to order something?"

Hi said, "They'll come by in a minute."

"You want to wait till she does? Before we get started, I mean?"

"Bad news, huh?" Hi said. "I need a drink to digest it?"

Traian sat back in his chair. Could not get over how quiet it was downtown. Wondering where all the college kids were.

"Is it always this dead down here?"

Hi looked at the agent and smiled.

"I don't know, Agent Thomas. I don't make a habit of investigating anything outside my jurisdiction."

Traian thinking, *this will be quick.*

He said, "If you want to be smug, the entire state is my jurisdiction.

I tried to be polite about coming into yours and you did not see fit to call me back. To be honest, I probably would have let all this go if you had called and told me that there was nothing to be concerned about. But you did not feel that was necessary, so I did what I'm paid to do. Look into things."

"Well," Hi said and then stopped to get the waitress' attention. Ordered a draft and went back to Traian.

"I went up to the May's place. Asked them how things were going and they said that they were having some trouble keeping up, but that it was nothing that they couldn't handle. They're not much more than kids. I told them about Shanks and his concerns—left the GBI part out—and they acknowledged that he might have seen some bodies that were still outside, but they also said that they had gotten behind and that they would do a better job going forward. More professional. And they also said that Shanks drank and that he may not be the most credible witness. That was it." The waitress dropped the beer off and Hi picked up the mug and took a deep swallow and put it back down. "Except," he said, wiping his lips with the back of his hand. "Except for calling you back, that was it. I might have saved myself the trip up here tonight. Be home with my wife and son, but I failed to do that. So I guess it's on me."

"You talk to anyone else about it?" Traian said.

"No," Hi said. "Did not see the need for that."

"You talk to Shanks?"

"No. Figured he had told you everything that I needed to know, so I went straight there. To the Mays."

"We talked to Shanks," Traian said. "Spent some quality time in his trailer together. I can confirm that he drinks. From the looks of the place and of him, I'd say he has a problem with it." Hi nodded.

"So again, it's on me. Not being thorough enough."

Traian finished his beer and looked for the waitress. Spotted her near the stairs and waived the empty mug at her.

"You know," he said. "We're not so different. I grew up in a small town in Ohio. Same small-town stuff I saw in LaFayette and Noble today. Good people just trying to get by. But see, behind the corn fields and the overalls and good country folk—the county fairs and pine wood derbies, there was still crime. And that's the one thing that is clever about crime. It has a sneaky way of disguising itself, no matter where it settles in. And when I decided that I wanted to go after people committing crimes, I told myself that I would not let any contextual circumstances get in the way. Meaning, I would assume that it was there until I could prove that it wasn't. If I were looking at crime as an actual person, then I would assume him guilty until I could prove him innocent. Our justice platform in reverse. And from what I learned today, I think that I have some more digging to do with the Mays." He paused and chuckled.

Hi said, "My turn?"

"Sure," Traian said. The new beer appearing from behind his right shoulder.

"I don't think that your philosophy is wrong. A bit wordy, but not wrong. But in this case, you are coming into this community with no relationships and only the word of one lonely man in a trailer. We have lots of lonely men and lots of trailers in Walker County. We got homeless men living in makeshift camps by a creek cooking drugs in old drums, and countless other shit birds causing inconvenience for themselves and the people around them. But the Mays? Those are good people. Black people who made something of themselves when most of the blacks around these parts are lucky if they have a section-eight apartment. So, when you got aggressive about this tip you called me about, it rubbed me the wrong way. I know you have a job to do. I can appreciate that. And I'm sure most places you show up around the state, hick Sheriffs like me look at you sideways and talk behind your back when you leave the room." He drank and wiped his mouth again. "If I really think about it, situations like this come down to aspirations. You have yours and I have mine. But you have someone telling you what to do, and that person has someone telling them what to do and that person has someone telling them what to do and on and on and on. Me? I'm elected. So, my boss is the people of Walker County and I don't have the luxury of assuming their guilt and rolling up into their place of business sticking my chest out so they can get a good look at my badge. Or second-guessing their answers when I ask them a question. You see the difference?"

Traian said, "Yes, but what I don't see is how that absolves you from looking into something further. We both have a responsibility to find resolution." Thought, *Jesus, this guy.*

"No, it does not absolve me," Hi said. "But seeking resolution when there is evidence is one thing. Seeking it based on speculation is another. I don't work off speculation."

Traian looked at the second beer and decided to leave it. "Did you know that Tri-State does not have a license which means that no regulatory body in Georgia is checking up on them?"

"Are they in violation of something?"

"Not in that regard," Traian said. "They were not required to be licensed when their father opened the place back in the seventies. But given the information that we both know now, and the fact that no one is making sure that they are doing their job correctly, don't you think that maybe ensuring everything is running correctly is important?"

"And that's the GBI's responsibility?"

"Jesus, Lewis. What do you think? GBI, sure. EPA possibly. Maybe the state medical examiner's office. Who knows where something like this goes. The point I'm trying to make here is that we don't know until we look. How do you not see that?"

"What I see," Hi said, "is a small-time crematory getting a few things wrong and it being called to your attention and then to mine. I went out and looked around. Talked to the people running the place and decided that aside from the assertions made by a man who I believe may lack credibility, there was nothing more for me to look into."

Traian said, "You know Lester Peacock at Turner's?"

"Yeah, I know Lester. Why? What's he got to do with any of this?"

Traian considering going into it and then thinking, *Fuck it. Go around him.*

Hi said, "You don't think that you might be getting a little ahead of yourself?"

"No, I don't," Traian said. Having a hard time now keeping an even tone. Lewis being intentionally thick. Saw no point in furthering the conversation. Couldn't believe that Lewis had anything to do with whatever might be going on at Tri-State, but obviously more than hesitant to do much about it.

He said, "I'm sorry that you drove up here for this."

"What does that mean?" Hi said.

"I'm *speculating* here, Sheriff Lewis, but I think that maybe that crematory warrants a closer look. And I'm going to get a judge to grant it. You can help me, or you can get out of the way. We'll keep you informed of how we plan to proceed." He stood. "I'll pay the check on the way out. You have a good night."

"You're not going to finish your beer?" Hi said, Traian starting down the stairs.

"It's flat," he said.

•

Hi sat upstairs and finished his beer and then drank the one Traian had left. Had two more on his own dime and then went down the winding stairs and out onto the street. Walked toward his car, feeling the beer and the colder air. Knew he should have brought a jacket with him. He got to the car and looked further down the sidewalk and saw the pay phone booth. Left it unlocked and walked down to call Sherry. Agent Thomas had been right. Dead down here. Some of the college kids had come into the bar before he left, but even they had been quiet. Sherry picked up on the second ring. Hi leaning into the glass of the booth.

"What's up?" she said. Sounded tired. Maybe getting ready for bed. He looked at his watch and saw it was quarter till nine. It had not taken half-an-hour with Thomas.

"Getting ready to come home," he said.

"What's wrong. I can hear something's wrong."

He let out his breath. "I don't know, Sherr," he said. "I think the Mays might be in trouble. Levi and Caroline anyway. Probably Shawna too."

"Why? What would Shawna May or her kids do to get in any kind of trouble?"

"It's a long story," he said. "And it may not be anything."

"Why don't you come home and tell me about it," she said.

"I will," he said. "I'm gonna walk around for a few minutes. I had a few beers."

"Does this have anything to do with what Robbie found in the woods? With Matt, I mean. The girl? Her skull?" There it was. Out of nowhere, the grade school teacher serving it to him on the phone. He had not thought about the bones he had taken down to Atlanta. Had not put the Mays and remains together. That and the coroner's gown. The one that they found at the homeless camp with Delbert Weir and his cooks. Those two things together and Thomas saying, 'Jesus, Lewis. What do you think?' Him acting like a smart ass. Telling the agent that he was getting ahead of himself—Thomas further ahead of it and didn't even know it. Hi looking like he was hiding something. Not hiding, just not showing. Shit, what would be the difference.

"Hi, you there?"

"Yeah, I'm here. I'll be home soon." She said she loved him and then he hung up. Thought about going back into the bar. He had his badge if he got pulled over on the way home. Walked back-up Market to the Pickle Barrel Door. Nobody on the street but him.

30.

LEVI ROLLED HIS FATHER'S WHEELCHAIR ONTO THE porch. Caroline and his mother in the kitchen, talking about the conversation that Shawna had at the church. Both of them nervous. Levi telling them he was going to take Rollie outside for some fresh air. Man did not smell like piss at the moment. His mind like alphabet soup. Could not tell them apart anymore. Even Matt, who would watch him from the corner of the room. Mixed with fear and curiosity. Rollie looking away from the TV and seeing the small boy, thinking maybe the child was lost.

Levi locked the wheels of the chair. The dusk like a warm bath. The old man's legs atrophied and arms like their spotted porch spindles compared to his time before the stroke. Levi sat on the swing and watched his father take in the color, the smells of the red earth and pine trees, the cape of quiet settling over everything around them.

He said, "Pops, I know that you don't understand what I'm saying and I know that you can't talk back very good. I got to tell you something, though, cause it's eating at me and I think," he stopped. "No, I know, that they are gonna find out what we been up to here." He waited to see if the old man would react, but Rollie's face was turned away from him. Focused on the yard, only it was not focused. Was more like a mask of wrinkles worn into a dark leather. His eyes a watery yellow. Levi got off the swing and went back in the house and took a bottle out of the cupboard. Took down one Mason jar, his sister and mother watching him. The Tri-State books on the kitchen table.

"He don't need any of that Levi," Shawna said. "And

neither do you."

He did not answer her, then thought about it before he went out.

"Ain't gonna hurt nothing, is it?" He went through the screen door and stood beside the wheelchair, pouring some of the liquor into the jar and forcing it between Rollie's legs.

"We gonna have a drink together," he said and sat back on the swing. Took a pull off the bottle and made a face. Bit through it and took another. The old man not noticing the jar between his legs.

"See, I should have been paying better attention about all this cremation work you was doing. But I was not here. I was playing football. Thought that was my way out. Then I come back and you got this deal. Gonna make us better off. All these bodies coming in and us sending back cinder block dust and cement dust, and all kinds of other shit to make those urns feel full. Fooling them funeral home directors. Them thinking that we's a bunch of dumb country niggers down here, just doing what we told. And they must have been making out good on their end, cause them bodies just keep coming and we just keep moving them around the property instead of doing what we's supposed to do which is burning them up and sending back ashes instead of..." He took another drink from the bottle. Feeling it now, knowing his mother and sister were listening. Matt upstairs with his books. "Instead of me busting up blocks and grinding them down and mixing them with dry cement. Me hauling bodies out in the woods and laying them around like they were decorations or some crazy shit like that. Buying supplies down at Turner's from that redneck motherfucker Lester. What I supposed to tell him, Popps? 'Oh, Lester. We just disguising the smell up there at Tri-State. Yeah, I know, I know. We supposed to be burning them up, but we got this thing going where we's making more money than we ever have and I can't be bothering with retorts or shit like that. We just scattering them.' Then you got to go mute on me. Stuck in that fucking chair and Caroline and me trying to hide all this shit. Got bodies all over the motherfucking place. White women, Pops.

We got white women out in the woods, man. I'm renting Bobcats and digging pits and driving to Alabama, Tennessee. Picking up dead people and dropping off fake dead people." He drank again, now reeling with it. Nothing on his stomach. Practice jersey from UTC stiff with sweat. "And you know, I'm gonna take the fall on all this. Not momma. Not Caroline. They gonna be alright. I'm gonna make them alright. But me? Me, I'm gonna take the fall on this and it's cause you took me out of school. Only you never actually took me out of that school. Momma did that for you. But, but, you might as well have cause you had to have a fucking stroke and leave all this behind for the rest of us to sweep up. How does that make sense, Popps?" The anger subsiding now. Emotion in his voice. "I'm gonna burn for this Popps. I think they call that irony, but fuck if I know that's right. They may not come today. May not be tomorrow. Winter weather coming. I can feel it. Can you? We went too far. We went..."

Shawna came out on the porch. Looked at Levi. Caroline inside not wanting to come out. She took the jar from between Rollie's legs and then came over and took the bottle from Levi.

"You don't know any of that to be true."

"Momma," he said.

"Momma nothing," she said. "You come inside and I'll bring Daddy in with me. Matt needs a bath before bed."

Levi stood. Shaky. The sun gone now and the dark creeping in where the light had been.

"We gonna be alright," Shawna said. "Me and your Daddy—we did this for you kids. We can make it right. Caroline gonna help you."

He walked past her and into the house. Caroline looked up from the table and then away from him. Started toward his room, then stopped.

"What we gonna do?" he said.

She touched the ledger book. "What you mean?" she said.

Shawna still out on the porch. No sound coming in.

"They talking about us up in Atlanta, Caroline. Funeral owners all over the goddamn place. How long you think we can hold out?"

"They's as guilty as we are," she said.

"Right," he said. "But they can say they was ignorant about what we were giving them all along. I mean, how many people you think inspect cremains, Caroline? Stick their head in a jar of ashes." Putting on a white voice, saying "Ah, looks good to me." Voice louder now, a little drunk. Too big for the kitchen

"They gonna say how the fuck would we know that they was sending back *fake* cremains. Why would they do something like that?" Then, answering his own question in the white voice again, "Oh, wait, are they fucking us more than we're fucking them?"

She was watching him pace back and forth, working through it like he had worked through it with Rollie on the porch. This time caught in a circle. Kept bumping into the same wall. Like a manic comic.

He said, "But they can always just go back to being ignorant, Caroline. Can we? With all these scammed motherfuckers laying around the property in clothes or piled up in a pit. Fishing out by the lake. Caroline, look at me." She looked. "There is some old woman in her wedding dress back there taking a nap under a fucking tree. Half gone now, but you can see what she used to be. She a hundred yards from this fucking house, Caroline. Now you gonna tell me that that weird fucker in Gadsden—Tyler Arnold, or another one of those crook motherfucking directors is gonna witness for us?" He stood. Quiet and worn out. He started to say something else, but turned and went toward the back of the house.

She let him go and thought about all of the dead out in the woods—dead she had not seen herself—and then thought about Clarence and how he might be able to help. Thought harder on it and knew he'd be too smart to get close to something like this here. *You'd have to be crazy*, she thought.

31.

JACK CHAMBLISS, TWO YEARS OUT OF OLE MISS WITH A degree in history, knocked on the city editor's door at the Chattanooga Times's downtown building. Said, "Dutch, you have a minute?" The City Editor looked up and motioned the young reporter into his office.

"So," Chambliss said. "I think I might have something."

"That so," Dutch said. He took a pack of cigarettes from his shirt pocket and offered one.

"No thanks. I'm trying to lay off."

"Smart," Dutch said, pulling a heavy green ash tray closer to him. "What do you think you have?"

Chambliss said, "So last night I'm in the Pickle Barrel talking to this bartender I used to date some. I'm trying to get her to go out with me after her shift. The whole place is dead for once. Nobody in there. And then this guy who just left comes back in and sits down at the bar. At first he's keeping to himself..."

"Is there a story pitch somewhere in here?" Dutch said. Plume of smoke above his head.

"Sure. Okay. Sorry. I'm kinda hung over."

"Ahh," Dutch said.

"So, he's keeping to himself and then he orders a shot and starts talking to me and Jill."

"Jill is the bartender?"

"Yeah."

"The one you are hoping to lay?" Chambliss stopped. Dutch said, "Go ahead."

"So he's talking and drinking and it turns out that the guy is the

Sheriff in Walker County."

"Okay," Dutch said. "Now we are getting somewhere."

"Right," Chambliss said. "So, Jill is making him shots and I'm taking shots and she's taking shots and this guy, this sheriff, starts talking about how the GBI is all in his shit about a case in Noble, Georgia."

"Noble?" Dutch said.

"Yeah, it's some unincorporated town near LaFayette. I don't even know if it's actually on a map."

"Okay. So, what about this case?"

"Well, he would not get into the specifics about that, and I was not going to ask too many questions since he did not know I was a reporter, but he went on and on about his responsibilities to the people down there and how agents out of Atlanta didn't understand and didn't care—always sticking their nose into other people's business. Showing off. That kind of thing. And he was drunk, right, but he wasn't getting sloppy. It was like he just wanted to get something off his chest and we just happened to be sitting there."

"So you think that the GBI is investigating this Sheriff?"

Chambliss thought, then said, "No. I think they're getting ready to investigate something down there and he does not like it. From the way he was talking, it sounded like something was coming. Imminent, you know. And he was getting drunk before it happened, cause I think that he just found out. Or maybe he was figuring it out. I don't know."

"What makes you think that?"

Chambliss reached across the desk and took one of the cigarettes out of the pack and then used the City Editor's lighter. "Because I think that the man he came in there with the first time was the one who told him. The agent."

"There was a second man? What man?"

"Yeah, this guy in suit clothes came in first and then this sheriff came in and they went upstairs. Then the other guy left, then the sheriff left and then he came back in."

"Jesus," Dutch said. "They ever talk about the upside down pyramid in journalism class, Chambliss?"

"I majored in history. And I told you I was hungover."

"Right," the editor said. "I forgot to account for the hangover."

"So, what do you think? Is there a story here?" Chambliss said, not sure what the comment had meant. Head too fuzzy to put it together. Dutch always saying things like that to the reporters. Old sage and all that shit.

"I don't know, Jack. What's this sheriff's name?"

"Lewis. Hi Lewis."

"Hi?" Dutch said.

"Uh-huh. Like the greeting."

Dutch said, "Interesting." Tipped the ash of his smoke looking out through the office glass to the newsroom. "I'll put your question back to you. Do you think this is a story and where would you take it?"

"I don't know. That's what I came in here for."

"This is not something for the city desk."

"I know. I didn't come in here to talk to the city desk. I came in to talk to you."

"I'm touched," Dutch said. Reached over and picked up his phone and called his assistant. "Genie. Get me Charlie's desk, please." He hung up. Looked at Chambliss, stubbing out his smoke. "Did she go?" he said.

"Did who go?"

"The girl. The bartender. Jill. Did she go out with you after?"

32.

WILSON WAS SITTING AT THE BAR BY HIMSELF. ON HIS second Seagrams. Pack of Kools next to an ashtray with a few butts. *Bumpy Face and a pack of what I am,* he called the order. Bartender everyone called Buddy, getting ready for the night crowd. Wearing a tight t-shirt. Hair cut short. Listening to Wilson run his mouth.

"Hey, Buddy?"

"Yeah, Wilson?"

"Where Missy at?"

"It's her night off."

"Shit," Wilson said. "You ever get it on with her?"

Buddy soaking some glasses, drying them with a dish towel and turning them upside down on a black rubber mat. "That's an inappropriate question."

"How that inappropriate when it's just me and you sitting in here talking? Ain't that what men do—talk about pussy when pussy ain't around?"

"A gentleman does not talk about his conquests."

"Who said that? Bill Clinton?"

"My father," Buddy said. "You want another one?" He pointed at Wilson's glass.

"Yeah, man. Hit me."

Buddy took the glass.

"Load it with ice man." Wilson waited on the drink, drumming his fingers on the bartop.

Buddy said, "Here you are Sir."

Wilson said, "Why you talking like that—*Here you are, Sir?*"

"Talking like what? English?"

"Fuck you man." Smiled and shook the ice in his glass. Turned toward the sound of the door opening and said, "Hey look here." He pointed to the door. "That's my boy Alan."

Jack Chambliss pulled his Citation into the gravel lot. Defrost heater going full blast. Windshield smeared with wet dust and grime. Rain coming steadier now. He had left Dutch's office after talking with Charlie the managing editor, forty-year newsman with stains on his white Oxford, stretched tight over his stomach. Buttons missing. Nose a roadmap of thin red lines. Hair a mess. They had talked about his encounter at the bar with the Walker County Sheriff and they told him to call down to GBI in Atlanta, see if he could find out anything about an investigation. Talked to a woman named Eunice who told him that she could not tell him anything about an investigation in Noble. Pressing her, saying "By that do you mean there is an investigation that you can't talk about?" She said she would pass his inquiry on to an agent and hung up. He went back to tell Charlie and Dutch and they told him to look into it if he wanted. Story might or might not be there. Told him to nose around if he felt like it. Non-committal. Chambliss's hangover thinking about lunch. Took a map out of his desk drawer in the newsroom. Found LaFayette and the best route to take. Bought some chips and Coke in the vending machine and made the drive down, listening to the rock station on the radio. No sun out and the cold finally arriving after teasing about coming. Good two months of it ahead of them. He looked at the roadhouse bar and figured he could start there. The lead had started in a bar, so maybe follow it up in one. Have a few beers and kill the headache. He got out and went inside, leaving the Citation unlocked. Hustling to the door, his jacket pulled up over his head. Pushed inside and saw Buddy sitting on a stool reading the paper. Two men, one white and one black, sitting on stools, talking. The black man reaching out and putting a hand on the other man's shoulder. Consoling. They did not look at him come in.

Buddy put the paper down and stood up, eyeing him.

"Hey," Chambliss said.

"Hey," Buddy said. "Get you something?"

Chambliss wiped at the rain on the jacket, pulled it off and looked for someplace to hang it.

"Put it on the back of one of the chairs," Buddy said. "We're not too busy." Chambliss hung the jacket, came back to the bar.

"You got a Miller Light back there?"

"You want a draft or can?"

"Draft," Chambliss said. He took a stool a respectable distance from the two men. Put his elbows on the bar and waited on the beer.

•

Wilson was saying, "Shit, man. What you got to worry about—You ain't done nothing, have you? They always like to fuck with you, police do. You ought to try being black. Might as well have a sign on you reading *fuck with me, I got nothin' better to do.*"

Alan said, "Yea, I know. Just kinda threw me, you know. Having the GBI in the trailer. Felt like they was looking at me. Like maybe I had something that I was not telling them."

"That's how they always do," Wilson said. Then, "Hey Buddy, how about you stop reading about your stock portfolio and hook me and Alan here up with another round. My man is nervous."

"Nervous about what?" Buddy said. Pouring the drinks.

"He done a good Samaritan type deal and the feds came in and fucked with him." Looked down the bar at Jack Chambliss. "Who you?"

"Me?" Chambliss said, pointing at his chest. "I'm nobody. Just came in for a beer."

"Nobody," Wilson said and laughed. "Like Odysseus and that Cyclops man wanting to eat him."

Chambliss smiled, and Alan glanced down the bar at the man.

Turned to Wilson and gave him a look.

"You don't know what the fuck I'm talking about, Alan?" Sipped from the fresh drink. "Hey Buddy, you know the Cyclops story."

Buddy said, "Sure." Went back to his paper.

"You from up in Chattanooga?" Wilson said.

"Originally?" Chambliss said. "No. South Pittsburgh."

"South Pittsburgh?" Wilson said. "That in Pennsylvania?"

Chambliss said, smooth, making conversation, "I don't mean to be rude, but overheard you talking about something with the feds. Mind if I ask what?"

"Why, you a cop?" Wilson said. Buddy picking his head up from the paper. All of them looking at him now.

"No," Chambliss said, seeing his reflection in the bar-back mirror. Wondering now how he would play it. Decided on straight. Nursing the beer. "I'm a reporter."

"No shit," Buddy said. "Where?"

"Chattanooga Times." Buddy turned to the front page of the paper.

"How about that."

"Hold on," Wilson said. Picking up his drink and stepping around Alan. "What you doing here then? You working on this story me and Alan talking about."

"What story would that be?"

"About them bodies Alan seen up at Tri-State. The May place. That one."

Chambliss said, "Can I join you?"

"*Can I join you,*" Wilson said, mimicking the reporter. All nasal. "But of course. Be my guest." Chambliss got up from the stool and walked down the bar, Buddy following on the other side, leaving the paper. They clustered around Alan, the gas man looking sheepish. "Tell the man, Alan," Wilson said, clapping his back. "You can't make this shit up. What's your name?"

"Jack," he said, getting up again and going to his jacket for his pad and pen. Came back and sat down. "You mind if I take some notes?"

•

Alan was slow to respond to the questions. Tired of telling it over and over. Kept wishing he'd kept his mouth shut. Now it seemed like he could not keep it closed. The reporter wanting more and more detail, Wilson pushing him. Buddy keeping the drinks coming. Alan feeling better about things until Hi Lewis' name came up. What was the sheriff doing about it? Had Alan talked to the sheriff? Had the GBI? *Christ, he didn't know.* Not like he was being briefed about anything. Reporter, nice looking kid. Skinny like a tennis player. Kept flipping back through his notes, asking the same question a different way. Made Alan think about what his life was gonna be like after all this. People wanting to know what he had seen. Maybe nothing. Maybe he was more drunk than he thought working the route. *Jesus, seeing things,* he thought. Coming unglued living by himself in that shitty trailer park. Ball-busting landlady being friendly with the cops. Little dog of hers shitting in the flower beds. Asking him when he planned on cleaning up around the trailer. *Shit, never.*

Chambliss said, "Anything else?"

"That ain't enough?" Wilson said.

"I'm a reporter," Chambliss said. Wanting to get out of the place and call back to the newsroom. Tell them he might have something bigger than just the Walker County Sheriff. How big he didn't know. He said, "I get paid to ask questions. That's what I do." Hangover gone.

"Yea, well," Alan said. "I answered them. We're done."

"Hey, man" Wilson said, holding the empty glass out to his side then gesturing at the reporter with it. "I got a question. You gonna put me and Buddy in the story too?"

33.

Hi had gone back into the bar and sat on a stool, making small talk with a couple of young people. The girl behind the bar and some guy that seemed to be hitting on her, but listening to Hi talk in vague terms about the meeting with Agent Thomas. Now he was sitting on the toilet, holding his head in his hands. Headache pounding behind his eyes. He got up, flushed, washed his hands and then threw water into his face, leaning over the sink bowl and feeling the coldness loosen his taught skin. Take some of the heat out of his eye sockets. Taste of the bourbon furring on his tongue. He turned out the bathroom light and went down the hall to the kitchen, boxer shorts and an undershirt with yellowed sweat stains under the arms. Sherry was over by the stove, frying him a couple eggs and bacon. Turned around and looked at him and gave a half-smile.

She said, "Well, Sheriff."

He tried to think of something witty to say. Gave up. Went to the coffee maker and poured some in a mug.

"Not my proudest moment, Mrs. Lewis," he said. Sat at the kitchen table and looked out the window. Mean looking rain. Blowing against gravity, the color a cold metallic. Winter in North Georgia. Had a tricky way of bringing your mood down. Everything wet and solemn. Hi feeling the season heavier than usual.

"Listen," he said. Looking down at the coffee now. Not sure where to start. "I think that there might be some trouble out at the May's place."

Sherry slid the eggs out of the frying pan, picked the bacon out of a skillet with a pair of silver tongs and put that on the plate next to the eggs. Brought it over to the table and set it in front of her husband. Robe sleeve loose around her wrist. Frayed.

"You said that. Last night on the phone. What do you mean?"

He moved the plate closer then got up and went to the drawer for a fork. Came back and sat down. Started to eat, then put the fork aside.

"Sounds like maybe Levi has not been doing the best job with the disposal of bodies at the Crematory. Rollie not being involved I guess. Might be cutting corners. Hard to say."

"What about Shawna?" she said.

"I don't know, Honey. There's an agent with the GBI. Name is Traian Thomas. Sharp guy. Little slick for my taste, but he got a tip from someone here in Noble. Asked me to look into it and..."

"And did you?" she said. "Did you look into it?" Not sure why she'd pounced on him like that.

"Yes, I did," he said. Put some egg into his mouth. Not sure that he could finish them. Tried the bacon and the salty pork agreed with him. "I did go over there and ask a couple of questions. Took Ellis with me. Things seemed okay to me. They said that they had gotten behind and that the guy who called in the tip must have caught them at a bad time."

"What does that even mean?" Sherry said. "What are we talking about? Caught them at a bad time—doing what?"

"Bodies," Hi said. "Apparently they had left bodies outside and this guy saw them and called to express concern. Said it was not the first time."

"Oh God," she said. Had never seen a dead body that she could recall. Maybe a funeral with an open casket. But nothing like tossed-off people. Sherry had never asked Shawna about the Crematory. Had kept it strictly to education. Did not want to understand anything as morbid as burning dead people. Had a hard time putting her friend in a scenario where that's what the work entailed.

"Uh-huh," Hi said, chewing on the bacon. She stood up and got more coffee and sat back down. Holding the mug in two hands, resting it on the table.

"Robbie at school?"

"Yes."

"And what I asked you last night. On the phone. About the girl's bones?" She had not let that go since Hi told her that it was tied to a girl with no name and no explanation as to how she'd ended up in the woods only to have her kid find the skull playing army.

"I don't know, Sherry."

"But."

"I don't know."

"And you went out there—like the GBI asked you? You did that, so are you…"

"Clear?"

"I guess," she said. "I guess that's what I mean."

"Sure," he said. Sipping the coffee. Then he said, thinking about it, "There's not a lot that I could do aside from driving out there and asking some questions. I mean, I've known those people all of my life and the feds were not asking me to go investigate anything. Just check on the place, you know. See if the tip was substantiated. The whole things sounded so ridiculous until this Traian guy calls me to meet him. Says he thinks that it warrants looking into further."

"And what does that mean?" Sherry said. "What does that mean for Shawna and her kids—looking into it further?"

Hi pushed the plate away and looked back out the window at the rain.

"I suppose," he said, tired and needing to get ready for work, "it means they might want to come up here and look around for themselves."

She picked up his plate and scraped the uneaten eggs into the garbage can and he left the coffee on the table. Went back to the bathroom, undressed and got in the shower. Running late.

•

Carlisle said, "Gillis?" He shrugged. Back in the conference room in Atlanta. She looked to Traian and tilted her head.

"Look, I know it's thin," Traian said. "But there's something about this that I can't let go of. The interview with Shanks. The dodgy attitude he had. The purchases at the feed store. This sheriff that wont answer the phone. Wont ask any questions. All I'm requesting is some time to look into it further."

"Looking into it further requires a warrant," she said.

"Right, right, I know. But we've already discussed that it might involve multiple states and if that's not legit for our office..."

"Did you tip the paper in Chattanooga?"

"No," Traian said. Offended. Looked to Gillis for confirmation. "We didn't say shit to anyone about this. Only the people we interviewed and I don't see them leaking this to a reporter. Why would they do that?"

"I don't know, Agent Thomas. You and Gillis are the only ones that have been involved and now we have a reporter asking what we're doing poking around in Noble. Which is a really good question, I might add. You tell me."

"Nothing to tell."

"Director Haskins is out of the loop on this," she said, looking at the brief Traian had given her. "I let you move forward and I'm in your boat. You understand that, right?"

"I do."

"The reporter said that his source on this is local. Multiple sources. You have any idea who might be talking to him?"

They both shook their heads.

"It's too small of a town," she said. "Hell, it's not even a town. Somebody is talking."

"It has to be Shanks," Gillis said. "That guy at the feed store wanted nothing to do with this, plus I think he might be smarter than he lets on. Shanks, he probably got drunk and wandered down the lane to that landlady's building and told her the whole thing and by noon, half of Noble knew we were there."

"All the more reason for us to move," Traian said. "Either we have a case or we don't. But if the press is calling us, then the people involved—the Mays, I mean, they probably know as well. We don't act on this and they skate."

"Skate from what?" Carlisle asked.

"Don't know. But my guess is that they are working some angle with the money and the body disposal. They're hiding something and they got careless. I can't work it out—the scheme I mean. But everything down there is so backwoods and random that it's probably much more simplistic than I think. I'm trying to turn it into a coordinated effort and maybe it's not coordinated at all. Maybe… fuck, I don't know. There's something though. I know that much. All I'm asking to do is walk around."

"What about the funeral homes—people supplying the bodies. They have a role don't they?"

"Yes," Traian said. "But I don't know what it is yet. I made some calls and came up with at least five or six that would confirm who handled their cremations. All of them Tri-State. And that consti- tuted funeral homes in Georgia, Alabama, and Tennessee. So, there's that. I don't know if they are involved or if they even know what's going on—if there is something going on." He was working through it out loud. Making the whole thing muddier for Carlisle. Better to wrap it up. "I've taken it as far as I can without setting off an alarm."

"Backwoods and random," she said. "This is a clusterfuck. You know that, right? We're chasing some black family that didn't follow protocol and some gas salesman saw a corpse and decided to call his aunt one night when he was half-way through a bottle of Evan Williams. You see how this plays, right, Agent Thomas?"

"Is that a 'yes,'?" he said.

34.

CARLISLE GAVE TRAIAN HIS 'YES.' TOLD HIM THAT HE needed to strengthen the brief that he had outlined for her. Make a better case and define the scenarios that might be playing out. He wrote it up at home. Had Kim read it, asking her to punch holes in it. Revised it and then went over it again the next morning with Gillis before bringing it to a judge that Carlisle thought might be willing to listen. Two weeks and the warrant came back signed and official. He sat in his office looking at the order. Picked up the phone and called the Walker County Sheriff's department and asked for Hi Lewis.

"Agent Thomas," Lewis said.

"Sheriff," Traian said. Waited. Wanted to see if he would offer anything after their last conversation. Nothing. "We are going into Tri-State in the morning. We have a warrant to search the property."

Nothing. Then he said, "I guess my assessment was not convincing enough."

"I think you already know the answer to that," Traian said. "You may be right, and of course if you are then this will be one of, if not our last, conversation. But I'm giving you a heads-up out of courtesy. You can be there or not. It does not really matter to me one way or the other, although if you're wrong, I'm not sure how well your absence will play." Getting right to it. Tired of the whole courtesy approach, wishing he'd skipped the call. Feeling a superiority after making nice. Hick cop who was either to lazy or choosing sides. Didn't matter now.

"And if you're wrong? If it's nothing? Then how will you play that?"

"It's my job to investigate crimes, Sheriff Lewis. Possible and probable. I don't get to pick and choose."

"No, I guess not," Lewis said. Paused, picturing them showing up in the morning. GBI crawling around the May place. Looking for bodies. Levi, Caroline, Matt, Shawna confined to the porch. Rollie drooling in his wheelchair in front of the television set. Shawna reading over the warrant. Looking at Hi wondering if he woould stop them. Help a friend out.

"Alright," Hi said. "What time?"

"Sheriff," Traian said.

"Yea."

"Anything you want to fill me in on before we go in?"

"Meaning what?"

"Meaning is there anything that you want to tell me before we go in?"

"Meaning am I withholding something from you?"

"I did not say that."

"No," Hi said. Let the line hang open.

"*No*, meaning you have nothing to tell me?" Traian said.

"We done?" Hi asked.

"I need your fax number so I can send you a copy of the warrant. I'll put the mobilization details on the cover sheet." Hung up after Hi gave him the number. Went down the hall to Gillis' office to walk through everything. Anxious to be moving forward.

35.

JACK CHAMBLISS PULLED INTO THE PARKING LOT AT the Walker County Sheriff's department at the same time Agents Thomas and Gillis were coming out the main door. He parked toward the end of the building and watched the men talk to one another over the top of their car, the man closest to him wearing a dark blue jacket with GBI in white letters on the back. They got in the car and pulled out of the lot. He watched until they were out of sight and was opening his door when Hi Lewis and Ellis Carver came out, walking quickly toward one of the patrol cars. They got in, Lewis driving, and followed in the direction of the GBI car. Jack closed his door, waited until the sheriff's car was a ways down the road, then he followed as well.

He kept his distance, tailing Lewis out of LaFayette and then down into the maze of narrow country roads, tree canopies keeping the two-lane corridors dark and shadowy with limbs empty of leaves. Ahead, he saw the back end of the GBI's car. It had pulled into a break in the trees, the sheriff's car slowing and pulling in behind the agents. The four men got out of their vehicles and then began walking up the road from where they had parked. Chambliss stopped in the middle of the road, hoping they would not see him. When they turned and walked up a driveway some twenty yards from their vehicles, he looked for a place to pull his car off the shoulder. Then he got out and walked the rest of the way.

Traian was in front and was coming up close to the porch when Hi put his hand on his shoulder. Traian stopped and looked at the sheriff.

"I'll do it," Hi said. Traian stepped aside and let Hi go up the porch steps alone. He knocked on the door. Carver looked at his wristwatch. Nine in the morning. Saturday in February. The door opened and Hi looked down to see Matt May staring up at him.

Hi said, "Matt." The boy looked at the sheriff and then looked around the side of the door at the three men waiting at the bottom of the steps. "Can you get your mom for me, Matt?"

The boy left the door open and went back into the house calling for Shawna. Hi waited. When she came into view she was wearing a robe and some worn slippers. Looked like she might have just gotten out of bed.

"Hi?" she said.

"Hey Shawna," he said. "Can you come outside with me please?" He stepped back to let her though the door.

She saw the men at the foot of the steps and then looked back at Hi. "What's this about?" she said.

"Is Levi here?" Hi said.

"Yes," she said. "He's asleep I think."

"And Caroline?"

"No, she's not here."

"Okay. And Rollie?" She nodded.

"Rollie's always here," she said. Then, "What's this about, Hi? Who are these men?" Traian put one foot on the bottom step and Hi put his hand out to him.

"Shawna, these men are with the Georgia Bureau of Investigations. They have a warrant to search the property." She started to speak. Hi said, "Wait. I need you to go get Levi, please. Ellis will go with you. I'll explain once Levi is down here."

Shawna pulled at the neck of the robe. Started to speak again. Stopped and went back into the house.

Hi motioned for Ellis to follow her. Said, "Give her space," as the deputy went past.

They waited five minutes, then Levi was coming to the door wearing sweatpants and no shirt. Shawna behind him. Ellis looking over her shoulder at Hi.

"Levi," Hi said and went through it again. Telling them about the warrant and the reason for it. Shawna and Levi quiet through all of it, not looking at Hi. Shawna reaching out and taking Levi's hand, the large man nodding that he understood that they would need to wait on the porch or inside the house until they were done looking around. Not seeming to notice the cold without a shirt.

"You want to wait out here, Momma or go inside?"

Shawna looked up at her son. "Let's go inside with Daddy and Matt," she said.

Hi said, "Shawna, we'll need you to get Caroline back here please."

"Okay," she said and went in. Levi following her. Ellis going with them.

•

Lewis came off the porch and started walking toward the buildings in the back. Traian and Gillis fanning out to his left and right. The woods quiet. Cold day with a scent of wood smoke curling from the chimney of the main house. Jack Chambliss standing on the road, watching the men moving toward the trees. Had not heard anything said on the porch, but knew enough that a warrant had been served. Still watching when Gillis went into one of the buildings and came back out gagging and swearing. Then a shout from inside the trees followed by another and then all three men were going back into the building where Gillis had gone and back out again, sputtering and coughing. He could hear them now. All of them talking loud.

"Jesus fucking Christ," Gillis said. "I've never. Jesus Christ." The sheriff was walking back toward the woods, then stopped. Looking up at the sky with its thick gray cloud cover. Traian coming quickly down the slope of the yard, then up onto the porch and going through the front door, not bothering to knock. Chambliss stepping into the drive now. Carver coming out onto the porch and then down the steps and around the back of the house. Coming back with Gillis. Saying, "He's using their phone to call." Gillis walking ahead of the deputy, up the steps and into the house. Chambliss zipped his coat and Lewis heard it.

"What the fuck are you doing here? Who are you?" Did not seem to recognize Chambliss from the bar.

"What's going on?" Chambliss said. "Why is the GBI here?"

"Fuck off," Lewis said, starting down the driveway toward the reporter.

"I'm just asking what's going on."

"And I'm telling you to get out of here. Get off the property."

"Why is the GBI investigating a Crematory?" Lewis stopped and turned to look back at the house.

"No comment," he said. Did not seem to know what to do next. Traian and Gillis coming onto the porch together, talking fast. Traian seeing Hi and Chambliss standing at the foot of the driveway.

Called down, "Who is that, Sheriff?"

"Press," Hi said.

Traian frowned. Moved on. Said, "I need you to come inside with me." Hi nodded, spoke to Chambliss as he walked away. "Stay off the property or I'll have you arrested." Walked back to the porch. Climbed the steps and followed Traian inside. Silence in the yard, wind picking up. Chambliss went up the road to his car. Got in and turned on the heater, rubbing his hands together.

•

Ellis was having trouble. Words not coming out right and Tanya waiting on him to tell her what happened next. The deputy back in English class trying to make sense out of what the teacher was telling them about whales and Anne Frank and some kid in a boarding school sleeping with whores. Always talking about symbols this and that and Ellis trying to focus but finding his attention moving through an open window and wandering toward the parking lot where he had his Pontiac that needed work on the gear box.

"Ellis, Jesus, what happened next?"

"It's the damndest and the scariest and the weirdest thing that anyone has ever seen," he said absently. His hands scratching the top of his service revolver.

"Cause of all the bodies?" she said.

Ellis looked at her. "Well of course because of the bodies Tanya. I mean shit. What else?"

"Weeeeelllll," she said. Mocking him. "How would I know. You were there, not me. I'm just stuck in this office answering the phone that has not stopped ringing since this all happened and nobody telling me anything and then you come back in here and act like I'm speaking Chinese or something."

"Just shut up," he said. "Just shut up for a minute and let me think. I'll tell you. Just let me think for a minute."

He had been in the room with all the Mays. Watching television when one of the GBI guys came in and went into the kitchen to use the phone and then he was talking loudly into the receiver and telling someone that he was going to need as many people on site as possible and that this was going to be all over the news so they would need to send someone down from the Atlanta office to handle communications, and that they would need the medical examiner notified because it looked like he was going to have to be involved and that they also needed counsel to be made aware because he was *fucked* as to what they were going to charge this family with.

Ellis quit listening and looked at the Mays sitting close to him in the room. They were not listening either. Or at least it did not seem to Ellis that they were listening. More like they were pretending that nothing was strange about any of this. Not even this white deputy sitting in the room with them. And the man in the wheelchair as quiet as a prayer, not looking at the television but out into where there were now two GBI agents, one of them pacing around the small kitchen table and telling the other man on the phone what to say and what to ask and the other man on the phone saying 'fuck' every other word and then Hi was in the kitchen with them and he was not saying anything at all. Not even looking at Ellis, but holding his hat the way that he did when he was thinking.

Then the man on the phone, Gillis was his name, hung it up and looked at the other agent with the funny sounding name and they talked in whispers for a moment before coming into the room where they were all sitting and took Levi out and then Gillis came back and asked Shawna May to come in the back with him and Ellis was left with the little boy and the old man in the wheelchair and Hi. The boy looking like he was about to cry and then Hi came into the room and touched the boy on the shoulder and went back to where the agents were questioning Levi and Shawna and returned and stood the boy up and walked him into the kitchen and got him a glass of water and picked up the phone and called his wife. They waited in silence. Could hear them talking in murmurs in the back rooms, and then Hi took the boy out on the porch and came back by himself and sat down across from Ellis and after he took a few minutes to gather his thoughts, he told Ellis what they had found outside and in one of the buildings.

Tanya said, "So, what did they find?"

"They had bodies all over the place. Stacked up in the building where they were supposed to be cremating them, only they were just stacked on top of each other and there was stuff all over the floor. And they had them laying around up in the woods too. And Sheriff Lewis was trying to tell me all of it, but he kept stopping because I don't think that he could believe it either. And his wife came to get the little boy Matt, and then state patrol showed up and we all went outside together and started walking through the woods and Sweet Jesus, Tanya, I've never seen anything like it. I know that I keep saying that, but I can't think of any other way to tell it. It was like something out of one of the those movies where the dead come looking for teenagers and whatnot. Every time you came around a tree it seemed like there was a dead body just decomposing there. Some of them still had their clothes on and some of them had been picked at by animals, and it was just horrible. I mean horrible. And there was this reporter guy there walking around with us, and we just let him cause I think everyone knew what this was all going to amount to and he might as well see it cause we were all just fumbling around out there and some of the cops were throwing up and it was like someone flipped a cemetery upside down with all of it and... Goddamn, I don't even know. I don't know if I'll ever sleep again."

"Then what," she said.

"Well," Ellis said. "I guess everyone just knew around the same time that there weren't any use in wandering around the woods knowing what we already knew and so we came back to the house and stood around the yard and talked. I guess GBI called TBI, cause some of those boys showed up, and it was like a bullhorn went off across North Georgia and Tennessee cause it just turned into a circus all at once and more press showed up and Hi told me to keep them back on the road so we could control them, but they were giving me a hard time and so Hi came down and told them we'd be giving them a statement when we had one and they got all pissed off but held back." He stopped and took a breath. Went in the back of the building and returned with a cup of coffee. "You know what else?"

Tanya was standing. Had been waiting for him, ignoring the phone.

"What, Ellis?" she said.

"All this before lunch."

"What does that have to do with anything?"

"I'm just saying," he said.

"Where's Sheriff Lewis?"

"He went up to Chattanooga with them Feds."

"What for?"

"They arrested Levi May."

"But why are they in Tennessee. Not here in LaFayette?"

"Hell if I know, Tanya. Maybe cause this deal is gonna blow up all over Dixie and they thought they might need a bigger jail. I can't say. It all took off like a bunch of startled rabbits."

"What about the rest of them—mother and sister and whoever else?"

"I don't know. That girl Caroline was not there."

"Oh shit," Tanya said.

"What?" Ellis said, putting down the Styrofoam cup.

"Nothing," she said. "I guess I was just thinking about coming home to a yard full of cops and people being taken off."

"Yeah, Tanya. That would be weird. Nothing like the normal scene where an old woman in her wedding dress is propped up against a pine tree with her face gone to bone. Home fucking sweet home."

"You know what I meant."

"I guess," he said. "Sheriff wants us to be ready for the media when they come pouring in here. Says it's gonna be like Sherman's march to the sea."

"Who?"

"Exactly," Ellis said and took a pad of paper out his pocket to go type up the statement that Hi had dictated to him while they were bringing Levi May out and putting him in the back of the GBI car. Hands cuffed, Levi not making eye contact with anyone, but not looking away either. His mother on the porch by herself, staring like she'd been dropped on her head. People coming and going, everyone looking at the ground while they walked.

36.

CLARENCE SAT ON THE EDGE OF THE MOTEL BED IN HIS white boxer shorts. Caroline beside him half-dressed, crying. He reached across her and put the phone back in the cradle. Rubbed her back. Waited for her to catch her breath. Hitching with sobs.

He said, "Baby, what is it? You want me to get you something."

She shook her head. Started back with the crying. He stood up and went over to the built in drawers where the TV sat. Bottle of Jim Beam with the glasses from the night before. Took one and rinsed it out in the sink. Came back and poured some of the bourbon and took it to the bed. Handed it to her, standing still. She looked up, shook her head. He reached down and lifted her chin.

"Drink some of this. Calm you down."

She took the glass. Sipped at the liquor and coughed.

"Easy now," he said. "Get calm and tell me what that was about."

She took another drink and put the glass down by the phone. Wiped her mouth.

"Just calling my mother," she said. Taking in bigger gulps of the stale motel room air. Heater running. Something loose in it, making a rattle. She told him. All of it.

Stopped her half way through so he could get his own drink. Sat down in a chair, stretching out his legs, listening and smoking. Got up. Turned off the heater and opened the door part way to let out some of the smoke in the room. Came back to the chair and let her finish. Said, "I never heard of anything like that in my life. That's fucking crazy, girl. Why would you?" Stopped and watched her across the room. Got up and closed the door. Not going back to the bed. Taking it all in. Assessing it now. Trying to see it clear in his mind.

"I don't know," she said. "I don't know why. Just..."

"But," he said.

"Don't. Don't ask me to help you make sense of it when I can't make sense of it myself. It was about the money at first. Daddy started it and then Momma told us about it after he got sick, and then after that, it just got to be normal."

"Normal?" Clarence lit another cigarette. Went back for more of the Jim Beam. "Ain't nothing normal about that shit, Caroline. Don't got to have a degree to know that this sick shit is as far from normal as you can get. That's like saying—that's like saying. Hell, I don't even know what that's like saying."

"Right," she said. Then stood up. "I gotta go home. They arrested Levi and Momma says that they want me back there."

"They gonna arrest you too?"

She started to cry again. "Don't know. I gotta get going. Take a shower and drive back. Oh Jesus."

He sat in the chair. Watched her throw the clothes from the floor into the overnight bag. Pulled out some jeans and a t-shirt. Pair of panties. Laid them out on the bed and went to the bathroom.

He waited till the door was closed behind her. Then he got up and dressed. Took a shot of the bourbon out of the bottle and left some money next to it so she could pay the bill. Then he went out and got in the hearse. Smoking inside of it, window cracked. *Fuck it*, he thought. Turned onto the state road and drove back to Holy Family to see what Mr. Arnold would have to say about all this.

He parked in front of the building and went inside. Walked down to Arnold's office and found the little man sitting behind his desk. Talking on the phone. Laughing in that high-pitched way of his. Prissy little thing in his neat clothes and oiled up hair. Clarence walked in and stared at Arnold until he told whomever he was talking to that he would have to call them back. Hung up and smiled at Clarence. *What can I do for you? Little prick.*

Clarence said, "What the fuck is going on down there in Noble?"

Arnold feigned surprise. Straightened up in his chair.

"You heard?" he said.

"Yea, I heard," Clarence said.

"How?"

"What's it matter how I heard."

Arnold looked pleased with himself. "Well, I guess it doesn't. That was a colleague of mine outside of Huntsville. It seems that our friends at the Crematory have been—how should I put this—in dereliction of their duty. That means..."

"Man, I know what it means, you asshole. How you involved in it?" Considered the question. "How *we* involved in it?"

"I'm not involved in it and neither are you," Arnold said. Calm. Already thought all of this through.

"You shipping bodies down there and they not burning them and you taking whatever it is that they are not burning and selling it to dead people's families. Marked up and all of that. How you not involved?"

Arnold stretched his neck. Scratched at the side of his face. "I have always considered you to be a rather smart man, Clarence." Raised his hand when Clarence started to interrupt. "So I think you should provide me the same courtesy and respect my own intelligence."

"What the fuck you talking about, man? This ain't about none of that. Why you always going on about shit that ain't got anything to do with what we're talking about? Acting like the lord of the manor and all that fake aristocratic bullshit. Like we in some old movie nobody ever heard of. Maybe try answering the question straight up."

"Well of course, Clarence. Since you put it so eloquently. Let's start with why you think that we chose Noble in the first place. Do you think that it was because they were centrally located in a tri-state area? Do you think it's because of their years and years of proven service? Do you think it's because they are a trusted name in the industry? Do you think it's because of their technological efficiency and business acumen? Any of those things ring true to you about the Tri-State Crematory?"

Clarence was quiet. Seeing it now.

"Ahh, it dawns on him," Arnold said. Smiling again. Smug and giddy now that he was making his on-high speech. "That's right. It's because they are a backwoods outfit with inexperienced operators and they would not know exploitation if it knocked on their outhouse door. And even if they did, they are certainly not capable of seeing beyond what they assumed was a windfall for their piney-woods venture. And should something go wrong with anything at all—even something as unpredictable and insane as what has occurred, there would be no way for them to point the finger at Holy Family or any other reputable funeral home. What would they even say? How would they even make a case? How would they tie all of us together? Are they going to tell the state and federal prosecutors that there was some grand conspiracy by a consortium of funeral parlors that forced them to stop properly disposing of bodies and start decorating the woods with corpses? How do you think that plays out in court? Oh, we'll be pulled into lawsuits. I imagine a massive mess of class-action suits will name any and everyone who had anything to do with this *atrocity* but there will be so much to untangle in all of this that they will never go anywhere. And people are going to ask us if we used them and we'll say 'Yes Mam, we did, but we certainly had no idea what was going on down there. They came highly recommended and were always prompt in returning the cremains. We just never thought to check and see if they were real or not. Shame on us.' I mean, who would even think to do something like that, Clarence?"

Arnold wound up now. Floating behind the desk with how clever he was. Clarence looking out the window at the rain and the fog, laying thick over the Holy Family grass. Hills vague in the distance.

"So they gonna hang and you're gonna skate. You and that pack of creepy looking pimps you run with."

Arnold ignored the insult, waving his hand. "Oh certainly the Mays will. Not all of them. Probably just that man Levi. He'll take most of the rope, but if the feds don't destroy them then the families will. That cross has not even come to bear yet. They will be out for blood, my friend." He paused, looked at Clarence. "Don't quit on me over this, Clarence." He stood up and walked from behind the desk, starting toward the door.

Clarence said, "Is that some kind of threat?"

Arnold turned. "Heavens no," he said.

37.

DR. WENDELL SAT BEHIND THE WHEEL OF HIS SILVER BMW, parked as far from the building entrance as he could get it. Looked out the driver's side window at the clusters of people walking into the community center entrance. Rain holding off for now. Coldest day of the year. People swaddled in oversize jackets. Working class and white collar alike. Bent forward in the frigid air. Wendell sighed and waited for Traian Thomas to show up. He had spent the last two weeks in the woods and in meetings with everyone from the EPA to the attorney general. Press so far up everyone's ass that it was hard to breathe. Coming from all corners of the Earth. TV, print, radio. News story about what they had found in the woods bigger than the attack on Pearl Harbor. Him in the middle of it all. Talking about DNA and progressive deterioration. Dodging questions about litigation and who was going to account for all of this. Lawyers moving through the crowd like a stomach virus. Self-righteous. Professing their sympathies for the disrespect their loved ones had suffered. Maybe make some money out of it though. A *clusterfuck*. No other way to put it. Levi May in custody. Keeping his mouth shut. Lawyers of his own for him and his mother and sister. Prosecutors frustrated with how to charge them. No regulatory precedent for tossing bodies around the yard. Filling boxes with cement dust and charred bits of rock and sending them back with someone's name tagged on the top. Funeral homes circling the wagons too. Everyone pointing fingers. *Clusterfuck.*

Traian knocked on the glass. He slid it down.

"You ready?"

"I suppose," Wendell said.

"You don't seem happy," Traian said.

Wendell put the window up and got out of the car. Locked it. They walked together toward a side entrance that Traian had a key for. Come in through the big commercial kitchen and then into the meeting room without interaction. Crowd sitting in folding chairs. Press pushed back in the corner. State troopers keeping them in line. Relatives of the dead they had found in the woods on edge. Wondering whose remains they had sitting in their living rooms if it was not their great aunt or some departed cousin. Coming to Noble from all over the place. Dragging ghosts along with them. Looking for vengeance and a clearly defined lawsuit.

They came into the kitchen where Gillis and the Walker County Sheriff were waiting for them. Drinking coffee. The unrest of the crowd seeping through the double doors. Tired of waiting on answers and bureaucrats pushing around excuses. No word from the Mays. Levi May not offering an explanation no matter how many ways they asked. Stoic and resigned to it. Not feeling any need to expand on one- and two-word answers. Overly polite. Like talking to a well-mannered kid.

Traian said, "Okay, Dr. Wendell."

The medical examiner nodded, led the way, the cops following him in a line, Gillis putting a mug down on a steel prep table, Hi Lewis taking off his hat, turning back to survey the empty kitchen before following them in. The big room was steamy with radiator heat and the damp clothes. Chairs all taken and people standing along the walls. The crowd going quiet when the officials stepped behind the tables and podium that had been set-up for the meeting. Traian nodded at Wendell and the doctor tapped the mic. Full quiet.

"Ladies and gentlemen," Wendell said.

•

Jack Chambliss sat at the head of the table in the paper's dingy conference room. Editors lining both sides, carpet splotched with coffee stains, air like an ash tray. The men looking over the notes that he had Xeroxed after the medical examiner's press conference in Noble. Nursing a cup of weak coffee. Still jittery from the four-hour chaos—the families never letting up the pressure. Tension and violent rhetoric. People standing up making speeches. Some of them teary and soft-spoken. Most of them rage-filled and beyond frustration. The medical examiner playing it cool, sticking to the facts of the investigation and exhaustive search of the property. Laying out the protocol for identifying the remains of the bodies that they had found strewn over the May property. Law enforcement officials filling in the gaps where they could. No one having a good answer for how anything such as that could have gotten this far without being noticed. All kinds of accusations and threats. Wendell laying out the process. Sounded like an archeological dig. Telling the families that they would have to submit DNA samples along with the cremains that they currently had in their possession. Chambliss writing until his hand cramped around the ballpoint.

Charlie said, "Did he use use the word *strewn*?"

Chambliss looked at his notes and then to the managing editor. "I don't know. That's what I wrote down."

Charlie nodded his head. "It would make for a solid quote."

"We got enough to work with here, I think," Dutch said. "Chambliss, I don't have to tell you that we have a lot of outside interest in this story that basically unfolded in our back yard. We're not going to compete with TV or the big papers, but we can be right alongside them, if you follow me."

"I follow you," Chambliss said.

"Good," he said and slid the notes into the middle of the table and took out his cigarettes and lit one, looking at the newsmen who were looking back at him. He said, "This is about the most surrealistic thing I've encountered since we were reporting on Nixon. I want input from everyone involved. Get some people pulled off the cop beat and have them help on the follow-up interviews and stories. We need to emphasize the local impact. Keep out of narrative that the national guys are going to take. These are people who read our paper every day. I want the cops, the lawyers, the medical examiner's office, the victims—are we calling them *victims,* Charlie?»

"I don't know. Are we calling them *victims* Chambliss? You were there."

"I would say so," Chambliss said. "They arrested Levi May, which makes what is obviously a crime, a crime. So yes, I would say they are victims."

"What are they charging him with, exactly?" Charlie said.

"They don't know," Chambliss said. "There's nothing on the Georgia books that specifies exactly what was happening out there, so I think they are trying to figure it out. They have him on some kind of theft charge for the fake remains, and they are trying to work through what exactly to term the desecration of the bodies. I'll follow it."

"*Victims* it is," Dutch said. Stubbed out the cigarette and stood. "I have to go brief the publisher. Anything else for me?" He went to the door and then came back in, standing over the table. "Anyone in here affected by this? Anyone have a relative who was sent there?" Two hands went up. Dutch pointed at both of them. A gentle gesture. "Stay away from this until you know," he said. "Christ, you have our sympathies if it does not go your way." Turned to leave again. Paused and said over his shoulder, "Chambliss, have a draft ready to go well before deadline. I want plenty of time to read through it. No sensational language. Just tell us what happened."

38.

NOBLE, GA. — MARCH 19, 2002 – MORE THAN 300 BOD-ies have been discovered on the Tri-State's Crematory's property over the course of a three week investigation launched by the Georgia Bureau of Investigation with cooperation from the Walker County Sheriff's department, the Walker County Coroner's office, and the EPA.

The state's lead medical examiner, Dr. Richard Wendell, provided new information in a press conference today in Noble in which he outlined the conclusions of the Tri-State Crematory investigation.

A warrant to search the property was issued in January of this year after a tip was provided to the GBI by a local gas company delivery man who witnessed, on more than one occasion, multiple bodies stacked outside of several out-buildings on the property. State officials declared the Crematory property a disaster area in an effort to secure state funds to enable the mass clean-up.

Tri-State is owned by long-time Noble residents Rollie and Shawna May, but is currently run by their eldest son, Levi May, who was arrested on charges of theft by deception. He is being held in Hamilton County Jail and Detention Center pending arraignment.

Wendell described a macabre seen on the May property, stating "in all of my years in this profession, I have never seen anything like this. Never."

According to the investigative report, bodies were strewn throughout the property in varying states of decomposition. Some of the corpses were recent enough that toe-tags were still attached to their feet. There were half-dug pits that contained piles of bones, and a pond on the property was drained after remains, including a skull, were found. But officials said the true horror of the scene was relegated to the buildings that were located in immediate proximity to the May home. Specifically in a building known as a *retort*—the facility that was designed for the burning of bodies.

"Early in the search we found numerous bodies inside the retort building, stacked like wood," said Traian Thomas, the GBI agent in charge of the investigation. "There was no telling how long they had been there and the condition of those buildings was monstrous."

Dr. Wendell stated that there were a number of bodies that had reached a state of mummification which indicated that they had likely been left outside for more than a decade, confirming the investigator's suspicions that the Mays' practice of abandoning the bodies was systematic, common and long-lived.

"We had a mechanical engineer assess the cremation facilities, and none of them were operable and likely had not been for many years," said Thomas. "But for whatever reason, the Mays never had them repaired. Instead they were sending back fake boxes of cremains that typically contained cement dust, rocks and bits of charred wood. The lengths they went to to deceive people is appalling."

Those fake cremains were handed over to family members like Joseph and Ellie Carmichael of Fort Payne, Alabama. Mr. Carmichael's father's body was sent to Tri-State for cremation in 1997. His corpse was found on the edge of a small pasture and was identified by an ID bracelet around his wrist.

"We had my father's ashes interred in the church that he went to all of his life," said Joseph Carmichael. "Then we get a call that he's actually laying out in the woods, rotting. I mean, how do you even respond to something like that?"

Dr. Wendell outlined the protocol for the identification of bodies at the meeting this morning. All found remains have been collected at a makeshift morgue on the May property. Forensic personnel from across the state are working to establish firm identifications where possible. Those corpses that have reached advanced states of decomposition will require DNA matches with surviving family members, many of whom were in the audience seeking confirmation on the authenticity of their loved one's remains.

"It makes me sick to my stomach," said Nancy Everett of Lookout Mountain, Tennessee. Mrs. Everett's sister Edith Hamilton was sent to Tri-State in 2000. Mrs. Everett was at the meeting to find out if Mrs. Hamilton was one of the bodies awaiting identification. "To think that anyone could behave like this and not understand the anger and the sorrow that they are causing other people is just beyond me. There is a special place in Hell for Levi May."

Walker County Sheriff Hi Lewis attended the meeting but did not speak publicly. In a phone interview with the Times, Sheriff Lewis deferred comment to the GBI. When asked if he felt that there was more that his office could have done in light of the mass desecration, he offered only that he deeply regretted what had occurred and would be cooperating fully with the GBI and state lawmakers as they move toward prosecution. When asked what justice might look like for those families whom Dr. Wendell called "victims of the most heinous of crimes," Sheriff Lewis said that it was not for him to decide.

"Everyone is in shock, myself included," Sheriff Lewis said. "This is a small community, and we are doing our best to cope. There are a lot of people hurting right now. I thought that I knew them," he said. "I really did."

39.

HI LEWIS PULLED THE CRUISER INTO THE PARKING LOT of the hotel and waited. He knew that the agents were heading back to Atlanta that afternoon. He had called the county prosecutor's office and asked him for an update and he told him that they were getting nowhere with Levi May and that his mother and sister had hidden behind their lawyer. Depositions a script of questions and non-answers. Told Hi that Gillis had said they were done as far as they were concerned. That getting a motive and figuring out what and who to charge was not in their scope. Said he was kind of an asshole about it.

"I don't blame him though," the prosecutor said. Hi ready to hang up. "They broke this open and then they have a legislature that is almost as incompetent as the Mays. These fucking state reps are all pointing their fat fingers and tripping over each other, and Walker County and of course the funeral homes and the regulatory body there and that's just Georgia. Christ, it's anyone's guess when this is over."

Hi said, "Okay," and hung up the phone. Told Ellis and Tanya he would not be back and had driven the twenty miles north to Chattanooga. The weather warming up so that he could ride with the windows down. Hint of spring air soothing and fragrant on the road.

Traian and Gillis came out of the side entrance of the hotel and walked toward their car. Hi got out and met them as they were opening the trunk. Both rolling neat little suitcases. Looking up at him as he came forward.

"Howdy Sheriff," Gillis said. Big fake accent with black sunglasses on and a smirk. "You come to wish us goodbye? I'm touched."

Hi said, "You mind if I speak with Agent Thomas a minute?"

"Sure," Gillis said. "I need to hit the bathroom before we vacate this lovely part of the territory. I'm gonna hate to leave it all behind." He walked away, Hi and Traian watching him go.

"He's a good agent," Traian said and turned to Hi. Smiled.

"Well," Hi said.

""How can I help you, Sheriff Lewis?"

"I wanted to say goodbye."

"That all?" Traian said. "Seems like a long trip to make just to tell me *goodbye*. Nothing else on your mind?"

"You mean like an apology," Hi said.

"See," Traian said. "That's what I'm talking about with you. Someone asked me about you and I told them that I thought that you were probably a pretty decent guy when you were not busy being a prick. Acting like everyone is out to take your badge or take a shit in your backyard. I was just doing my job, Sheriff. That's all it was and if you can't appreciate that, then I don't have much for you." He picked up one of the suitcases and placed it in the trunk. Looked at Lewis. "And I don't remember asking you for anything that even resembled an apology."

Hi removed his hat.

"I'm sorry," he said and Traian laughed. "I am," Hi said. "You were right about this and I was embarrassed that it happened on my watch. I had a personal relationship with the family and I was hesitant to push anything. It should not have happened that way and I know it."

"Okay," Traian said. "Is it my turn?"

Hi thought about the Pickle Barrel meeting and knew the agent was recalling it as well.

"Sure," he said. "Go ahead."

"Thank you," Traian said, and picked up the other suitcase and tossed into the trunk next to the first one and closed the lid. Gillis came back across the lot with two cups of coffee and handed one to his partner and nodded at Hi as he went around to the passenger door and got in. Traian looked at the coffee and smiled.

"Like I said, he's a good agent." He looked over Hi's shoulder at the greening bulk of Lookout Mountain and at the neatly scaled buildings of downtown Chattanooga. "This is a pretty spot," he said. "I think I will have to find a reason to come back." He stuck out his hand and Lewis took it. Then he climbed into the driver's seat and waved at Hi as he pulled past him, turning the sedan onto the street toward the on ramp south.

•

Shawna sat at their kitchen table and held both hands around a mug of coffee. Caroline had just left, and Matt was staying with her sister who lived in Dunlap, Tennessee with her husband and three boys. She had rolled Rollie into the kitchen with her to keep him company. Give the TV a break for awhile. She was going to shower and drive up to where they were holding Levi. The trial about to start and all signs pointing to her son going to jail. The prosecutor telling her that as far as he was concerned they were going to leave the women out of it. Shawna had thought about getting in his face. Telling him that they did not need his special treatment. They would handle their own defense. But she had stopped, looking at Caroline's expression while the prosecutor talked down to them. Told them that they were inconsequential. He would have gone after Rollie if he was still standing. She knew that. But he wasn't. He'd lost more ground in the last couple months than he had in the previous year. She did not expect him to see Levi out of prison.

She let it go. Let Caroline have a life. Her sister said Matt could stay with her as long as he needed to. Even if he had to go to school up in Tennessee. She had said that would be fine until she could figure out what to do next. They had left her alone, but they seized the money that they had made. The money that was supposed to get them out of Noble. Now there was nothing. Not even her job with the school system. They had called her about that not long after everything broke apart. Said what she expected them to say. Not going to wait around until they gave out the guilty verdicts. Everyone in the world knew they were guilty of something. You just had to look at the TV for that. She wondered if Rollie saw it when it came on the news. Didn't matter.

The coffee had gone cold. She reached over the table and took Rollie's hand. Silent as usual. Lips had a little tremor in them. Like maybe he was trying to speak. She stood up and went to the coffee maker near to the kitchen window and looked out. It was like a tornado had come through and claimed everything. Trees down as far as she could see, piled on top of one another, laying this way and that. Knocked down every-which-way. The buildings and the vehicles and everything gone. They had bulldozed the buildings and hauled everything off. When she asked one of the men working what they were doing, pretending that she did not know, he said they were clearing everything all the way to the ground. "Gonna make it like this place never happened is what they told us. Make it look like this never happened."

They did. The only thing that they left was her house and she could keep that for now. She did not know what would come of the trial and everything that it entailed. It was beyond her understanding for the most part. There were people smarter than her and Rollie that had no idea how to proceed. Her mind was focussed on Levi and how quiet he had been through all of this. She supposed that there was no other way for him to be when she really thought about. He had not chosen this path. That had been her doing. She and Rollie. Rollie who had told her that it was just until they got the retort fixed. Rollie who was over at the table sitting in his own piss and her looking out at a land full of dead trees that would need to be burned. Too many to haul off.

40.

WILSON WAS WAITING FOR HIM WHEN HE CAME INTO the office after the late morning sermon. He had poured them both some bourbon and he was sitting with his feet up on the Reverend's desk when he came through the door.

"Hey now," Wilson said. "What you tell them today?"

Reverend Righteous came around his desk and looked at the bottom of Wilson's size eleven sneakers.

"You mind removing those filthy things off of my clean desk."

"Sure thing," he said, "Made us a drink. Figured you might need one after all this consultation you been providing to the community in the wake of this disaster."

"Wilson," he said. "Those people are grieving. You could try and show some respect."

"Grieving my ass," Wilson said. "They was hoping to get a look at one of them Mays in church this morning. Ain't no one seen them since they got busted. What them people got to grieve about? That the Mays tarnished this black community? Damn. We colored folk is lucky they don't try and charge all of us for that evil, crazy zombie shit they been pulling up there in the woods. I mean what the fuck?"

"Wilson, could you please give your mouth a rest."

"Say," Wilson said. "You going back down to Atlanta after this mess is over? Once you got your flock organized and through the dark wilderness of dead people?"

Reverend Righteous looked at him across the desk.

"See, the reason I'm asking is cause I'm thinking about getting out of here."

"The church?" the Reverend said, sipping from the drink. Liking the warm feeling of it. Liking the idea of Wilson being gone even better. Wilson cackled.

"Naw man. Not the church. Noble. I'm thinking about getting out of Noble, brother. Thought maybe you could hook me up with a job in Atlanta. You know, some gig in one of those clubs you belong to. How would that be? I could recognize my true potential and you could come and visit me when you have strayed from the path and need some strange pussy."

"Jesus," the Reverend said.

"Yea, him too. Bring him along too. He probably like a change of scenery from all this lunatic, back from the dead crazy going on around here." He finished off the drink. Stood.

"You want another one?" Reverend Righteous looked at his glass. Swirled the liquor and then finished it off. Handed it over to Wilson.

"Why not?" he said.

41.

HI LEWIS HAD DRIVEN SOUTH ON INTERSTATE 59 TO
Birmingham to attend a regional law enforcement conference. He
had been there for two days and stopped for gas on the ride home to
ask Sherry if he needed to pick anything up before he came through
Trenton, Georgia and crossed over Lookout Mountain, then back
down the other side into Noble. She told him they needed peanut
butter, milk and some Frosted Flakes. He took the exit ramp and
pulled into a grocery store. The sky had started to lay down a light
misty rain. The parking lot puddling up the pot holes and the overhead lamps murky in the creeping fog. He got out of the cruiser and
walked through the nearly empty Sunday night lot, then in through
the automated doors. The black mats greasy and slick.

A teenage girl sat behind one of the registers, chewing gum
and reading one of the tabloids from the rack. Hi nodded at her
as he went past and found the peanut butter and cereal aisle and
then went to the back of the store where the coolers were. He saw
the milk and pulled out a gallon and then looked down the row
and noticed the beer. He opened a second cooler door and had
to balance a six pack out of the cold opening, hands full with the
other items. He shifted the milk to a free hand and turned around
and stopped, looking down at Shawna May from beneath his wide
brimmed hat.

Shawna stared up at him and for almost a full minute, neither
one of them spoke.

Hi said, "Shawna?"

She nodded, lips tight together. No make-up. The fluorescent
light made her face look stark. Almost alien.

Hi said, "Well, what are you doing over . . . "

Shawna May said nothing.

He said, "I guess I, well, I guess I understand *why*. You by yourself?"

"No," she said. "Got Rollie in the car. He's sleeping. Seems like all he does is sleep."

"How is he? I mean," he shifted the groceries. Thought about putting something down so he could move his arms. Feeling tight and trapped in the broad aisle. A man with a push broom was coming toward them from the section of low coolers where they kept the meat.

"He's the same Hi. Don't know anything about anything. Kids, well, I guess you know about all that. The trial. Levi going away. Me and Rollie back where we started, I guess. Caroline too embarrassed to be seen. Matt with some relatives. Don't know when or if I'm gonna bring him back."

Hi felt an opening.

"Robbie was asking about him," he said. "He misses him."

"Yea," Shawna said. "He's a good boy, Robbie is."

"They are both good boys," Hi said.

Shawna clenched her hand over the top of her purse.

"How Sherry doing, Hi? She still teaching school?"

Hi nodded. Started to speak then quit.

"Good," Shawna said. "That school needs strong teachers like her."

"I'll tell her you said that," Hi said.

"You do that. Can't imagine I will get the chance to tell her myself."

"Listen," Hi said.

"Don't," Shawna said. "Don't do that. We both know where this road we were on parted. I don't blame you Sheriff Lewis. You're a good man. My husband looked up to you. Considered you his friend. I like your family very much. You were kind to us and never cast any judgments—well before all of this." She swung the purse like the grocery store was *all of this*. "And when it came right down to it, you were doing your job."

Hi started to speak again.

"Ahhh," she said. "Don't ask me what ten lawyers already asked me, and Levi, and Caroline. I can't give you an answer. Way I see it, there's not an answer out there that anyone would believe anyway. We got a good lawyer. He has the state chasing their tails. But that's all red tape bullshit and people looking to place blame like they was holding something hot." She paused and then let out a very long and unhealthy sounding sigh. "Let's just say that sometimes things happen. We don't always know why or how we got there or what motivated us, or even when we lost our way. They just turn out one way and not another." She paused, then said, "The dead don't know they're dead." Then she laughed like she had caught herself in a private moment. Something funny then but strange to recall now.

Hi stood quietly feeling the damp in his shoes.

She reached out and touched his shoulder.

"You take care, Hi."

"You too Shawna," he said, and watched her walk toward the meat section, her compact frame moving slowly, passing the man pushing the broom. The choppy piano music tinny and small through the speakers overhead.